The
Wedding
Date

Zara Stoneley was born in a small village in Staffordshire and wanted to be James Herriot when she grew up. After completing an IT degree, working as a consultant, running a dog grooming business, teaching, and working at a veterinary practice she decided she had more than enough material to write several books even if she would never qualify as a vet!

She now splits her time between a cosy country cottage in Cheshire and an apartment in Barcelona, and writes fun, romantic stories set in the British countryside that she loves so much.

Zara Stoneley is the author of the Tippermere series (*Stable Mates*, *Country Affairs* and *Country Rivals*) published by HarperCollins, as well as several standalone novels.

🐦 @ZaraStoneley
f www.facebook.com/ZaraStoneley
www.zarastoneley.com

Also by Zara Stoneley

The Wedding Date

ZARA STONELEY

A division of HarperCollins*Publishers*
www.harpercollins.co.uk

Harper*Impulse* an imprint of
HarperCollins*Publishers*
The News Building
1 London Bridge Street
London SE1 9GF

www.harpercollins.co.uk

This paperback edition 2018

First published in Great Britain in ebook format by
HarperCollinsPublishers 2018

A catalogue record for this book
is available from the British Library

ISBN: 9780008301033

Printed and bound in the United States of America by
LSC Communications

19 20 21 22 LSC 15 14 13 12 11 10 09

For my parents. With love.

ACT ONE – THE INVITE

Chapter 1

Reasons I, Sam Jenkins, cannot go to this wedding:

1. I'm too fat, and just don't have time to get down to a look-okay-in-a-posh-summer-frock weight.
2. Lemon is so not my colour (which is the colour theme – Jess knows my aversion to over the top dresses and so has gone for a theme rather than providing the type of dress she loves and I hate). Mum says it drains me.
3. I have far too much work to do. And house-cleaning, and gardening.
4. I don't have a date.
5. The last man I dated ripped my heart out, stamped on it and is going to be the best man.

Reasons I have to go to this wedding:

1. Jess ~~was~~ is my best friend.

I could add 'and my hair looks crap' but that one is easily handled. Much more easily handled than losing the choc-olate-cake-and-chips stone in weight that has very comfortably settled itself round my stomach like an unwel-come lodger who intends to stay. Healthy food is on my to-do list, it just hasn't made it on to my shopping list yet. I mean, you have to prioritise, don't you? And I'm not quite ready.

Now don't get me wrong, I can be pretty determined when I want to be, and show amazing self-control (last summer I lost 5 lb in weight the week before we went away, which meant the 7 lb I put on during the week was totally acceptable), but there are times in life when only a super-size bag of crisps and a bottle of wine will do, and the last few months has been one of those times. It has also been a time for espresso martinis and bumper bags of gin and tonic popcorn.

I was dumped, and now *this*.

A wedding invite. Well, advance warning of a wedding invite to be more precise.

Normally I love a good wedding, who doesn't? But, right now, cheering on *any* happy couple would make me feel slightly hopeless and weepy for all the wrong reasons. And this is worse. This is *the* worst.

This isn't just any wedding invite; it's from Jess. My bestie.

We've known each other forever. She told me some time ago to 'save the date' (when I was still the deluded half of a happy couple), and now she's emailed to tell me why.

4

She is getting married! The invite is in the post! It will be here any day! She is excited! Dan is excited! Everybody is excited! Her mum has already bought a hat!!! The wedding is going to be A-MA-ZING!! (The exclamation marks are hers, not mine – she is excited.)

Normally I'd be pretty thrilled too – after all, I love her to bits. I want her to be happy, I truly, truly do, and she will be. But *normally* was the time before Liam shredded my heart, hopes, and the perfect future I'd created in my head, as thoroughly as he shredded his very private and confidential banking documents – and pretty much every other sheet of paper left carelessly lying around. And Jess is marrying Dan. Liam's brother. And Liam will of course be the best man. Not that 'best' or 'man' are words I'd voluntarily apply to him.

So I am not thrilled. I am imagining walking up the aisle behind my best friend towards the man who cheated on me. And everybody there will know he cheated on me. I will be the elephant in the room, the person that everybody stares at but avoids talking to because it is all so embarrassing and we are all so terribly British.

And if I'm totally honest I actually feel like an elephant, as in big and an anaemic shade of grey - and I don't have time to remedy the situation. I'm not sure any spray tan or control knickers are slimming enough.

For the sake of my own battered self-esteem I need to be that kitten who looks in the mirror and sees a lion. Except in my case I need to see the sexiest pre-break up version of me possible. Liam and all our friends and family need to see that girl too. I need to be *me*, not the girl Liam dumped.

And I do not have time.

In two months' time, Jess will be saying 'I do'.

I'm halfway to work when my phone starts beeping.

Did you get my email? Isn't it amazing?! Can't wait to catch up with you, it's been ages!

It has been ages. Five months, three days, five hours and thirty-seven minutes (give or take the odd minute). That was when I'd waved goodbye to Jess and her boyfriend Dan, just five minutes before his snake-in-the-grass wanker-banker brother Liam dumped me.

He'd put his hands on my waist and pulled me in for what I thought was a pre rumpy-pumpy kiss. Liam liked to work to a routine which could, if I'm brutally honest, be a bit long-winded and anti-climactic (though the last bit is only true for me, he peaked as regularly as clockwork). The foreplay started at the pub, lasted the entire walk home with increasingly amorous snogs and squeezes, there'd be a brief grope as we stumbled up the stairs, then it culminated in a five-minute shag, a groan of satisfaction – his, and only occasionally mine – before he collapsed on his back and fell asleep.

Anyway, I thought that's why he'd grabbed me, so I puckered up and closed my eyes. And nothing happened. I opened one. Liam was giving me his spaniel look. Beseeching. So I opened the other eye, wondering what could be so earth-shatteringly important as to disrupt his foreplay routine (those two words shouldn't really sit side by side, even I know that).

'Samantha—' he only called me Samantha in front of my parents, his parents, and his boss '—you're a lovely girl—' I could feel my body stiffen, as though it was expecting a blow, though my brain hadn't twigged why '—but this has started to feel like a habit.'

Ahh, maybe at last my subtle hints about our all the way home warm-up session had sunk in at last. 'I know what you mean.' At last! A chance to add a bit of spice to life. Impulsive just isn't a word you'd breathe in the same sentence as 'Liam', but maybe he'd seen the fun his brother was having with Jess, and decided to go for it.

I loved Liam with all my life, he was kind and considerate, but we *were* in a bit of a rut. Maybe he had realised that a rut isn't good when you're not yet thirty. Perhaps it was time to buy some new sexy underwear, a little black dress, some slightly higher heels. 'Maybe we should walk back a different way? Across the park?' A fumble in the bushes would make a change, and Mrs Tribble from number 26 wouldn't be able to peer out and tut. Why do people insist on watching things they know they don't approve of? Pull the curtains, love. Watch the weather forecast.

Anyway, we could even spend a romantic moment on the bench by the pond. But I *was* dying for the loo, so it would only be a fleeting stop.

'I don't mean the route.' He gave me his sad smile, the one he normally reserved for customers he was just about to turn down for a loan. I half-expected him to start his next sentence with 'regretfully', but he didn't. 'I mean our relationship. It's not really going anywhere, is it?'

He liked his routines. He thrived on routine. We had our own sides of the bed, his toothbrush had its own side of the mug, every second of the day had its place in his organised life, and he was saying this as though it was my fault? He was saying he was bored? But I knew I could put a positive spin on this. Maybe I had been a bit lax, not determined enough to shake us both out of our complacent little life together.

'We could have a mini-break, go to Spain, or Paris? Ooh la la!' I did a wriggle which could have been sexy French, or the start of a Spanish flamenco. 'Spice things up?'

'I didn't mean go anywhere as in travel.' The sad look was now turning into one of annoyance, and he was gazing straight over the top of my head – not looking me in the eye. 'There's no easy way to say this, and you know I like to be straight.'

I did. Liam wasn't one to soften the blow – he liked to say exactly what he was thinking, which could be embarrassing at times. He was the man who'd agree with the hostess that the meat was on the tough side, and told my mother that yes, her bum did look a little bit large in her new trousers, but at her age it didn't matter. She'd laughed it off, but the next time I saw those trousers they were in the charity shop – I swear they were hers, they had the faintest of stains from where she'd slopped the coffee she'd been passing to him.

'I think we've reached the end of the road.'

We'd not even reached the corner shop. 'But we're only…'

'Samantha, I've met somebody else.' The blood had the decency to rush out of his face at roughly the same speed the words shot out of his mouth.

I stared in astonishment, pretty sure that my mouth was gaping open.

'I'm sorry, I do wish you well.' And he held his hand out. Held his bloody hand out! I suppose it was habit, the bank thing.

I hadn't seen Jess after that. We'd swapped texts, even had brief, slightly awkward phone conversations where she'd tried not to mention Dan in every sentence, and I'd tried to ignore it when she did, and to act normal and jolly. And not ask if she'd seen Liam.

The trouble was, we'd been a foursome. For ages. And now we were a threesome and it didn't quite work the same. We hadn't had separate girly dates for years. Our social life had been double dating, and though she did sympathise, and she did call Liam several nasty names (she was actually far more inventive than me), I couldn't expect her to join in a bitch fest about her boyfriend's brother all the time, could I?

I'd gone on a spectacular drunken bender with Sarah from work, then I'd booked some leave and sat in my flat for a week, because going out meant putting eyeliner on, and there is no eyeliner known to woman that could cope with the rate at which my eyes were leaking.

The only thing I didn't do was lose weight. I hate every woman who sheds the stones like a snake sheds its skin when they break up with a boyfriend. Because I pile it on. Wine, chocolate and every carb known to woman flock to my side to comfort me – then settle on my stomach, and under my armpits.

Anyway, so that was then and this is now, post exciting-wedding-news email.

Fantastic news! I text back to Jess. *I'm so pleased for you!! You and Dan make the perfect couple!!!* I always find exclamation marks can make up for any lack of enthusiasm when you can't think of anything to say, and all you can think about is the groom-to-be's bastard brother who will be at the wedding. *Can't wait to see you!!!*

A text comes back straight away, as though her fingers have been poised over the send button. *Just so you know, but I know it won't bother you seeing as you've got a new man* (I'd lied – when Jess had texted me about 'the break-up' I'd told her I was over Liam, so over him, I had a new man, I was happy, deliriously happy!) *Liam's new girlfriend will be with him, she's preggers. HUGE!*

Shit. My feet have become disconnected from my brain and stopped working, and the nearest wall looms towards me.

Pregnant? How could she be even a teeny bit pregnant,

let alone huge? It had only been five months and three and a bit days since we split, and Liam never rushes into anything. Anything. It took him half an hour (minimum) to get into bed, because the sheets needed straightening and his teeth needed brushing and his clothes needed folding. I'd never yet had a hot meal with him, because if the table wasn't laid properly and the cutlery perfectly aligned then he couldn't get stuck in. I mean, who needs fully coordinated tableware when you're tucking into bangers and mash?

Liam was a man of habit. The more I list his habits (which I do a lot these days), the more I wonder why I was so mad about him, why I went to bits when he dumped me, why I ever put up with him.

But love's weird like that, isn't it? And I'm beginning to think there might be a tiny bit of hurt pride shoved in there as well. Dumping in your own time is one thing, being the dump-ee is altogether different. But I had been happy with Liam. Lazily happy.

Jess has obviously got bored of waiting for a reply, or is worried I've gone off to top myself. *He's a prat, I wouldn't have invited him but he is Dan's brother.*

I know. It is the best response I can do under pressure. No exclamation marks.

I'd known he'd be at the wedding. He'd told me he'd met 'somebody else' – met, not shagged. To be honest a tiny part of me wants to see this girl. The part that could scoff and say she wasn't that pretty, that thin, that clever. A bigger part of me wants to run a mile in case she is all that and more.

But pregnant? Huge?? No part of me had expected that.

At least I wouldn't have to look at some willowy beauty hanging off his arm, I suppose. Although, shit, don't pregnant woman have this 'glow'? I can't stand next to a glowing girlfriend if I'm all fat and spotty. And alone. Everybody will be looking, nodding sympathetically at me, and whispering 'you can't blame him' behind their hands.

I can't wait to meet your new man! Jess is still texting.

Nor could I.

How the hell am I supposed to hook up with somebody new before the wedding? And the more excited texts I get from Jess, the guiltier I feel about even thinking about saying I can't make it.

Not long!!! See, what did I say about exclamation marks? I suppose between now and the wedding I could say my mystery man and I had split up, or I could actually find a real man, or the imaginary one could die, or rush off to care for an ill relative, or get run over by a bus. Or all of the above. The possibilities are endless. *Sorry, got to rush, late for work.* I do usually tell the truth. *Call you back later for a proper chat xx*

My 'reasons I can't go' list needs updating. There's a new entry at number six.

1. My ex has impregnated somebody else. Hugely.

Shoving my mobile in my bag, and pushing my shoulders back, I paste a 'happy as Larry' grin on my face and throw open the door of the travel agency.

Chapter 2

'What's up?' Sarah, my other best friend, is sitting behind a desk that has two mugs of coffee, three Danish pastries, and several travel brochures open on it. She has pink hair (it changes regularly, I think she's naturally blonde, but I can't be sure, I've only known her three years), and a T-shirt that says 'Windsurfers do it standing up'. Most travel agencies would insist on a uniform, but Sarah's aunt owns this one and is as potty as she is. For her sixtieth birthday, she (the aunt, not Sarah) celebrated by going parasailing in Crete and taking the thirty-five year old instructor to bed. My mother celebrated hers with afternoon tea in a posh hotel. I fear that I am more like my mum than Sarah's aunt.

Sarah isn't fooled by my radiant smile.

'Here. Just what the doctor ordered.' She pushes a coffee towards me, and holds out a sticky pastry. I'm not sure any doctor would order anybody to eat this. 'There were only three left, so I couldn't leave one on its own could I?'

'Jess is getting married.'

'Fab. So the problem with that is?' Sarah only knows what I have told her. She moved into the area when she left college and her aunt offered her the type of job that would let her go backpacking *and* get a discount. 'You look like you've swallowed a lemon.'

'Thanks.' I take a bite of sugary pastry to combat the sour look. 'She wants me to be maid of honour.'

'Oh hells bells.' Sarah tends to say some odd things. 'You don't have to dress up like an extra from *Frozen* do you?'

'I don't think so.' I take another bite of pastry, and a gulp of coffee and plonk myself down in my swivel chair. And swivel. 'Liam is best man.' I try and say it casually, but I rotate a bit too vigorously and nearly end up in the potted plant behind me.

'Ahh.' We chew in unison, once I've stopped spinning. 'But you don't still care about Liam, do you? He's a shit.' She gives me the beady eye. 'A total shit.'

'Oh no, no of course I don't care.' Well maybe a teeny bit. 'I've not seen him since...' Sarah nods encouragingly. She knows seeing him again might be an issue. I mean you never know how you will actually feel, do you?

In my head I am so completely over him. He is a complete twat who I never really loved, but in real life what if he makes me feel wobbly? Or sick? 'It's not Liam, it's just everybody will be looking, and knowing.' Sarah nods, breaks the last pastry into two and passes half to me. 'And I haven't got round to that diet yet.'

'Well, I don't think you need to lose weight.' This is easy

for Sarah to say as she is stick thin. I know I have a got a bit over-rounded.

'Photos put pounds on you, I can't look like this.' I have let myself go since the split, I know I have. In fact I let myself go before the split. I got boring and fat. Both Liam and I had, but neither of us had really noticed. 'I never used to look like this.' Being lazily happy has been bad for me. Being heartbroken has been very bad for me. I seem to have totally lost the real me in all of this, and it is time I found myself again. Preferably before my current state is immortalised in wedding snaps.

'Well, you did say last week that you wanted to get fit again.' That is true, good intentions have been surfacing, popping their heads up like baby seals, then disappearing again. 'So maybe this is the incentive. A countdown!' Sarah spins round, kicking her legs in a very unprofessional way. 'We could go jogging?'

I pick a flake of pastry off my boobs and eat it. The idea of me and Sarah jogging is hilarious, unbelievable. But it's nice of her to offer. She'd probably turn up in Doc Martens and pink tights. I swallow the last bit of my calorie-laden breakfast. 'Maybe.' I am not good at saying no, which is part of the problem. 'There is another tiny problem.' If I call it tiny it might become tiny. They call it visualisation, don't they? 'I told Jess I had a new man.'

Sarah grins. 'Well, that'll be a piece of piss to sort.'

'Will it?'

'Hire a guy!' She has completely lost it. More off the

wall than ever. 'Oh my God, this has to be fate, you won't believe what I've just been reading. Look, look.' She starts to delve through the paperwork on her desk, pamphlets flying in all directions, then holds a holiday brochure up triumphantly. 'Voila!' She likes to throw in the odd foreign word when she speaks to clients, to create the right atmosphere and sense of anticipation.

'What?'

'Look!' The brochure is shoved into my hand and I am spun round at speed. Through the blur I can make out that it is actually a magazine. She clutches the arms of my seat so that I stop so abruptly the g-force hits, then pokes at the page. *Studs for Sale – how the modern woman solves the dating problem.* There's a photo of a famous movie star, with a hot to trot man gazing at her adoringly. 'She paid for him, can you believe it? Her! She hired him just for the night. *Everybody* is doing it. You just need an escort. Oh God, this is so frigging cool.' Her bracelets jangle alarmingly. 'It's karma!'

'It is?'

'It's meant to be, me having this mag and you desperately needing a man. Fate!'

'I wouldn't say desperately.' No woman in this century should ever admit to desperately needing a man, should they?

'Whatever. Shit, Sam, this is perfect.'

'I'm not sure everybody is doing it.' Escort sounds seedy. 'Especially not in the Surrey suburbs.'

'If they can do it in Hollywood, then why can't we?'

'Well, for one I can't afford it.'

'How do you know?' She's got a point, I haven't got a clue how much you have to shell out for a fake date.

'And somebody looking like that won't be remotely interested in a small town church wedding followed by a nosh up and boogie.' Okay, I'm being a bit unfair here, dragging Jess down to my level. It's because I'm panicking. It will be a lovely wedding, in one of the posh hotels. There will be nothing small town about it. But there will also be nothing Hollywood about it.

'Oh rubbish, I'm sure we could find somebody who'd do it. We should investigate, let's get...'

Luckily an elderly couple open the door and head straight for my desk. That tends to happen; I handle upmarket cruises and quiet retreats, Sarah gets booze cruises and 18-30 raves.

'Well?' She waves the magazine in the air in one hand, her other poised over the keyboard and mouths 'Google' at me. 'Sounds great to me – you'd never have to see him again!'

'And that could be a godsend,' chips in the lady, who has sat down and is rummaging in her handbag. She produces her glasses, puts them on and peers at me. 'I sometimes wonder what my life would have been like if I'd never had to see my Albert again.' She pats his knee in apology, and he smiles. 'Daft bugger has got flat batteries in his hearing aids so I can say what I want. Now, dear,

Albert wants to go to Brighton, and I want to go to Lake Garda. What do you suggest?'

I look at the couple, but my mind just isn't on the perfect holiday that combines the attractions of the south coast of Britain, and the Italian Lakes.

Studs for sale. Huh. Honestly, does she really think I'm so desperate I'd hire a date?

Chapter 3

I don't really believe in all that fate and bad luck stuff. Well, I do think the number seven is quite lucky, and I don't walk under ladders, and thirteen is a bit of a weird thing, and I don't step on cracks. Oh, and I do pick a penny up if I see it. And I have been known to follow the odd black cat, and trample over my friends in a bid to catch a bridal bouquet. But in general it's all a load of guff isn't it? I wouldn't say I believe, or let it rule my life in any way whatsoever.

But now I do believe bad luck comes in threes.

I have just got out of bed and picked number three up off my doormat. A thick, cream, embossed, exceedingly posh envelope. I reluctantly slide the thick, cream, equally posh card out of the envelope. I read the words on the front.

Wedding Invitation.

I open the card.

Number one was that save-the-date message, and number two was finding out that not only was Liam seeing the girl he'd 'met' while he was still supposed to be seeing me, he would also be taking her to the wedding. And she is huge. As in hugely pregnant. (Number two is a biggie in all senses of the word).

It's not the fact it's the actual wedding invite that qualifies it as number three (because I was expecting that) – it's what I read when I open it.

Jess and Dan aren't getting married in the local church, with some posh nosh up the road. Oh no. My imaginary partner and I are cordially invited to join the happy couple at Loch Lagwhinnie Country Estate.

I don't like the look of the word 'loch', it sounds ominously Scottish.

I am still clutching the invite as I Google the estate's name. It is Scottish, as in Scotland Scottish.

It is a remote estate in the wilds of Scotland, miles from civilisation. Well, the website I found doesn't exactly say 'wilds', but that is how I tend to think of Scottish estates. It's all Queen Victoria and her ghillie Brown, and shaggy ponies. And Braveheart. Hairy men in kilts. Oh my God, kilts.

I turn the invite over and it gets worse. Far worse. The celebrations are to last a week so that we can partake in the many activities on offer. There will be opportunities to shoot, fish, gallop across the estate, walk beside the loch, and sample the local whisky.

A WEEK!

Bloody hell, a whole week. I will need whisky. Not just a sample, gallons of the stuff.

I slide down the wall until I'm sat on the floor, because my wobbly legs don't give me much choice. Invite of doom in one hand, mobile phone in the other.

An actual week. How can Jess do this to me? My ordeal as a singleton is to last days.

My face will crack if I have to pretend-smile for seven days. My new jeans will split with the amount of alcohol and food I will be forced to consume as a coping mechanism. I will run out of supposedly waterproof mascara and eyeliner, and make-up remover.

She might give birth dramatically.

I'm slightly distracted by the thought of a mini Liam, already in tartan, entering the world whilst a bearded, kilted bagpipe player plays some mournful kind of music, when I realise my phone is vibrating in my hand. Still staring at the invitation, I answer it on auto-pilot without even looking at who's calling.

'Darling, it's me, Mum.'

Bugger. 'Oh, hi.' I can't go. Not for a whole week.

'Are you okay, Samantha? You sound distracted.'

Distracted is too small a word. 'Fine, just tired.' Tired always works well where my mother is concerned.

'Oh dear, you do work too hard. You need a break. That's why I'm ringing actually.' I can hear the excitement start to leak into her voice. 'Are you still there, Samantha?'

'Yes, I'm here. Sorry.' What do you do on a Scottish estate? Falling off horses (not that I'd get on one, given a choice) and marching through the heather in green wellies with a shotgun over my shoulder isn't exactly going to show Liam what he threw away, is it? I've got the type of calves that never look good in wellingtons, even when I'm at my thinnest and fittest. And I wouldn't know where to start when it comes to shooting, apart from that bit when they yell pull. It will probably be the nearest I get to pulling the whole week.

'Samantha! Did you hear what I just said?'

Unless I turned it into an Agatha Christie murder mystery type of week and shoot him. Although there might be a bit lacking in the mystery department.

'Samantha!'

'Sorry, what Mum?' It probably wouldn't be very fair on Jess though; births and deaths tend to be pretty messy affairs from what I've seen and could completely spoil the joyous occasion. And it is supposed to be *her* week, *her* big day. I sigh, I can't be that selfish. Even if she is practically shoving the means to destroy him into my hands.

'Did you hear what I said? Honestly darling, sometimes I think you're turning into your father.'

What did she say? My mind is blank. Oh yes. 'You're ringing cos I need a break?'

'I'm ringing because you are going to *get* a break.' She pauses melodramatically. Mother always fancied her chances on the stage. She's a member of the local theatre group, but has never yet got her big break. I think it might be too late, but nobody is going to dare tell her. Dad just throws me a wink behind her back, pours her a sherry and says they don't know what they're missing when she's cast as 'third woman in the corner shop' again. 'Oh I'm so excited, have you had your invite? Isn't it perfect?' The pitch gets higher, she'd be clutching me if she was here. 'A week in Scotland, how extravagant is that? I always did say Juliet and John knew how to do things in style, it's so nice they've stayed in touch over the years as you and little Jess have grown up. Aren't they beautiful? You can get a week off work, can't you?'

What? Scotland? Invite? A week off?

Oh. My. God. I stare at the cream card in my hand. If she knows all this, then it means my parents have been invited as well. Just when I thought it couldn't get any worse.

When I'd told Sarah everybody would be there I'd meant Jess's parents, Dan's parents, our friends. Liam. Her hugeness. Not my *mother*.

I definitely can't go now. Even if Magic Mike and his gang and all the Chippendales agree to back me up.

My little bit of mojo that has been creeping back has been bludgeoned to death.

This will be total humiliation. 'Well it might be a bit tric—'

'Oh of course you can, what am I saying? She's your best friend! And that Dan is such a lovely chap, such a shame you and Liam...' The words trail off, but then after an intake of breath she picks up again. 'Well never mind, some things aren't meant to be. But isn't it lovely?'

Lovely. Super.

'Is it cold in Scotland in June?'

I'm going to need a whole new wardrobe for a week. 'Er, I don't—'

'I can get your father to do that googly thing on his laptop can't I?'

'You can.' I need help from that googly thing myself.

'It looks incredibly posh, like a castle. Do people still wear Harris Tweed? I can't have your father looking out of place now, can I?'

Too many questions. My father is the least of my worries. A castle, how can Jess do this to me?

'Samantha? Samantha are you listening?'

'Oh no, yes, I mean no you can't, and I don't know about tweed, can't you buy *Country Life*, or *Horse and Hound* or something and check?'

'I'll ask Juliet. Oh this is exciting.' She's practically clapping her hands, I can tell. 'You'll look lovely on a horse darling, you can get some of those breeches, you might find a nice lord or something.'

'I won't.'

'Oh don't be so negative, Samantha. You have lovely hair, and teeth.' She's struggling, I can tell. Whoever had to stoop to listing her daughter's teeth as a selling point? 'And you're so clever.' Definitely struggling, she'll be bringing up my GCSE B grade in maths any second. 'And you do need a date, or you'll mess up the table plans.' And we couldn't have that could we? It would be my fault the whole wedding was ruined, the bride in tears ... because I, the friend, the maid of honour no less, had a spare seat next to me, or, worse, we'd gone woman-woman because of the odd number. Maybe I should suggest a lesbian table? A woman only table? A sad singletons table? Then it wouldn't matter. Maybe not. Maybe it would be a table for one.

'I've got the answer! You can take Desmond.'

Desmond, who the F is Desmond? And who calls their child that in this day and age? Now all I can think about is Desmond Tutu. I can't date a man who reminds me of a bishop.

'If you'll let me get a word in, Mum, I can't because—'

'He's very nice. Got lovely manners, and I'm sure it's not his fault that silly dating site can't find—'

'Mum!'

She stops. A miracle.

'I can't go with Desmond because I already have a date.'

There is silence. Total silence. I am just beginning to think we must have been cut off, because my mum is never stuck for words, when...

'Oh.'

Shit, what have I done? Why did I say that?

'You never told me.' There is a slight hint of hurt in her tone. 'How lovely. Although you might find a Scottish lord or laird or whatever they call them as well. No need to rush into things with this new one, it would be so nice to live in a castle, that would put Mrs Bracken next door in her place. If she's told me once, she's told me a million times about her new son-in-law going to Oxford. And you could have some of those Scottish wolfhound dogs.'

'I think they're Irish, Mum.' See, one invite and this is where it's taken her, into a complete fantasy land.

'Don't be silly dear, I'm sure some of them are born in Scotland. I've seen pictures of them in the Sunday supplements, outside castles. With kilts and ... David ... David, what are those purple prickly things? Oh don't be ridiculous, pansies aren't prickly! Prickly I said, not pretty. See, what did I say? He never listens properly. Thistles, that's what they are, thistles. So it has to be Scotland, not Ireland.'

'It doesn't matter, I'm not meeting some castle-owning laird, and I don't want a big dog. I've already got a boyfriend.' Why have I repeated the lie? Once could be a mistake, twice means it is a truth.

'Well, if you say so Samantha. That's wonderful, well done.' She's obviously hankering over a highland estate to boast about to the neighbours and I've thrown a spanner in the works. 'What's his name? Do I know his mother?'

Bugger. I should have thought this through. Brad, George? 'No, you don't know his mother. Hang on a sec, there's somebody at the door, might be him!' I might have shouted that a bit too enthusiastically. I do some door opening and shutting, and mutter a bit.

I need to make a name up and write it down, what kind of girlfriend doesn't know her boyfriend's name?

There's silence when I finish my door banging. I know she's waiting for a name, probably a surname as well. She wants to Google him. Or get Dad to check if he's on Tinder. She is the Hercule Poirot of her neighbourhood.

'Oh no, not him! Just a lost cat. Well it wasn't a cat, somebody has lost a cat, all go here!'

'You'll have to bring him round for supper.' She's brightened up. I don't know where 'supper' has come from though. When I was growing up we had breakfast, dinner and tea. At some point dinner became lunch, and tea became dinner. Now we have supper. 'Then we can meet him before the wedding.' Interrogate him more like.

'Yes, er, I'll ask him.' After I've managed to meet him. 'I'll have to call you back, Mum. Got to dash, I've er—' in for a penny, in for a pound '—I've got to get changed before I meet him.' I will have to get changed, I'll probably have to get changed several times before I meet my mystery man. See, I'm not exactly lying, just slightly misleading which is perfectly acceptable, and natural, in a mother-daughter relationship.

So what do I do?

I book an emergency appointment at the hairdresser's. The cheapest form of therapy known to man (and, of course, woman).

I am on the way for a cut and blow, hoping a pamper session will leave me feeling less like devouring the contents of the fridge and more like joining in the celebrations. It will also give me time to decide whether

Sarah has a valid point, and I am now actually desperate enough to put an advert on Gumtree: 'Desperately Seeking Stud'.

Chapter 4

'How are you gorgeous?' Tim, the loveliest hairdresser in the world, gives me a very unprofessional hug, then holds me at arm's length. 'A little snip here and there and you'll be all bouncy again.'

It will take more than a little snip to give me back my bounce, although a snip in Liam's direction might help cheer me up. In fact a snip several months ago might have meant we were still together. It's dawned on me in the last few minutes that for anybody to be *hugely* pregnant, they would have had to be shagging my boyfriend *long* before he became my ex.

This is not a good thought.

My plastered-on smile must have slipped a bit because Tim is frowning at me.

'I think you need a bit of colour in your life. How about a hint of pink?'

I nod. Pink, purple, bright blooming blue. I'd say yes to anything right now.

'Chantelle will run you some colour through, won't you,

darling?' Chantelle is nodding. 'And I'll get you a nice little glass of prosecco.' He pats my hand. 'Then you can tell Uncle Tim all about it.' Uncle Tim is probably a good few years younger than me, but right now I'm happy to play along.

Prosecco in hand, with Chantelle gaily adding streaks of colour to my boring hair and life, and Tim sitting looking intently at me, I am already starting to feel a bit better. Tim might be gay, but he's the only man who's run his fingers through my hair this year. And that's fine.

'It's that lousy Liam, isn't it?' I nod rather too vigorously, then freeze, hoping Chantelle hasn't added a highlight the size of a zebra stripe. Tim knows all about 'the break up'; he's my hero – he supplied me with fags, wine and a good haircut as I wept in front of his mirror, and never once suggested I wasn't good for business before wheeling me into a dark corner of the salon. If Tim didn't have a boyfriend I'd have suggested he move in with me by now.

'You know, don't you?' Shit. He knows. Everybody knows. How come I'm the absolutely last person on the planet to find out about the huge girlfriend?

'His mum was in here last week, she's putting a brave face on it babe, but... *She. Is. So. Fuming.*' He spaces the last four words out, then shakes his head before patting my hand. 'Such a dick, you are *so* well rid.'

Logically I know I am well rid, and I know that his mother disapproves of all his girlfriends (including me), but in my heart there is still a tiny illogical Liam-shaped

31

hole. I've been hanging on to that hole, I haven't been ready to stitch it up and shut him out forever. 'He's going to be at the wedding, with her.' And it. The unborn. The prosecco seemed to have lost some of its bubbles. 'I can't go.'

'Oh, girlfriend, you have *got* to go. Hasn't she, girls?'

There is a nodding of heads and chorus of consent. I suddenly realise that the dryers have gone quiet and all ears are tweaked our way.

'But I can't.' I know I'm being a bit feeble, and it's a bit of a wail, but Tim is not to be deterred. 'My parents have been invited as well, and I can't face them all unless I look amazingly fabulous, I will totally be the centre of attention and I'm fat and...' Tim holds a hand up to stop the flow, but he knows what I'm getting at. The next time I see Liam I have to be slim, glamorous, drop-em-dead gorgeous. The one that got away. For my sake, not his. My voice drops to a whisper. 'And I have to have a man.' It isn't that I think my life isn't complete without a man. I'm not that hopeless. 'I've told Jess I've got a new boyfriend, and Mum.' Christ why did I do that? 'And everybody...'

'Will be looking at you?' Tim sums it up in one. He stands up, triumphant. 'We're going to make you look fab-u-lous, and—' he waves his hand flamboyantly '—we're going to find you a man, aren't we girls?'

Sitting with gunge plastered all over my head, a rather hot heat lamp threatening to singe my hair, and a glass of prosecco in my hand, I don't feel fabulous.

'Right gorgeous, describe your perfect date.' He's back in his seat. 'Hit us, babe. The full works.'

I wriggle in my seat (it does feel a bit like my head is burning, and for a moment I wonder if he's got carried away and turned me up high). 'Well, Jude Law's very nice.'

Chantelle tops up my glass. 'Oh my God, did you see him in *The Holiday*? I mean he's a bit old for me—' anybody over twenty-one is probably a bit old for Chantelle '—but I wouldn't have said no.'

'Daniel Craig is more my taste.' A lady at the far side of the salon puts her copy of *Harper's Bazaar* down. 'I didn't know I liked blonds until I saw him stride out of the sea in those swimming trunks.' She fans herself with the magazine.

'Isn't he everybody's, darling?' Tim joins in the fanning melodramatically.

'He has got quite nice, er, pecs.' I'm never quite sure which muscle is which, but I do know Daniel Craig has plenty of them. And I do know he scares me a bit. 'He's not quite my style though.' An image of Liam jumps into my head, totally pec-less. I shake it away – I can do better than that. 'I mean I like muscles, but I like cuddles as well.'

There's a collective sigh. Don't you love hairdressing salons? Guaranteed support, *and* a haircut.

A burst of loud music launches itself at my ear drums and Chantelle whisks away the heat lamp as the timer goes off. 'That's you done, don't want you too intense, do we?' She ushers me over to the backwash unit, and points at my right thigh accusingly as I settle myself into the chair.

I'm just about to apologise (several packets of cheesy wotsits have found a home there) when she leans over and jabs a button that I hadn't noticed (my thigh was in the way). 'New chairs, you even get a massage. How good is that?'

I'm not actually sure it would rate in my brilliant category, but after two glasses of bubbly and no bum fondling or back kneading for a long time, the gentle vibration is actually quite acceptable.

'I like a man who can cuddle too.' Chantelle digs her fingertips into my scalp firmly.

'Hugh Grant was my type years ago.' The woman at the next backwash sighs. 'I'd have cuddled him and much more.'

I glance over, and she looks at least sixty. She grins back in a very naughty way, positively licking her lips. Then winks. Too much information, it's like your mum bringing up her sex life when all you agreed to was some bonding over handbag shopping.

'It's the hair, and the smile. He'd make you laugh, wouldn't he love? Can't beat a man who can make you laugh.' I'm not so sure on that point. 'That film when he's Prime Minister,' Miss Sixty-Plus carries on undeterred.

'*Love Actually*?'

She nods. 'And he's doing that bit of dad-dancing, bless. Ooh, I could have grabbed him, I could.'

Tim whisks me and my drippy hair back to my seat in

front of a mirror, so luckily I don't have to come up with a response.

'Liam Hemsworth is cute.'

Tim's gaze meets mine in the mirror. 'If he was one of my clients, he'd be yours, gorgeous.' He combs my hair through. 'When I was working in London, we had actors in and out all the time.' The way he says it lends a definite double entendre.

'You could always borrow my little brother for the day.'

The words come out of the blue. For a moment I think I've misheard as I glance round wildly, then realise it's the girl opposite me, hidden by the mirrors. She leans to one side, so I can see her. My first impression is perfect smile, perfect make-up, and perfect hair. My second impression is money.

'Oh my God, Amy. Yes!' I think Tim's about to orgasm as he clamps his hands over his mouth. His gaze switches from her to me. 'He is SO gorgeous, SO you.'

I dread to think what he thinks 'me' is, and I daren't ask, because if this man is anything like his sister Amy then he's nothing like me at all.

'And that man can act, can't he Amy?'

'Oh yeah.' She rolls her eyes. 'He's an actor, he can play anything from cuddly uncle to porn star.' I'm not sure either of those fits my particular bill. 'He'll do anything to practise his craft – and throw in a party and he'll think he's in heaven.' She winks. 'And he's broke.'

'If he wasn't straight I'd have had my hands on that butt

of his years ago.' I've never seen Tim quite so animated. He's snipping away at my hair with gay abandon, a lustful smile on his face, and I'm wondering if it would be safer to ask him to stop now before I end up with a pixie cut that I haven't got the face for.

'Jake's a bit of a twat, but he's harmless.' Amy grins. 'He needs somebody down to earth and nice to put him in his place; you'd be perfect.' I'm not sure if this is a compliment or an insult, so I just smile nicely and try not to worry about the scissors. 'Those airheads he normally dates just simper and swoon when he tells them he's lined up to be the next James Bond.'

'Is he?' I know my eyes have opened a bit wider, and I've sat up a bit straighter. Holy crap, have I just bagged myself a real hunk? I've always been able to take it or leave it as far as James Bond goes, but I wouldn't say no to a date.

'Is he hell!' She laughs, and my backbone sags back into its normal curve. 'He's doing bit parts, waiting for his big break.'

Otherwise known as working as a barista. Licensed to handle a coffee machine isn't quite the same as licensed to kill. Or thrill. Although I'd probably get a good latte out of the deal.

'Here.' She stands up, showing off endless legs and a designer handbag. 'Take my card.' Even the card, framed by immaculate nails, looks expensive.

It would be rude to ignore it, but this is never going to work. The whole idea of a fake date makes me feel slightly queasy, and actor Jake is way outside my league. At least if I hired an escort like Sarah suggested, we'd all know where we stood. And he wouldn't be nearly famous.

'I'm not sure it will be up his street.' I try and match her posh tone, and just sound a bit like my mother when she answers the phone. 'And er, it's not for a day, it's for a week.'

'Even better, he could do with a change of scene! Honestly, he'd love it.' She puts the card down, then blows Tim a kiss. 'Let me know if you're interested and I'll sound him out, though he's anybody's for a free lunch.'

'Oh she's interested, aren't you gorgeous?' Tim hugs me. 'He's just what you need.' We watch Amy leave, and Tim wields the hairdryer until I look streaked and sleek.

'Divine.' He holds a mirror so I can see the back. 'I can just see Liam's face when you walk in on Jake's arm looking absolutely fab. The dream team.' He sighs.

I stare at my own reflection. I do look quite good, and Jake might look like a young George Clooney, or a Brad Pitt, or a cute Alex Pettyfer. After all he is an actor.

Tim spins me round. 'You can do this, I'm not taking no for an answer.'

I grin back. 'I can do this.' I swan out of the salon on a high, hair all swishy and a spring in my step. I *can* do this. I have to.

I shall go to the wedding. I shall take a date.

What could possibly go wrong?

Chapter 5

There are obviously loads of things that ~~will~~ might go wrong if I take a fake date called Jake to my best friend's wedding.

1. I might hate Jake.
2. Jake might hate me.
3. Somebody might know him.
4. I could become a laughing stock.
5. Everybody will despise me when they realise I've tried to dupe them.

There are of course positives in any situation.

1. Everybody will admire how well I have moved on (if they don't guess it's a sham), and how little I care about Liam and his huge girlfriend.
2. His mother might regret being nasty and be insanely jealous when she sees me with another man, and realise that I can no longer be her daughter-in-law.

The fizz has worn off a bit by the time I get home, and the frizz has set in. There is no hair product known to man that will totally stop my hair going all frizzy when it's damp outside.

I feel a bit daft, and all flat and deflated. I got totally carried away with Tim and his plan. I know he loves me and means well, but it's a mad idea. Who in their right mind would take a total stranger to a wedding? This is practically a family wedding. Everybody knows me, everybody will realise that I would never meet a young, posh George Clooney lookalike.

I decide I need to forget all about Jake, and take my new hairdo out for a glass of wine while it still has a tiny trace of swish factor left.

'What's up?' This seems to be Sarah's opening line at the moment. I am obviously not hiding my concerns as well as I think I am.

'I can't decide whether to have another Aperol spritz, or have one of those espresso martinis.' I'm eying up the one on the next table as I suck up the last drop of Aperol through a straw.

'Well hurry up and decide before that sexy barman does a runner on me.'

'Which sexy barman?' I've been coming in this wine bar on a regular basis for the past year with Sarah, and I've never seen anybody I'd rate as even mildly sexy. Some of them *think* they are, but they need a reality check if you ask me. I mean, being able to toss a cocktail shaker in the air doesn't make you anything more than a tosser, does it?

'There is definitely something up with you if you've not noticed. Look, there.'

I glance over the top of my glass, trying not to be too obvious. 'The one that looks about eighteen?'

Sarah nods. 'Soo cute.'

Okay, maybe he is quite cute. In an eighteen-year-old way. 'You can't!'

'Watch me.' She winks. 'Some men like a mature woman, I could teach him a trick or two.'

'I bet you could.'

'But I was looking for you, not me. You could take him to the wedding, it would be way cheaper than going to some agency. I Googled and it's scary how much these people charge, and that's just the normal places, not the type of guys that mag article was on about. I mean you can't even get a quote from some of those places without producing your birth certificate, statement from your bank manager and proof you've got a million followers on Twitter.'

'Really?' It's starting to look like if I'm going to do this, then it's Jake or nobody.

'And you have to swear on your dog's life that you won't tell anybody.' Sarah has obviously spent some time researching this.

'I haven't got a dog.' I haven't even got a hamster.

'See, I knew it was impossible. I mean you're not going to get a dog just so you can hire a guy, are you?'

'And you already know, so it wouldn't be a secret either.'

'Exactly.' Sarah has what I can only describe as a look of mischief on her face. 'So taking the cute bartender is an ace idea – they'd all be drooling, you'd be the centre of attention.'

Okay, feeling good about myself is what I'm after, attention is not. I've told Sarah about the wedding invite, and the 'huge' complications. I have not told her it's got worse. I've not told her about my mother, or Scotland.

'I don't want to be the centre of attention.' I am hoping to sneak in under the radar and hardly be noticed. I don't want drooling any more than I want pity.

'I'll get you a surprise.' Sarah is on her feet. 'And his number.' She's off to the bar before I can stop her, and comes back surprisingly quickly which I think means wonder boy isn't available to be whisked off for some private tuition.

The drinks are green. I'm never quite sure that anything I eat or drink should be green. Apart from M&Ms.

'Appletini. Callum reckons they're the in thing.' Oh, so he didn't blow her out of the water completely. 'Vodka and apple schnapps.' She takes a sip and sucks air in through her teeth. 'Yikes.'

'So you had time to discuss ingredients?'

'And what time he finishes!' She grins like a cougar that's got the kitten and smacks her lips. 'That has got a bit more kick than a V&T.' She sits back and watches as I toy with the slice of apple, then leans forward. 'You don't have to go, Sam.'

We both know what she's talking about. Sarah saw me through the break up, she fed me pizza, and supplied tissues and wine. And she listened. A lot. Sarah deserves a saint-hood.

'I do, Jess is my friend. And I'm supposed to be maid of honour.'

'She'll understand.'

'Would you?'

'Suppose not. In fact I'd think you were a bit of a selfish cow putting your broken heart above what's supposed to be the happiest day of my life.'

'Exactly.' I know she's said it tongue in cheek, but every word is true. 'And I told her I was over Liam and had a hot new man.'

'True.'

I take a big gulp of my drink, and my eyes water. 'Wow.' It comes out all spluttery and weak, I think my vocal chords have been damaged. 'That has got a kick.' It's got a knock-you-over, brandy kind of kick. Maybe I should take Callum and just let him wreak cocktail havoc, nobody will remember a thing.

Sarah puts her hand over mine. 'Sam you're gorgeous, loads of men would kill for a date.' We both know that's the green cocktails talking.

'Sarah, it's got worse.' I swig the rest of my lethal cocktail.

'I haven't just told Jess I've got a new man, I've told Mum as well.'

'Shit.' There is a long silence. 'Your mother, why?' Sarah knows what my mother is like (despite only meeting her once), because I have told her. And she has spoken to her on the phone.

My mother makes a habit of ringing me when I'm at work, and I make a habit of trying to avoid her calls. So she's got sneaky and rings the travel agency number, and not my mobile. Sarah actually thinks it's fun talking to Mum, so is more than happy to answer, and they're practically on first name terms now. Getting Mum off the phone practically requires a degree in evasive manoeuvres though, so Sarah knows her pretty well.

She knows that my lie is now folklore.

'I had to tell her, she rang to tell me she's been invited to the wedding as well.'

'Oh, double shit.'

We get another round of drinks, and by the time I'm halfway down I know I have to tell her about Amy. And Jake.

I take a deep breath. 'I can't take Callum.' She looks slightly disappointed, but resigned. 'And I think your escort idea is out, isn't it?' She nods glumly. 'Even though it was a brilliant idea.' I don't want her to think I don't appreciate her. 'But, well, there is another option. A definite possibility.' This is also the green cocktail talking. Cocktails have a serious role to play in society. I need a detached, independent opinion and Sarah is as detached as they come. And she's all in favour of fake dates. 'But it has to be a complete secret.'

If I ever do this, and I'm totally not sure I will, Sarah is the only person I know who definitely won't drop me in it. She also tells the truth, apart from the bit about the stampede of men who'd kill for a date with me, but I know that is to cheer me up.

'What kind of possibility?'

'Tim knows this girl who's got this brother.' I can see her gaze wandering back to the cocktail shaker, I'm losing her. 'Who's an actor.' She's tuned back in. 'Who would do it. You know be a fake date, but cheaper than those agencies.' I hope. Maybe I need to ask Amy how much he'd charge. If we could work it out on a sliding latte scale I'd be okay, but if he wanted film star rates... 'And I wouldn't need a dog, and I'd know him.' Kind of. 'So it wouldn't be as weird.' Maybe.

'Wow, a hot, sexy actor—'

'I didn't say...'

'Picture?'

'I haven't...'

'What's his name? Come on, let's Google him. God, I can't believe you haven't done that yet. I Google everybody.' She does. Everybody and everything.

'I've got his sister Amy's number, she said to get in touch if I decide...'

'Well, you've decided. I can't believe you didn't tell me

straight away. Come on, let's get another round of those apple things in and give sister Amy a call.' Sarah giggles. 'This is amazeballs.' Sarah often gets carried away after a few drinks and 'amazeballs' is her latest word; at least she's moved on from calling everything 'sick'. I blame it on spending too much time playing online video games with teenagers. 'The dog's bollocks.' See? 'What if it's Brad Pitt?'

'It isn't Brad Pitt.' I reluctantly wave Amy's card in front of her. 'She's called Amy Taylor-Smith.'

'But he'll have an acting name. Gimme.' She snatches the card before I can stop her. 'You go and get the drinks in, I'm going to ring Amy. Oh God, this is SO much better than just going to an escort agency, this is SO exciting.'

By the time I've walked to the bar and back I've changed my mind. Again.

'I can't do it.'

'Bollocks, stop being a spoilsport. You know you want to!'

A little part of me does want to, but the logical, sensible part doesn't.

'It'll be a right hoot!'

'You're not the one doing it. There are so many things that could go wrong, and he might be ugly, or gay, or have horrible blubber lips that I won't want to kiss.' I feel slightly sick at the thought of big fat lips heading towards me. 'What if I agreed to this and then totally didn't fancy him?'

'Or what if he's a sexier male version of his sister? I mean

I'm firmly in the hetero camp, but she is seriously good looking. Family genes and all that, he can't be a total minger, can he?'

'How do you know what Amy looks like?' I frown at her, suddenly suspicious.

She grins. 'She didn't answer when I called her, so I sent her a text, and she said she was in the middle of something. I had to do something while I was waiting, so...'

'So you went on Facebook.'

'Damn right I did. Look!' Sarah shoves her mobile phone in front of my face. I look. 'This is her, isn't it? I have got the right woman, haven't I? It would be so embarrassing if I'd got the hots for some totes different Amy.'

'Yep, that's her.' She's looking even more gorgeous than she did in the hair salon, and she's got her arms draped round two very hunky men. Some girls have all the luck.

'If her brother is dire, though I don't see how that's even possible, maybe she'll lend you one of these? Or,' Sarah pauses mid-sip, 'maybe one of these *is* Jake.' She enlarges the photo and we both peer. 'They are seriously hawt.'

They are indeed quite hot. Easy on the eye, as my mother would say.

'Isn't this a bit stalkerish?'

'Definitely not. It's essential research. Right girlfriend, let's get digging. If this is Amy's profile then there's bound to be a photo of her brother, isn't there?' She scrolls down, and I can't help myself. I have to look. What if he is actually nice? More than nice? This could maybe work.

'Have you seen this? Bloody hell, she was at the opening of that new bar, she's a real mover and shaker, isn't she?' Sarah has got distracted from the mission. 'Do you think she could get me an invite to some of these things, now you're friends?'

'I've only met her once.'

'But you're dating her brother.'

'I'm not exactly...'

She carries on undeterred. 'Or do you think she needs a holiday? I bet she could afford something really top of the range. Aunt Lynn would be seriously impressed if I could sell to her and her mates.'

'Sarah!' I try and grab her phone, but she's got a firm grip. 'I need to see him. Now!'

'Don't get your knickers in a twist.' She holds her phone in the air out of my reach, a big grin on her face. 'This is such a good idea.' I realise I'm grinning back. 'Oh God, we're being seriously thick here. We should look at her friends list, if he's on Facebook they're bound to be friends are they? And what kind of an actor wouldn't be on Facebook?' She's tapping away as she speaks and suddenly lets out a shriek. 'Oh my God! It's him, it's him!'

I nearly shriek as well, because she's clutching my arm. But she is bouncing about on her seat so much it's hard to see anything at all, apart from a blur.

'He is frigging gorgeous. You have got to do this, Sam, you have seriously got to do this.'

I take the mobile phone off her, and even though my hands are shaking, I can see him.

Jake Porter.

His gorgeous tawny-brown eyes are gazing straight back into mine as though we're face to face. Which is stupid, it's a picture. I touch it, I can't help myself, and we ping on to his page. Where there are lots more pictures. Jake winking, Jake laughing, Jake with his arm round Amy, Jake gazing at a woman who has to be his mother, Jake looking cute with a puppy, Jake on a horse.

I scroll back. A horse?

'He's on a horse.' It has to be an omen, apart from the totally sexy gorgeousness.

'So?' Sarah reclaims her phone. 'He's a real dish, isn't he?

'So, we have to do horse-riding and stuff in Scotland. He could fit in fine.'

'Fit in?' Sarah giggles – then stops and raises an eyebrow. 'You never said anything about Scotland, that's miles away!'

'I know it's miles away, and it's for a whole week.' I lean in closer to Sarah so I can stare at Jake. A whole week with a man like him could be quite nice. 'Maybe I can do it.' My stomach has gone all squirmy, so I take a big gulp of cocktail to try and distract myself.

'Oh God, yes you can girl.' Sarah is grinning slightly manically. 'You defo can Sam.' We both stare at his profile picture. His brown hair is tousled, casually sexy. He's in a casual shirt, open so you can see his brown neck, the hint of a smattering of hair. The sleeves are rolled up, showing indecently strong, toned forearms. And those eyes...

'Maybe he just takes a good photo?' I have to be prepared for disappointment.

Sarah giggles. 'Lots of good photos. He looks sexy in all of these, but we can always stalk him to make sure he doesn't act like a douchebag.'

She says it like it's an everyday thing. Stalking. Which is a bit worrying.

'What if I can't afford to pay him for a week?' I'm saying it, trying to be sensible, but knowing that if I can raise the money then I have to. There's a dimple at the corner of his full, firm looking lips. A naughty quirk to his eyebrow. He doesn't just look hot, he looks fun. Mischievous. Everything that I'd forgotten to be when I was with Liam.

'He'll give you mates' rates, he has to.' Sarah says it with conviction.

A little, very indecent, shiver goes down my spine. This could be fun, this could be brilliant. I could have the hottest date at the wedding, in the whole of Scotland, and I don't care if it means we are the centre of attention.

'Okay.' I take a deep breath. 'I'm going to do it.' I cross my fingers under the table. 'Let's get stalking!'

Sarah leaps in the air with a squeal (I swear she's related to this mad springer spaniel we had when I was a kid) and punches the air. Everybody looks our way. I'm very tempted to pull her down and sit on her, which is roughly what I had to do to the dog once or twice. Well, not exactly sit on it – before you report me to the RSPCA – subdue is prob-ably a better word. Strongly subdue. Pin down.

Sarah has not been subdued. 'Go you! Wow, I'm seriously jealous. Let's get another drink to celebrate!'

I feel slightly sick, but more excited-bubbling-stomach sick, than get-me-out-of-here sick. 'I still want to see him, in the flesh, before I talk to him.'

'We'll follow him.'

'He'll think I'm crazy.'

Sarah giggles. 'You are crazy, but I don't mean follow as in crazy-woman follow; I mean just happen to be in some bar where he just happens to be, and observe him. From afar.' She flings a hand in the air as though this is everyday, normal behaviour.

'My eyesight isn't that good these days, and it's dark in bars.'

'Not that afar. Come on, text Amy, find out if she knows what he'll be up to the next few days.' She reaches for my bag, to rifle for my phone, and I grab it protectively. Hug it to my bosom. 'Oh do it, do it now. You've got to! This is so exciting.'

We're grinning at each other like children about to unwrap the presents on Christmas day, and I feel a bit lightheaded and giddy. Which could be the cocktails.

I do it. And a message pings back from Amy before we even have time to order another drink. She has the perfect solution, they're having a family get together. A meal in the Italian restaurant up the road. I can see the whole family.

I can see him at his most normal (her words not mine, which rings a few warning bells) when he's not acting a part.

Thursday at 8 p.m.

I show Sarah, and she squeals again, then grabs me for a hug.

This is really happening. I am planning on spending a week with a fake date.

And my fake date is far, far better than Desmond (I've seen him, Mum sent me a photo in case I changed my mind. He has a combover. The type designed to hide a thinning patch, not the trendy type. Nuff said) or the idea of being on the spinster and lonely hearts table.

ACT TWO – THE DATE

Chapter 6

Reasons this could possibly work:

1. He has not got a combover (so infinitely better than Desmond).
2. He has a pert bum (and the rest of him is more than a little okay).
3. He loves his family (which is a definite positive as he will have to cope with mine).

Jake has got a full head of his own hair, and makes the type of confident entrance that makes people stop what they're doing and glance his way. And he's not even famous yet (as far as I know).

We know it's him because he looks exactly like you'd imagine him to from his profile picture on Facebook (which has to be a first in the history of social media) and because, to eliminate all doubt, Amy has stood up and rather enthusiastically shouted 'Jake, Jake, we're here. Where've you been?'

Even though the restaurant is a bit dimly lit, I'm pretty sure Jake would have spotted them, his family, unless he was pretty dim too. But it's nice of her to make sure we're in the picture, I just hope she doesn't blow our undercover mission out of the water.

'O-M-F-G, swoon-worthy or what?' I think Sarah is trying to sell this to me rather over-enthusiastically, probably because I look like I'm about to duck out. I was actually so excited that I didn't sleep last night, but now I've got what I can only think of as first date nerves, even though it isn't a date.

So far we've only seen the back of him, as he heads over to his family, straight into a hug and kiss with what has to be his granny. Which I suppose is a point in his favour (see point 3, above). Being demonstrative is good, doing it in public is even better considering the role he will need to play. 'I wish he'd turn around so I can see his face.'

'Forget his face, just look at that cute arse.' Sarah stops waving her breadstick and starts to eat it in a very suggestive manner. 'That wasn't in any of the photos.'

I am looking at his arse. I can't stop staring at his arse, in fact. But that is not the point. 'I have to look at his face, not arse. It's a wedding. It's a week.' I bury my head in my hands (but can't help peeping between my fingers at his very nice back view, he has a broad back, the type that is toned and probably tanned – not that I'll be getting to see that). This is a mix of scary and exciting. 'A week.' With a total stranger. And my family.

It sounds a bit like a wail to my own ears, and I hope nobody else has noticed. Sarah has. She pats my hand. 'You'll be fine. Just think what you could get up to in a week.' She winks, then goes all swoony again. I think I need to get a move on, or she'll be taking matters into her own hands. Literally.

'And eyes are important. I can't make lovey-dovey faces if I don't like his eyes.' Although I did like his eyes in the photos. I could quite easily gaze adoringly at him for a week if he really does look like that and it isn't all down to photoshopping. Because, you never know, his agent could check every photo before he's allowed to post it online.

'You're just so bloody fussy. Any minute now you'll be saying he needs a brain and—' she puts her posh voice on '—good conversation.'

'Sod off, Sarah.'

'A man's not for life, Sam, he's just for a wedding.' She giggles and tops up our wine glasses. 'Are you eating that bruschetta, or shall I?'

'You think this is funny, don't you?' To be fair, I probably would if the roles were reversed. 'And yes, I am eating it, hands off.' I need any carbs I can get my hands on, to soak up the wine I suspect we're going to be drinking. I also might have to tell her to keep her hands off my man as well. Not that he's my man yet. 'What...'

Then he turns around and I forget whatever I was going to say next.

The main issue with staring at a man's pert bum, is

that if he spins round you find yourself staring at his crotch.

I once looked up 'crotch' in the dictionary. Don't ask. I think I was in the waiting room at the dentist's and read it in some countryside or gardening magazine. It was an article about tree pruning, with photos of some very masculine looking types hanging off branches dangling chainsaws. I was confused, and bored, so I Googled. Anyway, it means (if you ignore the obvious) a fork in a tree, road, or river. As in the trunk where it splits into two branches, get it? This fork was very snugly encased in the jeans that are also caressing his rear.

'Oh fork.'

Sarah splutters crumbs. Christ, did I really say that? And in that way?

'Fork indeed.' Her eyes are watering as she spits the words out between what sounds like a cat coughing up fur balls, but I think it's a mix of laughter and tears, and trying not to make too much noise. At least it stops the suggestive breadstick sucking.

I glance upwards, just to check he's not looking at us because of the noise she's making, and he is. Looking at us. Well, he's looking straight at me, and he has got the dirtiest grin I have ever seen on his face. All Hugh Grant and awfully British, but awfully naughty. It is way, way sexier than the grin he had on his Facebook profile.

Then he winks. And my face is on fire, along with several other parts of my body.

Shit. 'I can't do this.' After I've been caught ogling him like that, he'll think I'm sex-starved. He'll turn me down.

'He is seriously gorgeous.' Sarah is now licking the end of the breadstick in a way that could get us thrown out.

He is. 'He thinks I'm some sort of perv before he's even met me. He'll probably say no.' I stare at the very interesting tablecloth and try and peek through my eyelashes to see if he's still looking our way. He isn't, he's got his arm round a woman who's brought more bread to the table.

'Honestly, what a flirt, what a chauvinist, I'm not sure I'd want to be seen with him.' Does he hug everybody? I mean, I want him to hug my mother, but not spend all his time embracing other women while I look on.

'What does it matter?' Sarah shrugs, and stabs a piece of penne pasta. I hadn't even noticed our meals arriving. I really, really hope she doesn't start to suck on that. 'He's probably used to women staring, and he's not going to think you're that normal anyway, is he?' She laughs. 'Anyway I know you don't mean it, you can't stop looking at him.'

Exactly. What normal woman would think of doing this? But thinking I'm not normal is one thing, thinking I'm some kind of sex-starved not-normal is another.

'He's probably very big-headed, and shallow.' I don't think my face is glowing quite as much now, it's calmed down to a simmer. My red blotchy chest is another matter though. Why didn't I wear a high necked top? Embarrassment, lust and heat always make my chest blotchy. Not that this is about lust. Now he'll think I've got some strange disease, as well as being sex-starved. He'll turn me down even if (and it is an 'if') I do offer him the equivalent of a down payment on a bachelor pad.

How excruciating would that be to admit to? Even worse than admitting I didn't have a new fabulous boyfriend and having to spend a week in Scotland trying to ignore pitying looks. 'We won't have anything in common.' Oh gawd, now he has a little girl on his knee, and she's giggling and looking at him adoringly as he balances a breadstick on his upper lip and I don't mind him hugging her at all. He's not at all self-conscious or flirty. I admit it, I wouldn't mind at all being seen with him. Spending a whole week with him. But will he feel the same about me?

'Methinks you doth protest too much.' Sarah is watching me now, not him. 'You fancy him don't you? Go on, admit it!'

He laughs, a full-throated kind of laugh that makes me feel tingly, and I forget to take a drink from the glass I'm holding up to my mouth.

She's right. I do fancy him. Who wouldn't? I fancy him even more as he leans down and picks up the napkin that his mother has dropped, then leans in to replace it and whisper in her ear. He really would be the perfect date, the type of man who would have my mother in raptures and my father's nod of approval. Even if it is all just pretend.

Sarah is still staring. Openly. 'And anyway just think of loser Liam and up the duff Delia or whatever she's called; he will totally buy into you two as a couple, you'll look great together.'

To be honest, I've stopped caring about Liam. I can't take my eyes off Jake. If anybody could prove to me what a total waste of my life Liam was, he's sitting right across the room.

I grab my mobile phone.

'What are you up to now?' Sarah whips away my last bit of chocolate brownie before I get a chance to object. To be honest, I've hardly noticed the food, I'd be hard put to say what I've eaten.

'Texting Amy. I want to do this, I need to do this. Taking Jake to the wedding is a brilliant idea!'

Sarah grins, then raises her glass. 'I couldn't agree more!'

I get a return message from Amy just after I've got home. Jake is up for it. He's suggested we meet on neutral ground so we can discuss details. The address is a bit weird though. Waggytails Wescue, sorry Rescue, Centre.

Jake is a volunteer dog walker, and he's suggested that I either join him or meet him after his shift. Rather rashly I have agreed to be a dog walker as well, and Sarah has insisted on joining me for moral support, because she loves dogs, and because she's nosey. She has also promised not to spy on us when I'm chatting to Jake – this is weird enough without having an audience. I think her main reason for coming is to make sure I actually go through with it because she thinks this is such an ace idea. Personally, after seeing Jake in the flesh I tend to agree, but it's still a bit awkward, isn't it, hiring a date? It has to rate as the most embarrassing thing I have ever done.

***

'Amy said Jake will meet us here.' I've still not corresponded directly with Jake, so I hope Amy isn't having me on. How disappointing will it be if I don't get to look into those lovely eyes of his close up? And of course, I have to remember the important bit, I will be back to square one as far as the wedding plans go. 'She said to go to reception and give our names, they'll hand over the dogs and then we'll meet him on the walk.'

Simple. What could be more perfect than a nice stroll in the fresh air, with some happy dogs and a gorgeous man?

So why do I feel all wobbly inside, and have fingers that are incapable of doing the simple things like my shoelaces? It took me an hour to get dressed this morning! I only had minor butterflies in my stomach at that point, but they have started to flap harder as the day has progressed. Now they are a tsunami of insects.

I don't know whether it's anticipation, excitement or just fear. I imagine this is how I'd feel if I was about to bungee jump off a big cliff. I want to jump, I need to jump, but the sensible bit of me is saying it might be a little bit dangerous.

Anyway, I started off with jeans, Converses, T-shirt and hoodie, then tried every combination of vaguely sensible (and some not so sensible) dog-walking outfits, and ended up back where I started.

I am also knackered after a bit of a jittery night. I had this dream (and I hardly ever remember my dreams) where I was denounced during the wedding speeches for being a fake and a liar. Jess was in tears, Liam had this massive head which he literally laughed off, and Johnny Depp made me walk the plank. I was grabbed by the Loch Ness monster, but then rescued by Jake who gave me the kiss of life, then slung me onto the back of his horse.

All of this has to be a good omen. He rescued me. And Liam's head fell off. I'm therefore feeling extremely positive this morning, and know that this will definitely work.

If Jake passes the basic criteria of good manners (for the parents), good looks (I think that box is well and truly ticked) and the ability to deceive (normally the complete opposite of what you look for in a man, but this isn't normal) then I will sit down and discuss terms with him in a very business-like manner over a cup of coffee.

The dogs' home apparently routinely turns down unsuit-able adopters, despite them offering money and good homes, and I do not intend to suffer the same fate. Not that I'm offering him a home, just food and board for a week. And not that I'm calling him a dog.

The girl on the desk, who is wearing a badge that says 'Em', looks at us with slight suspicion. 'What did you say your name was again? You definitely rang?' Anybody would think they had a kennel full of Cruft's champions that we wanted to steal. 'You'll have to fill a form in. Here.' Her hand is halfway to the form when it stops, suspended in mid-air, and she is suddenly transformed into Mrs Smiley-face.

'Hey, there.' It's a deep, very masculine voice, with the hint of a drawl that makes you want to turn around and look. And from Em's swoony face, I'd say it might be worth doing just that. Any minute now she'll be rolling over to have her tummy tickled.

A tanned, muscled forearm lands on the desk, next to my own much smaller one, so I look. I mean, I might as well, I'm not going to get any sense out of reception girl.

He winks at me. It is him, definitely him, and somebody has turned the heating up in here.

I resist the urge to flap my T-shirt to let some air in, and stare.

'Everything okay?' He glances from me to Em, and she edges closer. I no longer exist in her world.

'Epic.' Em is much cooler than I am, in all senses; her blush is a light smattering of pink along her cheekbones, I think I've gone beetroot-coloured all over. 'Are you taking the girls out next, Jake?'

Gawd. She knows. How can she know?

'I certainly am.' He smiles, a lovely warm smile that looks

totally genuine. 'But I just wanted to check Sam and Sarah had arrived before I go and put their leads on.' Phew, so the girls are dogs. 'Okay if I meet you at the start of the Woodland Walk, Sam? I've got to make a quick phone call but I know Em here will take good care of you.'

All I can do is nod.

'See you shortly then.' He raises a hand, and smiles again, and the dimples at the corner of his mouth deepen.

I could stare at him all day, if he hadn't just headed off. O-M-G I could end up taking this man to the wedding! It is really happening. He is even more gorgeous close-up in the flesh, and he hugs puppies. He couldn't be more perfect if I'd handpicked him out of an escort catalogue (if they have such a thing).

Sarah is nudging me, and I realise that Em is talking. She has reverted to grumpy teenager mode.

'I didn't realise you were with Jake. Why didn't you say?' She is sounding slightly miffed. 'Jake and his sister Amy help us out lots.' She emphasises the last word, and shoots me a 'hands off' look. I feel a totally irrational twinge of possessiveness, then tell myself that she's far too young for him. 'He's wonderful.' Her voice loses its edge, then the phone rings and breaks her out of her daydream. 'Come on then, I'll take you through and we'll find some dogs that need walking. You are used to dogs?'

We both nod. Honestly, how difficult can walking a dog be?

'Oh yes.' I wave an arm flamboyantly to make my

case more clearly. 'We've always had dogs.' She doesn't look overly impressed, though teenagers don't often, do they?

'Retrievers, collies, rescues … difficult dogs.' I'm getting carried away. We had a very old Labrador at home that used to steal sausages off my plate and lie on my feet snoring and farting. The most difficult thing about him was his inability to resist food of any kind. And we had the mad springer spaniel. By the time he was six months old my parents had made a strategic decision to 'manage' rather than 'control' his behaviour. Which meant he did what he liked most of the time and this caused less stress all round.

'We had a sausage dog when I was young,' Sarah sighed. 'She was so cute.' She shrugs her shoulders in a 'want to squeeze cute dogs' kind of way. 'I used to dress her up, and take her to bed with me.'

'Awesome. I'll give you Tilly then.' Em grins, warming to this new cuddly side of Sarah that I didn't know existed. Dogs do that to people. 'She really misses her cuddles, you'll love her. She is just so sweet and sensitive.'

She says something else, but her last few words are lost as we round a corner to where the kennel blocks are, and are met with a wall of barking. I never knew dogs could make such a racket. Terriers are leaping up and down as though they're on springs, a collie is quaking in its boots, and a brindle Staffordshire bull terrier eyes me up silently as though he has seen it all before.

Em doesn't seem to notice the chaos. She carries on talking, and we nod in the gaps when her mouth stops moving. I haven't got a clue what she's saying, but it can't be that bad.

It turns out it is that bad.

She was asking if I thought I'd be okay with Tank, seeing as I was experienced and he could be tricky.

I must have nodded.

Tank sat down as she put his lead on, cocked his head to one side and stared as though to say, 'I've got the measure of you'.

'Go across that field, just follow the signs, the woodland walk is that way. Do a couple of laps, half an hour will probably be enough, but I suppose Jake will tell you. See you later, have fun.' And she's gone before we have time to say anything, not that I could have said anything as Tank is off, intent on yanking my shoulders out of their sockets. Half an hour of this? You've got to be kidding me, I already feel like one of those rubber stretchy men that kids throw at windows.

It's also raining, that drizzly stuff that makes you feel a wimp if you put your hood up, but leaves you soaked if you don't. My hair has started to curl, my fingers are numb and I've got a nagging twitch at my temples which normally heralds a headache. And we've not started the walk yet. But there is a bright light on the horizon. Jake.

'Do I look like a drowned rat?' Will he change his mind, when he sees me like this?

'A bit.' Sarah laughs. 'Chill, he liked you, I could tell. He'll do it.'

There is a big problem with walks in rescue centres, even when you're doing the corner of the field bit and not the under trees bit, and that is everybody walks along the same path. Which means it is muddy, unless you're in the middle of a dry summer. Which we are not.

Now I like dogs, I love dogs, but this is no normal dog. Sarah has a cute, nervous whippet which is side-stepping the boggy bits daintily, while me and the Tank-mobile wade straight through like a Sherman tank, scattering well-meaning dog-lovers as we go, saying sorry a lot. Me, not Tank. Tank doesn't care. He is having the best time ever. Tank is a donkey crossed with a hippo, a hippo who has discovered freedom and a mud bath. He has been along this path before, he knows the way to the woodland walk, and nothing is going to stop him.

'Look!' Sarah has stopped dead in her tracks. Well, not dead. She's bouncing on the spot.

I look, it's hard not to though it does involve taking my attention off the Tank for a moment.

Mistake. Up until now I've been slipping and sliding a bit, in fact I probably look a bit like a first-time water skier, but now Tank leaps forwards, and I'm yanked off my feet. For a split second I'm airborne, then I'm eating mud.

'Noooo...' Tank is away, dragging me along in his wake.

'There he is! It's Jake.'

And we are heading straight for him. Jake is standing

by one of the signs that marks the woodland walk, and he's not looking at all like a drowned rat, or wimpy. He glances up, and sees us. How can he not, when Sarah is about as subtle as a panther in the snow, and I'm hurtling towards him like a bobsleigher, determined not to let go of the leash?

Even at this distance and with the mud that's being kicked up in my face, I can see he's got three dogs of assorted sizes at his side (all beautifully behaved), and half the staff are milling round him, though he absolutely doesn't need any kind of help at all. Unlike me.

Tank barks a welcome, speeding up, and I'm pretty sure Jake's jaw has dropped as we hurtle towards him. I'm not sure if he's amazed the dog can pull me, or worried he's going to get trampled.

'Oh shit.' He throws the leads at one of the bystanders. 'Hang on.' I am hanging on, that's the problem. But I can't catch my breath to say it. I close my eyes, this is going to end badly, I just know it is.

It hasn't. We've stopped.

'Settle down, settle down, good boy.'

I open my eyes. He has got Tank by the collar, and he's crouched down, peering at me with a worried frown on his face.

'Are you okay?' My God, he's strong. He's stopped the unstoppable. He's holding the dog with one hand, and now he's managing to pull me to my feet with the other. 'Sam?'

'Sam, Sam.' Sarah has caught up with us, and I can see

she's not quite sure how I'll take it if she collapses in hysterics. 'Wow, I've never seen anybody do that in real life before.'

'Tank has.' My rescuer shakes his head and very gently tucks a bedraggled strand of my hair behind my ear, his warm fingertips brushing my skin, which makes me shiver. 'All in one piece?'

I swallow hard, and blink. I'm not quite sure if it's his touch or that smooth, concerned voice that's responsible for the weird sensation. I think even my scalp has got goose bumps.

'No harm done.' It comes out a bit shaky, with a very nervous laugh at the end that I didn't intend at all.

Sarah looks like a cat watching a ping-pong game, her gaze switching rapidly from Jake to me, and back again. 'I'll er, leave you to it, shall I? Catch you later?' At least I think that's what she says, but I can't really concentrate.

He's staring at me. 'I think you need to sit down, you're in shock.'

'I, er, do feel a bit wobbly.'

'I'm sorry, I should have met you at the kennels, but I never thought they'd give you Tank. I'll have words.'

'Oh no, no, don't have words.' Jake being all masterful is sending goose bumps down my arms (they seem to be getting everywhere), and it would be quite nice to see somebody wading in to support me. But not very fair on the staff. 'It was my fault, I said I'd be fine, I am, er, used to dogs.'

'Are you sure? You could have been hurt.' He's looking at me like he seriously cares, and my legs are going a bit wobbly.

'I'm fine.'

'You sound breathless.'

That is probably down to my close proximity to him, not my adventures with Tank. He even smells good.

My dream was sending out the right signals, he's already saved me, and we're nowhere near Scotland yet.

His eyes really are as amazing close up as they were in the photos and from the other side of the restaurant. He's got this steady gaze that makes me feel like he knows exactly what I'm thinking. Which could be dangerous.

'Well, if you're sure.' Eek, his thumb is on my cheek. 'Mud.' His smile is so familiar, I feel like I've known him for ages. 'There, that's better.' My face might now be clean, but there is no hope for the rest of me.

'We'll walk round slowly, shall we? Then grab a coffee? I'll take Tank, I'm used to him. Here, you hold little Angel, and somebody else can take the other two dogs.'

Angel who is about six inches tall, and looks like a waft of breeze would carry her away, looks up at me trustingly. I like Angel. I also like Jake.

'You did a great job of hanging on to him, most people would have let go.'

I rather wish I'd been most people, but Jake thinks I've done a great job, which makes me feel warm inside.

Miraculously though, just like that, Tank seems to have

lost his head of steam. Maybe Jake is also a dog whisperer, as well as an actor.

Even at a slow-for-Tank walk, we lap most of the other volunteers who are sauntering along as though they're on a Sunday morning stroll – which helps to dry me out. At least I'm going too fast to feel embarrassed. I really wish I'd gone for a date that involved wine, not fresh air and four-legged furries in need of a good home. I need to lie down.

'So...' Jake is studying me out of the corner of his eye, which is a bit unnerving and distracts me from the need to lie down. 'You've not been here before?'

'No, does it show?' We both laugh, at exactly the same time.

'I don't know what got into Em, giving you this thug.'

I have got a feeling I know what got into Em. 'It's not a problem, honest. I'm fine.' And I now know that he is more than capable of rescuing me from Loch Ness monsters, or any other attacks. His protective streak is a definite mark in his favour, not that I've found any reason not to beg him to come to Scotland with me.

'He's a nice dog really.'

'Just big.'

'Just big.' We walk along in companionable silence for a bit, and it doesn't feel awkward at all. 'Amy tells me you work at the travel agent's in town?'

'I do, so if you ever need a discount...'

'I might take you up on that sometime, must be handy.'

'And you're an actor?'

'I am, you might have caught my finest TV moment.' I glance at him. If this is a test, I've failed; I haven't caught any of his TV moments.

'Erm.'

He's grinning, the faintest of lines fanning out from those mesmerising eyes. 'You don't mean you missed it? Tut. Watch Holby City?'

'Well, yes.' I'm wracking my brain, trying to picture him with a stethoscope and failing. Well, I can picture him with a stethoscope, but I certainly can't picture him in an episode of Holby. Maybe I missed one.

'I was in the third bed along, second episode this season.'

'Ah.'

'Arm in a sling.' He laughs, and Tank jumps up and licks his cheek.

'So is that what you want to do? TV?'

'Jake!' A girl yells his name and I realise with a jolt that we're back near the kennels. Which is a shame. I'd quite like to know what he wants to do.

'I'll take the dogs if you like, and you can clean up?' He's grinning as he speaks, which he seems to do quite a lot, and I look down at my clothes. I'd almost forgotten about the mud. Almost. 'I'll catch you in the café, and we can chat more?'

'Great, I'd like to.'

'And you can tell me more about your indecent proposal.' The way he says it makes me blush, and the wink leaves me dithering between objecting and wishing it actually was supposed to be indecent.

He whisks Angel up into his arms and has gone before my mushy brain can think up a suitably snappy reply.

Chapter 7

When I get back to reception it is to find a new teen-ager-cum-twenty-something, who is just like Em. She is trying her hardest not to smirk, and makes no comment whatsoever about the wide strip of mud that covers the front of me from head to toe. She does tell me where the bathroom is though, and where to find Sarah.

'I hope nobody filmed that,' I whisper to Sarah, suddenly having visions of it being on their Facebook page. 'It could be all over the internet.'

'I doubt it, I mean it was funny but it isn't going to help with rehoming him, is it?' She grins. 'I might have tweeted a picture though.'

'You didn't?'

'Naw, don't worry, I was too busy laughing, couldn't hold my phone steady. Well?'

'Well what?' I studiously avoid her gaze in the mirror and concentrate on washing myself down.

'Well, what did you talk about? Is he nice? Will he do it?' She pauses, and leans in closer. 'Do you fancy him?'

I don't know which bits to ignore, and which to answer. I decide to offer highlights. 'His name is Jake Porter, not Taylor-Smith, because Amy is his half-sister, they've got the same mum. Her dad was a writer and he ran off with his agent, and it was a massive scandal. Jake doesn't know his dad as his mum had a fling, but now she's met somebody that everybody likes and they've got this enormous family.'

'Wow, you two must have hit it off, you got up close and personal.'

I frown at my own reflection. When I say it, it sounds like we did, but I almost feel like Jake was brushing over things. It's a weird feeling. I can't quite put my finger on it, but I'm sure I've got the edited version, as though he's used to saying it to deflect questions later. 'Not really, maybe it's on his CV, you know, ready prepared for the press.'

'And do you fancy him?'

'Sarah! It isn't like that, I'm paying him,' I drop my voice, suddenly worried we might be overheard. I mean, it's not the type of thing you broadcast, is it?

'That means you do. You do fancy him! I don't blame you, I fancy him and Em definitely fancies him, and it's good you fancy him. It'll make it dead easy, you won't have to pretend.'

I sigh. If I object, she'll go on even more. And I do fancy him a tiny bit. He's very fanciable.

'So will he do it?'

'We're going to have a coffee and chat.' I can't help myself, I look at her and grin. 'I think so though!'

'Yay!' She gives me a hug, ignoring all my muddy bits. 'Oh God this is brilliant, I'm so excited for you, I wish I could come to the wedding!'

'He hasn't said yes yet.'

'He will do, I know he will. Come on, come on, don't keep him waiting.' I look down at my jeans. We've scraped the worst of it off, and there's not much I can do apart from get changed. 'I'd better get off as well.'

'Where are you going?'

'I'm off to play with puppies! They've got a secret kennel area for all the babies, like a giant nursery and they've said I can go and see. I'll come over and find you later, shall I?'

'Do I look passable?'

'Best of a bad job.' She starts laughing again. 'Oh God, you should have seen yourself zooming across that field.' Sarah is practically crying, which is very mean, then gives me the thumbs up. 'Good luck!' Which is nice, and I know she means it.

I would quite like to play with puppies too, but I have a job to do. A different kind of play date. The indecent proposal type.

'Feeling better?' Jake, I've decided, is quite posh. He's sat at a table in the small café which is attached to the reception area and although he looks at home, there is something about him that says he's not short of a bob or two. Though at the moment he probably is, as playing a patient in the third bed along can't pay that well, can it?

But there is nothing the slightest bit hoity-toity about him. He has the type of voice you can listen to without wanting to yawn, or walk away. Now I think about it, Liam has a bit of a whiney edge to his.

He will fit into a country estate perfectly. I can imagine his sister Amy, who is definitely posh, in long boots and cream breeches standing in front of a castle with a couple of Labradors or spaniels at her feet quite easily. Jake is probably more the quadbike type, although I can picture him wading across a lake, his white shirt moulded to his muscled chest, his hair slicked back...

'Sammy?'

He's waiting for a response, his tawny-brown eyes slightly puzzled.

Nobody calls me Sammy apart from Tim, I think it makes me sound a bit like a dog, or a hamster. This is probably a good time to act a little bit sophisticated myself.

'It's Samantha, or Sam.'

'Not Sammy?'

'Definitely not Sammy.'

'Shame, I quite like Sammy.' The corner of his mouth twitches. 'Cuddly.'

See? Cuddly does not say Ferrari and Monte Carlo, cuddly is what pyjamas and puppies are. And hamsters. 'It rhymes with hammy.' I puff my cheeks out. Sammy the hammy.

'Ahh, I get where you're coming from. Amy used to call me snakey Jakey.'

'Oh. And are you?'

'What?'

'Snakey?'

'Well, I don't eat live mice, if that's what you mean.'

'But are you sneaky?'

'Only in the way brothers are to bratty sisters. She also called me fakey Jakey when we were kids, and Jake the rake, and on-the-make Jake.'

'Ahh.'

'She loves me really. So is it Samantha or Sam?'

'Sam to friends.'

'Friends?' He grins and a cute little dimple appears in the middle of his chin. Very cute. Gawd, I am pretty sure I shouldn't be considering my potential employee in that way. 'From what Amy told me, I gather you're suggesting we get to be a bit more than that.'

I know now that this could work. Jake doesn't look at all like a young George Clooney, which was one of my concerns as me meeting a Clooney lookalike would not be credible at all. He has got the same crinkly bits round his eyes, which suggest he smiles a lot, and that confident air, but there the similarity ends. He looks cheekier. Unsettling.

Which could be a problem, because even though he's incredibly dishy, this isn't really an indecent proposal, and I really don't want him to think I'm *that* kind of girl.

'No!' Oh my God, what has Amy said to get him here? 'Oh no, no, just like friends, but...' Does he think I want a f-buddy (I can't say the word, not even in my head, while he's looking at me like that). 'I'm not sure…' This isn't going quite how I expected, it was easier chatting to him on the dog walk, about his family, dogs, things like that. But now we are sat down here, and I need to explain, it all seems a bit trickier.

He seems a bit … well, a bit (lot) *unmanageable*. Like Tank. Jumping up at everybody. Ignoring the rules. Who knows what chaos he could cause in the wilds of Scotland?

'Of course you're not sure.' He's gone all serious and sensible for a moment, and my little niggle melts, along with something else as he puts his hand over mine. 'Are you okay?'

I don't want to grab my hand back, because he's got the warmest of warm hands, but it seems like a good idea. I'd rehearsed this, but in real life it isn't quite as easy. And the fact that I want to wriggle in my seat isn't all down to his capable looking hands.

'A bit soggy.' Major understatement. Everything down to my knickers is damp – and not in a good way. If there is such a thing in polite society. It's obviously the cold, sogginess and aching arms that have made me feel a bit pathetic and quivery.

I also know I look a complete disaster, *I* wouldn't go out with me if you paid me. 'I'm fine, that's dog-walking for you, haha.' He looks immaculate. Not a hair out of my place.

'Wait here. You need warming up.' He winks, and I'm

right back in that Italian restaurant, warming up rapidly. 'A coffee might help, or I hear they do a good hot chocolate here?'

How did he know that whipped cream, chocolate and marshmallows are exactly what I need right now?

Apparently he knows what every woman needs. He's bounced up to the counter, and the girl serving him has gone all giggly as she whisks the cream, and the woman behind him in the queue is staring at him adoringly as he passes her a slice of cake she can't quite reach (talk about obvious moves, honestly, whoever heard of anybody not being able to stretch that extra inch or three for a chocolate brownie?), and a loose dog runs up to him like he's the last man on earth. Which is when it hits me. I need rules. If this is to work, if I'm going to be able to keep him (and myself) under control, I need rules. Boundaries.

This is where I have gone wrong in the past. I need fake-date rules. Like you would if you got a puppy – not that I'm saying he's a puppy. No jumping on the sofa, no bad manners, no leaping over the fence and humping the neighbour's dog…

Okay, so sometimes rules get broken now and then, but a broken rule is better than not having one in the first place.

'There you go.' He's back, complete with hot drinks and a slice of chocolate brownie. If I wasn't supposed to be interviewing him, I'd kiss him. 'So, Amy says you've got a problem?'

I like the sound of that. Describing this as a problem, rather than an indecent proposal, makes it sound much more acceptable. I have a problem, and problems should be viewed as opportunities. And I now have the opportunity to date an extremely dishy man.

I can't answer straight away though as I'm up to my nose in hot chocolate, thinking about rules. And of course getting a chocolate hit.

But when he leans forward and brushes the cream off my top lip with his slightly salty thumb (sorry, my tongue kind of brushed against it) it's a bit distracting. Like a puppy giving you kisses when you've told him to sit.

I mustn't think about kisses. Or tongues. This is a business deal. Nice eyes and arse or not. Although I do now know without a doubt that this is a face I could stand to gaze at for a week. 'Er, bit of an awkward situation really, rather than a problem.'

He sits back, his head slightly tilted to one side. 'She said you didn't want to go to your mate's wedding on your own.' I nod. 'But why do you need a fake date?' He sounds more interested than judgemental, and I suppose it is fair enough, him wanting to know.

'Well...' I concentrate on my marshmallows but can't help noticing (when I peep up) that his steady gaze never leaves me. 'I told Jess, that's my best friend, the one that is getting married, that I've got a boyfriend and I haven't.'

'I'm surprised about that.' His voice has softened, and when I look up, the corner of his mouth lifts. 'The "haven't" bit.' The gentle tone makes me blink, which is horrible, I'm not supposed to be feeling sorry for myself. I don't feel sorry for myself. I'm totally fine.

'Well I did have, until five months ago. He dumped me, for another woman.'

'Ahh.'

'A woman who I've just found out is pregnant. She's huge apparently, hugely, hugely pregnant.'

'To be honest, does it matter if she's hugely pregnant, or just a little bit? If she's pregnant, she's pregnant.'

'Well yes it does, actually, because it means he, he...' I pause and take a deep breath, because this is the really horrible bit. 'Well, she's huge, as in more than five months pregnant. So that means he was poking her when he was still with me.'

'What a total shit.' I look up at him properly then, because there's a harsh edge to his voice that I haven't heard before. He looks genuinely angry, and his soft tawny eyes have gone hard. Wolf eyes.

'And...' I waver. 'He's going to be there, at the wedding.'

'You have got to be kidding?' It's not just his eyes, his whole body has stiffened. 'What kind of best friend is this Jess? Inviting your ex to her bloody wedding. That is totally out of order.' He leans forward, and gives my hand a gentle squeeze, and some of the tension seems to ebb out of him. It feels nice, reassuring. Supportive.

'It's not Jess's fault.' I can't help but sigh, as I stir rather too vigorously and marshmallows pop up and down like corks on a rough sea. 'My ex happens to be the groom's brother.'

'Oh, tricky then.'

'And the best man.'

'Ah. That's a tough call.' His thumb is rubbing the base of mine, almost absentmindedly. It's mesmerising and almost makes me forget the story and just ask him out for a real date. But then he stops.

'I also told my mum I had a boyfriend, so that she wouldn't insist I took Desmond.'

'Desmond?'

'He's nobody. But Mum and Dad and all my mates will be there, and Liam of course.' He looks blank. 'My ex, with his girlfriend.' I shrug and try and make out this isn't the most important thing in my life at this precise moment. 'Anyway, that's why I want a date.' I stop all my messing about with my hot chocolate and look at him. 'I *need* a date. I don't want them all feeling sorry for me, and whispering in corners. I'm so over him, and I need to show them I am.'

'You could just not go?'

'No!' I think I shout it a bit too vehemently, because he freezes. 'She's my best mate. I can't let her down just because of some stupid man.'

He nods.

'I have to be there for her, she'd do it for me, and besides, I love her to bits. So I am going, whether you say yes or not.' I stare him in the eye, so there is no doubt. 'But, I would like to show them how totally over the heap of...'

'Shit?'

'Shit, thank you, I am. So, are you up for it?' Please say yes, please say yes. I'm holding my breath; he might say no now he knows just what he's letting himself in for.

'Well...' There's a long pause, but he's gazing into my eyes still, so at least he's man enough to say no to my face. But then I realise I've missed out a crucial bit. If I don't say this now, and he does say yes, then he might change it to no later.

'Oh, and it's in Scotland, a whole week.'

'A whole week of mischief?' His eyes are all twinkly and naughty again, which is very disturbing and makes me feel a bit giddy. 'Well, just so you know, I did say no when Amy first asked.'

I lose my giddiness. 'But she told me you—'

He holds his spare hand up to stop me. 'I actually laughed and told her she was crazy.'

'Oh.' I am deflated. He's right, it is crazy.

'I dunno, it seemed a bit odd, I've never done anything like this before.'

'Believe me, nor have I.' I'm not sure if he believes me or not, he's giving me a strange look. 'Honestly.' I'm very worried about what Amy might have said. It might have been along the lines of 'sex-starved and desperate woman I met while I was having a cut and blow.'

'I believe you. Honestly. Er, you're gripping my hand a bit, I think my fingers are going blue.'

Sugar, I've been hanging on to his hand for dear life.

Willing him to say yes. Which is why he's looking at me strangely. Not because Amy has told him I'm sex-starved. Or maybe that as well.

'Sorry.' I let go. 'But you did, er, agree to meet me.'

'I did.'

'You've changed your mind?' If he says he thinks I'm out of my mind now that he's heard the full story, then my whole plan is scuppered and I'll be going to the wedding alone. Or with combover Desmond. I have a sudden desire to grab his hand again and plead. But I don't. I grab a piece of the brownie and stuff it in my mouth to stop the words from forcing their way out.

'Okay, I want to be upfront with you here, which I guess is best seeing as this is just business?'

The 'just business' bit jars a bit, I was hoping he found me a teeny bit attractive and wouldn't keep reminding me that he is only here for the money. I notice he's totally reclaimed his hand, and it is now wrapped round his mug of coffee. You see, this is the problem with dating an actor, isn't it? You don't know which bits are real and which bits are, well, acting. He might not have been genuinely angry about Liam, he might just have been practising his art.

The truth? He *is* only here for the money, and I am only here, walking the dog and swallowing too many calories (I have a maid of honour dress to fit into, and sewing in a strip down the side would be so uncool), because I am desperate.

But we still don't need to spell things out and be too honest, do we? I mean, I'm not going to be completely honest and start saying that although he's gorgeous, his ego is probably bigger than my spare room. That he is no doubt shallow and big-headed and thinks every girl will fall at his feet, that we are totally unsuited in every single way. Am I?

'I'm not sure we need total honesty.' After all this whole thing is dishonest, and so is business. I sell holidays for a living, and let's face it, there is a tiny bit of stretching of the truth now and again. What you see isn't always what you get. Infinity pool and tin bath on the edge of a cliff aren't the same in everybody's eyes.

'I think we do need the whole truth.' He grins. 'How many times do you get a relationship where you can be totally honest? No white lies.'

The man has a point. 'O-kay.' I can take this, I am strong.

'Well, like I said, at first I told her to get lost.'

'Oh.'

'My sister can be bossy, and I don't like being told what to do.' His eyes glint.

Bugger. He's going to hate 'the rules', if he ever gives me chance to come up with some.

'But though I hate to admit it, she is right, it is the perfect distraction.'

'The perfect distraction from what?' I can't help myself, I mean, any normal person would want to know, wouldn't they?

'Life.' There's a wry quirk to his mouth, and he moves on before I can push it. 'And then of course, I saw you.'

'Saw me?' This was sounding better.

'Stalking me.'

'Ahh.' Worse.

'In the restaurant, and Amy seemed to know you, so I grilled her. I'm intrigued.'

Intrigued isn't quite 'knocked off my feet by your presence', but it's a start I suppose.

'And you sealed the deal out there with Tank.' His eyes are all lit up and shiny. Which could be his brilliant acting skills, a sip of too hot coffee, or just the fluorescent lights. 'I couldn't sleep with a girl who doesn't love animals, dogs in particular. That's why I thought this would be a great place to meet.'

'Sleep?' I've gone all croaky. I don't love Tank, but we can skip that for now.

'Sleep. I presume you don't intend staying awake for a whole week so you can keep an eye on me?'

'Well no, but...'

'And we will be sharing a room?'

'Well, yes, but ... just sleep, as in sleep?'

'As in sleep. Unless you're offering?' I don't know whether he's just teasing, or he's the one that is sex-starved.

'I most certainly am not!' I definitely need rules. 'Sleep, bed, asleep, fine.'

'Fine.' He grins. 'You were great with Tank, I love a girl with guts.'

'I don't need loving.' It's killed me to say it, when he's looking all cute and nice, but it's a fact. He's not a date. I will keep reminding myself of that, before things get complicated. That's rule number one.

'Everybody needs loving, Sammy.'

'I need rules, and don't call me Sammy or I'll call you snakey Jakey in public.' He's grinning. That might not quite work over the wedding breakfast though. Unless it's said in a lip-licking way, which is frankly not how I should be thinking.

'I have er, rules...' Best to get it over with now, if we're going to be totally honest.

'Rules?'

'No, er, loving.' He raises an eyebrow. 'Or sex.'

'Is this with you, or in general?'

'Ever!'

His eyebrow goes higher.

'Not ever, ever. Just while we're at the wedding. You can't go off and shag the other guests. If Liam hadn't gone off waving his willy in the wind, then ... don't you dare laugh!' I glare, and he holds a hand up in surrender.

'No laughing going on here. Promise.' He's gone all serious again. 'But I don't think it's waving it in the wind that was the problem.'

He has a point. But if the one-eyed trouser snake had stayed in the cheating bugger's trousers, then I wouldn't have to be here, doing this. Splitting up is one thing, splitting up because your boyfriend has put his *other* girlfriend up the duff is another. 'No sex in general.' I know I'm muttering, and stabbing marshmallows like I'd like to stab a certain person's dangly bits. 'You're supposed to be my boyfriend. My adoring boyfriend.'

'Smitten?'

'Totally. Yes, that's rule number two. How could you not be?' I'm going to have to write these down before I forget them.

'How could I not be?' I can hear the smile in his voice, and when I look up from my hunt-the-marshmallow search, he's grinning.

'Exactly. Stop laughing at me.'

'That's honestly a rule? The smitten bit? You just added that one.' He is grinning in a way that suggests he might not be very good at sticking to rules. 'How about we forget rules? We just need to get to know each other a bit.'

I knew he wasn't the type to stick to rules. 'The no sex rule is non-negotiable.' But if I don't see this through, then I've had it. This is make or break. I'm running out of time.

'Shame, but who says I want sex anyway?'

I decide to ignore that bit. It was him that mentioned the loving bit, I just embellished. I mean that's how it goes, isn't it? Love, sex, marriage? 'So, you will do it?'

'Look, Sam.' His smile looks a bit sad. 'I'm not being flip here, but I really get how you feel. I know what it's like to be betrayed, I know how shitty it is.' He's looking past my right ear, and there's a hint of that harshness back in his voice but this time it's tinged with something else. Hurt.

His gaze drifts back to my face, and he looks straight into my soul. 'What you're doing is incredibly brave.' The smile lifts, and his tone softens. 'Far braver than tackling Tank. And I love that you're such a good friend to this Jess.'

I smile back. I can't help it. I want to hug him.

'I want to help, I want us to go up to Scotland and show this Liam just what a stupid twat he is.' He leans forward, earnestly, like we are co-conspirators. 'I want us to have a wild time.' He's gone all twinkly again. 'We are going to have so much fun. I am definitely up for it.'

'A whole week, in Scotland, with me and my batty friends and family?' I need to be sure. 'Horse-riding and fishing and stuff like that.' He's looking amused. 'On a big estate, miles from anywhere.' He's still not said no. 'With no sex.'

'You're really selling this.' He's chuckling. 'I can't wait.'

'And everybody does have to believe you're my real boyfriend.'

'Of course.'

'It's top secret, the only people who know are Sarah and your sister, of course.'

'Good.'

'And my hairdresser, and everybody who was in the salon.'

'But it is top secret?'

'Nobody at the wedding must suspect. We'll have to get to know each other, practise.'

'Practise?' Jake raises his eyebrow. He really has to stop that, it makes me wriggle. And when I wriggle I realise my knickers have dried into something more like cardboard than cotton. Which is not a good sensation.

I ignore his naughtiness. 'You need to be...' I pause. I had originally had in mind just a boyfriend, any kind of boyfriend. Okay, I hadn't really thought about it in detail. But now I am thinking about it I realise that Jake isn't like just any kind of boyfriend. Jake is posh, Jake is good-looking, Jake has endless possibilities that I need to have a think about. Jake is an actor. 'You need to be the type of boyfriend who would drive a Ferrari, and adore me, and watch chick flicks on a Friday night, and...' I really do need to think about this.

'Whatever your heart desires.' I'm pretty sure that warm huskiness is purely a demonstration of how good an actor he is, and nothing more.

'Pizza and a bottle of wine normally.'

He laughs, a deep throaty laugh. 'A girl after my own heart.' Oh heavens, any more of this and I will be booking him for a lifetime, not a week. 'Except I'd rather have the footie than a chick flick, but hey, I can pretend.'

'Good.'

'How about Thursday then, for the first getting to know you session? I can tell you about my rules then, as well.' He winks, it's a bad habit.

'Your rules? You can't have rules!' I haven't even got rules yet, and I'm the one who's supposed to be in control here. It is part of my plan, to be in control of my own life.

'Just watch me.' He's chuckling as he stands up and

shoves his hands in his pockets. 'How about Thursday then? You can come and watch the play I'm in, then we can go out after?'

'Thursday.' Watching him act seems like a very good idea, it will prove just how well he will be able to pull this off. 'How about that new pizza place?' Much as I like the way he's being all assertive, I feel I need to be more that way myself. I'm the one that is supposed to be running this show. And I want pizza. And I'm a bit concerned about his rules.

'If you like, not quite sure that's where Ferrari man would take you though.'

'You can start off being Mini man and we'll work up.'

He laughs again. I could get used to listening to that laugh, it makes me feel happy inside. 'Nothing Mini about me.'

'But you are an actor, aren't you?' I try and look sweet and innocent. 'I'm sure you could pull it off.'

He just shakes his head.

'Jake?' He stops, raises an eyebrow. 'Why have you said you'll do this?' I've got a feeling this distraction must be something important, or why would Amy mention it?

'Money? You know, penniless actor and all that.'

Even I can tell that's not the whole truth, and we did say this was going to be an honest relationship. 'And?'

'And...' He studies the crumbs on my plate for a moment, then lifts his gaze back up to mine. 'Like I said before, I know what you're going through, and what this means to you. Really.' We stare at each other, for a long moment, and I believe him. He gets it. And I really want to know why. Except it would seem really rude to ask him, and I take it from his angry reaction that whatever happens still smarts, and is off bounds.

'And I've got some time off, before I start filming.'

As a way of diverting me from quizzing him, it's brilliant. I go after it like a terrier that's seen a rat. 'You're going to be in a film?'

'I am, I'll tell you about it over the pizza.' He shrugs. 'Sam.' I hate it when people just say your name, then pause. It nearly always means they're going to follow it up with something you don't want to hear. 'This is just business though, okay?'

I nod. A part of me wishes it wasn't. He's funny, he's cute, and I can already see that he's not just sexy but he's a nice guy. A *really* nice guy.

'Definitely.' I do not need a man in my life right now, not even a really nice one. I need to rediscover the real, pre-Liam me.

'I'm not looking for any kind of...'

'Me neither.' I take a deep breath. 'Which reminds me, we need to talk about, er, money.'

'We do.' He fishes in his pocket and drops a ticket on the table. 'For the play. That one's on the house though – I'll warn you now, it's not exactly a masterpiece. Very modern.'

'Oh, I'm sure—'

'No, really. How about thrashing the money details out on Thursday?' There's a glimmer of his cheeky side, then he sobers again as he pushes his chair under the table. 'Sam, if I *was* looking though...' He half-smiles. 'I couldn't think of anybody I'd rather date than you.'

Which leaves me feeling all warm and fuzzy inside. It's the kind of feeling that I really wish I could bottle, and whisk out on the rubbish days.

Chapter 8

Things I need to do this week:

1. Work out how to avoid 'supper' with Mum and Dad.
2. Work out how to raise enough money to pay Jake (once we have agreed an amount, that is. I have to admit I hadn't really thought this aspect through).
3. Find out what Jake needs distracting from.
4. Find out more about the type of acting Jake really wants to do (he was just about to tell me when we were out walking, and I'd really like to know).
5. Make a list of rules, and things we need to know about each other. (Like which side of the bed I sleep on, because no way am I going to let Liam think we haven't done it while he's been busy sowing his seed like he was planning on feeding a third world country. Oh no, Liam is to see me in a new light, as a tousle-haired irresistible sex goddess – the hair bit I've mastered, not sure about the rest yet).

It is already Thursday and this has been a good week in that I've hardly thought about the 'huge' girlfriend or the banker-wanker at all, because I now have a boyfriend. But, all my spare time has been devoted to working out what I need to know about him, and worrying about the six-hundred-and-seventy-eight ways it can all go wrong when we get to Scotland.

I've also been trying to work out just how I can afford to buy a wedding present, clothes suitable for a week of shooting, fishing and drinking whisky in Scotland, *and* pay for my employee, because after meeting up with him at Waggytails Wescue, I went home and Googled 'equity rates' and 'reasonable expenses'. If I was you, I wouldn't.

If I'd just wanted him to do a TV trailer (which now I come to think of it, is a possibility. Does he really have to be there? Could I not just share videos of the two of us happily loved-up?) then it would have been a snip compared to a live performance, and by the time I'd added on travelling expenses, clothing allowance and God knows what, I've run out of spreadsheet (no spreadsheet should cover more than a sheet of A4 in a font size I can read without holding it up to my nose).

Looking up escort rates with Sarah had just got me into an area of the world wide web that I really didn't want to know about. I didn't think it was possible to physically do some of the extras, let alone be able to request them. But he's an actor, isn't he? Not an escort. Which is infinitely better. But not cheaper.

My quandary is about to be solved though, as it is Thursday and I am about to go on my second date with him!

I feel sick. I have made a dreadful mistake. I should leave a note for Jake saying there has been a change of plan, and totally abandon the whole fake-date idea, because I have just sat through the most awful play ever. And I have been to a lot of awful plays; mainly the ones my mother has been in, before reassuring her that she was wonderful.

I am not sure I will be able to reassure Jake about this play. He was right, it was not a masterpiece, it was not even a minor triumph. It was totally weird. Hamlet meets Alien, with a lot of street dancing and graffiti.

I am confused.

I could see that Jake had thrown himself into it, but he did not convince me that this type of space and time distortion is either a good thing, or possible.

There were only a handful of people in the theatre when I arrived, and fewer when I left.

'Ready for that pizza then? I'm starving.' Jake no longer looks like the love child of a Martian and the Prince of Denmark, he looks like Jake, but with slightly more ruffled hair than normal, and a smear of green paint on his cheek.

I reach out to rub the paint off, and he catches my hand and studies me.

'Don't say you've changed your mind.'

'I wasn't go—' I was actually. It isn't that I don't want to share a pizza with the dishiest man I've seen in a long time, but I have got seriously cold feet. Ice blocks. If this is the type of acting he does, we are never going to pull this off. Plus, he is hot enough to fancy and possibly fall for, but this is only business. He did check on that several times the other day, as though he really wanted to be sure that I wasn't trying to sneak under his radar and date him on false pretences.

'Yes, you were.' He glances round to check nobody was listening. 'Look, I know it was crap. I did it as a favour for this guy I was at college with, promised it ages and ages ago so I really couldn't get out of it. But Sam, I don't exactly need to act my guts out to make this work, do I? I just need to pretend I want to spend time with you and take you to bed.' He pauses. 'It'll be the easiest role I've ever played.' We stand for a long moment in eye to eye conflict, except it's a nice conflict, more a silent negotiation.

'You are such a smooth talker.' I have to say something to break the spell, and remind myself that this is Jake acting. It's not real.

'I do need the money, don't I, doll?' He winks.

All I can do is shake my head. 'Honestly, I'm not surprised Amy calls you names, and who says doll?' I don't give him time to answer, because I can tell it will be something cheeky. 'I suppose if I have to do this—'

'And you do.'

I smile. 'You're as good a bet as anybody, even if you do make a crap Shakespearian alien.'

'You leave my alien alone. He has feelings.'

'But you'll have to smarten up a bit.'

'Cheeky sod.' He smiles back. We're good.

'And you mustn't do that creepy alien voice in front of my parents, or in the middle of the service.' I shudder, and it isn't acting. 'That was seriously creepy.'

'Good.'

'What do you mean good?'

'It means I got under your skin. Come on, food time.' He angles his elbow out, inviting me to slip my hand in, and I hesitate. Suddenly feeling a bit, well, shy. Awkward. 'We might as well start practising straight away, I thought you'd told everybody we'd been dating for ages?'

'Well yes, but...' This is a bit odd, I hardly know him. We've barely touched hands, and now we're going to have to get all touchy-feely. And kiss. Gulp.

'I won't bite.' He leans in closer. 'Honest. I'm not really an alien hybrid.' He grins, and some of the tension disappears.

'I might like being bitten.'

'It's going to be fun finding out.'

When we get to the restaurant, they find us a table for two in a corner. Probably because of the way Jake keeps looking at me. He has obviously slipped into role, and is treating this as an audition.

'So, you've always wanted to be an alien?'

'Always.' He is straight-faced. 'It is what every actor

aspires to, you can't claim to be a proper actor until you've played an alien. All the greats would give their right hand to be an extra-terrestrial.'

'Though not necessarily a Shakespearian one?'

'Not necessarily, those parts are like gold dust.'

'And what do aliens charge?' I am dying to find out more about what he's acted in and what he really wants to do, but I also need to get the money bit out of the way. What if I can't afford to do this? 'You know, if they are whisked away to a very posh country house, a castle, and they get free food and drink?'

'Hmm, well food doesn't feature high on the normal alien agenda.' He is not being helpful.

'And travel expenses, plus a clothes allowance?' Please God, I hope he doesn't only dress in Armani or some other designer gear I can't afford.

'Ah, well are we talking about a classy alien?'

'Definitely.'

'And what standard of performance are you expecting from this alien?'

Ha, bloody ha. 'Entertaining...' I pause. 'But without weird alien voices, and no extras.' I mention that so that we are clear about the sex thing.

'But with smooching?'

'Who says smooching these days?'

'I'm an actor, darling.' The waitress comes over at that precise moment and does a double take. I can tell she's heard what he said and is trying to work out if he's famous.

And she's taking far too much time sprinkling the pizza with parmesan and pepper. If she doesn't stop soon I'll be sneezing all evening.

'He was third bed along in Holby City,' I say, helpfully. 'Arm in a sling.' It does the trick. She loses interest and heads off with her pepper grinder to listen in on somebody else's conversation.

'You should have mentioned the alien.' He looks pretend hurt.

'She's not an alien type of girl, I can tell.' I take a big bite of pizza, I'm starving. 'No smooching, can't afford it. I won't even be able to afford pizza after this.'

'My treat.' He says it lightly.

'But you're only here because of the job, my treat.' I try to sound assertive.

'I wouldn't say "only".' He shrugs. 'You're not bad company, and you had to endure the play, so I think I need to pay.'

'But this is business.' He made that quite clear, and so did I of course. I don't need a man in my life, and definitely not one I've had to tempt in with the offer of payment.

'Sam.' He puts his slice of pizza down and leans forward slightly. 'It is business, but we can be friends as well, can't we? Won't it make it easier?'

'True. And I split the bill with friends.'

'God, you're stubborn.' He grins. 'But the no smooching bit is boring. I might throw some in for free, for authenticity.'

'You aren't being very helpful here.' It's my turn to sigh now. 'And people don't smooch their friends.'

'They don't, but they don't do a lot of what we're going to, do they?'

Which reminds me, we're supposed to be agreeing his fee here, not who pays for the pizza.

'I'm not very good at negotiations, am I?'

'Nor am I. My agent normally does it.'

Oh gawd, he's not suggesting we arrange this through his agent?

He laughs. 'You should see the look on your face.' Then he looks all serious again, apart from the glint in his eye. 'This is one contract I don't want him to have anything to do with, though I am thinking about sacking him anyway.' He looks at me earnestly. 'I know you can't afford to pay me loads, and I don't expect you to.' His voice has softened, and I know that he's the best person I ever could have found to help me out like this.

'I want to be fair, pay you what you'd be earning on a job.' I look him straight in the eye. 'It is business after all.'

He sighs. 'But I am taking a break, and I am getting something out of this as well. A fun week away, nice company.' His fingertips touch mine.

'A distraction.'

'Like I say, a fun week away.' His fingers move away. All the way across the table.

He's being evasive, something in his eyes has kind of shut down. There's a no entry sign which I'd really like to knock down. My stomach feels all empty again; it's almost like being on a proper date, one minute you're on a high and the next it feels like you've said the wrong thing. Which is weird, when I hardly know him. We're not even friends, really.

I swallow. I just have to be business-like. 'I did look on the internet at equity rates.' I quote the daily rate and expense allowance I found. Just saying it out loud makes my skin clammy and leaves me with a desire to eat *all* the pizza.

'Half of that is more than enough.'

'But you need to live. You can't have been paid much for your part in that play I've just seen.'

He grins, back to his normal open self. 'You'd hope not, wouldn't you?'

'I didn't like to say it but...'

'I'm not a penniless actor, Sam.' His hand is back on the table. 'An uncle of mine used to act, and when he found out I was following in his footsteps he set up a fund for me. It's not masses, but he wanted me to have some backup if I needed it.'

It makes sense; he and Amy definitely look like they come from a rich background, so he's probably better off than I am.

'Now, shall we order dessert, seeing as you've polished off the pizza?'

'Oh God, I didn't, did I?'

'You've been frantically munching as you talk.'

'I do that when I'm nervous. Hell, did you have enough?'

'I'm fine.' He is grinning, and his dimples have appeared. 'It's nice to eat out with a girl who actually eats.'

'I suppose your girlfriends are usually slim, gorgeous actresses and models?'

'I don't really have girlfriends.' He tops up our wine glasses, and for once isn't looking me in the eye. 'I got stung once and realised the whole commitment thing wasn't what I wanted.'

I stare at the menu and ignore the slight lump in my throat.

'That's partly why I want to help you out.'

'Oh.'

'But I did want to be straight with you, because—'

'Oh goodness gracious me!'

I do not get to hear the reason (which is bloody frustrating) because I am grabbed from behind and assaulted. Or rather smothered, by my mother's bosom.

'Samantha, fancy that, and you're with a man!' Mother is excited, but I do wish she wouldn't make it sound like seeing me with a man is such an unlikely occurrence. 'A real man!'

Jake is desperately trying not to laugh, but the quirk of his eyebrow is making me want to giggle.

'And there was I thinking you'd made him up.'

'Mum!'

Jake winks at me, so I scowl back. 'Somebody as gorgeous as your daughter must have men queueing at the door.' He blows me a kiss. 'I'm a lucky man.'

'You are indeed.' My father, who has been lurking behind me steps forward. 'David, Samantha's father, and you must be?'

'Jake, Jake Porter.' Jake stands up and they shake hands, and he kisses Mum on the cheek which makes her go all fluttery, which she never used to do when she bumped into Liam.

Dad pats me on the shoulder. 'Let's leave these lovebirds in peace, shall we Ruth?' He winks at me as well, it must be catching. I just feel like I've got a nervous twitch.

'Oh yes, yes of course, darling, but we must make plans.' My heart plunges down to floor level. 'Now, now Samantha, let's organise supper.'

'Mum!'

'I know you'll ignore me if I send you one of my little texts.' Her little texts are like novels. 'She's a naughty girl.' She smiles at Jake as she pats my hand, as though I'm five years old. 'But you both must come over for supper. How about Saturday?'

Jake raises an eyebrow in my direction.

'Sure.' I only say it to get rid of her, I'll work out later how to cancel. Supper with Jake and my parents is definitely not on my 'to-do' list at present. Or ever.

'Wonderful.' Dad is steering Mum away. 'Speak to you later darling, enjoy your meal.'

There is a long silence. Jake is trying not to laugh. I know he is.

'Don't you dare say I am just like my mother, or I will dump you.'

'So heartless.' He grins. 'I was going to say you look like you need something sweet.'

'I'd better not have a dessert.' The puddings sound amazing, but I have a wedding to go to soon. I might have sorted my date, but I think the 'looking my sexiest' isn't quite there yet.

'Death by chocolate sounds just up your street,' he says as if he hasn't heard me trying to deny my cravings.

He's right though. It is. I was practically drooling as I read the description.

'I need to lose at least four more pounds before the—'

'Rubbish. You look perfect.'

I let him order dessert. He is my date, and he says I look perfect – so surely that has to be good enough for me?

I text Jake after I get home, and confirm what I will be paying him. It is more than half, but less than what I had originally calculated. He doesn't exactly send an orgasmic thank you, but he doesn't say no. Which solves one problem, and leaves me with another MASSIVE one.

Knowing that this would happen, I planned ahead and have made an appointment with my bank manager. Tomorrow instead of spending my lunch hour comparing diet plans with Sarah, I will be sat in the bank, working out just how much grovelling I need to do to get a 'home improvement loan'. I'm now worried that not only could all my family and friends hold me in contempt for lying to them, but I could be arrested for falsifying information for material gain. It all sounds terrible, doesn't it?

I'm beginning to think that Jake could be one 'kitchen update' too far. No way will he add value to my house. I haven't told him he's an appliances update, because he'd probably rather be a new sports car than a top of the range oven, but I wanted the bank manager to think I was sensible and looked after my money, and would spend his loan wisely on something that would last.

Jake is only going to last six days. Well, last as in 'feature in my life', I'm sure not even my mother is capable of killing him off in a week.

I will be spending the money wisely though. Just not in an approved manner. Last time I looked at the 'reasons you may want a home improvement loan' on the bank website, 'pay for escort services' was not on the list nestling between 'loft conversion' and 'restyle interior'. It wasn't on the leaflet either, I checked just to be sure.

I feel strongly that this is an oversight, as surely if said escort was good with his hands (most are I'd imagine) then they could do a bit of DIY in between other essential servicing, and make the house far more appealing? I know for a fact, though, that it would make Liam go a funny puce colour with indignation if a client ever requested money for anything that didn't have a resale value on eBay.

Anyhow, my bank manager is built in the same mould as Liam, so I know it will be a total waste of breath trying to persuade him I've got a valid need – so I'm going with kitchen update, though I'm normally quite an honest person. In fact I was very honest until this wedding, and the huge girlfriend, cropped up.

I wonder if offering a cut-price deal on a Caribbean holiday will swing the deal, then decide that adding bribery to white lies probably isn't a good idea.

Chapter 9

Hooray! Friday has been brilliant so far. I have a bank loan – I can afford to take Jake to Scotland. This is excellent news.

Luckily when I got to the bank, I discovered that my grumpy bank manager had been transferred and instead I would be seeing Zoe.

Zoe turned out to be infinitely nicer than I could have imagined.

She was roughly my own age and wearing the exact same shade of nail varnish as I was. In fact, once I pointed this out to her, it turned out she was mates with Jasmine who did my nails, who is besties with Sarah, and she really would be over the moon if I could sort her out a cheap deal to Crete.

I got the money for my new kitchen, henceforth to be known as Jake, and she will get the best room I can wangle for her, with a view to die for and cocktails on arrival.

To celebrate, Sarah and I decide to go out for the evening.

The only confusing bit is a text I get from Jake, just as Sarah knocks on my front door.

He seems to have got confused, or maybe it is meant for somebody else, or maybe we are not on the same wavelength at all. I'll ask him. Later.

*****

'Why have we come here?' Sarah is ushering me into the newest bar in town, rather than our normal cocktail bar. 'What about Appletini Callum?'

'I need to avoid him for a bit. There are only so many apple cocktails a girl can take, and ... he is only doing it part-time, he's an astrophysics student.' She rolls her eyes. 'Honestly, who wants to talk about stuff like that all the time? Geeky is only good when it sounds dirty, and he doesn't know a thing about horoscopes.' She gave a fake shudder. 'He hasn't got a clue about how compatible Leo is with Pisces. How strange is that?'

'Well, I'm not being funny but I'm not a Leo, so I haven't a clue either.'

'No, but he studies astrophysics, which is about stars, isn't it? He doesn't know anything about horoscopes, *Star Wars* or *Star Trek*. I reckon he's looking at a totally different sky, all these objects he goes on about in outer space are just confusing.'

'He probably thinks you're confusing.'

'That's the intention.' She opens her eyes wide. 'Come on, we need to celebrate, and this place is supposed to be totes on trend. You've got yourself a date! Woohoo!' And with that we're in.

'What do your parents think about Jake?' Oh shit, I've just realised what that text from Jake meant. He said *Fish and chip supper, or posh? Cazh or classy? x* I quite like the way he always tags a kiss on the end, though this could be because somebody might see them – or it could just be an actor thing. Buggering hell though, I've just realised that 'cazh' means casual, and he's talking about supper at Mum and Dad's tomorrow. I was supposed to be working out how to wriggle out of that one, and I've run out of wriggling room before I've had the chance.

Unfortunately the new 'on trend' bar is playing music loud enough for my deaf gran to make out every word. This is shouting territory, and I'm not sure I want to share facts about my fake date at full volume. I definitely don't want to start talking about supper with mother.

'They've not met him properly yet. Just said hello at the pizza place.'

'Made him wet?'

'Met him yet!'

'He's the best hot stew around, your mum's bound to love him.'

'Hot stew?'

'What?'

'You called him a hot stew.' Hot I could understand,

from a purely business-like point of view, but stew? For a moment I do wonder if she said 'hot screw', but not even Sarah would say those words and mention my parents in the same sentence.

'No I didn't. I said he's the best of what's around, tons better than wanker-banker Liam.'

I heard that bit, well mainly the last three words, as did most of the restaurant. She yelled it out in that teeny weeny gap between tracks.

It was at that point, when the word banker left her lips, that I remembered I had to tell her not, under any circumstances, to discuss this with Jasmine, her nail-technician bestie. Because if Jasmine found out about Jake, and accidentally told my new friend, Zoe at the bank, then I could have a lot of explaining to do. And possibly no loan. Which meant, possibly no date.

'Can a bank ask for a loan back early?'

'A low backed what?'

'Oh shit.' All of a sudden I've forgotten all about the dangers of Jasmine and the risk of early repayment, or criminal charges.

I half-slide under the table, and Sarah joins me. 'Oh shit what? And low backed what?'

Miraculously the noise levels are much better down here near floor level. 'He's just walked in.'

'Jake?' She pokes her head above table level.

'No.' I pull her back down. 'Why would I be hiding from Jake? Liam.'

'Liam, here? Where?' She's up and down like a bride's nightdress as my grandad used to say. I don't actually think it's a very tasteful thing to say but it's the first thing that comes to mind, probably because all I can think about it this bloody wedding, and how it's going to ruin my life and leave me destitute.

I pull her back down. 'By the door. With a bloke in a grey pullover.' Figures.

'Let me go and tell him what a shit-face he is, and show him a picture of your new man.'

'No!'

'No?' She looks at me with suspicion. 'I thought you were over him? You told me...'

'I am. Really. I am so over him. But I don't want him to see me...' *Like this* are the words I don't add. I am still a tad overweight (even if Jake is happy with me as I am), my roots need doing (I was hanging on until the day before I go up to Scotland), and I am slightly tipsy.

Next time I see Liam I want to have swishy hair, perfect make-up, control pants and a man holding my hand.

I don't want him back, but I don't want to look pathetic. I don't want him to realise that when he dumped me I let myself go a little bit. I have to be the fully restored version of myself – and I'm not quite there yet. Call me shallow, but I want Liam to look and weep. To regret doing what he did.

Sarah gets it without me saying another word. 'He's got his back to us. You make a dash for the door and I'll pay the bill.'

I peep over the edge of the table, look longingly at the last bit of my very fancy kebab and half a glass of very expensive wine.

It's Liam's laugh that breaks the spell, and puts me off my food. It sends me scurrying for the door like a crab that's scared of being stranded.

How did I ever think that laugh was remotely funny?

To be honest I don't think I ever did. It's a bit like a hyena, but one that's been to public school. With added snorty bits.

Chapter 10

I have not managed to avoid supper with my parents. It has occurred to me though that this might give us a chance to have a dry run. If my parents, the closest people to me, believe that Jake is my boyfriend, then surely everybody else will? It will also be a test of Jake's durability. If he can survive this and still have a grin on his face then I honestly believe he will be able to survive whatever Scotland throws at us. It will be, as Sarah said, a baptism of fire. I'm not altogether sure I like the sound of that though, I would hate him to spontaneously combust and go up in smoke. It will not be, as Sarah also said, awesome.

On the positive side, I have had a hint about why Jake needs a distraction. I know that he does not want commitment because he has been stung, and so I am now wondering if behind that grin he is hiding a broken heart, and if, like me, it has hardened his resolve to be true to himself and not let a relationship lead to compromise and complacency.

However, I still haven't got any rules established (which

I think could be important, as I am a bit worried about Jake's idea of having his own rules), and I don't know if his acting aspirations stop at patient-in-the-third-bed-along and strange alien. Not only is knowing this essential for our wedding trip, I'd also quite like to know just because I can't imagine him being happy with a Wikipedia listing that doesn't include anything slightly more exciting. And I don't expect the uncle who has supported his dreams would be either.

I have therefore suggested to Jake that we meet at the local pub for a drink before enduring supper. It will also give me a chance to have a nerve-steadying glass of wine, and prepare him for what lies ahead.

Unfortunately he calls to say he's had a 'family emergency' and has had to rush round to his gran's as her dog is 'stuck up next door's tree'. This sounds like a very strange excuse to me, and I'm beginning to feel a bit worried that he's not going to turn up at all, when there is a knock on the door.

'Will I do?'

I don't quite know what to expect for 'supper', as it isn't a concept I was brought up with. I had therefore suggested to Jake that we go for 'smart-casual' as I would like him to make a good impression, but not look like he is trying too hard (I don't want Mum to get carried away and buy a wedding hat, then be grief-stricken when we split up after the trip to Scotland).

Jake does smart-casual very well though, as I thought

he might. He is stood on the doorstep holding a large bunch of flowers and carrying a bottle of champagne, and he is wearing a very nice leather jacket (that looks super soft and lived in, and smells wonderful when he leans forward to kiss me on the cheek), a shirt that is the mauve-ish-pink that straight men will only wear if they are seriously confident or good-looking, and black jeans.

'Well?'

I pretend to give him the once-over for parental approval reasons, but really it's just a good excuse to give him a good ogle. There is no trace of his normal five o'clock shadow (see, I am starting to know something about him), so he has obviously shaved. I quite like his usual slightly-rough-around-the-edges image, a trace of stubble and mussed up hair, but it is nice to see that he has made an effort in the way any boyfriend should when meeting his potential in-laws.

'Definitely.'

'I thought we could chat in the taxi?' He grins. 'We can tell him to go round the block a few times?'

This feels a bit like I imagine a speed-date would. There are lots of questions I want to ask, but as the taxi pulls away from the kerb I now feel completely tongue-tied. 'Dog up a tree?' This is not what I intended to ask at all.

'He's a border collie and was chasing her neighbour's cat. He's actually pretty nimble and scampers up quite high, but I think he got carried away.'

'So you had to climb up?' I've got an image of him

heroically scaling the heights, desperate to rescue the poor animal, totally disregarding his own safety. Then wrapping it up in strong arms and...

'No, I got the tin of biscuits out. He decided to just let go and allow gravity to do the rest.'

I now have an image in my head of a crumpled furry body. 'Oh my God, the poor...'

'He's fine. He bounces, though she did cuff me round the head and told me she could have done that herself. She's a right one, my gran. Left here, or round the block again?'

'Block. When do you start doing this film?' Knowing that his gran has a dog, and is a bit feisty is enough knowledge on that front, there are more pressing matters.

'Two weeks after we get back from Scotland.'

I like the way he says that, it sounds couple-y, natural. I think he must have been practising.

'It could be my big break, I've had umpteen screen tests and my agent finally confirmed it a couple of weeks ago.'

'You're not an alien in it then?'

'Nope, I play an author who has holed himself up on a Greek island to finish his book. My turn, how long have we been dating?'

'Two months, no, it'll be three now. I needed time, you know, I didn't want to date you on the rebound, did I? I'm not that kind of girl.'

'Of course, so we've taken it slow.'

'We have.'

'Have we, er, you know?' He raises an eyebrow, and I get a hot flush.

'Well, of course, I'm not a prude you know.' Liam has to think we've slept together. 'There's slow, and there's...'

'Dead from the waist down?'

'Sex—' I peer at him, it would be over my glasses if I wore them, which I don't '—starts in a woman's head, not below the waist.' The taxi driver chuckles. I always suspected that they could hear when you closed the screen, they just have them so that we *think* they can't hear and say all kinds of private things that they can store up and laugh about in the pub.

'Sex, I find, starts right here.' Jake's gone all husky and dirty sounding, and he closes in and drops the tiniest kiss on my lips, the kind you might have imagined, it is so light, but it makes your stomach squish and something clench at the top of your thighs. Or is that just me? Anyway, it is extremely disconcerting that he can turn me on like that. Especially as I have forgotten to shout out 'round the block again' directions. Oh bloody hell, we have pulled up outside my parents' house.

'You're here!' Mum is waiting at the front door. Which means she was spying, and probably saw the kiss. 'I could swear I saw a cab that looked just like yours going past the house only minutes ago, well I saw it twice, now isn't that funny?' She laughs and gives me a pointed look. 'I said that to your father, didn't I David? It's not often you see one cab driving past our house, let alone two in as many minutes.'

I am debating whether to start the evening off with yet another lie, when she gives a little shriek. 'Oh, how lovely.' Jake has produced his gifts, and kissed Mum on the cheek, which has made her forget all about the taxi. 'Flowers, and these don't look like they came from the petrol station, do they David?' Despite all the comments she has made over the years, my father still gives her bouquets that he has spotted by the till when he's paying for his petrol, and it still hasn't occurred to him to take the price label off.

'They certainly don't, and nor does this bubbly. Splendid, splendid.'

'Oh my goodness, champers!' Mum giggles. 'Are we celebrating something?' She did see the kiss, and is now clutching my hand as though she expects a solitaire diamond to materialise any second.

'We certainly are.' Jake winks at me, and I try to glare back surreptitiously. Which is bloody hard. Lying about our relationship is one thing, but letting my mother imagine she can hear the ding-dong of wedding bells is dangerous territory. 'First bottle of many, hey darling?'

I cosy up, so that I have the opportunity to dig him in the ribs and stand on his foot. Unfortunately, being bigger and stronger than me means he can get me in something akin to an affectionate headlock and ruffle my hair. He is so going to regret this.

'I just love how enthusiastic Sam is about this, don't I darling?' Why is he still talking? 'Can't stop jumping about, can you?'

'She always did get a bit over-excited, you should have seen her at Christmas when she was three.' My mother is warming up.

'No, he shouldn't, Mum.'

'Up at three in the morning she was, we found her surrounded by torn up bits of wrapping paper, didn't we David? Surrounded she was, and crying. Sobbing her little heart out because she'd opened ties and slippers and didn't realise they weren't for her!'

I think Dad wanted to sob his heart out too when he saw that tie.

'Aww how sweet, I can just see it. That's what I love about you so much, your impulsive nature, the way I can see every emotion on your lovely face. So honest and open.' He kisses the tip of my nose and his eyes are practically twinkling.

'Now, haven't I always said that, Samantha? Like an open book, you are.'

'Now Mrs Jenkins—'

'Oh, call me Ruth, call me Ruth.' She is practically simpering, this is so embarrassing.

'Ruth.' Jake smiles. 'I think we need to crack this bottle open and you can help me celebrate, it's not every day a man gets his first big film contract!'

The flicker of disappointment on my mother's face, as

she realises we are not about to announce our nuptials, is quickly replaced with excitement that she practically has a film star in the family.

'Oh my goodness me, come through, come through. Haven't you got that champers open yet, David? Honestly, chop, chop dear, we need to celebrate.' She shoos us through towards the lounge. 'He does dither, doesn't he dear? Sit down, sit down, anywhere you like. Oh no, not there Jake, you come and sit here with me, and we can chat about show business.' She pats the arm of her chair.

'Leave the poor man alone, Ruth. I'm sure he'd much rather sit next to Samantha.' Dad manages to successfully herd Mum one way, and Jake the other. He always did enjoy watching *One Man and His Dog* and he's found the positive reinforcement exercises very effective when it comes to my mother. 'That wasn't burning I could smell in the kitchen, was it?'

'Burning, burning? Oh good heavens, silly me, the cheese straws! They'll be a crisp. Samantha loves cheese straws, don't you darling, although they aren't on any Weightwatchers list I've seen. Although Marjorie says you have to take those lists with a pinch of salt, if we all stuck to those we'd waste away.'

There is a lovely silence while we listen to the oven opening and closing, and some clattering of dishes, and then my mother returns with Pringles and twiglets.

'I think there's something wrong with the oven again, David. You really need to have a man out, I don't think you knew what you were doing when you looked at it last time. Never mind, I'm sure these will be lovely. Pringle, Jake?'

Jake has pulled a master stroke with the bottle of champagne. By the time Mum remembers to put supper out she is already tipsy (excellent), and very giggly and flirty (not so good), which means she seems to have forgotten about interrogating us about our relationship, which I know she fully intended on doing. Mother views her role as an advanced screening service.

'This is amazing, a fabulous cook as well as finding time to act and look incredible.'

'Oh nonsense.' But I know she doesn't mean it. Mother touches her hair self-consciously and basks in Jake's admiration. She already loves Jake, which is a good sign. 'Get away with you! Such a shame the black pudding disintegrated.'

'Excellent as a crumb, what a brilliant idea! You'd pay a fortune for this in a restaurant, wouldn't you Sam? Delicious.'

'And the bacon was too crispy to put on, in the picture it was balanced on top of the scallop.'

'Bacon is overrated. Isn't it sweetie?' He squeezes my knee and I nearly jump out of my seat, but recover enough to squeak a response. 'And the wine is perfect, David. I bet you've got quite a cellar.'

Dad has never had a cellar. He has a small wine rack (the type you build yourself with dowels that collapses on a regular basis so you have to prop it up with junk) under the stairs. But he nods. 'Very kind of you to say so, Jake. A good little find this one, might have to lay a few bottles down.' Bottles do not 'lay' in my parents' house, they are drunk.

By the time we are on dessert, I feel like a lay down though.

'Now then, tell us how you two lovebirds met?'

I open my mouth and nothing comes out. We can't do this yet, we haven't talked about it. I don't know how we met. So I pretend to chew an imaginary mouthful of bread and butter pudding.

'Dog-walking.' I glance at Jake in surprise. He is brilliant! It's not technically a lie.

'But Samantha hasn't got a dog, have you?' Mum doesn't think it sounds so brilliant, she looks at me accusingly, as though there is something else I have kept secret.

'No, but—'

'She's not that good with dogs, not quite assertive enough, the man at the training class said when we took our spaniel.'

'I was four, Mum! You only made me take him because he embarrassed you!'

'Well, she is absolutely brilliant with dogs now, Ruth. They gave her one of the most badly behaved dogs at the rescue centre, they could see she knew what she was doing. Putty in her hands, he was.'

'Putty?' Mum looks confused.

Putty is not a word I'd use in describing Tank. Ever.

'Putty. Never seen this dog so well-behaved, and I've been helping out at the centre for years.'

'Well, that's nice, isn't it David?'

'Excellent. Brandy, Jake?'

'So you help out at a dog rescue centre? Aww isn't that kind of you, I can tell you're kind, you've got a kind face. Hasn't he, David?'

I can tell she is quite drunk, there are far too many 'kinds' in that sentence.

Jake has settled for a very small brandy with his coffee, and I have settled for the 'lovely exotic drink that I've just discovered, so fruity and foreign' that mother insists I try. It tastes suspiciously like Cointreau.

'Now isn't this nice?'

It actually has been quite nice. My parents both love Jake, and he has said all the right things and looked like he has meant them.

He has also chatted about his work at the rescue centre (I didn't realise quite how dedicated he is), his wonderful mother (who he clearly loves), and the gran he adores (he pops in at least three times a week to check she's okay). And when mother mentions Liam, he brushes it away with a slightly contemptuous look on his face. 'That man sounds an absolute idiot, he doesn't deserve somebody as lovely as your daughter. And—' he smiles at me '—he sounds far too boring for Sam, no fun at all.'

'Hear, hear.' My father nods in agreement. 'I always suspected the man was a waste of space, weak he is. Weak.'

I open my eyes in astonishment at the minor outburst. 'You never...'

'Not our place to comment, my dear, and I have to admit at first I thought the lad was a good 'un like his brother Dan. But I, for one, was glad to see the back of him.'

'We'll be seeing him again soon, David.' Mum has poured herself another fruity drink, while nobody was looking.

'More's the pity. I'll give him short shrift if...'

'Oh don't cause a scene, Dad!'

'You don't need to say anything, David.' Jake has that steely look in his eyes, they're tawnier and less brown. Something about Liam really seems to make him cross, which I guess must be to do with him having been betrayed himself. He did say he knew exactly how I felt. 'I'll make sure he knows what we think.'

Oh, this is quite thrilling, my father and my boyfriend standing up for me!

'We must meet up again.' Mum has necked her Cointreau and is now regaining control of centre stage. 'Before the wedding – we will take afternoon tea at that nice hotel up the road.'

I try not to roll my eyes, then catch sight of Jake – who is grinning. I grin back, it's impossible not to.

'We'd better go, Mum. Work in the morning.'

'Thank you, you were great.' Our taxi has pulled up outside my house, and Jake, ever the gentleman, has got out to hold the door, and it all feels very formal.

'My pleasure. It was fun.'

'Really? Oh, I suppose it was, but...'

'Your parents are lovely.' He smiles. 'Just like you are.' His lips brush over mine, gossamer light, and my mouth opens of its own accord. Waiting for the full blown kiss that never comes. 'Night, Sam. Sleep well.'

And with a brief wave of his hand, he climbs back in the taxi. I watch the tail lights until it reaches the end of the road, turns and disappears from sight. Taking my knight in shining armour with it.

I hug my arms round myself and realise I'm smiling.

This wedding is going to be brilliant!

ACT THREE – THE WEDDING

Chapter 11

As it turns out, Jake and I do not get a chance to meet my parents again. I have a real, valid, honest excuse. Well, Jake does.

He has a job that doesn't involve making coffee, being a pretend date, being an alien, or walking dogs. Jake has to stand in for the lead in some stage play where he was understudy. The guy broke a leg (I always did wonder about how wise it was to wish that on people, maybe understudies say it and it qualifies as a lucky break. As in career, not leg, obviously), and so Jake has been rehearsing and acting, until there are only two days before we go to Scotland.

Not only does he not get to meet my parents again, we haven't had much chance to get to know each other in a non-sexual way. It's been limited to a few snatched coffees, before he's rushed back to rehearsals, and we really haven't made as much progress as I had planned.

I realise that I really want to see more of him, he's good company, and it's weird when we're not meeting up for a chat. Or a pizza. I miss him.

Our meetings have been brief, but better than nothing. He's been distracted though, asking me to test him on his lines, and I've gone on about Liam, and Jess, and Jess's mum, and how I've completely failed on the losing weight front and at the last dress fitting everybody else's dress needed taking in, and I kind of took up the slack. I remember at school being told in a science lesson that energy cannot be created or destroyed. It is there, somewhere, transferred or in a different form. Well, I am fairly certain this applies to fat; one person might lose it, but it goes to another person.

Luckily my diet plan and the gym sessions have had some effect, so I've not got fatter, I just haven't got thinner. And Jake has said he doesn't know what I'm talking about, I look fine to him.

On top of all of this, on his first free day Jake has 'stuff' to sort, and I need my roots doing and a last minute pep talk from Tim.

'You are so not fat, gorgeous lady. Is she girls? You are statuesque, Rubenesque, burlesque.' I think he ran out of valid 'esque's' at this stage, but whoever it is that said gay men only like stick insects is wrong. Or maybe they said gay fashion designers? Either way they are wrong, or Tim is an excellent liar. I don't care – I'll take it. 'Now give Jake a kiss from me and strut your stuff!' I definitely wasn't going to start kissing Jake on behalf of anybody, but the round of applause did rather go to my head (or that could have been the Bailey's iced coffee that came free with a cut and blow) and I practically strut down the high street.

Then I get home, see my suitcase and it really hits me that tomorrow is *the day* and I feel like Jon Snow in Game of Thrones – 'I know nothing'.

I still don't know why Jake needs a distraction, but I have now got the most healthy bank balance I am ever likely to have. I am going to stare at my statements and wallow in my pretend wealth – until I have to hand it over to the man who is about to demolish or help me build my self-esteem and reputation to incredible heights.

I've been a bit worried that at this rate he'll be the only person at the wedding who does not know much about me at all – apart from the fact that I like chocolate brownies, and am not good with dogs (though he thinks I am). And he does know a lot about Liam. And Jess. And the fact that when I am unhappy I seem to lose my last vestige of self-control where food is concerned.

This is good in some ways (stops him pulling out), but very bad in others (increases the risk of being found out).

So the day before we're due to head across the border and the far north I'm knocking at his door in a state of mild panic.

He ruffles his fingers through his hair, so that it sticks up in all directions and he looks like a confused puppy that's just woken up. Cute, and mildly disturbing. I must be crazy. It's late and I'm door-stepping a hunk of a man I hardly know.

A near-naked hunk, who is standing in front of me in trackie bottoms and very little else.

I have never seen him nearly naked. And it is distracting. Very distracting.

And I'm in my pyjamas.

It was a sudden, impulsive decision. Mum had rung not long after Tim had massaged my scalp and my ego.

'You are still coming to see us in the morning, darling?'

Sugar, I'd forgotten about that bit. 'Yes, Mum.'

'Early. You know your dad likes to allow plenty of time.'

'Early.'

'Such a shame we couldn't get to see Jake again before the wedding.'

'Yes I know but...'

'We were so looking forward to finding out more about him. He seems such a nice young man, and I never got a chance to ask him about his acting. I'm sure with all my experience I could give him some useful tips. We all need to start somewhere.'

'It'll be fine, Mum. We'll come round half an hour before your taxi is due, and then you can have another little chat.' This had seemed a good idea when we'd agreed it. I'd thought the fact that they'd already met him, and *seemed* to know him would add authenticity. Thirty minutes had also seemed long enough for pleasantries, but well short of what was required for a full-blown Miss Marple style interrogation.

'Such a shame we aren't travelling up together.' Her sigh

was that old familiar sound of disappointment in me, of 'oh well, I'm sure you'll do better next time'.

'I know. But Dad doesn't like driving that far, it's a long way, and my car isn't big enough for all of us.' There are times when I am SO happy I have a two seater, even if it is old and crappy. It had made sense for my parents to fly, less stress all round.

'Well, I'm sure Jake has got a car big enough for all of us, hasn't he?'

She said it in a way that suggested if he hadn't, then he was lacking in some way. It was a question I couldn't answer though. I didn't know if he had a revved up engine and was firing on all cylinders, or if he had an environmentally friendly, but far less impressive, push bike. 'I think his is electric.' Which I think was a pretty inspired thought, given the pressure I am under.

'Oh, are those tiny, dear?'

'No, but the battery might run out.'

'Oh.'

'It's a long way to Scotland.'

'Those Duracell batteries are supposed to be very good darling, they last all day and night so I'm told.'

'It's a car, Mum. It's different.' Any minute now she'll be offering to pop down to Aldi and buy a bumper pack of AA's.

I haven't asked Jake whether he has a car because I had said we would go in my car – after all, I'm the boss here. But I can't own up to that.

'Or we could have all flown together, Samantha. That would have been nice.'

Excruciatingly nice. There can only be one thing worse than being stuck on a country estate for a week with a fake date wondering if it's all going to go wrong, and that has to be being stuck in a tin box at thirty-five thousand feet with a fake date and your parents. 'Yes but we thought...' I was struggling, we'd actually thought a few hours stuck in a car together might help us get to know each other. 'We thought it would be romantic, a little road trip.'

'Oh.' That does the trick. 'Well, don't put the roof down, it makes you look wild with your hair blowing everywhere. Men don't like wild.'

I don't know what planet my mother grew up on, but I'd beg to differ on that one. 'I'll bear it in mind.'

'You have packed that pretty dress, haven't you? I like you in that. It shows off your figure, I don't know why you young girls insist on wearing jeans all the time these days. When I was your age I...'

'Look Mum, it's late, I've not packed yet. Can we chat tomorrow?'

So I'm standing outside Jake's place. With a jacket over my PJ's, and a taxi waiting, with its clock ticking over.

He frowns. 'What's up?'

Well, his bare chest is up for one thing, and the fact that he's got that dark shadowy stubble effect which means he hasn't shaved for at least twenty-four hours. See, I don't know exactly how long because I don't know how often he shaves. As a girlfriend I should. It is little things like this that worry me.

'I can't do it.' I must add that the half a bottle of wine I downed after I'd finished my call with Mum hasn't steadied my pre-wedding jitters at all. It has set them into overdrive. I now have hyper-fidgets, which could be nerves, or could be partly down to staring at that chest. I want to touch it. Just a quick fondle.

'It's the bride or groom that are supposed to get cold feet, not the maid of honour.' He's looking bemused.

'Mum and Dad will realise, everybody will realise.'

'Did everybody realise Liam was a jerk?'

'Well no, but...' I bite the inside of my cheek as this thought sinks in. It is true, they had never noticed. Well, not until fairly recently, Dad said. But then neither had I.

'There you go. So why should they realise that we're not an item?' He opens the door a bit wider, and steps back, and I kind of fall in. I think my eyes are so focused on his body that when it moves, so do I. Which could have been embarrassing, but he sidesteps neatly and steadies me with a hand on my elbow.

'I thought I could tell them you'd stood me up?' This thought had occurred to me while Mum was going on about pretty dresses and wild hair.

He shakes his head, and looks disappointed. 'I have *not* stood you up.' He's still holding my elbow, which is rather nice.

'Yes, but, hypothetic—'

'I'd never stand you up. Never, not even hypothetically.'

His tone has softened and I really do want to touch that slightly hairy chest, to sink against his warm body (I just know it will be warm), to somehow believe him. Believe this can work.

The wine has obviously gone to my head.

'I'm not going to let you give up, Sam. We can do this.'

I get it. He's broke. That's why he took this job, and he wants to see it through. 'Don't worry about the money, I've got it, I'll pay you even if we don't go. I mean you should get at least some of it, for inconvenience and well, whatever.'

'There's no inconvenience. But you're going to get your week in Scotland, you're going to be there for your best friend, and you're going to show the world that you don't give a monkey's about that arsehole.' He brushes his knuckles against my cheek. 'I told you, this isn't just about the money Sam. I like you, you're mega brave and gutsy and prepared to do this for Jess.'

'It's not just for Jess, it's for me.'

'Good. I don't like the way you've been treated. I know how it feels.'

'And I am over him.'

'I know you are.'

'But everybody knows he used to be my arsehole and now he has—'

He puts his spare finger on my lips.

'Now he has screwed his own life up, and you should be very grateful he didn't screw yours up too.'

I hadn't thought about it like that before. Did Liam want to be a dad? He hadn't even wanted joint ownership of a goldfish when we were together. Too much mess, he said.

'I'm sorry, but I'm totally shagged, I need to sleep, Sam.' He lets his hand drop, and my poor cold elbow is abandoned. 'I've had a hectic few weeks and we've got an early start tomorrow. Go home, get your head down. Go on, bugger off.'

Now he's trying to send me away. We've only been talking for ten minutes tops, and he's bored. 'Mum wanted us to fly with them.' For some reason I don't want to go. Talking is an excellent way of delaying things.

'The drive will give us time to chat, get to know each other, and it'll mean we've got a car handy when we get there. And I, er, well, I might have a bit of a problem, a minor complication.'

'Complication?' Problem? Complication? I thought we had a deal. I could give in to hysterics now, or I could take deep breaths. More of them. At this rate there won't be enough oxygen left for everybody else.

'Don't worry, I'm sure I can sort it. Honestly. Forget I said anything.'

Only a man could put the words 'complication' and 'don't worry' together. How can I not worry?

'I shouldn't have mentioned it, should I?'

'Yes, yes, it's fine.' No, he definitely shouldn't have

mentioned it. Now I will sleep even less than the not-sleeping I was expecting.

'Hang on.' He turns around and I'm treated to a view of his back, which is nice and broad, and hair-free, and kind of muscled but not too much. And tapers down to his bum, which I already know is quite pert but solid looking.

Solid-looking. That about sums him up; not too slim, or jeans hanging off jutting out hipbones (or groin, I mean who thinks hanging your clothes off your groin is a good idea?). Just all round solid.

'Here.' He holds out an envelope.

'I'm not going by a post—'

'Read it, Sam.'

I read it. The bold, slightly flamboyant writing leaps out at me: I CAN DO IT.

'You can.' He's studying me, and nodding.

'I can.' I nod back. Tim told me I could do it. Everybody has told me I can do it. I can.

'Stick that up above your desk, or your mirror, or in your handbag or whatever. Read it whenever you have doubts.' He gives a slightly self-conscious shrug, which is SO cute. 'It worked for me.'

'Oh.' I look at him more closely, and wish I was sober. 'But you never have doubts, you're an actor, you were in the third bed along, and you're going to be in a film.' I can't imagine he ever needed to tell himself he can do anything. He is Mr Quietly Confident.

He laughs. 'It took me three years to get into stage school, then a few more before I got even a crappy little part. I'm no overnight sensation, Sam. My uncle had little signs scattered round his study, with words of wisdom like this. He gave me a plaque with these words on when he told me about the fund he'd set up. He said that some people are lucky enough to have a special somebody in their life who will tell them they can do it, but the rest of us need to tell ourselves.' He held a hand up to stop me speaking. 'He also said that self-belief is the strongest gift you can have.'

'But you don't have somebody else to…'

'I had my uncle, and then…' His gaze drifts across my face, as though he's trying to imprint it in his mind. 'I did have somebody else for a while, but what you see isn't always what you get, is it Sam? Sometimes it's all just skin deep.' The tips of his fingers cascade over my cheek and I want to grab his hand, but it's gone before I can. And so is the serious, thoughtful look on his face. He smiles, a bit lopsided, but a smile. If I've ever really wanted to hug him it's now.

'Sometimes people aren't who you think they are, but sometimes…' I pause, feeling all philosophical in the way I often do after a few drinks. 'But sometimes I think they're who they were all along. We just didn't want to look too closely.'

'You could be right. Which is why I guess I've decided it's easier not to get into anything heavy.'

'But wimpier.' Good God, what am I saying? I don't want heavy. Definitely not.

Jake just laughs though, a deep-throated chuckle. 'You're funny. Call me a wimp then.'

But I don't think he is, not really.

'Which is why you want a distraction...' I hold up the envelope in front of me, as though I'm meeting somebody at the airport.

'I want a distraction from something I can't do anything about. It is out of my hands.'

'Which is?'

He is still chuckling. 'Go on, go! Before I drag you off to bed, rules or no rules.'

He puts his hands on my shoulders and spins me round, then pats me on my bum to send me on my way. Which is rather nice. But distracting. God, he's cute. Or did I say that already?

Which reminds me.

I don't know what his complication is. And I definitely need to find out why *he* needs a distraction.

Chapter 12

It's a good job I've been keeping a lookout, because Jake turns up indecently early at my parents' house. And from my spot by the window the first thing I notice is that there is something wrong. Very wrong. He isn't carrying a bag, or any luggage at all.

I glance down behind his feet, check out his back. Not the teeniest-weeniest rucksack in sight. And from the fit of his chinos and shirt I'd say there isn't a place suitable to smuggle even a toothbrush in.

He's changed his mind. It's the only answer. He's decided he doesn't need a distraction, or his complication is just too big to ignore.

He's reaching out to push the doorbell when he spots me. It's hard not to really because I'm frantically rubbing away on the glass to clear up the steamed-up bit, as my nose has been pressed against it. Mum hates smudges.

I'm considering climbing out of the window so that I can frisk him and demand co-ordinating travel accessories. He freezes, arm outstretched, a welcome grin on his face.

'Stay!' I'm not sure if he can lip read or not, but I'm out of my seat like a whippet from a trap. Okay, maybe not a whippet, but for me I'm fast, out of the lounge, and tripping over the suitcases that Mum has strategically placed in the hallway before she's had time to take a bite out of her toast. I know she's done it on purpose, it's a trap. Nobody is getting in or out of this house without her noticing.

Which is why I'm rubbing my elbow when I open the door.

'You okay?'

'Slipped.' I point at the cases, which are now not so strategically placed, or so artistically piled up.

'Ouch.' He winces.

All I can do is point to his feet, where his own luggage should be, then back to the scattered pile. My parents have two large wheelie cases, one cabin bag, a couple of those posh suit bags, a small bag with emergency rations in (they like to be prepared) and what looks like Dad's old briefcase. For a moment I'm distracted, why does he need a briefcase? Are we going to be tested when we get there? Should I have packed a laptop, or pen and paper?

'Is that Jake, darling?' Mum has also left the kitchen door open so she can hear every move I make.

'Yes, er just a minute Mum, you finish your breakfast. Where's the...?' I know it's rude to hiss, and to point, but he's getting both.

He frowns. I mime picking up a bag in each hand and the furrows on his brow disappear.

'Ah, I left my luggage in the taxi. I'll go and get it. It's just, er, you know I mentioned last night that I'd got a bit of a problem?'

'Ye-s.' The word drags itself from my lips unwillingly. I had added his problem, his complication, to the long list of nightmarish scenarios that kept me awake until the early hours. 'The one I wasn't to worry about? The one you would sort?'

'That's the one. I had a bit of an issue on the sorting front I'm afraid.' He pulls a wry smile. 'I'm really sorry.'

'The complication is in the taxi as well?'

'It's a him, not an it.'

'A him?'

'Come on.' He holds out a hand and I automatically take it. 'Come and meet Harry, I was hoping it would be okay to bring him? That it wouldn't be a problem.' He raises an eyebrow my way, but I can't answer. 'He's no trouble, he'll be good. He's not very old so it's great for him to meet new people, socialise a bit. Can never start too early can you?'

Can't you? He's got a kid! We're taking his kid to the wedding – how the hell do I explain that one? This is one up on Liam's hugely pregnant girlfriend.

I haven't got a car seat. More importantly, I haven't got a seat. As in a spare seat in my convertible. It is a car made for two. It is not child friendly. He will fly out of the open top as my hair blows wildly.

'Are you okay, Sam?' Jake has stopped, and is looking at me weirdly, as though he's expecting me to keel over.

'He's not been invited, I mean it's just us, me and a guest. It would be rude to just turn up with...' I flap my hands because I cannot say the word.

'Sorry, seriously. Shit, I mean I wouldn't have brought him if I didn't have to. I can try and sort something, give me an hour. Two. I didn't want to be late, so I just bunged him and his stuff in and ... we've got a bit of spare time, haven't we?' He shrugs. 'Although, I know this is a bit daft, but I wanted you to meet him anyway.' There's a faint frown. 'You're not allergic are you?'

I am. Definitely allergic. My skin is already prickling, I think this is how it feels when people come out in hives.

How could he have not told me this?

'Sam? You've gone a bit pale.' I am devoid of blood. The worst situation in my life has just dipped into new territory.

'I tried to say no, believe me, in fact I said a very firm no after you'd been round last night and I thought it was sorted. But he turned up this morning, and I just thought Scotland would be er...' And with that, he flings the taxi door open and out falls Harry.

It isn't as bad as it sounds. No need to call social services.

Harry is all black fluff and curls. Harry has a waggy tail and a bark.

I laugh a slightly maniacal, borderline hysterical laugh, and sink down on the kerb as Harry put his paws up on my chest and tries to stick his tongue in my mouth. I can't breathe. Partly because I am hyperventilating, partly because I have a furry snout in my face.

'I thought the place would be dog friendly? I knew you were a bit of a dog lover seeing as you wanted to help out at the rescue centre, I mean that's why I wanted to meet you there and said...'

'You wouldn't sleep with a girl who didn't like animals.' My voice is all weak and pathetic. It was a test. It all makes sense now.

'It clinched it for me when I saw how you were with Tank.' He blows me a kiss. 'You're unbelievable.'

I quite like being called unbelievable.

'Incredible.'

He's pushing it now. 'You're just trying to get round me.'

His boyish grin is back, full force. 'Yup, and I thought it wouldn't be a problem, with it being an estate. But if you'd rather cough up for a dog-minder, I can ring round and...'

I hold a hand up, fend off the dog with my other one. 'You've persuaded me.' My bank loan does not extend to dog-minders. 'Pack the dog, or whatever you have to do with it. Fine, it's fine. I'll text Jess and double check before we set off.'

'Sure?' He smiles as he hauls me to my feet.

'Oh my goodness, aren't you the cutest?' I hadn't heard Mum creep up, but I shouldn't have been surprised. She can be a ninja when she wants to be, she can hear through walls and approach silently.

I think the 'cute' comment is aimed at the dog, but I can't be sure. 'Oh Jake, it's so nice to see you again! Samantha has told us all about how busy you have been.' He raises an eyebrow in my direction and I shake my head, they've heard nothing, it's a trick. 'Do come in, such a shame you two lovebirds couldn't come for afternoon tea, but we can make up for it this week.' She giggles in what I can only describe as a flirtatious manner and I could swear she's got a bum wiggle going on as she heads back towards the front door. Bum wiggles should be banned for all mothers, at least when their daughters are there. Particularly if the wiggle is for the benefit of their daughters' boyfriends. Honestly, it's indecent, even if he isn't a proper boyfriend.

Luckily he's too busy to notice as he's dragging his case out of the cab and paying the driver. We finally all get inside and there's hand shaking and dog patting, then that silence. The 'we don't know each other very well, what do we say next' kind.

'I hope they won't mind me bringing Harry. I was rather put on the spot.'

'Oh heavens no, of course they won't mind.' Mother does tend to make decisions that aren't hers to make. 'How could anybody mind? Of course they won't. They love dogs in Scotland.' A bit of a sweeping statement, but who am I to argue? She frowns. 'I hope he doesn't get lice.'

We all frown. 'Lice?'

'They get them up there, I read about it in one of those country magazines I bought, didn't I David?' Mother stores completely random information. Ask her the capital of Spain and she won't know, but then she'll trot out something completely obscure. She could be a secret weapon in pub quizzes. She looks at Dad, who doesn't comment. 'Hang on.' She picks a magazine up, she's got a bigger collection than the corner shop stocks. 'No, no, not that one, ah this one. Dog friendly places in Scotland!'

'But you didn't know we were taking a dog, Mum.' One day I could be like this, this is my future. Like mother, like daughter. Oh God.

'Oh, I just bought every magazine that had an article about Scotland in it. You know, for the pictures. One has to be dressed right, and it is a different country.'

I try not to roll my eyes, anybody would think we were off to the Himalayas or the Arctic Circle or something.

'Oh silly me. Ticks not lice!'

'I'll look out for them.' Jake is managing not to laugh. Or run away. The running away bit is one of the reasons I initially didn't want him to meet my family in advance. He did survive supper though.

I give him a sharp nudge in the ribs with my elbow, and hear a satisfying squeak. But he's grinning. He's encouraging her, we'll be sitting down discussing sporrans next.

'I did ask Juliet if they had midges there at this time of year.'

The mention of midges is making my scalp itch. I am having horrible visions of all the guests being supplied with free nets, white obviously, as it is a wedding, or pink to match the confetti, to stop us coming out in a nasty rash. So not good on a wedding day.

'Sun, breeze and keeping on the move is the remedy I think.' Jake replies smoothly.

'Oh wonderful. I could tell you were clever. We'll keep on the move, won't we David? Although I do hope there isn't a breeze. You are going to pin your hair up, aren't you dear?'

That is directed at me. I wasn't actually.

'And I do hope you've packed enough hairspray, you know what your hair is like if it rains.' Yeah, one big frizzfest. 'And the nearest supermarket is a thirty-minute drive away, you can't just pop out if you forget something. Can you credit that? Isn't it exciting?'

It isn't exciting. It is frightening. I am going to be trapped. Thirty minutes from civilisation. With a man I hardly know. And my parents.

'It will be like being stranded on a desert island!'

With midges and strong winds.

'Cup of tea, Jake? You can tell us all about your family and future plans.' She winks at me. 'You look like the type of man who'd make a lovely father.'

This is worse, much worse than the lice conversation, or midges or having to go to the end of the earth.

'Your taxi will be here any minute, Mum. Don't you need to powder your nose or go to the loo?'

'Nonsense, we've got lots of time. Sugar? Milk?'

'Stop embarrassing them, love.' It's the first thing Dad has said, and it wins him a frown.

'I'm not embarrassing anybody, David. Am I?'

'Plenty of time for that later, eh? I want to know more about this acting lark. My lady wife here—' he puts an arm round Mum '—has the acting bug. Quite the drama queen, aren't you, Ruth?' I glance at Jake, he's trying not to laugh, we all are. Apart from Mum, who has taken it as a compliment.

'Oh I am, I am.' She preens. 'Rather good, though I say so myself. You should have seen my performance in *Taming of the Shrew*.'

'You shouldn't,' I mouth, and he gives me a conspiratorial wink. Nobody should have had to sit through that. Dad had to though, I consider it a sign of true love.

For the first time in my entire life, I'm happy to hear a step by step account of her stage highlights. All of them. From the day she decided that drama was for her, up to six weeks ago when they cast her in a key role. Fourth down on the programme!

By the time she's got to her credits the taxi has arrived and Dad gives me a hug and a wink as he bundles her in. He shakes hands with Jake, and gives a nod as though he's satisfied. Handshakes are important to Dad, he says you can tell everything from a handshake.

I bloody well hope this one hasn't told him anything it shouldn't have.

Chapter 13

'I can drive if you want?'

'No!' I don't mean to shout, but I've got a thing about men suggesting they take the wheel – when it isn't their wheel to take. I mean, it's the start isn't it? It can look like consideration, but before you know it they might be taking liberties all round, grabbing the remote control, taking charge of the fridge and re-designating the wine shelf as a beer shelf, insisting the loo seat is best left up, resetting the central heating, and suggesting you don't know what you're doing.

I never used to think about who did the driving at all, but I have now realised it is a metaphor for my life. Or at least the bit of my life that I had with Liam. It was the thin end of the wedge. The day I let him take my steering wheel was the day I gave him permission to change my life. In a relationship you're both supposed to compromise, aren't you? But I realise now that it was only me that was doing the compromising. I now intend to take full control of my own wheel again.

Of course, a man suggesting he'll drive because you want to hit the cocktails is altogether different. But when did that last happen?

'Up to you.' He smiles as he does his best to jam Harry's basket onto the parcel shelf. The dog has more luggage than the both of us put together. 'I just thought you might be a bit tired and want doggy cuddles.'

I am a bit tired, but I haven't got time for doggy cuddles. 'We need to get to know each other.' Why does that sound such an ordeal?

'I told you, Sam.' He gives my arm a squeeze. 'Chill, we'll sort it. We could say we've only just met.'

'I told Jess we met months ago, like not long after me and Liam split up.'

He grins as he opens the driver door for me. 'We can say we've been too busy shagging to talk?' There's a hopeful, questioning lift at the end of the sentence.

I turn the key a little forcefully. 'So when Liam asks about that noise I make, what will you say?' Concentrating on pulling away from the kerb means I don't have to look at him. Until he makes a funny noise himself, and I realise he's not properly in the car. I stop and let him sort himself out. It wouldn't do to lose him before we're even out of the town, would it?

'I didn't notice it?'

'Noooo!' I crunch the gears. 'It's the noise I make when, you know, when…'

'When?'

'When we've, I've, you know…'

'You come?'

I glance over and he doesn't look disturbed, but boy do I feel it.

'If we'd spent our entire relationship in bed together then you'd know, wouldn't you?'

'I'd hope so.' He grins. 'So what is the noise? Do it for me, baby.'

'Don't call me baby. I can't just do it, it happens, you know, not on purpose.' I try an experimental noise, but it comes out slightly wrong, and with a yelp Harry leaps from his spot in the footwell, over Jake's shoulder and ends up on the parcel shelf burying his nose in his basket. Oh well, at least I know if I ever get a dog, it's not going to interfere with nookie. 'It just…'

'Ahh, so we'll have to, you know, so I can hear the real thing?' He strokes Harry reassuringly. 'Is that what you mean?'

'No that isn't what I mean! It was just an example of—'

'And a very valid one.'

I ignore him. 'Of what can go wrong.'

'Look Sam.' I can sense he nearly said Sammy, and stopped himself just in time. He places a big capable hand over the one I've got resting on the gear lever. 'Stop stressing. If anybody asked me a question like that I'd tell them to take a hike. I'm not the kind of guy to discuss the noises a lady makes when I show her what sex can really be like.'

'Show? You?' I suspected, at the start, that Jake might be really big-headed. He is, after all, good-looking, charming, and an actor. His need for an 'I can do it' message has obviously long passed, now that he has actually 'done it'. So much confidence in one man, it's indecent.

The trouble is, he probably could show me. But I don't want to think about that. I need to resist his charms, and capabilities. This is business.

'Me.' He squeezes my hand and I know I need to pull away. Quickly. Except I need to change down gear for the traffic lights. 'Believe me, you'd be making all kind of noises.'

'Harrumph.'

'But I've not heard that one yet. Okay.' He coaxes Harry down, and the dog leans over to give me a doggy kiss before it nestles in his lap with a sigh. 'I'll play along, if it's going to make you feel better. We'll take it in turns, me first. Where are your ticklish spots?'

'No way, I don't tell anybody about those.'

'Aha, so you have got some, I'll just have to find out for myself.'

I decide he's best ignored. I will ask sensible questions. 'What food do you absolutely hate?'

'Boring.' He fondles Harry's ears and stretches his long legs out as far as they will go in my small car.

'It's the type of thing normal people know about each other.'

'Rubbish, it's what they think they should know.' He gives me a sideways look and I know that he knows that

I am thinking that was exactly the type of thing I knew about Liam. 'I'm more interested in what makes you laugh and what turns you on.'

Watching him stroking that dog is having a funny effect, but we'll not mention that.

'I'm not the type of guy who does food preferences, I'm more interested in the intimate stuff, and what makes you happy.'

'Food makes me happy.'

'I noticed.' Jake laughs. 'Don't tell me, chocolate brownies and pizza top the list?'

'I do sophisticated as well.' I pretend to be offended. 'I am partial to an oyster.'

'You sound like your mum.'

'Any more talk like that and I'm stopping the car!' We share a look. He's funny, I like funny. I'm beginning to quite like Jake. 'I really like those tasting menus when you get loads of little fancy things, with wow flavours.'

'Wow, very sophisticated.'

'Although I also like scampi.'

'I love steak, hate olives.'

'You don't like olives?'

'What's the point?'

'Martini? You can't have a martini without an olive.'

'So, you said your ex is the groom's brother?' He really doesn't like olives.

'Yup.' He has already heard quite a bit about Liam. 'His brother Dan is really nice, and so is Jess.'

'And when you split up...' He pauses, he's watching me. 'You're okay to talk about this?'

'I am.' And I actually am. Seeing Liam again might be a bit weird, but I can talk about it all now without hardly cringing at all.

'So you knew about the pregnant girlf—'

'I did not!'

'I thought...'

'He did tell me he'd met somebody else, but I didn't know she was pregnant until Jess told me.'

'Oh.'

'When she rang about the invite, and told me how huge she is.'

'Bad.' He shakes his head. 'Did you love him?'

I think about that one, while we go round the roundabout, and join the motorway. And while I'm trying not to think about Liam doing his undressing routine in front of somebody else. Maybe it wasn't the same. Maybe he ripped his clothes off in a fit of passion. Or maybe not. 'I thought I did. But, it was more like very fond than madly in love kind of love.'

'It was a habit?'

'Say it like it is, why don't you?' He's getting a bit close to the bone now. 'You're supposed to be my date, not my analyst. Anyway, what about you?' Maybe I shouldn't ask, but I want to know more about him. I want to know why he's really here, what he's running away from. 'Did you love the one you need a distraction from?' I'm guessing it's a woman. A cheating one. He did say he totally understood about betrayal.

'I did.' There's a long pause. 'I thought we really had something good.' He is staring out of the window, but then glances back my way. 'Laura was the first woman I'd imagined living with, starting a family with.'

'Oh.' It's the first time he's shared something so personal with me. We sit in silence for a moment. 'I guess sometimes you see what you're looking for, not what is actually there. At least that's what I've ended up deciding, and I reckon I tried too hard.' I shrug.

'But that's the idea, you're supposed to try hard, aren't you?'

'You are.' I nod.

'You can love somebody, care about somebody, but still be the person you want to be. The person you should be. In fact, if they love you back, then they should want you to be you, shouldn't they?'

'True. That's the part I messed up though, I forgot about what I wanted.' Who I was. 'And I don't think Liam wanted the real me, he wanted his version.' I stop and think about the words I've just said. I've never said them before, in fact I'd never realised that was how our relationship had been. It's odd, but talking to Jake seems to make things clear in my head.

'Laura never forgot what she wanted.' He gives a short bitter laugh, and Harry licks his chin. 'You still don't expect the people you thought you knew to cheat on you though. Nobody deserves that.'

'No.' His words sink in, and I forget about Liam. 'You said people? Did you know the guy who Laura cheated with?'

'Oh yes.' He hugs Harry closer to him, and I wish I could join in the group hug. But I'm driving. 'Anyway enough of that crap, this week is about fun.' He opens his eyes wider, which instantly makes him look exceedingly naughty. 'What sports do you do?' He really doesn't know me at all, but it seems like he's determined we move on. 'Favourite one? Apart from the obvious of course.'

I ignore the suggestive wink. 'I don't swim, I hate water it's too—'

'Wet?'

'Definitely wet. I can't throw a ball straight and have never ridden a horse.' I rummage around in my brain trying to find something. Jogging is so boring, gyms are too competitive. 'I used to enjoy playing football with my dad.'

'Any good?'

'Excellent as a four-year-old. My dribbling was superb.'

'Rugby?'

'Are you mad?' For a moment I take my eyes off the road and stare at him. 'Rugby is just weird, who wants to get squashed under a pile of men?' Probably the wrong choice of words. 'All that scrambling about getting plastered in mud.' Still wrong. He's grinning. 'You're enjoying this, aren't you?'

'I am. Any birthmarks I should know about?'

Talk about speed dating, even my mum doesn't know some of this stuff, and Liam definitely doesn't.

'No, but I've got a tiny tattoo.'

'On your ankle?'

'Now that would be predictable. No, on my hip.'

'Right or left side? Just for research purposes, of course.'

'Right.' It's there to remind me, just before I take the plunge.

'Butterfly?'

'No, bluebird.'

'Oh.' He pauses. 'And?'

'And what?'

'You're not the type of girl that does things without a reason. Why the bluebird?'

'It was a song that Gran used to hum, by The Monkees. Okay, okay I know they're ancient, it was called "I Wanna be Free."'

'Like the bluebirds flying by me?'

'You know it?'

'Not that well, but … and do you?' He's looking at me intently, I can see out of the corner of my eye. His tawny gaze steady. 'Want to be free?'

'Gran used to tell me to remember that I could always be me, even if I wasn't free to do whatever I wanted. She said that was the secret to a long relationship.' Not that I was having much success on that front.

'Short break?' He points at the motorway services sign.

'My mum doesn't know about the tattoo, so don't you dare mention it!'

He glances sideways at me, and he's got a look of mischief about him. 'I wouldn't dare...' He pauses and raises an eyebrow. 'Anything else your mother shouldn't know about?'

'Depressingly enough, not a lot.' There isn't these days, but there used to be. Oh God, I really am turning into her. 'I was never bad, but I did used to be the kind of girl who acted on impulse now and then, and did mad things like get a tattoo.' I pause. 'Before I met Liam.'

He smiles. 'I think that girl's still in there, and I fully intend to winkle her out and let her free!'

We have burger and fries, and Harry has a pee and a poo (on command) then I kindly agree to Jake's request to drive my car. He might have actually been dying to have a go because it was his favourite model, or he could have just been trying to charm his way into the driver's seat because he thought he was the better driver, but I decided I didn't care. Either way, I somehow drop off to sleep and am woken up with doggy kisses. Well, I call them kisses, but I think he was probably licking the dribble off my face.

'Refreshed?'

I wouldn't say refreshed. More hot and smelling of dog, and with a sticky face. But to be fair I do feel a bit perkier and more positive. Especially when I look out of the window.

'Stop for a brief break and stretch our legs?' Even as he speaks, he's pulling off the road into a layby. Turning off the engine.

All around us the stunning scenery is bathed in soft afternoon light. I get out of the car and stretch, and I'm suddenly glad I've come. It would have been criminal to miss this, to miss my best friend's wedding.

Harry shakes himself then jumps on top of the stone wall, and looks at us, asking us to follow.

'Sorry mate.' Jake ruffles the fur on his head. 'Tomorrow. You can chase all the squirrels you want tomorrow.'

'He's not your dog, is he?'

'Nope, looking after him for a—' there was the tiniest hitch '—friend.'

'You look after him a lot?' They seemed to have a bond that went beyond the paid dog-sitter thing.

He strokes a hand over his eyes, then looks at me. 'Okay, I said we should be honest. He belongs to my ex.'

'He's your ex's?' I didn't expect that.

'Well he was...' He pauses, one of those big, fat, pregnant (no, I'm not obsessed) pauses. 'Ours, then...'

'You've brought your ex's dog to my best friend's wedding?'

'Is that a problem?'

One of us with an ex in residence is enough to cope with, and this just seems weird. She betrayed him. I wouldn't look after Liam's socks, let alone something like a dog after what happened between us. 'But why would you want her—'

162

'Our.'

'—dog, after what happened?'

'It's just a dog.'

Harry put his head on one side, so I cover his ears. 'He's not just a dog!' Why am I hissing? 'But he's hers.'

'Ours. Well, she got custody and I got visiting rights. Look, hang on, you're saying you don't mind me bringing a dog, just not Laura's dog?'

It's the 'ours' bit that bothers me. Though it shouldn't. 'It's not that at all.' Maybe he can't let go, maybe he's hoping that though she betrayed him, she will come back. And Harry is his way of keeping a connection between them. I feel irrationally angry. I don't want any part of her, the woman who hurt him, butting into our week away.

'Well?'

'What if she decides she wants him back, comes to pick him up?'

'She won't.' He sighs, and leans against the car.

'You've not packed her away in here somewhere as well?'

He raises an eyebrow, and doesn't look like he's going to answer. 'In a car with a boot this size?'

He deserves the scowl I give him. Just as I was about to get reasonable, he spoils it.

'Okay, okay, sorry. That was out of order. But we split up ages ago.'

'Ages?'

'Ages. Look. Bringing him along wasn't my idea at all, though I have him quite a bit. She asked me yesterday to look after him, because she's got a busy week on. She's away, stuff.' I wonder what 'stuff' is. Is that 'stuff' the thing he needs a distraction from? 'I said no, then after you'd been round I said no again. But when I got up this morning she was knocking on the door. She just passed me the lead and said she'd tie him to the gatepost if I didn't take him, and that I was being a selfish bastard and trying to spoil her special day because I was jealous.' He sounds quite gruff now. 'Okay? I didn't feel I had a choice.'

'Do you still love her?' I say it quietly, because half of me doesn't want to hear the answer, but the other half of me has to ask. And offer him hugs.

'It's complicated Sam.' I hate that word 'complicated'. 'I fell out of love a long time ago, but you know, well, there are still twinges.' Yeah, I do know, I know all about stupid twinges. 'And maybe hanging on to Harry isn't the best thing for either of us, because it means we still have to see each other, and she's still taking advantage, but I love the daft mutt and...'

'I'm being stupid.' I feel horribly guilty for pushing this, and stirring up things he doesn't want to talk about. 'It's fine, you bringing him. Fine. He's a cute dog.'

'You are being a bit daft.'

'You're not supposed to agree. But what if somebody asks?'

'Really?' He's brightened up. 'Somebody might want to know who he belongs to? I'll say he belongs to a friend, nobody is going to care, Sam. Are they?'

I look at Harry. He looks back. All cute button nose and dark brown eyes.

'I miss him.' Jake shrugs, but he's looking at me all sad dog eyes as well. 'That's partly why I go to the rescue centre. I'm too busy to have a dog, but I do miss H.'

'Oh for heaven's sake, let's get back in the car.' Any minute now I'll be tempted to throw away my rulebook which would be a disaster. He is *so* not my type. And I do not need a man in my life right now, I just need a man for the wedding.

'Any sexual fantasies?' He asks as he starts the engine up.

'What? Why?' No way can I tell him about the fireman and pole thing, or the chocolate smothered... 'You can't ask that!'

'I just did.' He laughs, a deep, rumbling, sexy, dirty laugh that is very disconcerting and makes me feel even hotter than I did when I was trying not to think about my unrepeatable sexual fantasies. I think he's trying to distract me from the Harry and Laura thing.

'Well, I'm not going to answer. You don't need to know.'

'True. I know I don't. I was just curious.' He's chuckling away to himself and I end up smiling. It's impossible not to. He's impossible.

I probably shouldn't ask. But he's asking stuff he shouldn't. 'So, this stuff you need a distraction from?'

'It's a long story. Later. Look.' He points. 'I think we're here.'

Here is a bit misleading because we don't actually seem to be anywhere, apart from at a large set of stone gateposts. We're in the middle of nowhere. Ahead stretches a road, across nothingness. There is grass, and heather, and trees, and, well sky. Rather a lot of sky. The horizon seems to have dropped, maybe it's because we're so far north. I nearly share this thought, then decide it might be better not to.

I now understand why it takes thirty minutes to get to the supermarket. From here we can't even see the castle, or whatever it is, that we're staying in, let alone a loch. And they're both pretty big aren't they? As in bloody massive type of big?

I take a deep breath as he turns the car in through the entrance and repeat my new mantra in my head. I can do it. I wish I actually had stuck his envelope in my handbag so that I could stare at the words and not just think them. Then they'd be more real.

'This is going to be fun.' He rubs his hands together and grins. I grab the steering wheel, as we veer towards the grass, and he puts his hands back over mine, and winks.

I have just realised that it is perfectly possible to control my direction in life, even if a man appears to be sat in the driving seat. So I smile back. 'This is going to be awesome!'

Chapter 14

Holy crap. 'You are *not* wearing that!' I sound like my mother already, and I'm not even thirty. Normally I would be embarrassed about unpacking my knickers in front of a man I hardly know. But I've seen what he has got in his own suitcase and completely forget that I have a lemon bra in one hand (to match the maid of honour dress), and black knickers in the other (because black is more me, and nobody will know).

I'd been lulled into a false sense of security, thinking that maybe this would work. This was because:

1. There was no welcome party when we finally stopped in the parking area of the castle, so we could sneak in with the help of a butler and without any kind of interrogation.

2. Our room is big enough for a family of four who never want to bump into each other. There's even one of those screen things to change behind, and a bathroom that's nearly as big as my entire house.

I am wrong. Not about points 1 and 2, just about the possibility this will work.

'That's a bit sexist, you wouldn't be happy if I said that to you.'

'I have one word for you.' I give him my schoolmarm look, and drop the knickers quickly hoping he hasn't seen them. 'Honesty! I'm not saying it wouldn't look good on you, that you wouldn't look great, er, sexy...' I say er a lot when I am flustered. 'But, but...'

'But?' He's picked up the offending article.

'It's a skirt!'

'It's a kilt.'

'A kilt, a man skirt, what's the difference?' David Beckham is the only man I've ever seen pull it off, and that was a close run thing. But it didn't put me off my porridge. This might, that's if they really serve as much porridge as I've heard they do in Scotland. 'People will be able to see your knees, and er...' I gulp. Well, is it true about what a Scotsman wears under his kilt? Or is that irrelevant seeing as he's English? Maybe I need to phone a friend, ask Sarah. She'll know, she's full of facts that are totally useless apart from the one per cent of the time they're useful.

'We *are* in Scotland.' He says it in his reasonable tone of voice.

'You're not Scottish.' My hiss isn't quite as reasonable, in fact it's verging on sarcastic, which my father says is the lowest form of wit.

'Who says?'

I try saying Porter in my head in a Scottish voice and

can't do it, even when I put an 'och aye' and a 'mac' in front. Even Jock McPorter doesn't cut it.

'I think you'll find we have a tartan.' OMG does that mean he really does know how to do things properly? Is he going to do the full Monty? Go commando? I've heard of method acting, but this is going too far. He points at the kilt. 'We're proud of our ancestry.' He does that wink thing.

If he is a real, proper Scot then I'm in trouble. 'What if somebody knows you then? Recognises you? That.' I point at his kilt. 'All Scots know each other, don't they? All those clans, it's like the mafia – but hairier.'

'Don't be daft.' He's chuckling, any minute now and it'll be a belly laugh and somebody will come to find out what we're up to. In fact, it wouldn't surprise me if my mother is eavesdropping at the door right now. 'This is Scotland, not some remote tribe in the rainforest.'

I wish I was in the rainforest. Give me face paint and war dances any day over pretend boyfriends with drafts up their skirts.

'Chill.'

I want to tell him that chill is not an appropriate word – it'll be him that's chilly if he wears that.

'It'll work. Trust me.' I want to trust him, I really do, but look where that got me with Liam. At least none of the men will be in a fit state to put a bun in anyone's oven if all their bits have shrivelled up and gone into hiding because they're used to being wrapped up all snug and warm.

I wave a sheet of paper at him, which was on the bed when we arrived. 'Well. I bloody hope so, because our itinerary says we've got to be in the bar for drinks at eight, so we can all get to know each other properly.' I already know everybody pretty well, apart from him, and Jess's Uncle Bert and Aunt Edna.

'I'd grab those back if you're going to need them.' He points, and grins.

Harry is wrestling with a rat on the bed. Except it's not a rat, it's my knickers. I make a dive and he's off, hurtling round the room with his trophy in the air. 'Oh God, those are one of my favourite pairs.' As in one of the few pairs that hasn't got a hole in the lace where I stuck my finger through trying to pull them up too quick, haven't gone a funny colour (that's why I buy black), don't have a shag-memory attached, and don't creep up between my bum cheeks like a cheese slicer.

'Nice doggy.' I try and head him off at the table, with my best 'come and see what I've got for you' voice, but he's not having it. My fingertips brush his furry tail as he hurtles across the room and dives under the bed, woofing though a mouthful of black satin and lace. 'Come here you bugger.' I'm halfway under the bed, and he's just out of reach. One more wriggle and I'll have him, then I realise that if I go any further I'll be leaving my jeans behind.

'Shit.'

Jake's face appears, upside down, at the other end of the bed. 'Need a hand?'

'Can you just...' Pull me out by the feet? Grab Harry? My mobile starts to ring.

His face is replaced by his feet. Then his face reappears. 'It's Jess.' He waves the phone so I can see the contact name.

Double shit.

'I'll answer it.' And all I can see is his feet again.

'No, no.' Oh gawd, wriggling really isn't the answer. I'm getting carpet burn for all the wrong reasons.

'She's, erm, indisposed.'

I freeze, but I can't hear Jess's response.

'Honest?' He chuckles. 'She's stuck under the bed.'

I still can't hear what she's saying. All I can hear is Jake's muffled laughter.

'No, no you can't blame me, well you can, it was my dog she was chasing.' Pause, as I start to flush. 'Yeah, something like that, he had her best knickers.' His face reappears over the end of the bed. 'Better get out from under there, she's on her way. Wants to meet Harry. She went...' He gives a high-pitched squeal that is a remarkably good impression of an excited Jess. 'And said she'd be here in thirty seconds.'

'Go away, get my knickers off your dratted dog.' He goes. I wriggle again, and it's just not happening. 'Jake?' His face bobs back down. 'Pull me out? Please?'

Men are supposed to make you laugh, not laugh at you. Not laugh so hard they can hardly pull you out from under the bed. I don't know who I want to kill first, Jake or Harry, who is jumping on my head, barking.

Both get a reprieve because there's a knock on the door,

and my best friend flies through without waiting for an invite, to find me flat out on the floor, a pair of knickers in one hand, an excited dog licking my ear, and a man holding my ankles.

I struggle to my feet and pick bits of carpet off my boobs.

I suppose she's entitled to barge in. It is her wedding. She has paid for the room.

'Sam!' With a squeal she grabs me. 'Oh God, I am so glad you came, for a horrible moment I thought the Liam thing would mean you ... and she's so huge.' Jess often leaves sentences unfinished, but most of the time I know what she means. 'And she wants to be the centre of attention, and she might be you know, but it's my wedding, and he's such a dick, but of course you don't care, do you?' We all pause for breath. 'You've got... oh my God you must be Jake, I mean I knew from his voice I just knew he'd be gorgeous, but...' She looks between me and Jake frantically; any more of this and she'll crick her neck. 'Where on earth did you find him? Tell me, no don't tell me, I'm taken!' I'm doubtful Jess will believe the partial truth, the dog walking story, but I'm not about to tell her the full truth. Well, I can't exactly say my gay hairdresser passed him on, can I?

'If I didn't have Dan I'd be jealous. Oh, oh, oh, that's his dog! That's your dog!' Jake nods. Jess lets go of me so suddenly I nearly fall on the bed, and she's on her hands and knees, nose to nose with Harry. 'Oh my God, he's the cutest, he's so adorbs, oh the girls will love him, can I show them? Can I take him with me to show Dan, and the girls?

Oh no he's frothing at the mouth, oh my God he's bleeding! Jake, Jake, he's cut...' She stops short. Then giggles. 'Er, I think he's picked something up, Sam.'

He has. Another pair of my knickers. My red, silk, *I don't know what they're doing in my suitcase anyway* knickers. I'm tempted to say he can have them, rather than suffer the indignity of Jake seeing them, but they were expensive. Obviously not as expensive as him, but bloody expensive for a triangle of material that only one person sees, two if you're lucky. Three if you're unlucky and there's a dog in the room.

At least I'm good for entertainment value; Jess and Jake are in stitches. I can guess what the conversation over drinks is going to be.

'Oh, I'm so pleased to finally meet you Jake.' She gives him a quick hug. 'I'm Jess.'

'I thought you might be. Pleased to meet you too, Sam has told me—' If he says 'all about you' then we're in deep shit. She'll be dredging up all the childhood memories he should know about. '—what a brilliant friend you are. She wouldn't have missed this for anything. How about we bring Harry to the bar later for introductions? To be honest, I think he needs a bit of chill time after the long drive.'

Don't we all?

'Aww, you are so cute.' Luckily she's cuddling the dog again now, not Jake. 'Hope you're not too tired. Sam, we thought that with everybody arriving at different times it was daft to have a formal dinner tonight, so we're doing cocktails, a buffet and...' She pauses and switches her gaze to Jake. 'You're going to love this – whisky tasting! How Scottish is that?' I try not to look at the kilt on the bed. 'See you later.' Harry gets a hug, Jake gets a hug, I get a longer hug, and a whisper in my ear that's a little on the loud side. 'Oh Sam, I'm so happy for you. I can hear more wedding bells, he's perfect, this is so exciting!' I love Jess to bits, honest. I've known her since we were little, she was always the one that was excited about everything and right now I want to be excited too. But I also need a lie down.

She stops at the door just as I'm teetering, about to collapse into a chair. 'And you have SO got to wear that, Jake!' Oh crap, she's pointing at the kilt. 'It's tartan and whisky night!' She grins at me. 'Even Liam is wearing one. Can you imagine? With knees like that!'

I don't ask her how she knows what his knees are like. Jake doesn't ask me what I'm imagining. He just opens my hand and places my soggy knickers in it.

The door reopens. 'Cocktail dresses for the girls, how glam are we? Oh, and look on the list.' She points at the piece of paper again. 'Look, look!' I comply. 'It's spa time tomorrow afternoon, girl time, you can fill me in on *everything*.' She nods dramatically at Jake and raises an eyebrow as she edges back out of the door.

To be totally honest, right now I don't feel at all glam.

Jake smiles, but in a nice way. 'It'll be fine.' He places his warm hands on my shoulders and gently turns me around. His soft voice is close to my ear. So close that I'm sure one centimetre back and I'd be leaning against him. It's very tempting to just lean. And go to sleep, and forget everything. 'Honest. Go and have a long soak in the bath.' I'm not sure the best bubble bath will help right now. And I'm not sure that any spa treatment known to man will reduce my inches enough for my cocktail dress to do up.

***

There is a burglar banging on the bathroom door. Except burglars don't knock. Do they? I hang on to the sides of the bath in panic. If he comes in I'm not going without a struggle, nobody is drowning me in my own bathwater. Who wants that on their tombstone? Died in her own...

This isn't my bath.

This isn't my home.

This is...

'Are you okay? It's ten to eight?'

'Christ, ten to eight? Are you sure? Why didn't you tell me?'

The water is bloody freezing. How on earth did I not wake up before hypothermia threatened to set in?

'I am telling you. I thought you were having a relaxing bath, so I left you to it. Took Harry out for a run.'

Oh hell. I let the plug out with my toe, then clamber out, splashing water everywhere.

There's a full length mirror next to the bath (what kind of masochist has a full-length mirror next to the place where you are most likely to be naked?) and I am all wrinkled. All wrinkled in a more prune than raisin way, which means it hasn't helped with the slimming, it has just made a few bits of me look far older than other bits. If this is how I'm going to look when I'm eighty then I want to be put to sleep before it happens.

My face has gone all blotchy red, which is what happens when I go near hot water and steam. The rest of my body has obviously not transmitted the message to it that the hot and steamy phase ended quite some time ago, we're now at the frigging freezing stage and the tip of my nose is blue. Very fetching.

'Are you going to get ready?'

Shit. 'Yes, yes, nearly done, we don't have to go over the top you know.' Bugger, bugger, bugger, cocktail dresses, castles, what do I mean not over the top?

There's a tub of moisturiser next to the sink (which shows how posh this place is) so I slap as much of that onto my face as I can, and pat it, hoping it will sink in. Dry skin is bad, greasy slick is worse. It's not happening. I pat hard. Rub. I'm still blotchy, if anything blotchier because of all the face slapping. And my hair looks like rats' tails.

Rats are not glam.

I'll pin it up. Yes, up. If I had pins. Mum said bring pins. Why do I never listen to her? How can I get pins? It's thirty miles to the nearest supermarket.

'Will you go and ask Mum if she's got some hair pins?'

'Hair pins?'

'Hair pins. To pin your hair. She'll know what you mean.'

I don't just need hair pins, I need him out of the bedroom so I can dive in and get clean undies and a dress. If I've got any underwear left that hasn't been slobbered on.

The door clicks shut. It is now seven minutes to eight. I've got seven minutes, although it will take him at least seven minutes to get away from Mum.

Find knickers. Where did I put my knickers? They're not in the case. Stop. I have to be calm. Seven minutes is fine. Six minutes, well, six minutes is fine. I remember, I put all my undies away. Out of sight. Out of Harry's reach. Oh God, which drawer? There are lots of drawers, and cupboards.

No, I need to lock the door first, or Jake might catch me in my knickers. Or not in my knickers if I don't get a grip.

I lock the door and am halfway back across the vast room when I realise.

No, not knickers, I need to find shoes next. My shoes are high and strappy and impossible to do up unless you're a contortionist. If I'm holding the shoe, and it isn't on my foot, then it's easy-peasy to put the metal bit through the hole in the strap. If I've got the buggers on my feet then it's like threading a needle with spaghetti. Why is it like that? Why don't shoes have proper holes?

I stand most chance if I've not got any clothes on and can lift my foot closer to my face. I can't bend the same with clothes on.

God, why is this room so big? I'll have lost pounds and more importantly inches by the time I get to the bloody buffet. Which I shouldn't eat. But if I don't then the cocktails and whisky will have a disastrous effect on my ability to talk sense. Which wouldn't normally matter at a party, but does matter right now as I have the fake boyfriend situation to cope with.

The door handle is rattling.

Bugger. Go away. 'Yes Jake?' I have to say this in a sweet girlfriend way, in case they can hear my hisses in the next room.

'Why have you locked the door, Sam?'

'Shhh.' My whisper obviously does not penetrate walls to the next room, or substantial doors. In a motel we'd be fine. 'I'm getting dressed.' Well, I'm hobbling about in one shoe.

'Which room are your parents in?'

'Three doors down. What do you mean, which room? What have you been doing?'

'Got four doors by mistake. Lovely people.' He sounds happy, relaxed, like he's having a great time.

'Jake?'

There is silence. He has gone. No doubt to introduce himself to all the other lovely guests.

Crap. Who is four doors down? Who's he already introduced himself to? I haven't got time for this. Yay! The second shoe goes on easier than the first, and I've got one leg in my knickers when he's back at the door.

'No answer.'

'Well, go to Jess then, end of the corridor.'

We're down to two minutes, I've unlocked the door, my hair is a mess, I'm hot, sweaty and totally knackered, and I'm in the only nearly-cocktail dress I own.

It's black and it's stretchy, well stretchy enough to cope with the half a stone I've put on. And forgiving enough to not cop out on me if I decide to eat more of the buffet than I really should. I like dresses like that. If more men were like buffet-friendly dresses then there would be fewer problems in the world.

'Sexy.' I don't know how Jake managed to sneak in that quietly, but he's back with a handful of pins, and the type of hairclip you'd give an eight year old for ballet lessons.

'Jess gave you *that?*'

'No, your mum did. She was chatting to Jess and insisted she had just the thing.' His eyes are twinkling. 'She was also pretty intent on coming with me so she could pin it in your hair. But...' He's so close I can feel his warm breath on my neck, which seems to be affecting my air supply, and bringing the blotches back on my neck. I duck out of range and turn around just as he says, 'I dissuaded her.'

'Oh my God.' I do an eek noise, I can't help it. 'You've got knees!' I can hardly squeak the word out, and my eyebrows couldn't get any higher even with surgical help. 'Naked knees.'

'If I didn't have knees I'd fall over.' He does a twirl and I very nearly discover what a Scotsman wears under his kilt. Well, not quite. He doesn't spin fast enough to get it that high. And I am very, very tempted to accidentally drop something…

'Shall we?' For a moment I think he means try and get it higher, then notice the arm he's shoved in my direction. 'Time to go?'

'How long have you had that on?' Oh God, he's been wandering the corridors in a skirt.

'I got changed while you were in the bath. I'd drop that necklace if I was you.'

The necklace had been a last minute touch. I'd thought it might distract from my still messy hair. You know, like one can distract from a huge cleavage with something shiny. Though I've never known that to work, if a man is prone to boob-staring then even a punch in the face won't stop him, let alone a dangly thing on the end of a chain. 'Too much?' It was very bright and shiny, an impulse online sale buy and I don't know what on earth possessed me to buy it, let alone pack it. And now I have it on. It is more fancy dress than posh cocktail hour in a castle.

'Way too much. Come on, don't want to be late and attract attention to ourselves, do we?'

Chapter 15

Being late isn't a problem. Jake is. I can blend into the background with my nice dress and absence of glitzy gaudy necklace. Jake and his knees cannot. And, holy crap, all those knees. My eyes are boggling. I have never seen so many knees, so much tartan. It's no wonder porridge, fires and whisky are so popular here, and thank goodness it's not a winter wedding, that's all I can say.

I am secretly chuffed though, and feeling a bit smug, because I have the man with the best legs. I'm not biased, because he's not my actual boyfriend. As an almost impartial observer I can say that he has legs to die for, compared to all the other ones on show. Although that does include quite a few oldies (sorry Dad) and Liam. Jake has proper MAN legs. But what does he have in his sporran? And has he gone commando?

I need to take a photo of the knees though, and send it to Sarah. I promised regular updates and this is the type of thing she will appreciate.

'Well now, if it isn't our little Samantha.' I'm wrapped

in a bear hug and for a moment lose sight of all the legs. 'And where have you been hiding?' Jess's dad smothers me in tweed and I try and resist the urge to pick prickly bits out of my mouth. I also try and smile but I've got a bit of a squashed face, so I'm sure it's not my best look. 'And you must be Jake.' He doesn't give me chance to reply, but sticks a hand out in Jake's direction. 'John, John Price, I'm the father of the bride.'

'Lucky man.' Jake shakes hands. 'Jake Porter.'

'And you're not doing so badly yourself. You've got a little corker here, hasn't he?' He used to call me a corker when I was ten. His grip slackens off, and so does my face, but he's squeezing my cheek between his thumb and the side of his forefinger now which is worse. He used to do that when I was ten as well, and call me chubby chops. Although my own dad was worse, he used to squeeze my knees and say it. I wonder if my face is now a brighter shade of red than when I got out of the bath? Is there such a thing as tweed-rash? 'Nice tartan by the way. Is it—'

Oh no, any second now and John is going to start interrogating Jake about which part of Scotland he comes from, and he'll find out he doesn't. And then he'll be asking about how we met, and how long we've known each other. I'm starting to hyperventilate, I can already see disaster ahead.

'Lovely, isn't it? Shall we mingle, darling?' I wriggle free of John's grasp and slip my hand through Jake's arm. 'Oh now, look over there!'

'Who's over there?' He's looking, and not seeing.

I haven't got a clue who is over there, I just said it because I know that John is going to start the interrogation and it might be better after a few cocktails, and when he's had too many whiskies to remember the answers. 'I'll introduce you. Oh, and there's Jess, so many people you need to meet.'

'Hang on girl, you've got a whole week. Hasn't she, lad?' He guffaws at Jake and claps him heartily on the back. John is hearty about everything. He's quite short and solid looking (the tweed suits him), and he's also quite loud.

'The man's got a point, darling.' Jake slips one hand round my waist and draws me closer, and winks at John. 'I can't wait to meet everybody though, we've been looking forward to this wedding for ages, the highlight of the year. Done nothing but talk about it, have we?'

'Nothing.' Well, that is sort of true. Our conversations have totally centred on this occasion.

'Tremendous idea coming here, this place looks fabulous.' Jake is holding a glass of champagne and gazing round the room with genuine admiration. He looks like he was born for a place like this, and there's not a trace of nerves. He is totally at ease with Jess's dad, who was always rather too bombastic for Liam.

John preens, and I'm sure he has puffed out a bit. He looks a bit like a gorilla about to pound its chest with pride. 'Can't take all the credit, but it's really something, isn't it?'

'We were only chatting to Sam's parents the other day about it, looked amazing on the website but it's really something else when you get here.'

'Been bombarding my wife with questions, has Ruth.' John winks at me. 'You know what your mum and Juliet are like when they get talking, phone wires have been on fire! Now then.' He turns back to Jake. 'Got Scottish blood then, have you lad?'

'Just a trace.' Jake laughs. 'Haven't we all? Tartan belongs to my uncle.' I switch off a bit then, and look around. I don't know about phone wires, but Jake and Jess's dad seem to be getting on like a house on fire. I can't believe how easily they've just slipped into conversation as though they've known each other for years. Liam was the complete opposite, he had to weigh everybody up, work out if they were worth the effort. And it was almost like he worked off a 'pleasantries' script – which was pretty short and lead to a lot of awkward silences.

But now I feel an almost maternal pride. Except there is nothing maternal at all about most of my Jake related thoughts, which seem to have their own non-business agenda.

The room we are in *is* amazing though. It's like I'd always imagined a castle to be, but posher, and not as cold. It's all stone, with fantastically high ceilings, softened with strips of plush red carpet, and heavy drapes at the unbelievably big windows. The bar is oak, and blends in with the heavy door we've just walked through.

To say this place is stunning is an understatement. It is, as John said, really something.

I'm gazing around in awe when I realise that something, or rather somebody, who is equally eye-catching but rather less wonderful, is heading our way with a very determined step.

'Wow! Is that Ruby?' I throw the 'wow' in, not because I like Jess's brattish young sister Ruby, but because I know her parents totally adore her. In an over the top, she was the child we never expected, our little treasure, sickening way. Which is why she's a spoilt brat, and Jess and I used to play hide and seek but not go and find her when we were little. I say little, we were about fourteen and way beyond silly games like that, but she was five and a total pain in the arse, elbow and any other body part you'd care to name. Anyway, we're now twenty-nine, which makes her twenty (though I've not seen her for yonks luckily) but I imagine she's still a pain. And the apple of her father's eye.

Unluckily it *is* Ruby. And she is stunning, in a twenty coming up twenty-one, totally glam kind of way. Okay, in any way. She has totally sidestepped her father's solid gene, and somehow discovered the willowy tall one that has escaped the rest of the family. Her hair manages to be glossy *and* blonde *and* wavy, and her crooked front teeth are now all straight and ultra-white. But she's still a spoilt brat. I can tell. She's wearing it proudly.

'Wow, you've grown up!' It's the best I can do, if I try harder I will be cringing with resentment.

'Wow.' Imitation is not flattery in this case. 'It's you Sam, you've er…' She obviously can't think of anything polite to say, she never could. The little cow. 'Grown too.' Total cow. At my age we all know what 'grown' means. 'Oh wow.' I think she is overdoing the wow bit, and I'm not sure if she's being sarcastic or it's her latest favourite word. 'You must be Jake.' She slithers between her father and Jake, in her slinky satin dress, and slips a hand through his arm on the other side. 'Where on earth did you find such a gorgeous hunk?' She squeezes, forcing him over her way a couple of millimetres, and although she's speaking to me she's gazing at him with total adoration.

I squeeze harder so that he sways back my way. I can see we might end up having a tug of war here.

Jake looks bemused, then slips his arm round my shoulder in a very nice (though these two words shouldn't really go together) possessive way. 'I think it's more a case of where did I find such a fabulous girl.' There's a lovely husky edge to his voice, and I really don't have to pretend at all when I gaze back at him in admiration.

'Now, now girls, don't you take him away before I've had a chance to chat, come on lad, let's find you a nice glass of whisky.' Ruby, the little treasure, pouts as her dad extricates my boyfriend from her grasp. 'You girls can have a catch up.' We both have to watch as my boyfriend is led away, though he does wink at me over his shoulder, and totally ignores Ruby. Which makes me feel all warm and mushy inside.

Liam never ignored Ruby. Even when we were kids, and she was a total pain, he had a soft spot for her. I wonder what he thinks of Ruby now she's all grown up?

'Us girls' stare at each other. I'm not going to play catch-up even if she runs away.

'Honestly though, where did *you* meet a guy like that?' I detect a little too emphasis on the 'you' bit.

'Yeah, where?' The much more friendly voice of Jess cuts in. I don't know how such a nice girl ended up with such a nasty little sister. Maybe she's really the milkman's. Or the devil's spawn. 'He really is something, look at those legs.'

I look at the legs, and panic as they get nearer to the bar. And to Liam. And Dan. And my dad.

Liam looks exactly how I remember him. As in *exactly*. He's wearing the shirt that he bought when he got promoted at the bank, and the tie he let me buy him for Christmas (I did buy a slinkier silk one that I thought would make a change, but we took it back and swapped it for a blue one, M&S are good like that – blue ties *and* swapping), and a pullover like all the other ones. And a kilt. I've never seen him in a kilt, but that's the only difference. I didn't fall in love with him because he was drop dead gorgeous – he's normal. But I'd liked 'normal' then. Now I'm not *quite* as sure. He looks less-than-normal next to Jake, who is bigger, broader. Happier. Maybe this needs to be my new normal. But I do miss the knowing, that I had with Liam. The knowing that comes from growing up together, from a friendship that slipped into a relationship. I knew where I stood, what we were doing, what he thought.

Maybe knowing is bad. Maybe knowing is about accepting less than you really deserve. Maybe knowing just leaves you open to discovering that you don't.

'It's that yummy voice that gets me.' Sally, a girl we both went to school with, slips her arm through mine. 'I could orgasm listening to that.' She sighs.

'You're married!' She was the first one of us to get married, to her childhood sweetheart. Sweet. And now they have three kids. Not so sweet.

'Don't I know it? And believe me, orgasms aren't that easy to come by these days.'

'And when did you hear his voice?'

'Just now. I was snooping. And he knocked on our door earlier, by mistake. Looking for your mum.'

'Oh no, it's the way he looks at you, really *looks* at you, like he's listening. I'd forgotten what that's like.' Beth, who works with Jess and used to sometimes join us on our nights out has a wistful edge to her voice.

'To be looked at?' Jess giggles. Beth is always being looked at, she has curves in all the right places and a big generous smile to boot.

'To be listened to. Si doesn't even pretend these days.'

'So, Samantha?' Ruby breaks up the chat ruthlessly. She says my name in a weird sarcastic Sa-man-tha way that she knows irritates me. 'Where the hell did you meet him?'

Which is slightly offensive, because she says it as though

I'm totally boring and never go anywhere, and never meet anybody interesting.

Although she's probably got a bit of a point. I didn't in the Liam days, because I was happy and had a boyfriend. But since then I've been to all kinds of places with Sarah, and got drunk on many, many occasions.

Ruby is positively drooling, and licking her lips. In fact, I'm more popular than I've ever been, if you can measure popularity by the number of people you've got hanging onto your every word. I'd keep Jake on for ever, if I could afford him.

'What does he do?'

'He's a lifeguard.' I'm about to say I met him at the pool, but they all know I don't like water, so that's a bit fishy, and not very geeky. I'd rather like a boyfriend who is not just a pretty face. 'Part time, when he's not being a...' Is nuclear physicist a bit strong? An engineer is clever, sexy, good with his hands. 'An eng—'

'Hey, Sam,' Jake has somehow snuck up on us, and gives my waist a friendly squeeze that makes me yelp. 'Brought you a drink darling, all sparkly and fruity just like you. Are you going to introduce me?'

'Eek, hey, hi, you, er, caught me by surprise.'

'Oh, I always want to surprise you sweetie.' He nuzzles into my hair, and drops his voice to a murmur that's for my ears only. 'Honesty, Sam. Let's stick to the truth where we can eh? Keep it simple.'

'Haha, funny.' I try and shake him out of my hair.

Honestly, honesty has no part to play in this week, our relationship, at all. Luckily none of the girls are taking any notice, they're staring at him. So I nuzzle him back. 'I might have to kill you later.' After the wedding. 'Honestly.' Everybody is waiting. 'Er, Jake this is Jess, who you've met.' I ignore Ruby. 'And meet Beth and Sally.'

'And you're a lifeguard?' Ruby is looking him up and down like she might start to lick him in a minute.

'An actor. Lifeguard was one of my parts.'

'Parts?' She's not looking as impressed.

'Think Baywatch.' He winks, and she's putty in his hands again.

I'll give him fruity and sparkly. He thinks I'm up on my tiptoes to kiss him, more to hiss at him. 'Don't push it too far.' Ruby has already taken a sneaky photo of Jake, and I know she'll be Googling him later. Our cover will be blown before we've started if he's not careful.

'Aww, love you too, Sammy.' I really am going to kill him, before the wedding.

'Oh my God that is so cute.' Jess has her hands over her mouth. 'She lets you call her Sammy.'

'I don't let—'

Jess is not listening. 'She doesn't let anybody call her that. The last boyfriend that tried got threatened with castration.' She giggles and Jake gives me a squeeze. 'You two are so cute together.'

'Aren't we just?' He's doing the nuzzling thing again, and rather than annoying me it feels nice.

'I'm so excited for you both!'

Why is it that brides suddenly think all their mates need to be as loved up as they are?

'Oh get away with you.' I do my best fake laugh and punch him probably a bit harder than necessary in the chest.

'I'm so excited too.' His voice drops a couple of octaves and goes all gruff, and he's cradling my face in his hands. He's going to kiss me. Do I kiss him back? Is this a freebie or will he bill me? Oh gawd, he really is, and he shouldn't. It's not in the rules. He's leaning in and he smells quite nice and outdoorsy. He's the type of man who would suck mints, so that his leading ladies enjoy it. 'And the best is yet to come.' I shut my eyes and hold my breath. The things you have to do for your best friend. Honestly. 'Any of you girls want another drink?'

He's let go. The sod. How can he *not* kiss me? I was all prepared, waiting for mintiness and all I got was to rub noses.

We all watch him as he heads back towards the bar. Then he glances over his shoulder, grins and winks. Jess shrieks.

The trouble with actors is that they like to be the centre of attention. They positively thrive on it. I'm going to have to explain that this is a minor part, a blend-into-the-background part. A no-snogging, or nearly-snogging, type of role. The no-sex rule needs a few sub-clauses.

'How successful an actor is he?' Ruby prods me when

she doesn't get an instant answer. Maybe she's guessed? Maybe I should have swooned a bit more. But I never swooned with Liam. Is swooning even a thing these days? 'What's he been in?' Ruby isn't going to let go. If I get my hands on her, I'm not going to let go either. 'What's his stage name? Will I have heard of him?'

'He doesn't like to talk about it.' See, I can do sweetness and light too. 'He's very modest.' I think I've overdone it now.

'Who's an actor?' Oh crumbs, it's my mother, and Jess's mother. Where did they pop up from? You'd think in a castle, you'd be able to avoid people if you wanted. Shouldn't they want a comfy seat in a corner after such a busy day?

'Jake.' Ruby has her head titled to one side, and is sucking the salt off the rim of her margarita glass. 'Didn't you know?' She's talking to Mum, but looking at me, assessing.

'Oh, of course we did.' For my mum that's a remarkable recovery. I'd have put odds on her saying she didn't know a Jake. She even denied knowing my dad once when somebody telephoned and caught her in one of her dottier moments. 'I thought you meant there was another one here.'

It's then it hits me that she does actually know. We told her the truth. And if I'd said he was an engineer I could have already been in a mess.

'He's a very nice man. He's going to help me with my delivery.'

It's the first I've heard.

'I need to learn how to project.'

Mother has never had a problem with projection. In fact, everybody in the bar can hear her right now, because she's put her acting voice on.

'Drink, Mum?' I'll sacrifice my bubbly, fruity drink if it shuts her up.

'Oh, Ruth, aren't you the lucky one?' Juliet, Jess's mum waves a regal arm and miraculously a tray full of cocktails materialises. 'It's so lovely that Sam has a new man, after, after what, after that terrible ... oh look, who wants a Rob Roy?'

I'm expecting a bearded Scotsman, looking a bit like Liam Neeson, to appear, but instead she's waving a drink topped with a cherry. 'We thought we'd go with a theme. We've got five different Scottish cocktails, so drink up girls.'

I accept one without thinking, so now I've got a cocktail in each hand, but my mind is on the 'terrible business' bit. Liam. Her hugeness.

I look at Jess, and do the fat tummy gesture, and she shrugs. The huge girlfriend is nowhere to be seen, I'm pretty sure I'll know her if I see her. Liam meanwhile is draped over the bar and he's looking this way. I knock back Rob Roy, who is a real hit. Better than Appletini.

'Oh I am lucky, Jake is so charming.' From the way my mother is going on you'd have thought Jake was her regular supper companion, not that she'd met him twice, and the second time was for ten minutes flat, first thing this morning. She waves at him. He waves back. I want to die.

'Dan's charming too, isn't he darling?' Juliet gives Jess a

squishy smile and squeezes her shoulders. 'We're so happy!' This is where Jess got her excitement, her exclamation marks from. Her childhood was punctuated with happiness! Excitement! Thrills! Aren't you clever! Mine was on a much more even keel. We were always fine, okay, never thrilled. Exclamations did not feature.

'Oh, I know he is, such a nice boy.' Mum gives Dan a little wave, and studiously ignores Liam when he half-raises his hand. Liam is no longer a nice boy. 'But I'm so glad Sam moved on, aren't we darling?' Now that's what happens when my mum drinks cocktails. She gets an edge.

Juliet and Mum always had this slightly competitive thing going on. You know, playground stuff – as in the parents in the playground, not the kids, parents are much, much worse. 'Oh look, Jessica came top of the class in the spelling test.' 'Really, how nice, Samantha's knitted square was the best in the *whole school*.' (They always use full names in a competition.) To be fair, Mum didn't join in that often, especially as we got older (Jessica has got 3 A levels! Jessica has got a wonderful job! Jessica has got promoted, the youngest ever in that role!) which was probably because I wasn't doing much worth boasting about. Samantha has sold a holiday to Corfu! Samantha's boyfriend has dumped her! Hasn't got quite the same ring. But now, with the whole Dan and Liam thing, and the castle in Scotland thing, I can see she's determined. Not even she knew how determined until she'd knocked back a couple of drinks on an empty stomach.

'Canapé anybody?' As if on cue, Jake is back with a tray of something that I suspect are black pudding topped with quail eggs. I'm not positive, but there was a list of 'delights' by the door, and this can't be anything else.

'Oh scrummy.' I can tell Mum is pissed – not only because of her argumentative turn, but by the fact she's said 'scrummy' and she's stuffing her face with black pudding. If we were at home and she was sober she'd be asking what it was, whether it would upset her tummy or give her indigestion, why they called it pudding when it obviously wasn't, and couldn't they afford full size eggs?

'Everything okay?' Dad has joined us, and he's got his arm round Mum, which means he knows how much she's had. I'm not sure if he's doing it in anticipation of her toppling over, or because he's planning on amorous after drinks activities. Bleurgh, what made me think that?

'Oh fine darling, just telling Juliet how pleased we are that Samantha's moved on.' Dad knows the warning signs, he knows that sometimes, like after a bottle of wine, or a couple of cocktails, she gets stuck in and things can escalate. Like they did in Crete when Juliet said she'd dived in the Commonwealth games, so Mum said she'd dived for the Girl Guides and ten minutes later had to be rescued after a belly flop that half-emptied the pool of water. It added insult to injury when she recovered enough to find her saviour looked more Sumo wrestler than Hoff and he was determined to give her the kiss of life. For some strange reason we didn't sit by the pool after that; it was all sea, ice-creams and historical monuments.

'Oh, a change is as good as rest, don't they say?'

I'm not sure that's supposed to apply to relationships, though Mum doesn't notice.

'Blood and sand.'

We all spin round. Juliet does not swear, saying something like blood and sand must mean something terrible has happened. Which is good. Anything is better than listening to my parents.

There's nothing to see, apart from blinis.

'Blood and sand!' Juliet says it again, louder, and grabs the nearest waiter, who has yet more drinks… 'It's our next cocktail!'

'Who's up for a whisky challenge, boys?'

I can tell that Dad is torn between acting responsibly and refereeing the mothers, or throwing in the towel and enjoying some whisky. He dithers, but when John holds a bottle of what he bellows is a five-hundred -year-old (or something like that) malt aloft, he's distracted and before you can say 'shake a leg' Mum has necked her cocktail.

Breakfast is going to be interesting tomorrow.

And so might the next ten minutes. Bugger and damnation, it's like the changing of the guard. Worse than blood and sand. Just as Dad and Jake head back to the bar, out of the corner of my eye I can see that Liam is heading this way.

I knock back the cocktail, stuff a blini in my mouth,

close my eyes and pray that somebody up there can help me.

And when I open my eyes He has. Or rather she has. Blocking my view of him is a woman. A huge woman. Her.

All I really register at first is the bump. Which you really can't miss as she's side on. And the boobs. And the look on her face, which is the type of look I remember on Ruby's face when she was a toddler and we said no to her.

It was usually followed by her throwing herself on the floor and thrashing about.

This woman doesn't throw herself on the floor (understandable), but points an angry finger at Liam. As entrances go it's quite spectacular. 'What the fuck are you doing still here Liam, you said one drink!'

My mother would call her a potty mouth, which is strangely appropriate given what the not so distant future holds for her. I would call her the girl who use to work in the filling station up the road from Liam's bank.

And there was I, thinking he'd stopped walking to work so that he could spend an extra ten minutes in bed with me every day. 'Sod the fuel' he'd said very uncharacteristically – money and the environment both feature high on his agenda so I really should have twigged.

'Stella!' He's shouting for emergency lager. 'Stella, hang on.' Oops no, it's her name. 'I was on my way back.' He's obviously been working on his lying capabilities. Unless he always was a liar, and I never realised.

'Have you any idea how bloody boring—'

'Four horsemen on the way!' Mum and Juliet have stopped competing, they're propping each other up, and offering a united front. As good friends should.

Ruby has turned the colour of her namesake and is looking shifty, which I suspect means that Liam's been chatting her up, and Jess is giving me the secret signal. We've had it for years. It's horizontal V's in front of our eyes and it's the best thing we ever saw Batman do. And he did it just before he did a biff, boff and split. Which is why we do it, because we're going to do a disappearing act.

Before Stella has explained what it is that's so bloody boring, we're out of the bar and halfway up the grand staircase.

We haven't got a Batcave, but I have got a very nice room, where Harry has been having a nod, and from the way his back end is wagging I'd say he's pretty chuffed to see us.

'You do realise Mum has got two more rounds of cocktails lined up for us? Christ, I feel so pissed.' Jess flops onto the bed, and an excited Harry leaps on top of her (I'm not sure he's allowed on beds but it's a bit late now). 'I had to get away for a bit. I wonder how long we've got before Mum sends out a search party for us?'

'Well, to be honest I don't think either of our mothers will notice we're gone.'

'True.' She rolls over. 'Dan will notice though.' And that soppy grin is the smile of true love. I don't remember ever wanting to smile like that, which makes me feel all sad and lonely. 'I love you, Sam.'

'Love you too.'

'Missed you. Why do men always have to fuck things up for us? Liam is such a jerk. He deserves Stella.'

'He is and he does. But I'm glad.'

'Why?' She props herself up on one elbow. 'He's a total fuckwit.'

'Well, if he'd only been a tiny bit of a jerk I might not have realised until it was too late.' I stare at the ceiling as it hits me. 'Oh my God, I might have married him!' That thought is scary.

Liam dumping me meant I have had lots of time to think about our relationship, and to talk to Sarah about it. But I've just realised that it's in the last few weeks, being with Jake, that has made me see just how much I gradually changed.

Jake is fun, he makes me laugh, which Liam hasn't done for a long time. Jake listens, whereas Liam used to interrupt me and ask if I'd ironed his shirt. Jake says nice things, he doesn't mind if I eat too much chocolate, and he thinks I'm brave for wanting to do things my own way. Not silly. And he laughs at Mum in a nice way, and doesn't tell her she's fat. And he tells me *I can do it.*

And he lets me take the steering wheel. In fact, we share. We are a team. Even if we aren't a proper team.

If Liam had not done his dirty deed then I would never have realised that my mojo had been skipping out of the room for a long time, edged out by familiarity and that thing called compromise. As Jake said in the car, you're supposed to try hard, but you can still be yourself. I did the first, and Liam did the second.

That is it! I had been compromising on a major scale, and I've only just realised. I had merged with Liam in a not very complementary way. It was not a merger, it was a takeover. I had become the person he wanted me to be. I had given up on uber high heels, cocktails and proper giggles. I had stopped speaking my mind and thinking about what I really wanted. Oh my God, I think this is what they call an epiphany, and it has taken a fake date to make me realise!

'And you'd have missed out on falling in love with Jake?'

'Sorry? What?' My epiphany is rudely interrupted by Jess, who is grinning at me expectantly.

'Jake! You'd never have met Jake if Liam hadn't been a jerk. God, he is so hot, and he is SO into you.'

I lie down the other side of Harry. I'm not exactly drunk-drunk, but I am definitely tipsy. And tired. Tired means my brain doesn't work properly. I don't know quite what to say, I'm not at the 'inebriated enough to say anything' stage yet.

'Come on then, dish the dirt, that's why I really dragged you up here!' She leans in closer. 'How on earth did you meet him, Sam? You are mad about him, aren't you?' She giggles. 'I can tell.'

I want to tell her. I need to tell her. It might not be wise. It might not be clever, but I have had several whisky cocktails, plus a bubbly fruity drink, and she *is* my best friend.

And I love her, and I've missed her, and men don't always fuck things up for us.

'I'm not totally mad about him.' I take a deep breath. I need to say this. 'Jess, I lied to you.' Oh God, no. I mustn't. It will ruin everything.

'You lied to me?'

'Jake is, well Jake and me, we...' No. I just can't. I've only just got here, and even though I'm a bit tipsy I know I shouldn't. I just really don't want to lie to my best friend.

'Jake is what?'

'We hardly know each other.' It comes out in a rush. That's it! I can be more honest, just not totally. 'I've only just met him.' Which is true.

'Only just? But you said ages ago you had a boyfriend, the one you—'

'That was the lie. Oh, Jess, there was no boyfriend.'

'No boyfriend? But ... you split up?' She flops back on the bed.

'There never was a boyfriend, Jess. I made him up so I could pretend everything was okay, and I was completely over the shit bag.' I feel bad, like I've broken some kind of unspoken agreement and am practically saying I don't want to be besties any more. 'Sorry.'

'But then you met Jake?'

'Then I met Jake.'

'He's mad about you, the way he looks at you.'

'That's er...' I can't say acting. 'Because it's all new, and exciting.'

Best friends shouldn't lie to each other. We used to share everything.

I told her about the stubble rash that the sexiest boy in Year 13 left behind (he was the only guy in the sixth form that had more than the odd spiky hair jutting out of his face) which left me walking like a cowboy even though we hadn't actually done *it*.

She told me about the first disastrous shag with Dan that had been followed up by the second earth-shattering one. I'd told her about Liam's folding his knickers routine and my quest to turn him on so much he'd forget to do it (it never happened).

And then I'd told her I was so over him, and had a new boyfriend. And I am still not telling her the whole truth.

'I mean I know it was stupid but I didn't want you to feel bad about being all mushy with Dan, so I made up a boyfriend. He didn't exist.' I so want to tell her that the current one doesn't either.

'Oh.' She hates me. I can tell. 'So you did that so you wouldn't spoil my wedding?' She sits up cross-legged on the bed and stares at me. Her eyes are all shiny bright with tears.

'Oh Jess, I am sorry, I mean I don't know why, I should have…' I gulp and my own eyes are burning. We've known each other forever, and I don't want her to be upset at me, not now, not in a castle just before her wedding.

'Oh my God Sam, you are the best friend ever!'

I close my open mouth, and blink. I didn't expect that, I don't deserve that, but well, I suppose it's true.

'It was partly to make me feel less useless as well.' Better to be totally honest now I've got the chance. I'm not one hundred per cent sure she can hear, because she's flung herself across Harry and got me in a bear hug, but I think she gets the gist.

'Aww but it was mostly for me. Oh heck, how lucky I am.' She does a funny sniff, strangled sob thing into my shoulder. 'You made a boyfriend up for me. That's the best present ever.' I know this is partly because she is very drunk on cocktails, and very high on adrenalin with a funny mix of hormones stuffed in. But hey, weddings do that to even the most sensible of people. Then she grins. 'I am so pleased you've found a new man though now, and he's totally sexy.'

I just nod. He is totally sexy.

'Where on earth did you meet him?'

It is just like when we were teenagers, curled up on a bed, telling each other our secrets. Except I don't tell her quite all my secrets, but I do tell her about Tank, and Jake saving me, and his crap play, and supper with my parents.

And it hits me that hiring Jake, bankrupting myself, doing all this is completely utterly worth it, because no way on earth could I have missed my best friend's wedding.

Chapter 16

Reasons why I should not let Jake kiss me:

1. I don't fancy him...
2. He is big-headed (well, it might just be an actor type of confidence, but he did tell me that if he took me to bed he could make the earth move, or words to that effect. That means he is big-headed or, well, unbelievably good in bed – which I don't want to think about).
3. I might enjoy it (see point 2 above).

There are also two pressing questions that need answers:

1. Why am I writing this list? And
2. Where the hell is the man in question?

It is one thing to hire a boyfriend, it is probably a bit careless to lose him after one day. Will anybody see posters if I pin them up? We're miles from anywhere.

Lost – one boyfriend, hardly used. Please return ASAP as warranty runs out in 5 days.

If he's just done a runner, do I get a refund? They might have to dredge the loch to find him, scour the highlands, track him down with dogs. Which reminds me, where's Harry? Oh buggery bugger, I've not lost his dog as well, have I?

I hang over the side and look under the bed, which makes my head spin (note to self, do not hang upside down after a night on the cocktails), and have to lie down again to wait until I feel vaguely normal.

Maybe, if Jake comes back, he won't notice. After all Harry is not that big a dog, and not really his. Well, half his. So technically speaking I've only lost half his dog.

'You've surfaced!' Speak of the devil. He breezes in and I get a waft of coffee.

Okay, I do fancy him a bit. Scratch number 1 off my list. But I only fancy him in the way everybody fancies a guy like say Liam Hemsworth, or Kit Harington. It's not real-life fancying, it's just like, 'Oh my God, my poster boy has come to life in my dream, wouldn't it be amazing to snog somebody like that?' Which means it's perfectly acceptable. Not that I have any poster boys these days. And *surfaced* isn't a word I'd really use. My head is banging, and I'd quite like to climb back under the covers. Once I've had some coffee.

'I brought you some breakfast, wasn't sure you'd want to face the masses.' I do not want to face one, let alone masses. If I say *can you please leave the coffee and go* will I sound rude and ungrateful?

'Where's Harry?'

Bugger. He's noticed.

And then I remember.

Jess has borrowed him. I remember seeing Liam's huge girlfriend and realising who it was, I remember coming up here with Jess for a girlie chat and then I remember falling asleep. Oh shit, I also remember something far, far worse.

I told her about fakey-Jake. Oh hell. Oh no I didn't! I remember! I nearly told her everything, but stopped myself just in time.

'You and Jess must have had some party in here, I didn't have you down as a heavy drinker.' He grins.

We called for more cocktails to celebrate after I'd told her about meeting Jake – which explains my throbbing head. 'I am such a party animal.'

He laughs. 'You don't really drink that much, do you?'

He's got me in one. My wild party days are in my distant past, heavy drinking these days is reserved for those occasions when crying into a double espresso martini is the best way to forget you've been dumped. Once Sarah had dragged me through the self-pity stage we'd gone back to our more normal drinking habits. I'm a lightweight if I'm honest.

I can't believe we finished off so much booze last night. There are several empty glasses on the bedside cabinet which I really shouldn't look at.

The queasiness is not because of the clash of the titans battle between spirits that is going on in my stomach and threatening a revolt though. It is because I very nearly told her. Which is scary. Keeping this secret could be a lot harder than I thought. Unless I:

1. Abstain from alcohol
2. Avoid best-friend chats with Jess.

And I can't do either. Unless I pretend I am pregnant, which would land me in even deeper water.

'No, but you know me.' I attempt a light, jovial laugh. 'If a job's worth doing, then it's worth doing well.'

'I don't know you that well yet, but I'm beginning to see a pattern here. You don't do anything by halves, do you Sam?' He winks. 'You've no idea how sexy that is.'

The last thing I want to think about right now is sexy. I don't feel remotely sexy. Maybe I should claim alcohol poisoning and go home.

'Are you okay? You have gone a bit pale. Well, even more pale and pukey-looking than when I came in.'

I try and glower, which makes me feel worse. 'Pukey-looking?'

'Just being truthful.' He stabs a sausage and takes a massive bite. I'm not sure my stomach and sausages are on speaking terms. 'You do look like you might need to dash to the bathroom any second.'

'Thanks.'

'Apparently Stella has been puking all the way through her pregnancy, and made Liam late for work.'

'I don't want to know.' I pull the sheet over my head, then raise it up a bit, because I actually do want to know and it's all a bit sweaty and hot under there. This is one of my problems. Not the sweat bit – nosiness. 'He'd hate that.' Really hate it. I can't imagine Liam mopping brows, or being late for work. I also can't imagine Liam holding a baby.

'He told us all the whole story in minute detail after she'd gone.'

'Gone?'

'Just after you went. She had a bit of a hissy fit, then went back to their room and locked him out. Can't quite see what you saw in a guy like that, doesn't seem very exciting. He was a bit pathetic if you ask me.'

I don't really like to point out that I'm not normally that exciting either. Or that I hadn't asked him. But I am inclined to agree that Liam is a bit pathetic.

'He works in a bank.' I think that's all I need to say.

Jake starts to butter toast in a very loud scratchy way. 'He's got a spreadsheet so he can work out how much the baby will cost up to the age of eighteen.'

Why does that not surprise me? 'Do you have to do that?'

'A spreadsheet?' He raised his eyebrows in alarm. 'I don't think it's obligatory, in fact I don't think it's normal.'

'No, the buttering thing.'

'Yep.'

'It's too loud.'

'It's for you. Come on, try it.' He comes nearer to the bed, waves a bit of toast temptingly, just out of range.

Aww. I might kiss him after all. When I'm feeling better, and have brushed my teeth and eaten a few packets of mints and lost the sour breath. Liam never, ever brought me toast AND buttered it.

And he called me sexy.

'Is there a gym in this place?'

'Gym?' It takes me a moment to remember what the word means. My slightly befuddled head is still considering toast and kisses. 'Why?' See, he doesn't know me at all. I am the last person anybody would ask about a gym.

'I normally work out every day.' He winks. 'Ever ready, me.'

I ignore the last bit. 'This is a wedding not a boot camp. And—' that wink needs to be put in its place '—there is nothing you need to be ready for.'

'Oh, you never know.' He pauses, but not long enough for me to come up with a witty response. 'If there isn't a gym, we can always run.'

'Run? We can? We?' He's seriously confused. Have we not had this conversation about how I don't do sport?

'Yeah, we. You know, devoted couple, do everything together.' He's laughing at me. 'Anyway, it might help, you know...'

Help? Even my banging head is capable of working out what is going to come next.

I have realised I don't like him. I don't care how buff he is. I totes don't like him, and I am definitely not going to kiss him now.

'I know you're not going to want to hear this. It's just you're...'

Bloody right I don't want to hear it. Any second now and he's going to say the F word, and when he does, I've got an F word of my own. Actually I'm going to add another point to my not-kissing list:

1. He wears a skirt.

This will put me off if my resolve ever wavers and he tries to throw in a free extra.

Oh, and:

2. He actually said I was FAT!!!

Why didn't I include a clause in our agreement *not under any circumstances to insult me* then I could send him home and not have to pay him for breach of terms. Not that we have an actual contract. Just a *gentlemen's* agreement. Ha!

He plonks himself down on the edge of the bed. '...you're so stressed about all this.' He's just said stressed, not fat, or cuddly. 'And believe me, exercise does help.' I'm not sure I do believe that bit though. Last time I tried running it nearly killed me. 'Seeing as you're not going to let me get your pulse racing in some other way.' Now he's spoilt it.

We're back to the not kissing thing. 'Maybe a gentle jog would help?'

Since when were the words gentle and jog compatible?

'So where did you say Harry was?'

Oh bugger. Full circle. And there was I hoping he might have forgotten.

'Er, I didn't. I told Jess she could borrow him, after I, er...'

I think I might have gone pale again, because he's waving toast and staring at me.

'I suppose I'd better get up.' I say it as brightly, and distractingly as I can. Which is hard in my fragile state, believe me. It takes up a lot of energy. 'Lots to do today. Spa, running, stuff.' I haven't had a proper look at the itinerary yet.

'After you er...?'

'Nearly told Jess about us.' I abandon the toast and make a dive for the bathroom, swerving to grab a cup of coffee. Then I lock the door.

After drinking the coffee and taking a very, very long shower, I still feel like the walking dead, and when I come out Jake is still there.

He is stabbing what's left of his sausage as though he's trying to kill it. 'You *nearly* told Jess?' I wince. One slip and it could be fatal. 'What does nearly mean?'

'I didn't tell her everything.' I also have a bit of a banging head, and even the stabbing without the noise is making me feel worse. 'I stopped myself, but I told her we hadn't actually been dating for ages, I told her that we'd just met.'

'Wouldn't it have been better not to tell anybody anything?'

'I could do without the judgement. Who do you think you are?'

'Your boyfriend?'

'You're not—'

'I'd keep it down if I was you, unless you're planning on telling everybody?' I settle for a scowl. 'Look babe, I'm saying this because…'

'You care? Oh, give me a break.' I'm feeling tetchy, because I know I'm in the wrong. 'And don't babe me.'

'You didn't have to.'

'She's my friend, my best friend. I didn't want to lie to her, but…'

He's ruffling his fingers through his hair. 'What if she tells her mum? Dan? What if Dan asks?' God, he is really taking this seriously. And he's right, I nearly cocked everything up. 'You can't expect your best friend to lie to the man she's marrying in a few days.'

I know that bit.

'What if her mum tells your mum? How will that look, seeing as you've told your parents we've been dating for ages?' He shakes his head. 'Why complicate this, Sam?'

I hadn't intended on telling Jake that Jess and I had slipped away for a chat. Except we both passed out on the bed, with Harry in the middle, and he came back to find us 'snoring louder than the poor dog' as he put it.

This is a relationship first for me, a new low. One minute we're talking sexy and free kisses and the next we're having our first argument, and we've not even slept together! In fact, we've not even slept in the same room.

Originally I'd said he could have the bed, because he probably expected some level of comfort as part of the deal. And he's longer than me so wouldn't fit on the chaise longue (which isn't, if we're honest, that long – it is very inappropriately named). Then we (or I) thought about building a pillow barrier between us. But in the end we didn't have to decide.

He came in, saw me and Jess crashed out, and left.

'Anyway, where did you sleep last night?'

'I spent the night with Dan.'

Great, there's been more male bonding than girlfriend-boyfriend bonding. 'Dan probably knows more about you than I do.'

'Ah but I didn't start re-inventing our imaginary relationship, did I?' He shrugs. 'Up to you I suppose, you're the boss.'

I've never been called 'boss' before, but I don't think he's saying it in a complimentary way.

'I am.' It comes out all small. I don't want to fall out with Jake, we're a team. 'Oh God, I'm sorry.'

'Oh Sam.' He shakes his head, and his voice becomes softer. 'Look, I know it was hard and it rattled you, seeing Liam and Stella, and you had to get away.'

'You do?' I know my voice is tiny. And I know he's right. It was weird, and all a bit much after all the build-up of the last few weeks, and I'd really needed some girlie time. I needed to be with Jess, and be me. Not pretending. 'I know I shouldn't have said anything.'

'You're doing great, they all think we're a couple, and I made damned sure Liam thought we were. It'll get easier now we've got the first day out of the way.' He's right. I know he is.

'It wasn't as bad as I thought it would be, seeing him.'

'Good, but next time we see him we're going to show him what a twat he's been, okay?'

'Okay.'

'You know the real problem though, don't you?'

It's my turn to shake my head, but he doesn't seem to be waiting for an answer.

'You're just too nice to do something like this, aren't you?' He taps the end of my nose with his finger, and smiles, and it's almost like we're making up. 'I've never met anybody quite like you.' There's a soft chuckle which makes me goose-bumpy. 'I know you don't want to lie to your best mate, but you have done this all for her, haven't you? And if you don't keep our secret then you're wasting your money. I might as well just pack my bags and go home, mightn't I?'

I swallow hard. 'I don't want you to go home.' And I don't, I really don't. It's nice having Jake here with me.

'Okay.' His voice is soft. 'So no more owning up?' I shake

my head. He takes a step back. 'So where did you say Harry was?'

'What is it with you and that dog? That's at least the tenth time you've asked.'

'I'm responsible for him, and I take my responsibilities seriously.' I risk a look at him, but it doesn't look like it's a pointed comment suggesting I don't, but then again he is an actor. 'And he'll need a walk.'

'Like I said, Jess took him, she wanted to go for a walk she said.'

'But he hasn't had his breakfast.'

'Ah, smarty pants, there you are wrong. He's had sausage and bacon.'

'He's had what?' He drops his fork with a clang, which is totally unnecessary and dramatic if you ask me. 'You can't give him sausage and bacon.' He looks genuinely dismayed.

'Why not? Jess went and got it herself from downstairs.' Then I had another half hour nap. 'It was freshly cooked. Oh, and he had an egg.'

'He's on a special diet.'

'He's a dog.'

'I know he's a dog.'

'Dogs just eat stuff, like, like dog food.'

'Exactly.'

'And human food.'

'Laura likes him to eat sensibly.' Well, this is great, he's still bothered about what Laura thinks. It's obvious that

215

Laura is the key to this, not taking his responsibilities seriously. This is probably niggling me more than it should. He's right, I'm complicating things. 'She'll have a fit if she thinks he's been on junk food, she gave me all these special packets.'

None of our dogs ever ate 'sensibly', although maybe that's why they were hyper. In fact, I don't eat sensibly either. Which might explain a lot. My mum was always pretty slapdash about food, she was far too busy doing 'stuff', apart from on a Sunday when we had to have a roast dinner even in the middle of summer.

'It won't kill him.' Surely one meal of sausage and bacon can't kill a dog? Surely? Now I'm a teensy bit worried. I start to Google it, but he takes the phone off me.

'It might kill me, if she finds out.'

That could help. I can see the headline: '*Crime of passion – boyfriend killed by ex in fit of jealous rage*'. I could mourn and accept condolences; nobody (apart from Sarah) would know he had never been my boyfriend. Although I don't actually want him dead. That would be weird. 'Harry's fine.'

'So, why did you change your story for Jess?'

I thought we'd moved on from that. 'She's my best friend, I don't like to lie.'

'You don't like to lie?' He's got an eyebrow raised, and even though I'm a bit mad at him I have to smile.

'This is so big it doesn't count anymore, apart from with Jess.' I sigh. 'But then I realised I couldn't tell her, but I had to say something.'

'Whatever you say. Come on then, hurry up and eat that while I have a quick shower. We've got some outdoor activities to do.' I'm not sure I like the way he says that, there's a definite twinkle in his eye. I have noticed he didn't say the word 'sport' though. Maybe it's just a stroll across the estate, a wander along the banks of the loch.

As I am not exactly sure what we're doing, but it's a lovely sunny morning, I put on jeans, a T-shirt and a light sweater and hope I am dressed properly for the occasion. It is a nice sweater, cashmere. It's not my usual type of purchase, but the lady in the department store said it would be *ideal* for this time of year in Scotland, and very smart but casual in a way that will *take me through from afternoon to evening*. It was appropriate for *any occasion*. So that works for me. Even if it is actually still the morning.

Chapter 17

I have just heard four words that are guaranteed to ruin my day. 'Sandy will sort out a hat for you.' The Sandy bit was fine, I have nothing against Sandy, it was the *sort out a hat* that made my knees lean in to meet each other for support, and my stomach contract like it wanted to scrunch up and take cover behind my kidneys.

I look at the young girl who has just uttered the terrible words, then back at Jake.

Hat is not a word I'm particularly fond of, as they just don't suit me. But they don't scare me. It's the setting that makes the word alarming.

I'd thought we'd strolled into the stable yard by accident. Apparently not.

'Did you know?' I glare at Jake, who is gazing round without a care in the world. In fact I think he's being a bit *too* casual. 'You knew, didn't you? You bugger.'

'Jess thought it might be better to keep it a surprise.'

I'm going to kill her. Both of them. 'You've been talking to Jess?'

'Only briefly. She popped into the room to say good morning, on the way back from getting your breakfast. I thought there seemed a lot just for the two of you.' I decide not to tell him that Harry scoffed the lot. 'Dan agreed it was best to keep shtum.'

Dan would. I am going to kill all three of them. Carnage in the highlands.

'She said she knew you'd love it once you got on.'

How can anybody love having their thighs spread unnaturally wide by some beast (and this is not an affectionate term for a large man)?

There are also other considerations that make this something I won't love. Horses are big, very big. I do not want to be spread-legged several feet up in the air. It is unnatural and dangerous. They also bite and kick at ground level, so why would I go near them in the first place? And, lastly but very importantly, they go fast. Very fast, whilst bobbling about up and down alarmingly. I have watched the Grand National. I know. People die.

'Yay, Sam!' Jess does not share my reservations when it comes to horseback riding. She is dressed for the occasion in tight jodhpurs, chaps, boots, polo shirt and gilet, as though she does this regularly. Which she does. I did think it was a bit odd when she didn't reply to the text I sent her this morning asking what to wear, but decided she must be busy doing loved-up things with her husband-to-be.

She is bouncing about more than a horse does as she

grabs me. 'How's your head? Mine was banging but Dan got me some tablets and breakfast, and he rubbed my neck, and my feet.' This is a girl in love. 'And I feel fine!' She pauses for breath and looks concerned. 'You look a bit pale.'

'Or pukey, as Jake would say.' I feel pukey. I was just starting to stabilise – and now this. My stomach is churning like a washing machine, and gathering up all the lovely crumbs of toast ready to deposit them out again if I have to climb on a horse.

Jess giggles. 'Must be love!' Then winks very obviously. I look round a bit too quick, which makes the world spin a bit, but nobody seems to have noticed. 'A good gallop really will clear your head though. Come on. Oh I'm so glad you've agreed Sam, I thought you might cop out!'

I am going to cop out, once I work out how.

'You're so brilliant!' She hugs me and grins at Jake. 'Isn't she? Come on I've got you something quiet, and you'll love yours, Jake.'

From that comment I take it that Jake is not allergic to spreading his legs for a horse. Figures. Jake can do bloody everything. I am starting to dislike him a bit. It is one thing to have a smart, attractive accomplished boyfriend, but nobody likes perfection, do they?

Before I can think this over any further, Jess has dragged me along to Sandy the hat sorter, and my head has been encased in armour plating. I just wish the rest of my body was.

'Say hello to Nutmeg! Isn't he the sweetest?' This is not

sweet. This is a ginger horse of mammoth proportions in all directions. Nutmegs are small, and this is not. He's as wide as he's tall, with hair sticking out from places it really shouldn't be. It'll be like sitting on a piece of hard leather strapped to a giant scrubbing brush.

I've always been told horses are gentle, trusting vegetarians, but this one is giving me the evil eye and curling his top lip in disdain like he's thinking about taking a chunk out of me. Then he shakes his head, makes a funny noise and showers me in spit. My expensive jumper is no longer going to see me through from afternoon to evening.

I am working on the 'I can't get on' approach when I'm foiled. The horse has been manoeuvred in front of a large block of steps and everybody is waiting.

Everybody else is now on a horse, apart from me and Jess. And before you can say 'isn't this a bit risky just before your wedding day' she's vaulted, without the use of a private staircase, onto a big black animal. 'We've sent the oldies rambling.'

'I wish I was with the oldies,' I mutter under my breath. But I know Jake has heard.

'You'll be fine, we'll take it steady.'

'I can do rambling.' All of a sudden I love rambling. It sounds like the perfect way to pass a few hours.

'You can do this.' He winks. 'Remember?' He's there by my side. 'I know you can.' His warm hand rests lightly on my thigh and when I look into his eyes all I can see is total confidence, belief in me. Which sends a funny little shimmer into the pit of my stomach. 'We're in this together, Sam, I'm here if you need me. For anything.'

And the funny thing is, I feel like he totally means it. He is there, and he does believe in me, and for a moment nothing or nobody else matters.

He squeezes my thigh again briefly. 'Ready?'

'I can do it.' I do have to admit that my fingers are crossed, and I really wish it was my legs. But I am ready.

It's not quite knight in shiny armour stuff, him holding a lead rein as we amble along at the back. But he is nice, and doesn't make fun of me. And I will just have to imagine I am Queen Victoria on my hairy pony, and he is Billy Connolly. If nothing else he will be able to tell me jokes.

It is surprisingly pleasant ambling along through the estate on my shaggy pony. He isn't actually mammoth, but he is rather round, which is the only thing he has in common with a nutmeg. But this does mean it would be quite hard, as Jake points out, to fall off.

Jake also points out gorse, rabbits and osprey which I think is his way of trying to distract me. As a relaxation technique it isn't working. How can people talk and look around when they're sat on a moving horse? I need to concentrate or I might be caught unawares when it suddenly leaps over a hedge or something.

'Did you know they're expecting twins?'

'What!' I forget where I am and yank back on the reins and stand up in my stirrups in surprise (something I wouldn't have thought I could do if I'd planned it). The pony yanks the reins back, hard. 'Shit.' I'm tipped off balance. 'Ouch.' I've landed on the hard lump at the front of the saddle, and my legs have been left behind, my feet still stuck in the stirrups.

There's a funny noise and when I glance over, Jake has got a strange look on his face. He's trying not to laugh.

'Oh no!' The stupid animal has put his head down and I'm about to slide down his neck face first. My hands are heading for his ears, and my nose is heading for the grass when he abruptly jerks his head back up and smacks me on the nose. I'm stuck, wrapped around his neck like a strip of bacon on a mini sausage. Now I know why they call them devil on horseback. Or is that dates? I'm pretty sure it is. I think I've got confused with pigs in blankets, which means I am the blanket to this piggy pony. I was starting to get quite fond of him, but he's done this on purpose. Never assume a vegetarian is a pacifist, they can have evil intent. Or at least this one has.

What the hell do I do now? Just carry on clinging to his neck, without a clue about how to get back in the saddle?

Oh God. Something has just gone down the back of my jeans. Something warm. Something strong that's yanking me back onto the leather saddle.

'Are you okay?'

Oh my God, I know what it is. It is Jake's hand. And it's still in there.

I don't think I am okay. He has his fingertips only centi-metres from my knickers, and his knuckles are brushing against my naked back.

'No harm done.'

No harm! Luckily the rest of the horse-riders have just carried on totally oblivious. 'I've got a black eye.' And your fingers are on my buttock.

He pulls his hand out. 'I don't think you have.' I'm not sure how it happens, but his tawny eyes are now only inches from mine, and he's stroking along my cheekbone with a warm thumb. 'You're fine.'

I'm not, I'm melting. I've forgotten how to breathe.

'Twins!' It's a wobbly squeak. 'Two babies?' Partly because I don't want to say it, and partly because everything seems to have stopped working, even my vocal chords are trembling. I'd move away from him, to try and recover some of my abilities (I won't say senses, because every bloody sense is on high alert) but if I move as much as a teeny muscle I might fall off. Well, that's my excuse and I'm sticking to it.

'Yeah,' he stops stroking. 'That's why Stella is so huge apparently. Double whammy. I reckon he thought it was something to be proud of at first, double barrel shotgun. But now the reality has started to sink in…' He goes back to sitting on his own horse properly, and my brain starts to work again now he's keeping his hands to himself.

'She always was rather large though.' She was, I'm not being bitchy. It's probably because she sits in a petrol station all day, helping herself to Snickers bars and crisps.

224

I realise then that we, or the horses, have stopped and we're in the most perfect spot ever. The type of spot that you could share with somebody you love.

The mountains that loom high, offering a protective backdrop to the estate, cast a picture-perfect reflection on the smooth dark surface of the loch, and we're surrounded by every shade of green imaginable.

The yellow of gorse burns a bright path of colour like molten sunshine tumbling down the hills, and the pinkish-purple of rhododendrons are an artistic splash that trace the path back to the castle.

There's no sound, apart from the occasional call of a bird.

Even the wind is holding its breath.

Jake is watching me, and it's slightly unnerving.

I stare at the water.

'It's beautiful, isn't it?' His voice is soft.

'It's not as big as I thought it would be.' Unlike Stella. 'It would have to be more Loch Ness mini-monster or something to live in here.'

'I meant the scenery.' There's the smallest of quirks to his mouth. 'But apparently it's a lochan, just a small loch.' He's still looking at me, and making me feel squirmy.

'Apparently?'

'According to Dan, but we had drunk quite a lot of whisky so whether it's actually a thing or not...'

'I quite like lochan.'

'I quite like you.'

225

He says it so softly, I could have misheard. But when I dare to look, his gaze is fixed on me, and his horse is so close to mine our thighs are practically touching.

'You're amazing, you know. And you're the most beautiful thing out here. I need to kiss you.'

'Er, you don't, there's nobody watching, they've all gone—'

'I know. I mean I *need* to...'

His warm hands are cradling my face, and he's looking into my eyes as though giving us both a chance to change our minds, so I close mine.

And he kisses me.

Just like that. No ten minute preamble.

And oh God, if this is what *need* feels like then I've truly never ever felt it before.

This is warm, enveloping, tickle your tonsils and every bit of you that is capable of going all prickly and tingly.

How can thirty seconds of mouth-to-mouth contact leave me feeling like I need to jump on the man and rip his clothes off? This is so wrong. So bad. I am his employer.

'You deserve better than Liam.'

'I know.' Very squeaky. 'I know.' A bit too low.

'I suppose we'd better catch up with the other before we're missed.' He shifts back into his own saddle and squeezes my knee.

Bugger. If he'd fancied another kiss I would not have said no, it would have been rude when he'd been so nice. But he isn't going to. Does that mean he doesn't fancy me, or didn't enjoy the kiss? Probably better not to ask. I have already failed miserably with my latest list, which stated quite clearly that I should not kiss him. My sub-conscious knew more than it was letting on. Now all I can do is try and forget he did that, and strongly suggest to him he doesn't do it again. Or slip his hand down the waistband of my jeans on the pretence of rescuing me.

'Yes, we better had get cracking.' I say it in my best let's get on with it voice, wave my whip in the air, and give Nutmeg a totally ill-advised hearty kick in the ribs, which is a total accident. I do blame Jake in part, because my mind is on escaping further kisses.

Nutmeg throws his head in the air then lurches into action back up the hill so quick I nearly topple backwards over his tail, but manage to grab enough mane and saddle to stay on board.

Then we're on the flat and I never knew I really had seat bones until now, when they're bouncing on that bloody hard leather like they want to make a hole in it. Pneumatic drill is the one thought in my head, but without the noise, unless you count my groans and shrieks. That'll teach me to try and avoid a grown-up conversation.

'Rising trot.' Jake's bellow comes from not far behind.

'I know what he's bloody doing.' Why do people some-times state the obvious? 'How the hell does telling me what is happening help? Tell me how the fuck to stop him.'

'I've never heard you say that word before.' He's laughing. 'I meant do it.' He's alongside me now, and he looks like he's just going slowly, whereas I know he must be going as fast as me, which is bloody fast. 'Rise.' I've never been so pleased to see anybody in my life though, even if he does look annoyingly relaxed. 'Go up and down like I am, unless you like having your bottom spanked?' He winks, which is totally inappropriate and leaves my face the same colour as my bum no doubt is.

I do not like having my bottom spanked, and he's right, it is a bit like that. And I don't want him to get ideas. He's gone all twinkly eyed and cheeky. I would like to point out that spanking is not in our agreement, but it's quite hard to speak clearly when you're being jiggled about and your arms are being jerked out of their sockets. I will keep that conversation for later, when I am on safer ground in all regards.

Nutmeg appears to have got the bit between his teeth, literally, and he's heading for home. I now know why they call it a spanking trot.

I never knew you could get totally out of breath when your feet aren't even on the ground, but what with wrestling with reins, rising to the trot completely out of sync with the motion, and trying to hold my legs in a position where they don't get more bruises with every step, I feel like I've had a session with one of those bootcamp terrorists.

It's just like a scene from Wuthering Heights as Nutmeg gallops across the grass, heading for the entrance to the stable yard. Except I'm sure Catherine wasn't hanging on to her horse's mane like her life depended on it; she was probably sat still, not bobbling about like a pea on a drum, as Mum would say. She also probably wasn't red in the face and gasping for air like a goldfish. And her Heathcliff probably wasn't trotting along making bad jokes about hell for leather and hot to trot.

It is even less like Wuthering Heights when the pony throws in a dirty stop, and solves my problem of how to dismount. Apparently a forward roll is perfectly possible on a pony.

'All done then?' Sandy, with a completely straight face, puts one hand on the reins which are dangling over Nutmegs head, and holds out the other for the hat as I stagger to my feet and try to look like I did it on purpose.

'All done.' I brush myself down gaily. 'Jolly good. Such a nice day for a little canter over the heather. Quite bracing.'

'The other ladies asked me to let you know they'd be in the spa.'

'Jolly good.' I don't know where 'jolly good' came from, it's a bit like my mother and 'supper'. There must be a much more appropriate Scottish equivalent. Sandy has gone though, Nutmeg following behind him like a tired old dog.

I can't walk. I discover this problem as soon as I try to walk away. I don't think I will ever be able to walk properly again. My hips have parted company and between them there is a horse shaped space.

'Maybe a session in the sauna, and a deep massage will solve the problem.' I'm not sure if Jake is grinning because of the way I'm walking or because he's happy. But I don't care. I wobble off in what I know isn't a very dignified walk. A few hours of oils, face masks and afternoon tea sounds just perfect to me.

Chapter 18

Jake is looking totally hot. Whereas I am just feeling hot and bothered, which is what a sauna and hot stones massage has done for me.

He grins, and looks even more irresistible. His hair is mussed up, but in an exceedingly attractive way, and the top buttons of his shirt are open. I am just thinking that he has definitely got a bit of the bad boy vibe going on this evening when he proves it, by pulling me into a clinch and kissing my neck, which sends an indecent tingle all the way down to my knickers.

'I think it's time we showed your folks what a fun time looks like, don't you?' I'm a bit startled, and still recovering from the unexpected tingle, so I don't really know what he's getting at. Until he inclines his head towards the small, and empty, dance floor.

'Oh, I...'

'Oh, Samantha doesn't really dance, do you?' I spin round at the sound of Liam's slightly nasal drawl.

He is standing right behind me, with Stella in tow. We've

seen very little of Stella so far, but this evening she joined us for the buffet and is now hanging onto Liam's arm possessively. She is also wearing a scowl, and a very big floaty blouse.

'She's not much of a party animal.'

'Oh, I think you'll find she does all kinds of fun things,' Jake's hand fixes very firmly on my waist. I am certainly not going to get the opportunity to run off again with Jess this time. Although I don't want to. I really don't want to. With Jake at my side I feel strong. So strong I can feel my chin lift. 'Don't you, darling?'

I'm glad he's actually asked me, I didn't want this to turn into one of those conversations when people talk about you as if you're not there.

'Absolutely, I love dancing! I am the queen of the dance-floor!' I am pushing it dangerously here. I have been known to dance, even on tables, but that was in the pre-Liam days.

'Oh no, she never used to...' Liam carries on talking to Jake, and I can tell he's irritated at being contradicted.

'Maybe not with you.' There's a gritty edge to his voice that I haven't heard before. Not from my totally laid back, fun Jake. 'But you always were a bit too boring for her, weren't you?' He pauses. 'Staid.'

Staid sounds like the ultimate insult. Staid is middle-aged and totally boring.

'Oh come on, babe, you don't want to bother with them.' Stella is tugging at Liam's arm and he's undecided. 'Let's go and sit down.'

'Yes, off you trot Liam.' It's the casual indifference in Jake's voice that makes me blink, and completely confuses Liam. Jake has already turned back and he's looking at me as though nothing else in the world matters. It's nice.

I forget all about dithering Liam. 'Well darling...' That husky, deep smooth voice is bad for me. 'Ready for a bit of dirty dancing?'

I don't really have a chance to object, or explain that my heels are too high, or we'll be the only ones, or anything, because he's edging towards the dancefloor as he speaks. And he's holding on to my hand, so I'm going too.

There's some spluttering going on behind us, which has to be Liam, and when I glance up, Jake is watching me. His eyes are serious, even though he's grinning.

Then I realise what he's doing. He's opening the door for me, for the real me, the old me. He's giving me a chance to start to be who I want to be again. I did tell Jake that I'd lost the real me, the girl who had tattoos done on an impulse, and I wanted her back. And Jake, it seems, is determined to let her loose.

'Too right!'

'That's my girl.'

And I am his girl as he spins me round until I feel lightheaded and dizzy, then pulls me in against his strong body so that I feel totally breathless.

There's some whoops and shouts so I get totally carried away and try a dirty-dancing style leap that sends Jake flying.

I get the soft landing, him, but he's laughing as he looks up at me. His strong hands still on my waist.

'Bloody hell, nobody has swept me off my feet for a long time.'

'You're a pushover. Come on, I've not finished with you yet.' I scramble to my feet and tug at him. Jake gets up with a groan. 'Are you okay?' Oh God, I've injured him!

'Kidding!' He winks. Then grabs me by my waist and I'm off my feet and being whizzed around. 'Not finished with me! I'll show you not finished.' We're spinning, he's so close, our bodies are pressed together, his forehead against mine. His lips...

'I don't want tonight to ever end.'

'It doesn't have to.' His husky voice is in my ears, his warm breath against my neck and I don't care who is watching or what they think. Tonight I've felt more alive than I have for ages.

It's midnight when I look at my watch. I kicked my shoes off a long time ago, in the middle of a dance where me, Jess and the other girls flung our hands in the air and bounced about madly. I've done a brilliant twist, which Jake insisted on videoing, and now I'm slow dancing with the best dancer in the room.

Our bodies fit together perfectly. His chin is on my shoulder, his words for my ears only. 'Had fun?'

'It's been brilliant. Have you?'

'Fantastic.' He pulls back a bit, so that he's looking me in the eye. 'I really like the real Sam.'

'Me too.' I bury my head back against his chest. 'Thank you.'

'Nothing to do with me, it's all you Sam. Shall we go for a walk before bed, cool down?'

I need to cool down, or I might forget the rules I've never got around to writing, and rip his clothes off.

The fresh air hits us as we step onto the small deserted terrace at the back of the room we've been partying in. There's no moon, no stars, just a normal sky hazy with clouds. But it's beautiful. So quiet and still after the hectic evening.

Jake sits down on the stone step, puts his jacket down for me, and we sit in companionable silence and listen to nothing.

'You wound Liam up tonight.'

'I don't care about Liam, just you.'

'You seemed really angry with him.' I put a hand over his. 'It's nice, but there's no need. I can do my own shouting.'

'I was angry. I *am* angry. I know you can stand up for yourself, Sam.' He squeezes my hand. 'But he had no right to treat you the way he did.'

'Laura really hurt you, didn't she?'

'She did, but I'm over her, it was who she did it with that really punched me in the gut. You think you know somebody, and then pow, you realise you didn't know them at all.' He studies our hands. 'People eh? After what happened to my mother I never thought I'd trust anybody completely, then I met Laura and she turned my world upside down. Guess I should have stuck with my first instinct.'

'Your mum?' I remember then what he said at the rescue centre, when we first met (which seems ages ago now) about his mum being betrayed by her first husband. About him running off with his agent and abandoning his family. 'Oh, you mean what Amy's dad did to her.'

'Yep, what do they say, keep your friends close, but your enemies closer? But what do you do if you can't tell one from the other?' He's talking about himself again now.

'He was a friend, the guy that Laura went off with? Oh Jake.' I hug him. I can't help it.

He drapes an arm over around my shoulders.

'But we live and learn don't we?' His laugh is slightly harsh, and I'm beginning to see why he'd only help me out if we kept it on a business level. If I thought *I'd* been badly treated, what Jake had been through was probably worse.

'I'm happy as I am, and I've got my career to think about anyway. Fitting a relationship into that can be tricky. Not many women would be happy when their other half says he's off to Greece for a few months.'

'True. So you're going more or less as soon as we get home?' It's funny thinking that soon this will be over. He'll be off to Greece for his big movie project, and I'll be back at work. Finis. We'll never see each other again. 'Your big break?'

'It is. A really good director, and film is what I've always wanted to do. I know some people prefer the stage, but I love the big screen. When I was a kid I just wanted to be up there, I was mad about the movies. Still am. What about you then, Sam? What's your dream? How did you end up working in a travel agency?'

'By accident really. Well, I love travelling.' I shrug. 'I had a diary when I was a kid with a list of all the places I was going to go to. I used to read a lot, and I wanted to go to all these fab places that I could picture in my head.'

'So working at the travel agency meant you could get a discount?'

'It was Liam's idea really.'

'Well, at least he got something right!'

'Not really. He suggested I take the job because I was interested in travelling, but he didn't want me to actually do it. The travelling bit.'

'Oh.'

'It was like a consolation prize. He just wanted us to go on a package tour once a year, he didn't want me to do three-week trips away, like Jess and I had planned. He said it was selfish.'

'You're not selfish.'

'I'm going to write a new list when I get back. I've been thinking of doing one of those charity things abroad where you raise money, you know volunteering, for a month or two.'

'Sounds good.'

'I could teach English, and tell them all about other

countries. Or—' this is all getting a bit serious '—teach dance?'

He manages to keep a straight face. 'You certainly could.' We both gaze at the expanse of lawn. Both thinking about our dreams. 'Ready for bed?'

We walk up to the room hand in hand, and it just seems natural to get into bed and curl up with him wrapped round me. But there is no monkey business, and when I wake up the cushions are back in place, and he's in the bathroom. Singing in the shower. Loudly.

It sounds vaguely familiar, so I get out of bed and go to listen in.

He's singing 'You can get it if you really want', so I peer round the door to see him swaying away like a true reggae dancer as the water pounds down. It's funny rather than erotic, even though he is butt naked, and the butt in question (and thighs) are as well toned as any real man can be.

I can't help myself, I start to boogie around the bedroom. And when he joins me, wrapped only in a towel, it is the best start to a day ever.

Chapter 19

'Oh my goodness, this one will suit you down to the ground Samantha, you'll be good at this.' Mum says it as though I'm not good at anything, and this is my big chance. 'You used to have a bow and arrow, didn't you, darling? You were rather good with it, wasn't she David? Hit anything and everything.'

'I was six, Mum. The arrows had rubber plunger things on the end and stuck to things.'

We are all assembled on a very large lawn, and there is a row of big targets and a rack of bows and arrows. Today is archery day. There are also two archers (who don't look like archers – they look like the groundsmen I saw sweeping up the gravel earlier), who are there to hand out equipment and instruct us.

It has been decided that the men will shoot first, so Jake is lined up next to Liam, with Dan the other side, and John and Dad further along. They are all steely-faced, but pretending to joke, in the way men do. All joviality, with a background of pure male competitiveness. You can almost smell the testosterone.

Dan goes first, and is totally rubbish, but Jess tells him he's fabulous and must have a duff bow or a blunt arrow. I don't think he really cares though, being bad is just an excuse to have a commiserating kiss from Jess and gives her dad the chance to show off. John has done this before (which I reckon is why we're all doing it) and he walks up in a very business-like manner, hustles the archer (who is supposed to be helping us) out of the way, and narrows his eyes as though he thinks he's James Bond with a sniper rifle. To be fair, he does look quite professional as he pulls the string-bit back and shoots, and his first arrow hits just outside the bulls eye. Juliet screeches with admiration, and there's a scattering of applause.

Next up is Liam. Liam preens and poses, and messes around, altering his stance and limbering up in a very strange way. Stella hovers behind him. And Ruby is on his other side – shooting looks of adoration at Liam, and contempt at Stella.

'That man just said you have to keep your elbow level.' Liam ignores Stella. 'It's up in the air.' When he finally decides to go for it, the first arrow falls to the ground at his feet with a plop. Jake and Dan (who are getting on quite well after their sleepover) heckle and the rest of us pretend we haven't noticed.

'I told you.' Stella says it so loudly that everybody stops their chattering and stares. Liam turns a funny puce colour, and Stella folds her arms, resting them on top of her bump.

'You never listen to a bloody word, do you? Won't be told, you always think you know it all.'

'Well I'm not surprised he doesn't listen to you, all you do is nag.' Ruby rolls her eyes in a very exaggerated manner. 'How can he concentrate with that racket? Go on, Liam, have another go.'

The archer quietly hands over a second arrow, and this one nearly hits the target. John claps him so hard on the back he nearly falls over, and tells him to put some welly behind it. I actually feel a (little) bit sorry for him.

Ruby tuts exceedingly loudly, mutters something that sounds like 'crap' and edges up the line to admire somebody more capable. Jake.

Jake is much better. He looks like he was born to hold a bow and arrow, and does it effortlessly. I think he must have been Robin Hood in a previous life, or maybe in a previous acting role. He turns and winks at me, in a very sexy way that makes me feel a bit hot and bothered, then turns back to the target and shoots as casually as they do in the movies. There is a brief silence, then applause and a few whoops. One of them from me. He has hit the target right in the centre!

I can't help myself, I leap on him and kiss him, and bask in shared glory.

And then it is my turn.

Now I do not like to boast, but it turns out that my mother was right. I can do this. I think it helps that Jake is stood right beside me once the instructor has gone, and lifts my elbow a little bit, and quietly suggests how I change the way I'm standing a little bit (he does hold my hips and is so close I feel like we're about to samba or do some other dirty dancing routine), but my first arrow hits the target! In the centre!

'Bloody hell!' I spin round, give him a smacker, then turn back to check I haven't imagined it. 'Look! I've done it! I've done it!'

'Su-perb.' Jake high fives me and sounds so proud I could burst, then he's swung me off my feet, and is kissing me as we spin round. 'You're a natural.'

'Beginner's luck.' We all stop and stare at Ruby.

'Now, now Ruby.' John, who has just been patting me on the back, stares at his daughter, who slopes off muttering.

Once I've stopped feeling dizzy I have another go, and do it again! He's right. I am a natural. It is not beginner's luck.

'Hold the bow thing, Samantha, hold the bow, smile. Properly.' Mum has her camera in her hand and is nearly as excited as I am. 'And you in the picture, Jake!'

'Chip off the old block.' My father, who hit the target, but not quite as well as I did, is beaming. I am a success! Today is going to be the best day ever.

It is Ruby's turn next, and she is nowhere near as good as me. And she's swearing about a broken nail, but has suddenly realised we're all watching.

She thrusts the instructor out of the way, sticks her chest out and marches over. 'Jakey, Jakey, come and help me.'

Ruby is tugging at Jake's arm, and simpering. 'You're so good at this, much better than this man.' She waves a dismissive hand.

Liam looks furious, and Stella is sulking. The rest of the men rush in, determined to help their own partners, so that Jake doesn't get all the limelight, and I have to admit the session does turn a bit chaotic. The archery men are rushing round shouting about health and safety, as everybody grabs bows and clamours for Jake's attention, waving sharp arrows in a way that could take an eye out.

Ruby is shouting for him to 'get closer' and Dan is sneakily trying to move Jake's target further away. Then he helps Mum and Juliet, who both demand that he position them exactly how he wants them, which leaves Jess and me on the floor laughing so much we're crying.

'He is so naughty.' Jess wipes her eyes.

Liam, who is behind us, tuts loudly. 'Childish.' The word is a mutter, but me and Jess both hear him. Jess rolls her eyes.

'It's called fun, Liam.' I try not to sound snooty, but I can't believe him.

He ignores me, and gestures at Stella. 'Ready to go?'

That would have been me a while ago, being herded away from the fun by him.

'Hey, look at your mum.' Jess is nudging me.

'Now what did I tell you Ruth?' Jake currently has his hand under Mum's chin. 'Head up, you've got such a wonderful jawline, you need to show it off.' She starts to giggle, which makes her drop her arrow. 'Bottom in Juliet, or would you like me to help?' I haven't actually seen either of them manage to shoot yet, but it doesn't seem to matter.

I offer to show them the stance, because I don't think Jake is trying hard enough, and before you know it we're pretending to hula hoop (essential to loosen our hips), Jess has joined in with some squats, and then we've got them on the mark ready to go. Although I'm sure Mum thinks she's Cupid, she's more likely to hit the tree on the horizon than the actual target.

Dad manages to get a brilliant picture of Mum accidentally hooking her skirt up (Mother thinks Scotland demands tweed skirts, not trousers) with the bow and showing her knickers, and a video of Juliet looking like she is twerking, which Jake told her is the best way to work out where her hips should be.

By the time we've finished I'm exhausted, all the laughing and exhilaration is pretty damned tiring. But it has been a good day. Jake helps them pack the equipment away and then draws me into his arms.

'You were brilliant.'

'You weren't so bad yourself.' There's a bit of a pause when he's gazing into my eyes and I'm wondering if I should kiss him. 'It's nice to see you so happy, you seem to have got your bounce back.'

I grin. 'I think maybe I have. It's been good.' And it wasn't just today. Since we got here every day seems to have been better than the last, and I know it's because Jake is here. If

I was to have a boyfriend, Jake is the type of man I'd want. I know that now. I also know I can't have him, but I'm not going to settle for any less.

He tucks a lock of hair behind my ear. 'You know the sexiest thing in a woman?' I shake my head. I'm guessing that being Jake he isn't going to say big boobs, long legs or even a nice smile. But I'm not sure what he is going to say. 'Self-confidence. And I'll tell you for nothing, you are out and out sexy, Samantha.'

I quite like the sound of that. Out and out sexy.

I also quite like the light kiss he plants on the tip of my nose, and the way he casually slips his hand into mine.

Chapter 20

Jake has not tried to kiss me properly again. Which is good. Honestly. We had an evening of posh dinner and drinks in the bar, at which he behaved like a doting husband rather than passionate lover. Which I have to say was rather disappointing after our fantastic day.

He then kept completely to his side of the bed. I swear at one point he actually puffed up the pillow barricade between us so it was even higher. As a result I didn't get a wink of sleep all night because I was wondering what I should do if he made a move.

But this is good, he is being a gentleman and sticking to the rules. Or he just doesn't fancy me. But he did say I was sexy. Bloody rules, why did I have to invent rules? It isn't like I ended up with a proper list of them, I seemed to stop after the no sex or flirting with other guests bit.

The only rule he has mentioned of his own though seems to be the no-relationship one. I am seriously tempted to say we can stick with his rule, but abandon mine. For the sake of authenticity. Although everybody does seem to think we are a proper couple. Bugger.

Anyway, I am determined not to let this lack of rumpy-pumpy (as my mother would say) spoil the week. Now I have had my epiphany and realise that I have been guilty of trying to become the woman Liam wanted rather than the real me, I am no longer heading down the cul-de-sac of middle age, and I can do a U-turn.

Only weak men need a woman who will excuse who she is. Strong men like Jake find strong, confident women sexy. I no longer care about trying to lose a couple more pounds from around my middle before the wedding day (although it will be a bummer if they can't do the dress up), because as Jake said before, I am the right size for me.

I do not need to please anybody else, or make any apologies, I am free to be who I want to be, and not compromise. Apart from horse-riding of course, but I am prepared to compromise for Jess. This is her wedding week.

'You look tired, dear.' Mother is watching me over the top of her boiled egg.

'Nothing wrong with that Ruth, remember the days when we looked like that in the morning, eh?' Dad winks at her.

There's a muffled giggle. Jess is sitting at the next table with Dan, and gives me the thumbs up. Maybe Jake was right. Maybe I shouldn't have told her anything at all. This is already getting far too confusing. Mum and Dad think we've been together long enough to be at it like rabbits, and Jess thinks we've only just met and I'm crossing my legs until I'm sure he's the one.

'Oh David, stop it.' Mum slaps his hand. 'You're drawing attention to yourself. Men your age can be such an embarrassment.' She's tapping the top of the egg gently with the back of her spoon. 'Now I'm the last person to be racist—' she's not '—but these Scottish people are totally different to us, what on earth do they feed the hens up here? This egg shell is as hard as nails.'

'Something hearty to keep them warm in the winter, darling.' Dad is tucking into his full breakfast with relish. 'And plenty of oats.' He really is on form, the highland air must be affecting his brain.

'Rubbish.' And with that she gives it an almighty smack with her knife and the top of the egg flies off and lands neatly on the next table. Jess giggles louder, but before she can reach it, Harry is there. On the table.

He looks quite comical and totally astonished, but not as astonished as the rest of us. Jake makes a dive for him, knocking his chair over, but Harry is quicker. He's grabbed the top of the egg, and a mouthful of pristine white tablecloth with it and he's off. His head held high with his trophy, his tail proudly in the air as he hurtles across the room, tablecloth trailing behind. There's a spectacular crash, and Jess's granola is scattered across the polished floorboards, along with a pot of coffee, an egg, two sausages, two rashers of bacon, black pudding and some amazingly red tomatoes.

'Come here, you horror.' Jake puts a foot on the cloth,

and for a second there's a growl tug of war, then the dog spots the trail of food. Have you ever seen a dog hoover up the full works while hurtling along at top speed with somebody chasing them?

Harry gets to the tomato and spits it out, before veering off under a table after a rolling sausage with Jake closing in. Until he steps on the tomato.

'Oh hell.' And it's a sliding tackle, worthy of any rugby player as he follows the dog on his bum.

We all duck down to see what's happening.

Harry is in shock. He's not sure if this is a new game, or an assault.

He is sitting stock still under the table, the sausage dangling from his mouth. 'Got you.' Jake grabs his collar, and Harry gobbles down the sausage as fast as he can, and starts to choke.

'More coffee, Sir?' The waiter is stood over him, coffee pot in hand, on the only clean patch of floor.

'A strong one please.' He pats Harry hard on the back.

'I don't think I'd carry on doing that.' Even I can see that he's starting to heave like he's going to deposit his breakfast on the floor.

'Oh yeah, right.' Jake finally twigs and scooping him up makes a run for the door.

'Oh God, Sam.' Jess has relocated to a new table, and Dan has gone off in search of a new breakfast. She's wiping the tears of laughter away with the back of her hand. 'He's such a hoot, and so gorgeous, how can you not have shagged him yet? How can you keep your hands off him?' I'd told her this was a very new relationship, that we hadn't actually done it yet. That I didn't want to accidentally get carried away. 'If I was you I'd want to keep him at home, you're going to miss him so much next week when he goes off filming.'

I don't really want to think about next week.

I definitely am not going to admit to Jess that I *have* been tempted to have an all-round pants off session, but he doesn't think the same. It is getting quite frustrating that he is determined to keep to my no sex rule.

'What are you two in a huddle about?' Dan has returned with a new plate of food, and saved my bacon as it were.

'Oh crumbs, is that the time?' I don't know why I revert to saying the same type of things as my mother in times of crisis. 'Must rush and check where Jake is.'

'Can't spend a second apart, you two, can you?' Jess's uncle Bert has crept up unnoticed, and slapped my arse. I'd like to slap his face, but I'm not sure it would go down well. 'More's the pity. You'd make an old man very happy if you'd spend—'

'Oh put the poor girl down Bert, you'll give yourself indigestion gallivanting about before your breakfast has gone down. And I've not got any tablets left, you know.' Aunt Edna tuts and shakes her head. 'Has anybody got any marmalade? I do like that thick cut, very tasty. Tart. I had it yesterday.' She wanders off in search of marmalade.

Jess is trying not to laugh again, I can tell, even though she's got her sympathetic best friend face on. 'I don't blame you, he's such a hunk. If I didn't have Dan I'd be following him round with my tongue out.'

Dan laughs. He's used to her. And she does blow him a kiss as she says it.

'Oh well, yes, er, and I need to get changed. What does one wear for, er, shooting?'

'Plus fours, love.' Bert hasn't gone away. This time he wraps an arm round my waist and squeezes, his fingers creeping ever nearer my boob. I'm working out how to knee him in the groin in a way nobody else will notice when he's given a hearty pat on the back and nearly lands head-first in Dan's new breakfast.

Dan grabs the plate out of harm's way surprisingly quickly. Talk about jumpy.

'I've heard you're shooting blanks, old man.' Jake's best acting voice booms out, his hand on Bert's shoulder and the man turns the colour of the tomatoes.

Dan is choking on his breakfast and Jess is gazing dreamily up at Jake, and licking butter off her fingers.

'What? How?' Bert is spluttering, and is looking for a way out.

'We all will be,' Jake chuckles. 'They're not going to let us loose with the real thing, are they?' My hero is back. I do have to admit he is better than any real boyfriend I have ever had. Nobody has ever rescued me from a groper before. He pats Bert on the back again. 'More's the pity eh?'

'Air rifles.' Dan has recovered enough to say at least one word. He takes a gulp of coffee.

'Don't want the best man being shot, do we?' Jake gives me a friendly squeeze.

What does he think I am? 'I wouldn't dream of...' It's no wonder he doesn't want to kiss me again, or throw the cushion barricade away, if he thinks I'm capable of murder. Then I see where he's looking, over my head towards the corner of the room. 'Oh.' Stella has her arms folded and she does not look happy. In fact I haven't seen her look happy since they arrived. I thought pregnant women were supposed to bloom, be joyous, once the morning sickness stage was over? Quite honestly, it's hard not to feel a teeny bit sorry for Liam, and very sorry for the babies. Maybe she is just fed up of waiting, maybe she will be joyous once she has the bundles in her arms.

Although now I think about it, she was never very happy when I paid for my petrol.

Jake now has his arm draped casually over my shoulder, and his voice is husky in my ear. 'I've sorted Harry, so I think I've just got time to sort you before the day's activities start, haven't I?'

Bert splutters. 'I'd better go and help Edna find the marmalade, please excuse me.' And the poor man is off at high speed, looking very flustered.

Jess giggles. 'You are naughty.'

Dan shakes his head. 'Good on yer, mate.' Suddenly taking an Australian turn. 'Now will you all piss off and let me finish my bacon in peace?'

***

'Are you sure it's a good idea bringing Harry?'

Harry is now on a lead, but still looking very pleased with himself after his big breakfast. Laura would be horrified, which makes me secretly pleased. I must have a bad, until now largely undiscovered, jealous streak in me.

'It isn't a proper shoot, he'll be fine. We can keep him on his lead.' I feel quite smug that he has said 'we', it almost means we are in this together, he is *our* dog. As opposed to his and some other woman's. Hopefully though, that does not mean I'm partly responsible if he does something bad.

As Jake had announced at breakfast, we'd all be shooting blanks. They won't be letting me loose with a loaded shotgun. And I do think that Jake has a point. Liam is in much more danger from Stella than from me.

Anyway today is air rifle day, but tomorrow I might actually get the chance to shout 'pull' when we graduate to clay pigeons.

Although I might have pulled already. I'm not quite sure if Jake is a truly brilliant actor, or actually a little bit fond of me. He did say I was sexy...

Harry, it turns out, is not keen on shooting. Maybe he is a pacifist, or doesn't approve of blood sports. Although I know for a fact he's not vegetarian, and he's more than capable of killing a leather shoe when it suits him.

At first he whines, then he starts to bark, and now we have progressed to howling. I did try holding his ears firmly under his chin to cut down on the noise, but he still wasn't convinced. So, being the good girlfriend and caring partial dog-owner that I am, I decide to take him for a little walk. It has absolutely nothing to do with the fact that I seem much more accomplished at hitting the space between the targets, than the actual targets themselves.

It's nice away from all the noise though, with a companion who is an excellent listener and doesn't butt in at all when I tell him all about my quest to rediscover my true vocation. Now that I have found the real me again, I am determined to decide what I should do with my life as soon as this week is over. I did mention to Jake some charity work, but I need a long term plan. I have an exciting stirring which started after I had spoken to Jake, a tiny germ of an idea involving accompanying people to exotic locations, rather than just sending them there on their own. I love exploring, whereas a lot of people are a bit scared of this, aren't they? With my organisational skills I could take away the stress, and get to see the world whilst being paid.

'There has to be more to life than a dead end job, doesn't there?' Harry looks up and blinks knowingly. 'I can't keep settling for second best and doing what other people want me to, can I?' Harry gives a vigorous shake. He's with me on that one, he has a policy of doing whatever he wants – unless Jake has quietly threatened him with castration if he doesn't stop it. 'I'll be thirty soon, which is a third of my life gone.' I have good genes, my parents show no signs of dying young, they're just getting a bit eccentric. 'I really don't need a man in my life.' Harry looks doubtful at that one, and gives a little whimper. 'But if I do have a man it has to be somebody like Jake, doesn't it?' That gets a wag. 'Somebody who makes me tingle and somebody who can make me laugh.' I think back to that woman in the hairdresser's who was talking about Hugh Grant. She had been right, though I hadn't realised it at the time. I need somebody who can make me truly happy, who can make me giggle. Or I will just settle for a dog.

'Sam, can we talk?'

My conversation with the dog is interrupted, and Harry flops down with a heavy sigh.

'Oh, it's you.' Liam. The person I least want to have a chat with. In fairness to him, if he hadn't acted quite so badly I might never have realised what a hash I was making of my life, so he has done me a favour. But I still don't want to talk to him, because he didn't do it for my benefit. He was being selfish.

'I don't seem to have seen you on your own all week so far.' He scowls like a spoiled child. 'It's been impossible, that man won't leave you alone.'

'No, well, Jake's very attentive.' Harry sits on my feet at the sound of his master's name, and looks up at me. Then looks at Liam and barks. He's a way better judge of character than I am. 'And he is my boyfriend.' I feel I should be clear on that point.

'I noticed.' Liam is scuffing at the earth with his shoes, which isn't the type of thing he normally does at all, because it tends to leave dirty marks. 'You look happy.'

'I am.'

'You look good. Great. Really.' This was exactly what I'd wanted Liam to say when we saw each other, and yet now he's said it I realise I don't really care that much. I'd like to return the compliment, but Liam doesn't look great, and I don't want to add to the lies.

'Thanks.'

As he stands there, all awkward, and not like the old Liam at all, I realise that the way he looks is how I'd felt when we were together. He made me feel awkward, and not at all sure of myself. He took my sexiness away from me.

Being with Jake is what has made me look good, because he's made me feel good. It's not my weight, or my inability to achieve all the things I'd wanted to, none of that has really changed (although I am doing something about that). But something inside me has. I've rediscovered me. I have remembered how much fun things can be, I have remembered that wild, silly ideas can sometimes turn out to be good ones. I have remembered why I had my tattoo.

'We had something, didn't we Samantha, something good?'

He's looking at me as though this really matters. 'Well...' I pause and try to work out what to say. 'We had something nice, and safe, and comfortable.' It's the fairest I can do.

'A nice home?'

'A very nice home.' And it was. It was what I thought I really wanted. With his and hers nice towels, his and hers sides of the nice sofa, his and hers roles in the relationship. As though we were ninety.

'I've been such an idiot, I shouldn't have messed it up, we could have been quite settled.'

Settled? What kind of a word is settled? Settled is what you do when you start thinking about a massive mortgage, plan Christmas in July and think about your imaginary kids' education. I want to scream it at him, but instead I just smile in what I hope is a non-committal way, as opposed to a forgiving way. Because I haven't forgiven.

'I'm sorry, Sam. I've been so stupid. It was just her boiler had broken, and she was all on her own and asked me to have a look.'

'Well, her boiler isn't broken now, is it?'

He looks startled, which isn't surprising I suppose.

'Well no, I put a new washer in, and then the following week she had an issue with her gas, which can be quite dangerous.'

'I bet it can.' A gassy Stella isn't something I want to dwell on.

'It can be difficult for a woman on her own.'

That comment warrants a glare. 'I bloody know it can, what do you think I was once you left me?'

'But you've got friends, and family, people like you.'

I'm not sure if this is a compliment or not.

'And once she told me she was pregnant, what could I do?' He runs his hands through his hair, another very un-Liam like thing to do. Messy. 'Oh God, Samantha, I'm not ready to be a dad, I'm not ready to … to leave you and our nice life.'

'Shouldn't you have thought of that before you cheated on me and got her pregnant?'

'She said she was on the pill.' His face is twisted like he might start crying, and I am struck by a sudden lightning bolt of understanding. A lot of Liam's niceness is actually weakness. Why haven't I realised before? I could be Stella. That could have been me. Well not actually me being her, but if I'd been mysteriously struck pregnant he'd probably have gone to pieces like he's doing now. He looks like he hasn't slept for a month, so what's he going to look like when there's a baby, sorry, babies, in the house?

'Liam.' If this had been two months ago I might have thrown myself into his arms, two weeks ago I might have tried to strangle him, but now I can't be bothered to do anything. 'Would you have freaked like this if I'd got preggers?'

He blinks uncomprehendingly. 'But you wouldn't, you haven't. You're not, are you?' He looks even more freaked now. He takes a step backwards as though I might have something catching. Although if I have, it's a bit late for him to worry about it.

'You've always been the one for me, Samantha. I don't know what I'm going to do without you.'

A flash of colour catches my eye and stops me from saying anything rude. On the hill heading towards us with long, positive strides is Jake. My knight, not that I need one right now. I've got this.

He's been watching us, I'm sure he has. He's close enough to see properly now and for a moment he pauses, and he smiles and gives me a tiny thumbs up.

He's letting me know he's there for me, but knows I can handle it. He believes in me.

And then I know. If a man, any man, can make me feel that special, at that distance, when he's just doing a job – then Liam has never been within a million miles of being 'the one' for me.

'Liam.' I suddenly get another lightning bolt, I seem to be on fire today. I also seem to be lacking in empathy for the man I thought I was going to spend the rest of my life with. But he does deserve it. This is totally his own doing. 'Did your parents never tell you that you shouldn't dip your wick if you can't face the consequences?' Liam looks dumb-founded, this obviously wasn't the response he was expecting.

'Dip his wick?' Jake slides to a halt beside us, his eyes are twinkling. I quite like his twinkly look, when he goes all crinkly-wrinkly round his eyes. I can tell he's trying to keep a straight face. Apart from the eyes.

'Mr Double-dip here—' okay, I'm mixing metaphors, or facts, or whatever, but I'm on a roll '—was shagging us both, so he deserves whatever bed he's made and has to lie in.' After a few drinks I've been known to confuse even myself – this is good, by my standards. Particularly as I have not had a snifter of whisky today. But I know what I mean.

'So you don't want to get back together?' There's still the slightest whiff of hope in Liam's tone, something that needs stamping on.

'You have made your bed with Stella.' I try to sound lofty, but from the twist to Jake's mouth I think I might be failing. He's still trying not to laugh. 'And the twins.'

'Oh God. Twins.' Liam's wail is not that of a man prepared for imminent fatherhood. 'Two of them.'

I decide not to agree that twins normally means two. 'And Stella.'

'I thought you loved me.'

That does stop me dead for a while, and my jollity does a runner. 'So did I Liam, but…' I take a deep breath, knowing he can never be *the one*. 'Now I know I don't.' I pause. 'I'm sorry.' And I am. Once upon a time we'd both thought we'd met our perfect partner. 'And you can't love me, can you? Or you wouldn't have ever gone near her boiler, would you?'

Jake squeezes my hand. I hadn't even realised we were holding hands, which is a bit worrying. Have I really got *that* used to having him around?

'And anyway, I've got Jake now.' I squeeze back, and shoot him a look. I came here, to Scotland, for Jess, but I realise now that although I might not have gained a boyfriend,

I've gained a heck of a lot more. 'I've moved on Liam, I think you need to as well, don't you? Don't forget to send me the christening piccies.' But not the cacky birth ones though, oh no, no, please not those.

'Sure.' Liam nods and straightens up as though he's completely accepted the situation. But that's what he's like. Logical. This is the most emotional I've seen him for ages, and it's because he's on the verge of panic about his new life. A life he doesn't really have much control over. It's not me he really wants, it's security, safety, the same 'knowing' I'd thought I wanted. An escape route. 'I'll see you around then. I'd better get back to Stella.'

Something inside me deflates as he ambles away, up the hill. And it's not something like hope, no last flickering embers of desire or anything poetic like that. I just feel worn out. I am shocked to realise I am trembling.

'I thought things like this were supposed to be empowering, energising?'

Jake chuckles. 'I think you're getting confused with confessing your sins, or unburdening your soul.'

'Oh.' Though it is a bit like that, confessing to him and admitting to myself that I don't love him, probably never have, and it has nothing to do with Stella and what he did. 'I need a drink, a large drink.'

'I'm sure I can arrange that m'lady.'

'I'm so over him, he's going to be a—'

'Dad?'

'I'd really rather have a puppy, like Harry.' It's at that moment that I realise in all the emotional hoo-ha I have forgotten about my responsibilities.

I am holding a lead with no dog.

All that is left at knee height, where the black fluffiness should be, is a frayed, chewed piece of tartan nylon.

'Shit.' I look blankly at Jake, who looks back, then back down at the lead as though miraculously Harry might reappear. He doesn't. 'Where's he gone?' I spin round, but it's hopeless he could be anywhere. All around are mottled patches of dark and light, heather of different shades that is on the verge of flowering. 'Oh God, I'm sorry, he was here when Liam came, I swear it. He gave him a funny look, and...' Oh buggery bugger, he could be anywhere. The place is massive.

'It's okay, don't panic.' Jake puts his hands on my shoulders and looks reassuringly into my eyes. 'He can't have gone far.'

'Except he does.'

'What?'

'Go far.' He runs faster and further than any dog I've ever had. I can imagine him hurtling up the hillside, dodging the thistles, bouncing over the heather, into a distant part of the estate I've never been to.

'He's probably gone after a squirrel, or rabbit, and just headed off with his nose down.' Jake has got the faintest of frowns on his forehead, which from what I know of him so far means he is definitely worried. It's his version of panic.

Oh hell, what have I done? He loves Harry, and Laura will be furious, or heartbroken, or both.

'Oh no.' I clasp my hands to my mouth. 'He could be stuck down a hole, or up a tree.'

'Tree?' For a moment there's the normal glimmer of a smile on Jake's face. 'He's not a cat.'

Which reminds me of an article in one of Mum's magazines. 'There are big cats in Scotland aren't there? Wild ones, they might get him.' It was pretty graphic, with blurry pictures of prowling cats and torn bloody carcasses of sheep and deer. I grasp Jake's arm. 'I'll organise a search party, I'll get Jess. We need to find him quick before it gets dark.' All the pictures were at night, Scottish cats hunt when it's dark. Harry can't be an evil cat's late-night snack, he just can't, I love him too much already.

'Sam, calm down. He won't get stalked by a cat. He might even have headed back for his dinner, you know what he's like about food.'

'We need binoculars.' Why aren't I one of those people that goes fully equipped on a ramble?

Jake shakes his head and hollers. I holler. Our hollering bounces off the emptiness and there is no sign of a little black dog, or anything. Not even a rabbit. The big cats have probably eaten them all.

'Hang on! There, that's him isn't it?'

I spin round. 'Where?'

Jake is pointing in the one direction I hadn't looked. The loch. It takes a minute, but then I see what could be him.

A dishevelled black blob. A soggy doggy balanced on what looks to be a log.

He's okay, he's alive, just a bit damp. Nothing that can't be fixed with a quick blast from the hairdryer in our room.

'Shit, he can't swim.'

'What do you mean, he can't swim?' I trot after Jake, who is heading for the bank of the loch. 'All dogs can swim, that's why it's called doggy paddle.' I'm panting, this man can move fast when he wants to. 'Every dog I've ever known has been able to swim.'

'He'll drown.' There's a note of panic I've never heard before in Jake's voice, and he's not really listening to me, so I give his arm a tug. Partly to slow him down, and partly so that I can talk some sense into him. It's quite sweet though really, that he's so concerned.

'How do you think he got there in the first place?' It is my responsibility to be the calm one here (to make up for my lack of responsibility when looking after him). 'Flew?' I flap my arms, trying to make light of things, but Jake is a man on a mission. He's in a right paddy and is already stripping off his shoes and socks, and they're flying in all directions. I catch a sock that's flapping past my head, and dodge a shoe. His gilet comes off next and I must say he looks quite the part in his country shirt and thigh hugging trousers.

Unfortunately he doesn't start stripping those off. I don't blame him, it's not exactly warm.

'Christ, she'll kill me if he drowns.' He wades into the

loch, and Harry starts to bark. 'I'm coming, mate, hang on.'
Harry stands up and is wagging his tail with excitement,
threatening to submerge whatever it is he's standing on.
'Wait. Don't move.'

Jake dives, and Harry ignores his command and jumps.

It is now pretty apparent how Harry got out onto the
log in the first place. I thought lochs were always deep, as
in very deep. Some, it seems, are shallow in places. Like
this one. In this place.

There is an almighty splash, followed by spluttering, and
a lot of swearing.

'Christ.' Jake staggers back to his feet, spitting out water
and wiping green stuff from his eyes and Harry does a
good impression of walking on water as he bounds towards
his master, delighted that he's joining in the game.

'Oh my goodness me, it's Mr Darcy!' Mum's excited high-
pitched voice interrupts the barking and swearing and I
turn around.

There's a round of applause. Shooting must have finished
for the day.

Jake has an audience. There's quite a crowd, with the
obvious exception of Liam who has missed his opportunity
to see what a *real* man does.

I glow in the shared limelight. I've never been the centre
of attention for heroics before. I know the diving to the
rescue was him, and I know it was totally unnecessary, but
he's my boyfriend and Harry is *our* dog – the new me is
determined to see the positive side.

Jake has steam coming off him. Well, it looks like that in the sunlight as he lifts Harry up in the air, and bows. What else would you expect?

He heads towards me, bearing the wriggly dog aloft, and I really know I should take him, and we should embrace. But they're both sopping wet, and Harry does smell a bit, so I let Jake put him down.

He has a massive shake then starts to run round excitedly, and at great speed, in ever increasing circles. Which effectively disperses the crowd, who do a bit of shrieking and run up the hill.

'Oh my, oh my.' Mum unfortunately has not been dispersed. She's clutching her hands to her chest dramatically. 'Your father has never done anything like that.'

'I doubt many men have, Mum.'

'And so handsome.' She squeezes his arm. 'Oh goodness, I feel quite overwhelmed.' It's my turn for the squeeze treatment. 'You really must both come to supper when we go home.'

I'm not going to worry about that right now. When we get home I can say he drowned.

He grins, flips his dripping hair back and winks.

I can't say he drowned. That would be nasty, and tempting fate. I might just have to say he dumped me.

'Shall I take Harry and get him dried off?' This is very unlike Mother. One, offering to help and two, agreeing to do anything more than pat a dog. 'Then you two can have a moment. David, David, come and take this dog.' Ah, that's more like it.

Jake loops Harry's chewed lead through his collar, and Dad dutifully takes the end.

'You've never jumped in a lake to rescue me, David.'

'You'd never go in a lake dear, the only time your feet get wet is in the bath.'

'Well, Samantha wasn't in the lake.'

'Exactly. He went in to get the dog.' Their words drift as they get further away.

'You've never rescued any of our dogs from a lake either.'

'We haven't got a dog, dear.'

'Just like Mr Darcy, oh our Samantha is so lucky. Such a blessing that Liam did what he did, well not a blessing. I mean you can't call behaviour like that a blessing, but...'

I can't hear them now. There's just me and a very wet Jake.

'Are you okay, Sam?'

'I'm fine, fine. It's you that jumped in the lake.'

'But, Liam...'

'Is a stupid idiot.' I have stopped trembling now. The shock of the confrontation, and being so assertive, has been replaced by the dread that I had lost the lovely Harry, followed swiftly by awe at Jake's heroics, and I am now slightly stunned at the sight of him looking so hunky and masculine (and it must be said, wet) in front of me. I am all a kerfuffle. A mass of messy emotion, which is probably why I am stuttering and staring.

I want a Jake all of my own. I fancy him rotten. That is all.

'He certainly is. He's a complete dick if you ask me. How any man could do that to you, I don't know.'

'Oh.'

'That kiss, when we were out on the horses...'

'Oh it's fine, no need to apologise.' I don't really want him to spoil things by saying it was a massive mistake, or he felt sorry for me, or I'd have to pay if I want another one.

'I wasn't going to apologise.' He's so close I can feel the steam coming off him. Or is that me? 'I'm afraid now I've done it once, I really want to do it again.'

'You piled the cushions up higher.' I don't know where that thought came from, but it is true. Last time I thought that a bit of physical contact was on the cards (after our dirty dancing and archery triumph) I was let down.

'Cushions?' He's looking puzzled.

'On the bed, after the archery. You made the barrier higher.' And it is actually my barrier – I built it, and am maintaining it.

'I had to. It was a case of higher, or out of the window.'

'Oh. You're wet.'

'Wet is good.'

'Is it?' I'm going to need this whole outfit dry cleaned, or at the very least dried.

'Definitely.'

This kiss is even better than the first one. Our teeth do clash at first, because I'm not quite ready, but then his tongue starts to do this circle thing round mine and I couldn't give a monkey's what came first.

I never knew a man could taste this good, without mints or breath freshener, or beer. My nipples are acting very irresponsibly, and all I can think of is sex. And what his pert bum will feel like naked. And if his six pack feels the way it looks (I sneaked the odd peek when he was getting ready for bed). And whether the bit of him that's pressed against the base of my stomach is really that hard.

And whether this means he does actually fancy me, properly.

I don't think I care.

'Shall we get back, get these wet clothes off?'

Oh swoon. All I can do is gulp and nod. I am a disgrace to independent women, and I don't care. If he wants to throw me over his shoulder right now, I'll let him.

We walk back hand in hand. He's got very nice, firm, capable hands. Manly hands, the type you'd be quite happy to have undressing you.

'I should go and find Harry.' He kisses the tip of my nose, which is really quite sexy and not at all cutesy and silly like it looks on films. 'How about I get a nice warming glass of whisky and then I'll run us a hot bath when I get back?'

All I can do is give him a silly grin. He said us. Run 'us' a hot bath. And he can't mean Harry, he has to mean me and him, which means we are heading for hot sex. I haven't had hot sex for at least three years, and that happened by accident when Liam accidentally put the air conditioning on a heat setting he didn't know it had. I thought he was all hot and sweaty from excitement, and apparently he thought the same about me. But at least it made him forget his routines and do the closest to ravishing me that he was capable of.

Jake is tugging, and I suddenly realise he's trying to get free, in a nice way.

'Fab.' Oh God, who says fab when they've just been offered a night of passion? The only worse thing has to be 'thank you'. But he might not have heard, the second I let go he is off. Obviously in a rush to get Harry, so that he can be back quickly.

I soon realise though, once I get back in our room and start to rummage in my drawers, that I have a major problem.

I have nothing to wear! I should have bought a sexy nightdress or something. Not just posh jumpers, walking boots and tight dresses. I should have been prepared for any eventuality and packed some kind of slinky nightwear. Instead of the baggiest, least sexy, pyjamas that I could find. I was aiming for androgynous, now I realise that if I wear these I will have achieved forty-year-old-bag-lady.

Bugger.

Now what do I do? What if he comes back and kisses me again? What if he doesn't? I shouldn't think negatively, he will come back. He is bringing whisky and the promise of a hot bath. And we have an absolutely ma-hoo-sive four poster bed. Quite frankly the bed had been scary when we arrived, something that was impossible to ignore. Now we are about to use it properly – without pillows and a fluffy dog down the middle as a barricade! I throw the cushions and pillows willy-nilly across the room.

Shit, I need to do my teeth, and spray perfume, and ... I wonder if Jess has a spare sexy something-or-other? Although she is about a foot taller than me, and thinner. But I can't ask anybody else because they all think Jake and I have been in a proper relationship for ages, so I would have packed posh undies and nightwear. I could say I'd run out, that he'd ripped the others off me in a frenzy of passion?

I'll just have to dive under the covers, naked. Or is that forward? Isn't it sexier to undress each other? Maybe, but not when you're dressed the way I am. There is nothing sexy about peeling off sensible socks.

Oh bugger. I could text Sarah.

No, I have to ask Jess. Jess will have a boudoir's worth of killer undies. Surely that is a pre-requisite when you're getting married? And Jess is the only person who will understand why I don't have my own supply. But Jess is also a size eight and I am a twelve, but I am sure if she has some French knickers going spare, they will stretch to cover the extra. French knickers are accommodating.

I'll call her. No harm in asking.

There's a buzz and it's a bit confusing, because it's not coming from the phone receiver I've picked up. It's coming from underneath me, along with the hint of a vibration.

I am tempted to ignore it, because I really do need to

prioritise or I could lose my chance of passion, and having not had any for quite some time I'm feeling quite randy. I had felt perfectly fine before. I could handle no sex. It didn't bother me at all. But now Jake has kissed me, he seems to have flicked some inner setting to the 'on' position.

Whatever is under my bum has also been flicked to the 'on' position though. And when I fish my mobile out from underneath the rearranged pillows there are messages, lots of messages. Sarah messages.

Chapter 21

I have sent Sarah regular updates on the castle situation since we arrived. The first day I sent her a hastily taken picture of Stella, which was a bit blurry but very demonstrative of her hugeness. I also sent her a picture of Harry, and one of Harry and Jake in the loch. I have also sent pictures of men in kilts, and highlighted the fact that Jake has the best legs.

I have *not* mentioned that I do actually fancy Jake a little bit. Okay, make that a lot. That he has been the perfect boyfriend. I have not said a word about the new development. The snog. Well snogs, plural. I really should, but I'm not sure if I should share yet, or wait until after the hot bath.

Except if I read the WhatsApp messages then she'll know I've read them, and I'll need to reply. And then I'll tell her, because I won't be able to lie. So I could ignore them for now. Except I want to know what they say, because there are lots.

So I can't really ignore them, can I? Something terrible might have happened.

OMG you won't believe this! Sarah can be melodramatic, I probably can believe it. *I found out why he needs a distraction!*

I scroll down, and something terrible does happen.

A terrible, terrible something.

It's a picture. Of Jake. Cradling a tiny baby. With a massive caption. *Proud Daddy moment!!*

Okay, Sarah is right. I don't believe it.

As the need for distractions go, I'd say this was up there with the best.

I feel sick. I do not want a bath any longer.

Jake is a *daddy*? Jake can't be a father. Jake has half a dog and an ex. How can he be a daddy? Liam's nearly a daddy. Jake is a pretend boyfriend.

OMG I bet you can't believe it?! I saw this on Facebook!!

It's a bit fuzzy, because Sarah has obviously taken a photo of her laptop, with her pretty crap old phone. But it's him.

It's Jake!!!!

She's even added that, in case I'd missed the fact.

When duf u sew this? I'm typing too fast, with trembling fingers, but I know she'll get what I mean. I'm also locking the room door, and pushing the chair against it, which makes it hard to spell.

Just, but it was posted two days ago. Can you believe he's got a baby?

No. I can't. It can't be true. I don't want to believe it. *Two days ago? But he's here in Scotland. How can he be in two places at once?* He did go to the supermarket on his own the other day, but unless he's got a private jet or turned into superman then he couldn't have gone home, posed for photos, and got back here. And that's if you skip the messy labour and all that stuff. And he did bring Pringles back, in a bag that was definitely from the local shop (which actually isn't that local).

Who knows? I don't think she cares. *There's another pic here of a girl, she is SO glam even though she's just had a baby.*

Laura? He said she was his ex.

Who's Laura? She doesn't wait for a reply. *She's called Annabelle or Isabelle or something, some actress. Hang on. I'll look. They are just like the dishiest couple EVAH*

My heart has been doing this bouncing, palpitation thing, but it now sinks to the bottom of the deepest ocean, and Sarah is oblivious to my agony. Laura is an ex, but he forgot to tell me about the next woman in his life. The glamorous Annabelle.

Oh God yes!! She IS called Laura. How did you know? Has he told you about her? It's the baby that's called Annabelle.

Oh. Jake's ex is an actress, a real one. A glamorous one. And he has a baby. *They* have a baby. Not just a dog.

And even if she is totally his ex, he is still holding their baby. A very tiny baby. An absolutely gorgeous, edible kind of tiny baby.

When people present their offspring, especially ones they've just had, you just have to say they're pretty, cute or whatever, don't you? Even if they look a bit like ET on a bad day, or just a bit battered, or bald, or just plain ugly. I'm not being nasty here, but they don't always come out looking adorable to anybody but their immediate family, do they? But this baby truly is beautiful. Which makes it worse.

Off out with Appletini guy, catch you later?

Sure! I thought he was off the menu though? I feel sick. What kind of man needs a distraction from their beautiful baby?

After he'd talked dirty to me about the Milky Way and Uranus I decided to give him a second chance.

Have fun! I wish I was at home, and off out with Appletini guy.

I plonk myself down on the big, empty bed and stare at my reflection in the mirror.

I carefully pick the cushions up off the floor and put them back down the middle of the bed. With an extra layer. I might need to bury myself under it later.

Except I don't want to get in the same bed as him, and pretend I'm asleep. I don't want to share a room with him, let alone a mattress. In fact, I don't want to share a castle with him.

He kissed me. It was amazing. But that is all it was. A kiss. Two kisses. I need to get out, before he comes back with his whisky and bath salts. I need to work out what I should do next.

This is massive. This, on the scale of complications, is much bigger than bringing a dog. How could he talk about Laura, betrayal, Harry – and not mention his baby?

I can't go home and ruin Jess's wedding though.

I can't pay Jake and send *him* home, because then I will be poorer and I will have even more explaining to do than when I just had a fake date. And I still might ruin Jess's wedding.

I can't see him right now. I will burst into tears, or throw myself at him and try to batter him to death. And ruin Jess's wedding. I need to get out of here before he comes back with whisky and his treacherous smile.

So I go down the corridor, and push open the door that says 'fire exit only' and see the last person I expect to, sitting on the stairs with a glass in one hand and a cigar in the other.

'Dad! What are you up to?'

'Shh, don't tell anybody, Sam. Bloody impossible to find somewhere you can have a smoke.'

'I don't think it's allowed inside.'

He winks. 'Well, if you won't tell, I won't. Only place I could find without a smoke detector, and where your mother won't find me.'

'Ahh.' I sit down next to him.

'What's up, darling?' Dad moves in closer, and it is just like when I was ten years old and our rabbit had died, then again when I was fourteen and heartbroken over a boy, except now I am nearly thirty and we are in a castle. 'It can't be that bad.'

'It can!'

'Well, tell me, then we'll see. Nothing that can't be mended.'

'This can never be mended.' I know this for a fact, a bit like the rabbit. 'He's got a baby.'

He looks a bit confused at this and just squeezes my hand. I've discovered that the reason older people seem to know *everything* when you're little, is that they wait until you tell them, then they pretend they knew all along.

'I thought you were over him, love. We know he's going to be a dad, but...'

'He's already a dad!' And he was going to shag me! I hope I didn't say that last bit out loud.

'Oh my goodness, darling.' His eyebrows raise in alarm at the tear that's just spurted from my eye, and he delves in his pocket for a handkerchief. 'Arrived already have they? Boys or girls, or shouldn't I ask?' He's got a nervous twitch, the same one he used to have when I handed over my school report, or exam results. In fact, he used to say the same thing. The 'shouldn't I ask?' bit, not the boys or girls bit. 'One of each?'

'One of each? There are two of them?' I've got a bit loud, I can tell by the look of horror on his face. 'I only saw one!'

'I thought you knew? We all...'

'Everybody knows?' This is even worse. They all know my boyfriend is a father. It was bad enough that everybody knew about huge Stella before me, but this is ten times worse.

'Oh yes,' Dad doesn't seem to think it's horrendous, he's totally unbothered. He could at least pretend to be shocked, for my sake. Have his standards dropped so low? 'Jake mentioned it to us, when you went for a top up of toast this morning. He'd told everybody over a drink in the bar apparently, think I missed the announcement then. Your mother dragged me away before they opened the best whisky.' He's sounding quite miffed, which is quite unlike Dad. I make a muffled sob noise, to redirect him, and he remembers that this is far more important than whisky, or his crafty cigar.

'Twins.' How come everybody has twins, is there something in the water? 'How could he not tell me? Why am I always the last to know?' And why was there only a picture of one?

Dad has leaned in closer, because I'm down to a whimper now and he can't hear, and I'm screwing his handkerchief in the way I'd like to screw Jake's neck. He pats my hand, but I know he's staring at the handkerchief, wondering how he'll explain the state of it to Mum. I'm sure she thinks they're for adornment rather than use.

'Maybe he didn't think you'd want to know, darling? I mean he's been a complete heel and all that, but maybe he thought it was the right thing to do.'

I stuff the hankie into my mouth, to stop myself screaming.

'This Jake seems a much nicer chap.'

'Nicer chap than what?' Now, it's me who's confused. He's not making any sense at all.

'Than Liam. Much more upfront.'

'How can you say that, Dad, when I've just found out he's got a baby, well, two.'

'Has he? Well blow me!'

'You just said he had!'

'Liam, not Jake. Has Jake got children as well? My, my, not surprised you're a bit upset if you didn't know.' My dad only knows 'a bit upset,' out of your mind hysterical doesn't exist in his world. 'Well, that's a turn up for the books, I must say. Would you credit it? And you didn't know?'

'So he's not got twins?'

'Not as far as I know, Samantha. Well, he hasn't even got one as far as I was aware.'

'He has. Sarah sent me a picture she saw on Facebook.'

'Sarah?'

'Oh, you know David.' Oh, God, Mum is here now. How did she creep up on us? 'Sarah is Samantha's little friend from the travel agency. A bit odd I have to say, but well meaning. She told me she could get us a nice discount on a cruise, which is more than Samantha has ever offered.' She's giving me her disappointed look. 'With an ocean view.'

'Samantha's a bit upset, Ruth, aren't you, love?' He is now trying to wave smoke away, stuff his cigar out of sight and explain all at once. 'Had a bit of a shock. Appears her fella has got a baby he only just told her about. Bit rum that, isn't it?'

'He's got half a baby, and half a dog.' At least he's only got one I suppose, but I rather think it's the type of thing a man should mention before he starts breaking the rules of a business arrangement and entering into full bodily contact. Which I'm pretty sure he was about to do.

What really hurts though is that he knew all about Liam and Stella, and their imminent babies, and never mentioned this.

'So Jake has got a baby, not just Liam?' Mum never really listens, which means she quite often loses half the conversation. 'Oh dear.' Mum pats me on my hand. 'Oh never mind darling, you'll soon find somebody else. Though he is rather good looking. I must admit, your father and I were a bit worried about his prospects, I mean acting isn't the most secure of professions, is it David? But...' She stops, when she realises I'm crying more now. 'We are glad you left that Liam fellow, he really wasn't the man for you, Samantha. I mean, we didn't like to say at the time, you know we'd never interfere, but he always seemed a little bit boring.'

'He—' splutter '—is—' sniff '—boring.'

'Well, you're best forgetting him.' Dad is good at career chats, but I can tell my emotional outburst is worrying him a bit. 'And maybe I should leave you and your mum to have a little chat?'

'I don't care about Liam, he's just silly, and he tried to

control my life and nearly spoiled everything. But I really like Jake.' I do, which is why I'm so bloody upset. I know he's just a business arrangement, but I've just realised that being with Jake has been nicer than being with any other man I've ever known. He understood, he knew about broken trust and disloyalty, and being good enough as you are. And now this. I want to cry, lots more than I already have. It just isn't fair. 'I thought he just had an ex and a dog share.' I sniff. Sharing Harry is nothing compared to this. 'Now he has a baby!' I wail, I know I'm wailing, I can hardly breathe. Dad passes me a new bigger white handkerchief, Mum always insists he carries more than one. 'Oh, Dad.'

'He's got a very sweet little dog though, he does seem a nice man.'

Dad pats my hand. 'Your mother is right, dear. I'm sure it doesn't mean Jake cares for you any less, or he wouldn't be here.'

'He doesn't care for me at all!' Even I know I shouted that last bit rather melodramatically. Sarah would be proud. 'He's got a glamorous ex and a baby! He's a, he's a...' The man had said he needed a distraction, what kind of a man wants a distraction from their newborn baby? And he was using me as that distraction! He was even going to go as far as hot baths and whisky as a distraction. 'He's a complete basket!' I was going to say bastard, but thought at the last moment that this was a bit strong in front of my parents, and basket was the best I could come up with.

'Oh, no I wouldn't say that, he...' Dad is trying to be reasonable, I know he is. Everybody has a good side he always says. I don't think this observation is based on real life.

'He's not real.'

Now they both look very confused. I don't blame them.

'Well he is real, but he's an actor, Dad. And...' I take a deep breath and look him full in the face. 'He's not...' Oh God, I nearly told them. I nearly told my parents that this is all a fake, and Jake is not my boyfriend, and that I hired him. I can't do that, not yet. If I tell Mum, it will be as good as telling everybody. She'll tell people, even though she won't mean to. 'Maybe he's not serious, he's just been pretending he likes me?' It's a bit lame, but the best I can do. 'And it'll ruin the wedding if we have a big row, and he goes.'

'Oh.' He takes the handkerchief back (the most recent one that is only a little bit creased) and wipes his brow. 'Oh Samantha, I don't think he'd pretend. He seems a nice enough chap, and we don't care if he stays or goes, it won't spoil a thing. You've got to do what's best for you, and we love you anyway.' Dad rests his chin on my head.

'Such a shame, I have to say I am a little bit put out though, I did rather like him. More than I liked Liam, or that, what was he called? That one you went out before.' Mum is frowning, trying to remember.

Dad shakes his head. 'Oh yes. Funny lad. Limp handshake.'

'Oh well, look at the time.' Mum stands up and brushes imaginary dirt off her top. 'Chin up darling, we don't want to miss our cocktails. It's the wedding in a couple of days, Juliet has planned a nice little soiree for tonight she said. What did I do with that list David?'

'I don't know dear, but you're not going to find it in the stairwell, are you?'

'Well, we'd better get back and see what time it starts. You can come and sit with us, Samantha.'

'Mum, you won't tell anybody about Jake's baby, will you? Dad?'

'Tell them what, Samantha?' She frowns. 'You youngsters are perfectly entitled to the odd lovers' tiff, so I don't think it's strange at all if you're a bit at odds with him tonight. Do you, David?'

'Oh no, no, not at all, Ruth.'

'I've already told Juliet you're planning a September wedding. There is time for you to make up dear.' She pats my hand again. 'Although like your father says, it is up to you. But he is very nice.'

Oh hell. How could my mother do this to me? 'He might have more than one baby.'

'Or he might not. Don't you think you should have checked at the start? I mean, when I first met your father...'

'I didn't...' Oh God, what is the use? 'It isn't the type of thing he'd have on his CV, is it?' And at the start it hadn't seemed important at all.

'Now there's no need to be so melodramatic. And anyway,

why would you look at his CV? That's not very normal, is it? I never looked at your father's, did I David?'

Oh shit, I've nearly dropped myself in it again. I really need to stop, go for a lie down and calm down. This is a business arrangement. I shouldn't care if he has a dozen children.

Except I trusted him. And liked him, rather a lot.

A very lot (pardon my English), which means I've been totally stupid.

'I was joking, Mum. I just meant it isn't the type of thing you ask, it's the type of thing people tell you.'

'Oh well, don't worry dear, people split up all the time, get jilted at the altar.' She waves a hand dramatically. 'Come on David, and don't forget to pick up that cigar.'

Chapter 22

There are three questions I have for Jake:

1. Is Laura really your ex?
2. What do you need a distraction from?
3. Where did you sleep last night?

If the answer to the first one is no, and the answer to the second one is a baby, then I am rather cross (given his insistence on honesty, which now appears to have been for his benefit only). In addition to the lies, I have been cuck-olded (I have always wanted to use this word) and he is a bastard because he kissed me, and was going to run me a hot bath.

If the answer to the first one is yes, but the answer to the second one is a baby (I can't avoid this word) then this could mean that a) He's a total bastard who has abandoned his child, and not the man I want to be with. Or b) It was a mutual separation and he is not to blame for dumping his child, but he still has a baby. Which is quite a biggie by anybody's standards. I am not ready to be a mother, or a substitute mother, or a sometimes weekend mother.

I admit that I may have got a little bit carried away and our two kisses and possible bath have turned into a full-on relationship, with a possibility of living together. This is totally unreasonable, but surely it is better to project long term, cover all eventualities? I had been thinking long term with Liam, but obviously had not thought it through properly at the beginning or I wouldn't have been in this mess. I am not going to let that happen again.

I am also, categorically, not cut out for being left holding the baby. Not even for an afternoon, let alone a weekend. A puppy I could cope with. Puppies do not have nappies, or have to be fed with bottles. They do not bawl until they've gone a funny colour, and they're cute.

I am sure I do have maternal instincts and hormones, but they are currently dormant, or buried very deep inside me. A bit like the Loch Ness monster, they will probably surface one day. But as yet are only rumours.

'Are you okay?'

'Fine.' Which means, no not really, I am totally confused. If I ask Jake the questions now then the outcome can only be bad. And it is too late, far too late to get a replacement boyfriend before The Big Day.

He will either turn out to be a complete bastard, or a man with responsibility for half a baby, *and* half a dog. Neither is good.

'Where did you go last night?' I can ask the third question, this is perfectly acceptable over the breakfast table, in company. This is also friendly interest, as I do have to try and remain friendly and not scream at him, and hopefully he will not say something that will cause a problem and definitely define him as a bastard.

By the time Jake got back with whisky and Harry yesterday, I was dressed and told him my parents were waiting for us as it was cocktail time. I then somehow ended up dragging Jess back to our room, putting the *Do Not Disturb* sign on the door, and telling her all about the kiss, the nearly hot bath, and showing her the picture.

I had to tell somebody.

'Oh crap balls.' Jess stared at my mobile, then hugged me. 'He looks a bit rough though, in fact almost haggard. My God, look.' She's peering more closely and has zoomed in on the picture so much that to be honest he's more blur than haggard. 'This doesn't look really recent.'

I don't want to look though.

'Maybe the baby thing was a shock?' Though anything that takes nine months to cook can't be that much of a shock, can it? 'And don't a lot of them keep you awake half the night?' Even angelic ones like this. I don't know why I'm excusing his less than perfect looks though.

'I suppose so.' Jess sounds doubtful. 'He doesn't exactly look his normal chilled self though, he looks awkward. Are you sure this is recent? I mean he doesn't look quite as fit, does he?'

I peer over her shoulder, he does look a little bit flabby

round the jowls, but I hadn't really been looking at his jowls before. Just the thing in his hands. It had been a shock. I'd reacted rather hastily and just rushed off for a cry, and to tell my parents. Well, that bit was an accident.

'I reckon this is older than a few days ago, maybe it was last year and they split and he's got his act together? Maybe this is nothing to be bothered about at all.' She doesn't sound convinced. 'Oh God, Sam, I can't believe it's anything, I mean he really seems into you.'

He does. Because he's acting, and I've been an idiot. 'Maybe.' It seems a bit far-fetched to me. 'But why didn't he tell me then?'

'I mean people often post old pics don't they? Or it comes up as like a memory from last year. And you did say you hadn't been going out that long, I mean it's not something that's easy to slip into a convo is it?'

'But it's a major thing!'

'But did you ask?'

'Well no.' And I think he's asked more questions than I have. I went for the basics, music, food preferences. Olives. He went for tattoos, things that made me laugh, turned me on...

'You've gone pink!'

'Sorry, just thinking. No, I didn't ask, but it's not the thing you normally need to, is it?' I sigh. I thought I knew him at least a little bit, and lying does seem out of character when he was so keen for us to be honest with each other.

Maybe Jess is right, and he had been trying to work out how to tell me. He's obviously been really hurt in the past, *betrayed* to use his own word, so maybe it was just hard for him to come out with it. He has been very cagey about his distractions and complications.

'Maybe he was going to tell you when you got home? You know, now it's more serious between you two.'

'True.' I think about that, while Jess goes back to staring at the photo.

'I'm not being nasty here, Sam, but when I found out about Liam it wasn't a total shock or anything, but Jake seems different. I just can't believe he...'

'He is an actor though.' A very good one it seems.

'Yeah, but ... well, at least you didn't find out after you'd shagged.' She hugs me. 'Oh I am sorry, Sam. I like him.' The last bit sounds a bit plaintive. 'And he really seems to like you too.'

I like him too. More fool me.

And I was sorry too. Did I have a sign saying 'stupid' on my forehead?

'It was only a kiss.' I shrug. The kind of kiss you can't actually imagine until it happens.

'You should ask him, and soon. You need to know. Maybe there's a perfectly reasonable explanation?'

She is right. 'I'll ask him before we go home.'

***

'I slept with Dan. We're getting quite close.' Jake is grinning. He looks cute, innocent. He's shredding my heart even though he's not my boyfriend. 'Everything okay with Jess? Did you have a good time?'

'Oh yes, yes, we just wanted a catch up.' Again.

'You really are close, you pair aren't you?'

'We are.' I can't help it, I stare at him challengingly, but lower my voice to a whisper. 'Or I wouldn't have gone to all this trouble, would I?'

'This trouble?'

I glance around, but nobody is looking our way. Not even Mum. 'You!' He blinks, looking a mix of cross and sad. But I am not going to fall for it. 'Are you ready?' I point at his full cup of coffee. 'It's our 4X4 off-road experience today.' It's a good job we got 'archery' out of the way before I discovered who he really was, or there might have been a nasty accident.

'Has something happened to upset you? You seem a bit out of sorts.'

Something happened? A bit out of sorts? Words fails me. But I am not going to explode. I am in control of this situation. I will choose the time and place to have a rant. When I hand his cheque over is probably the time, when I drop him off at his home and this is all over.

I will be cool and collected. Well, I'll try.

'We've been looking all over for you two, come on!' Jess bounces up to the table and saves the situation. I am teetering on the edge of throwing button mushrooms at him, or emptying the coffee dregs over his head.

I am totally relieved to find, when we assemble outside, that we are to have expert personal tuition from an instructor. This means I won't have to be trapped in a Landrover, thigh to thigh, with Jake.

It's much harder to pretend that Jake is my boyfriend now that we've crossed the no-touching barrier. In fact we very nearly ended up touching all over, which would have been wrong on so many levels.

Before, I knew where I stood. I was pretending to like him, and he was pretending to like me, and it was fine. Well, as fine as that kind of thing can be. We were like best mates with a shared secret. It was fun.

Now it's bloody awkward.

I'm not sure I can pretend I like him, now that I've realised I *more* than like him but that there's the whole baby issue. And if he *more* than liked me he would have told me about it, wouldn't he?

It's all a bloody mess.

Maybe I should just pretend we're splitting up. But if I do that then I'll end up spoiling Jess's big day, and that is something I just cannot let happen. I have come this far and need to finish what I've started.

So I need to pretend.

To act.

I am obviously not cut out for it though. He keeps giving me strange looks, so if he's doing that, God only knows what everybody else thinks.

I'm also worried because Mum is sending him disapproving looks (I wish I hadn't told her about the baby, that was a major mistake. I am double glad I didn't tell her the full story – that would have been disastrous).

The more time we can spend apart doing 'activities' the better. Soon it will all be over.

'Now aren't you the lucky girl?' Ruby has a very sarcastic edge to her tone and she's looking even more sour than normal.

'Sorry?'

'She's just jealous, aren't you Rubes?'

If looks could kill, Jess would be heading for an early grave. She ignores the look and grins good-naturedly. We all know that Ruby hates been called Rubes, we reserve it for special occasions.

'Jealous about what?' I seem to have missed something while I've been trying to work out how to handle this mess I've got myself into.

'You getting to share the whole experience with Jake!' Beth has sidled up. 'I wish Si was outdoorsy like Jake is. He's just so, so...'

'Macho?' Sally has joined us.

'No not macho, just, well, just such a real man.'

I want to blurt out that he's more real flirt than real man, that he has abandoned his newborn baby, and stuck with the dog instead. But I don't. It might all come out if I start.

'What experience?' I hiss in Jess's ear instead. 'I'm trying to avoid whole experiences right now.'

'They're short of instructors, and as Jake has done it all before they said he can go with you.' She looks a bit apologetic, then leans in to whisper. 'But maybe it'll give you a chance to talk in private, you know, ask him about the B issue.'

'But he's not qualified, insured.' I look at her in desperation. There has to be a way to stop this.

'It will be fine, honey, trust me.' Somehow Jake has joined us unnoticed and has now draped his arm over my shoulder and is looking all 'real man' as Beth would put it. I had trusted him until now. More and more each day.

Ruby stalks off, Jess squeezes my arm and whispers in my ear. 'Maybe we've got this wrong?'

Beth and Sally scurry off to join their personal instructors, and I am left with mine.

'What have you got wrong?'

'Everything.' I march towards the Landrover which I assume must be ours. He raises an eyebrow and follows me. His long stride covering the ground in half the number of steps I need to take. I am so tempted, but I can't have it out with him yet.

'Are you sure there isn't something you need to tell me, Sam?' At least he's dropped the babe and honey.

'Positive.' I bang my door shut slightly too assertively. 'Is there something you need to tell *me*?' I regret the words as soon as they pop out of my mouth. What if he does tell me? What then? We will ruin the off-road experience day and not be talking to each other for the wedding day.

He doesn't. He shrugs. 'I don't think so. Is Liam the problem, has he upset you? I can talk to him if you—'

'Liam? Liam? Liam?' I've got louder with each exclamation, although crunching the vehicle into gear does make a bit of a noise, so I did have to shout. 'Why would Liam be a problem? I've completely forgotten about Liam. Liam was merely a hiccup in my life.'

'Good, well er, I'm glad.'

Glad, huh.

'The whole baby thing must have been a shock, but—' He stops short and flinches. I think I've just growled. Loudly.

'Babies you aren't expecting can be.' I say it between clenched teeth and wish he'd shut up. Throwing your personal tutor out of your off-road vehicle probably isn't allowed.

'It's not something I've done, is it?'

I stare ahead. Definitely something he's done. Lots of things.

There's a pregnant pause. I'm going to have to stop thinking of it as that. 'It wasn't the kiss that upset you was it? I mean, I thought...'

'And we all know what thought did.' He obviously doesn't because he looks puzzled. To be honest, I'm not totally sure myself. It's something my aunt used to say.

'Don't you mean curiosity?'

'No I don't!'

'Oh, so ... well, I'm sorry. But you did seem to enjoy it.'

'You caught me unawares. Where do you want me to drive?'

'Oh. So you didn't like it?'

'I didn't say that. Through this gate?'

'Look baby...' He really is doing his best to wind me up.

'Don't call me baby.'

'Oh come on, Sam, you know you can talk to me about anything. I thought we said we'd be honest with each other.'

I twist the steering wheel slightly more violently than I should and put my foot down hard so that we bounce through the gateway in a way that makes me grab the steering wheel tighter and makes him grab the door handle. I think my ribs have kind of concertinaed together. I shouldn't have done that.

I could push it, I could ask. This is the ideal time. I have two unanswered questions. I know the answer to the second one, the thing he needs a distraction from is his baby. Although why is anybody's guess. And I shouldn't ask the first one. The ex one. 'Laura isn't really your ex, is she?' I can't help it. I had to ask. I can't help looking at him either.

He looks shocked. Poleaxed, I think, is the term. His jaw has dropped. He wasn't expecting me to ask any more than I was.

'Yes.' His jaw has tightened in an attractive action-man kind of way. 'She is. Why do you say that?' His features soften slightly and he gives me that look that he gave me before he said he needed to kiss me. The meltingly gorgeous look which I know I have to steel myself against. 'It's totally over. I promise. Look if it's the whole Harry thing that bothers you...' His voice is soft and he's reaching out as though he might touch my face any minute now.

'It is *not* the Harry thing.' I might have shouted. That stops him in his tracks a bit. So now I could ask about the baby. I have the perfect lead in. But is it worth it? He doesn't owe me anything, he never asked for all of this. I don't want it to blow up, not now when the wedding is so close. I am obviously a hopeless judge of men, and liars. But I can survive. I can do this. That is my new mantra, this is what Jake told me to practise. I can do it.

'Why didn't you tell me you had a baby?'

'A baby?' He makes a funny spluttering noise. 'What makes you think I've got a baby?

'A photo! Look, I know this is just business for you, and you don't want to get involved with me.' He goes to interrupt so I glare and hold up a hand to stop him; I don't want the whole 'no relationship' spiel because it will hurt. 'But we said we'd be honest with each other.'

'I have been honest.' He looks a bit cross. 'I haven't got a clue what you're talking about, and believe me if I had a baby you'd think I'd have ... watch out, you're going to hit—'

It all happens so quickly. He lunges for the steering wheel just as I swing back to study the track ahead, and swerve at the same time, hoping I'm going the right way and am not about to kill or maim any innocent little Bambis.

There's a crunch, a lurch and a bang.

Then silence.

'Shit, what the hell? Are you okay?' He is rubbing his forehead, and looks a bit pale.

I nod. I can't speak, I am winded.

'Bloody hell.' He loosens his seatbelt and makes a 'phew' noise.

'Where is it? What was it? Was I going to hit a deer, or rabbit or something? I haven't hit it, have I?' I look round wildly, but there's no livestock in sight. 'I didn't have a chance to see it, I just swerved.' To be honest, the swerve just kind of happened because when I swung back to face the front I was gripping the steering wheel so hard I took it with me, and it didn't help that he grabbed out as well.

He is frowning and looking blank.

'You shouted that I was going to hit—'

The frown has gone, and he has started to laugh. He doubles up, laughing so hard that his eyes water and he bangs his hands on the dashboard. 'I just thought you were going to go to hit that rut. A rut!'

'A rut! You shouted because of a rut?'

'It was a big rut, and I was getting exasperated.'

'Well, there's no need to laugh at me.' I fold my arms in a huff, but can't completely stop the smile. That's one of the most annoying things about being with him; even though I'm mad at him, and he's misled me, and he's now laughing at me, I like him. He's funny. He cheers me up.

Makes me happy. And it won't do. 'Are you sure you're being honest?'

He wipes his eyes with the back of his forearm. There's a loud hiss and smoke.

'Shit, this isn't going to go up in flames, is it?'

'It's only steam.' He has stopped grinning. 'You'd better turn the engine off though, and I'll phone Dan and get somebody to rescue us.' He shakes his head. 'You are funny.'

I'm not trying to be funny, but he's clearly highly amused. I fish my mobile out of my pocket so that I don't have to look at him, and end up liking him again.

He's finished calling the cavalry. 'Sam, I have been honest, I don't have a baby, but...'

'Has Laura got a baby?'

There's an incredibly long pause and he ruffles his fingers through his hair. 'Yes, Laura's got a daughter, and I do love her like my own.' He stares at me and looks incredibly sad. Haunted. 'Or I did. But she's not mine. Okay? I'll explain later, not here. It's complicated. Can you trust me on this one? Please?'

I blink and nod.

'That baby is partly why I agreed to come here, agreed to your mad plan.' There's a slight twist to his mouth, the faintest trace of his normal humour. 'And why I needed a distraction.' He touches my cheek very briefly. 'But it's why I really can't...'

I put my finger on his lips. I don't want to hear him say

that it's why this has always just been about business. Why in a few days' time he'll walk away without a backward glance. Without me.

'I get it.' I'd like to show him the photo, ask more. But I can't. There will be time later. The right time, the right place.

I tap my pin code into my phone.

'What are you doing now?' Jake sounds tired.

'It's your fault we're in this ditch.' I try and smile, to lighten the mood.

'I don't think that's—'

'You did grab the steering wheel when it was only a rut.' And if I hadn't thought he had a baby, and we hadn't been having the conversation, then I wouldn't have swerved the way I did. I would have been concentrating on what I was doing, my driving. But I'm not going to say that, it wouldn't be fair. 'I thought they called these off-roaders? It's not very good off the road, is it?'

'You ran into a ditch, and a tree. Only a tank would cope with those.'

Which reminds me about Tank. 'I'm writing a list, while we're waiting to be rescued.' I need something to do, so I don't end up looking at him, wishing that things were different, and he hadn't been betrayed, and he did want a relationship. With me.

He tries to peer over, but I turn around so he can't see.

The Wedding Date

Things I need to do when I get home:

1. Adopt a dog (but not Tank).
2. Avoid men like the plague. I don't need one in my life.
3. Come up with a plan for my thirties.

I am going to be strong and independent in my thirties. I will be at my peak so I really shouldn't waste another second. I will plan out a new career and buy my own Ferrari and date guys like Appletini Callum.

I'm not quite sure what career I am going to pursue, but age is no longer a limiting factor. I have life experience and that counts for a lot. Look at the candidates on *The Apprentice* – some of them are positively ancient. Way older than thirty.

I am still thinking about my travel options, but I might even take up dog sitting, or walking, or grooming and settle for job satisfaction and fun. Although I might have to set a size limit – I don't want dogs like Tank, I want dogs like Harry. Or handbag ones that I can carry if I need to pop into a shop.

'You're biting your lip.'

'Shh. I'm thinking.'

'It's cute.'

I stop biting my lip and frown at him. I don't want him to call me cute any more than I want him to call me Sammy. It will give me false hope. Words like that between us can cause all kinds of damage. Mental as well as the type that's been caused to our vehicle. I hope the insurance covers this type of thing, and Dan and Jess won't demand more money. My bank account can just about cope with Jake, it can't cope with vehicle repairs.

'You did call Dan?'

'He said we'd be rescued pronto, as soon as he's finished going round the course he'll come and pull us out.'

Chapter 23

I can't believe that it is already the wedding day. How did that happen? One moment we're casting flies, and the next it's nearly over. Which leaves me feeling all flat and empty, like you do when you get back home after a party. And we haven't even had the party yet.

I have survived, and I should be happy. But now I know I have been very silly and taken this whole thing far too seriously.

A few short weeks ago I was dreading coming here and seeing Liam and his huge girlfriend, and now I realise that was totally ridiculous. Liam never really loved me, and to be honest I'm not sure he loves anybody that much. Not even himself. And he was never *the one* for me. I do hope he manages to love his babies. Children deserve to be loved. Children deserve big fat sloppy kisses from aunties they hardly know, cuddles from their fathers, and parents who love them for who they are.

And I hope Jake gets to love Laura's baby as well. We haven't had the full conversation yet, but I do now know that he is totally serious on the 'no relationships' front, and I think by mentioning the baby I have opened a whole new kettle of fish, as my mother would say. I am determined that when we have the conversation, I will be adult and do my best to help him, and be a good friend.

I feel a bit sad really, I've got quite used to having Jake around. Soon I will be going home, back to my house for one, and to mad cocktail hours with Sarah.

I'm going to have to get a hobby, and maybe a dog.

'Everything okay?' He's got his hands in his pockets and is casually loitering in the doorway. It suits him. Everything suits him, goddammit.

'Splendid! Last day!' I say it brightly, in the kind of way Jess does. It is not Jake's fault that I've become rather attached to him. That I have been totally stupid and thought that he was enjoying kissing me as much as I enjoyed kissing him, when all along he was just doing a job very professionally. Very thoroughly. Well, to be honest I suspect he did enjoy it a bit, but I am glad we didn't sleep together, as I think that would have made walking away even harder.

'Sure?' He's got an eyebrow quirked in that cute way of his, but I am going to ignore it. I am going to be professional, and enjoy my best friend's wedding. I am not going to get all silly and emotional. Well, I might for the actual wedding bit, but not for the Jake bit.

'Oh yes – and your money's over there by the way.

Wouldn't like to forget it!' This excited-voice lark is bloody hard work, I'll be exhausted before we even get to the altar.

I wrote the cheque out to him this morning while he was out with Harry, and I wrote a very polite note, on the posh hotel notepaper, thanking him for his services and wishing him well in what had to be a sparkling career as an actor. I can do professional. I even added that if he ever needed a reference, I'd be glad to provide one. And that he should consider me a friend if he ever needed somebody to talk to.

'There's no hurry is there?' He doesn't sound like he's in any kind of hurry at all.

'We'll be off first thing, don't want to waste time.' I point at my suitcase, which I have already started cramming things into. 'Might want to pack now, be prepared and all that! Don't want to be doing it with a hangover, do we?' I'm babbling, I know I am, to avoid having to have any kind of sensible discussion.

Talking of which, do I mention the baby again before we leave, or in the car? Or when I drop him off? Or not at all? If I mention it before we set off, and there's an atmosphere, it will be terrible driving all the way home playing loud music to try and make us feel happier.

He takes a step towards me and I panic and grab his kilt from where it's hanging on the back of the door, then thrust it at him. 'Better put your skirt on.' If he touches me now then my professional persona will crumble, along with my dignity.

'I'm leaving the skirts to the gorgeous girls today.'

'Ah, right.' He's doing that melting-eye thing that is designed to make girls go weak at the knees. I am going to resist though. Today is our last day together, tomorrow we will be heading home and this will all be over.

'I'm going with the boring suit look.'

It takes him all of two seconds and he's back, before I've even finished packing my underwear, and he doesn't look boring at all. He looks incredible. There's a lump in my throat that shouldn't be there, and a very horrible burning at the back of my eyes. I swallow and blink. He doesn't deserve to look this good, life just isn't fair sometimes.

'We need to talk, Sam.' He puts a hand out as though he's going to touch my arm.

That's my line. Not his. 'Do we?' I've just realised I've packed absolutely everything, and won't have any clothes for the morning. So I start to unpack, and ignore him. 'I need to go and have my make-up sorted, and my hair, and...'

He sighs. 'I'll see you downstairs then, in a bit? But be warned, I'm not going to let this drop.' There's a dangerous glint in his eye.

We have had a morning of hair straightening, followed by hair curling and twirling and pinning, and 'natural make-up' that has taken ages and more make-up than I actually own. Then we got dressed, with the help of my mum who was no help at all. Her constant cries of 'oh my goodness,

I need my reading glasses,' as she tried to thread the ribbon through the tiny loops of satin just made Sally giggle, which then made us all laugh, which is no help at all when you're trying to hold your stomach taut in order to be laced in as snugly as possible so that you have a waist.

By the time we were all tied in, we were thirsty from all the laughing and drank the glasses of bubbly that Juliet brought over rather too quickly, so we were all quite giddy.

I have to admit that I was actually chuffed when I lined up in front of the mirror with a grinning Beth and smiling Sally. My dress fitted perfectly. We all looked happy. Mum insisted on dragging Dad back into the room so that he could take a photograph.

Sally slotted her hands rounds our waists and pulled us in closer. 'It's great to be together again, isn't it?'

'It is.' It really was. I need to add another item to the list I made on the Landrover experience day. I need to make sure I find time to meet up with my friends more often. Even if we do all have very different, very busy lives these days, in different parts of the country, there are some people you should make time for.

In the background we could see grumpy Ruby who had a scowl on her face. She only agreed to be in the photo under duress, and Dad took another one without her in case she'd ruined the first one.

I don't think she's the female bonding type. She's also not the shooting or fishing type. I did feel slightly sorry for her actually.

'I'll be so glad to get out of this place, God knows why I thought there'd be any talent here.'

Only very slightly sorry. I know for a fact that she's made a move on Jake, plus was cuddling up to Liam until Stella made her presence felt, and according to Beth she gained rather more personal expert tuition than was in the contract on the Landrover experience day.

'I reckon we're ready to face the world, girls.' We high fived each other. It was time to head off to the church. We were going by car; Jess had a horse and carriage, and I couldn't wait to see her when she got there. I was also rather relieved that the carriage wasn't big enough for bridesmaids.

'You look amazing.' Jake is the first person I see when I get out of the car with Sally, Beth and Ruby. He is standing outside the little chapel in the estate grounds. The soft sunshine mellows the old stone, lending it a gentle glow, softening its edges and Jake looks like he was born to live in a place like this. It could almost be a film set, it is so perfect, so romantic.

I swallow down my thoughts and try and talk normally. 'You look quite nice yourself.'

He lifts my hand and kisses my knuckles, which sends a little shiver through my body. I shouldn't let things like this happen, but I am determined to enjoy today. I want to make the most of the last day of this amazing week, before I return to real life. Today I am going to ignore the disappointments because it is a day that deserves to be perfect.

'Oh God, do you have to?' Ruby is staring at us and rolling her eyes again. 'Can't we just get in there and get this over with?'

'We're waiting for your sister, the bride, remember?' Sally laughs. 'You're such a misery Ruby, lighten up.'

Ruby doesn't lighten up. She folds her arms, leans against the wall and looks very un-bridesmaid-like. 'Whatever.'

I reclaim my hand from Jake and try to ignore the knowing look Beth is shooting my way. She's now wiggling her ring finger and winking, which is beyond embarrassing. I am never going to lie to my friends again.

And then we all look up at the sound of the clip clop of hooves.

A small carriage appears round the corner, the sun glinting off the polished harness of the two horses, their coats gleaming and their manes silky long, floating as they toss their heads. But I'm not really looking at them, I'm looking at Jess.

One of the horses whinnies as they clatter to a halt and I forget all the lies and everything. Nothing in the world matters except this amazing moment. My best friend is smiling nervously and she looks absolutely stunning. Just like a bride should do.

Her dad holds out a hand and she steps down from the small carriage in a very elegant manner, her silver-white satin dress shimmying around her slender body, the beautiful sweetheart neckline showing the slightest hint of cleavage, her hair cascading in beautiful curls over her bare shoulders.

'Oh wow, Jess, you look beautiful.' My eyes suddenly feel all damp and gushy, which is not good after all the time that was spent on my make-up.

'Will I do?' Her own eyes blur over and she giggles nervously as her dad gives her a hug.

'Gorgeous.' His voice is gruff and he looks like he might burst into tears himself, and he really isn't the type of man who cries.

'You'll more than do.'

'Oh, Sam.' She hugs me, and her dad pats me on the shoulder slightly too heartily, and we all cough and splutter a bit and try to act normally.

John recovers first. 'Can you go and check they're all set, love?'

'Sure. Wait here!' I hug Jess again, and Jake is already in the chapel, holding the heavy oak door open for me so that I can dash inside.

'Oh, bloody hell and damnation.' Everybody looks round and Jake pushes the door shut hard behind us, shooting me a glance and I know we're both thinking the same. We hope Jess didn't hear that.

Stella's voice rings out clearly, her words bouncing off the walls in a very inappropriate fashion. It's not exactly what you expect to hear in a church.

'This dress cost me a fucking fortune and it's ruined.' I scurry down the aisle and Stella is glaring at Liam as though it's his fault, and for a nanosecond I feel a bit sorry for him. 'My waters have frigging broken.'

That does cause a bit of a stir. All the frowns of disapproval (apart from the vicar's) disappear, the hissing and chatter start, and Liam flaps his arms, goes pale and looks like he's about to cry.

The organist hits an opening bar and for a moment I think he's about to play the babies in, then realise he's actually playing the bride in.

'Oh cripes, stop, stop! Jake, stop him! I've got to make sure Jess doesn't come in.' Jake emits the loudest wolf whistle I have ever heard, and all noise (including the organist) grinds to a halt. I gather up my dress and do my best to run back down the aisle, although this is no easy feat in four inch heels and a fishtail frock. I must look like a flopping mermaid as I run, but I think most people are too busy looking at Stella to notice. Imminent birth in a church pew has a kind of can't-look-away attraction doesn't it? Will she get stuck? Will it be blessed?

But I don't really care, I just want to make sure that Jess doesn't pick this precise moment to walk down the aisle. This wedding is hers, I want it to be perfect, and I don't want Liam and Stella's offspring to upstage her and make an unscheduled appearance.

'Stoppppppp!'

Jess is teetering on the edge of entry (better her than

Liam's babies), and hangs on to her dad's arm to stop herself toppling. She does stop though, and is looking at me like I've lost my marbles.

I'd only gone into the church to check they were ready, and to pass on a last minute message to Dan, which I hadn't done.

'Shit, forgot to tell Dan! Hang on, hang on. Don't move. Hang on one sec, just a sec, please? Don't ask. Just don't ask.' I wheel back round, and get tangled up in my fishtail, and stagger into Ruby's clutches. I say clutches, but she sidesteps so I end up clawing desperately at her arm. 'Wait there!'

'What the fuck?' Ruby is not amused.

'Stella's waters have broken.' I think I hiss it softly enough so Jess doesn't hear.

'My God, some people will do anything for attention, won't they?'

Which is rich coming from Ruby, she's probably storing it for future use.

'I don't think she did it on purpose.'

'Now then, little Sam, what's all—' John looks like he's about to head in and sort things out.

'Something has come out—' bad use of words '—no, cropped up. Hang on.' And I head back in, doing my sideways leg flipping thing to try and move faster.

Jake does a thumbs up, Mum has a mop bucket, and there's no sign of Stella. 'Just give us five minutes, darling, everything will be fine. I'm sure the stains will come out, although this floor isn't the cleanest I've seen, you'd think in the house of G—' Dad, bless him, grabs the mop off her, throws it in Jake's direction and steers her back to her seat.

'It's fine Ruth. A little bit of dirt never hurt anybody. Look at where baby Jesus was born.'

It's as Dad holds her at arm's length that I notice her hat. It is ginormous. And as she takes her seat, behind Juliet, I see why. This is obviously hat wars.

This is not a time to think about hats though. This is the time for action, and putting poor Jess out of her suspense. 'But where's...?' I look round wildly, there is no sign of Stella.

'She's through there.' Jake points. 'Where the vicar puts his frock on. Liam's rung for an ambulance, and I've got the ring in case they need a best man stand in.' He winks, and for a moment something all gooey and gorgeous flows between us, and it's almost like it was after the kiss. But without the carnal thoughts – this is a church after all. I love him and hate him so much. 'Go get the bride,' he says. 'Go!' I go, and Jake does another of his whistles, and gives the organist a wave.

I run with my flippy flappy dress and give them the thumbs up, and Jess smiles, and as I waddle down the aisle behind her I know it's going to be alright. Even though I am now hot and sweaty and feel like I am in a straitjacket. Everything is going to be okay. One way or another.

313

There is a hush as we enter the chapel. We all pause for a moment, and then as the music hits its stride, Jess slips her hand through the crook of John's arm and the 'ooh's and 'aah's say it all.

I want to cry. Jess has the biggest smile ever on her face when she reaches the front of the little chapel and turns to glance up at Dan. But when I sneak a look under my eyelashes at the stand-in best man, it's not Jake who meets my gaze. It is Liam.

He's pale and pasty, and staring at me like he's seen a ghost. For a moment I think something terrible must have happened to Stella, but Jake gives me the wink, and blows me a kiss, and he wouldn't do that if she was screaming her head off in there, would he?

The sun is out, and it's the perfect clear blue sky when we emerge from the dim, cool air of the chapel, and back into the bright summer day.

There's a hint of a breeze which catches the bottom of Jess's dress and tugs at her veil, which I'd call romantic but Mum would call annoying.

Now I know I wasn't keen on the kilt idea, but Dan, Liam and John are posing for photographs and they really look quite good. Well, apart from Liam's legs, I think those might need some tonal adjustment and airbrushing. Amazing what you can do with digital photos these days, isn't it?

'Sam, Sam, come on, you're in the next photo!' Jess is waving madly at me so I head over and take my place.

Jake gives me a little thumbs up and winks, and for a second, him being here feels less like a dirty secret, and more like something we're in together. Which we're not. I am paying for this, and I shouldn't forget it.

But I've never felt comradery with a man before. Not like this. No boyfriend has ever been totally in my corner.

He's a brilliant actor. In fact, from the standard of those kisses I'd say he's got a promising career ahead, though perhaps not in dog-handling.

Talking of which, there's a flash of black as Harry zooms out of the undergrowth, where's he's been for a potter, and he aims straight for us.

Everybody freezes. Wedding outfits and muddy paws don't mix and who knows what he's been walking in?

'Harry, Harry, come here!' Jake lunges forward, but he's not quick enough. With an excited bark, Harry hurtles through the air, his jaws closing around ... Liam's sporran.

There's a yelp (from Liam), so maybe he's sunk his teeth into more than the fluffy bits, and then he's got all four feet back on the ground and is tugging like his life depends on it. And growling as though he intends to kill it.

'Stop him, stop him.' Liam is bouncing from foot to foot, hanging on to the top end as he's tugged from the line-up towards the photographer, who grabs his tripod.

For a second there's a horrified silence, and then Jess starts to giggle. Her mother, Juliet, joins in, and soon everybody is falling about.

'What a little belter.' The photographer has given up on

shouting for order, and is clicking away with a grin on his face.

This really could turn out to be the best photo session ever. Harry is doing exactly what I'd like to do, but because he's so cute (and a dog) he's allowed. If I did it I'd be locked away.

'Should I stop him?' Jake mouths at me.

Yes is of course the correct answer, but really?

And the trouble is, the more people laugh and shout, the more excited he gets.

Which escalates to a new high when the annoying whirr we'd been ignoring suddenly gets louder, and the breeze turns into a bit of a whirlwind that nearly leaves the bride garrotted by her own veil.

'It's a helicopter!' Trust Mum to state the obvious.

We all wait, open-mouthed as it gently plops down on the flat land in front of the castle.

Even Harry drops his trophy, his tongue lolling out.

'Oh my goodness, oh my goodness. Look!'

'We are looking, Mum.'

'No, look! Harry!'

'Oh God, what's that dog doing now?' Jake appears behind me, nearly knocking me off balance. He grabs me round the waist to save me from trampling over Harry, who is flat out in front of me.

'Not the dog.' Mum's got one hand on her hat and is gesticulating wildly with the other – any minute now she'll take off like a helicopter herself. 'There! Him!'

We all stare at the two men who are heading our way, ducking down like they do on the telly.

'It's, oh my goodness, it really is ... it's ... it's...' Mum is now clutching my arm and batting me in the face with her hat. She isn't often speechless; she doesn't usually have time to stutter, there are too many words that need saying.

'Holy crap.' Sally has her chin on my shoulder, and there's a note of awe.

'It's Prince Harry!' She and mum say it in unison, and before I can tell them not to be stupid we've all been elbowed out of the way.

'Where? Tell me!' It's Ruby and her pointy elbows, and they are proper pointy. Lethal weapons.

I wobble on my heels, and grab at the nearest thing, which is Sally and we nearly both go over. I can cope with heels, or fishtail, but not both at the same time. If this is what Ruby's like now, God knows what's going to happen when Jess throws her bouquet later. I am going to stand right at the back, out of harm's way.

Harry the dog rolls onto his back and groans. I don't blame him – as weddings go, this one is getting a bit out of hand.

'No it's not.'

'It is. He flies helicopters. And look at his hair!' I'm sure if you think somebody is royalty you're not supposed to point and scream 'look at his hair', Mum hasn't read the etiquette page.

'Mum, this is an air ambulance.'

But Mum is not to be stopped by mere facts. 'Maybe he's just visiting, he might have dropped in for a cup of tea.'

To be fair, the man does have a passing resemblance – well, a pretty close resemblance – to Prince Harry, but I'm pretty sure he wouldn't have given up the afternoon to cart a woman in labour off to hospital, and what are the chances of a random helicopter landing in the middle of the wedding photos?

'All these castle owners know each other, you know, these lords, and earls and whatnot, and he does own a castle.' She says it like it's an enthusiasts' club – *oh, all these Volkswagen owners know each other.*

A sudden thought hits her and she clutches even harder. 'You could marry him!' She seems to have declared an amnesty on the Jake front, and has not mentioned the baby, but she is obviously keeping her options open.

'I thought she had Jake?' Ruby says drily, but everybody ignores her.

'I think I'm a bit late, Harry's already taken, isn't he?'

'And he's the last one.' Mum uses exactly the same tone of voice she'd use to describe the last Rolo in the packet. 'What a shame.'

Damn, that's our chance of becoming members of the royal family scuppered.

Mum soon recovers from the loss, and brightens up. 'I wonder if Meghan is with him?'

'Not unless she's carrying the other end of the stretcher.'

Sally giggles, and Ruby snorts and stomps off to consider other options.

'She seems such a lovely girl. I bet Jake knows her, they might have acted together, you need to ask him. She's an actor as well.'

'I don't think he does know her.'

'Oh dear, what a shame. It would have been so exciting if she'd been here, we could have chatted about our roles.' For a second Mum looks disappointed again, then claps her hands. 'Oh, look at your naughty little dog!'

I'm not sure he's mine at all now, even though he felt very briefly like he was. I think I have lost all claim to ownership. But I still love him to bits. He must have taken advantage of the distraction and gone in for the kill. He now has Liam's sporran in his jaws and is holding it aloft like a trophy. There is no sign of Liam, who I think has dashed back inside to comfort the woman in labour. If he was that good a partner he shouldn't have abandoned her to be in the photos. I am well rid of him.

'Should we go and see how Stella is?'

My mother shakes her head. 'She told us to clear out in no uncertain terms when we helped her into the vestry. Very abrupt she was, if I was you I'd leave her to it. Steer well clear. I think she must be ... what do they call it ... vajazzled or something, to have led Liam astray like that.'

'Mum!'

'Well, the rest of her isn't that pretty, is it?' I'm quite shocked at the outburst, and I can see everybody else is, but we're all waiting to see what she says next. We can't help it.

'You do know what vajazzled means?'

'Of course I do dear. I wasn't born yesterday. Crystals for your crotch, it said in that magazine article I saw in the hairdresser's. I'm not sure it would suit me though dear.' From the look on Dad's face it wouldn't suit him either. 'I'm quite sensitive down there and if you start using super-glue you don't know where it will all end up, do you?'

'You don't.' Beth is giggling. 'I bet my Si would be inter-ested to find out though. Maybe that's what I need to do, get down to the arts and crafts place and buy some sparkles. He might listen to me then.'

'Oh, I'm sure it would prickle dear, and looking isn't listening, is it? There's enough foreign objects find their way round, without sticking them in unnatural places. I'd say it's a last resort for that girl.' Personally I'd say it is something Mother has made up, though I'm not 100 per cent sure on that. 'And she has a potty mouth and a big bottom, if you ask me. Right, now, what was the question?'

'Shall I go and check on her?' I wish I hadn't asked in the first place.

'Definitely not. I think that naughty Ruby has sneaked off to make sure it isn't Prince Harry, so it will serve her right if that woman gives her what for. Come on now, dear, I think they want more photographs of you and that lovely Jake.' She pats my hand. 'You might think I'm a daft old bat, darling, and I know parents don't know a thing, but I really do think you should clear the air with him. Such a nice boy. Maybe you've got the wrong end of the rod.'

'Stick.'

'Whatever you say, darling. But you should ask. I mean, I'm not saying all men are like your father but he's done the oddest things, complete misunderstandings they were, like the time I caught him in a clinch with his PA at the office party. We'd only been dating a few months, we had, and he always was a favourite with the ladies.' This is not how I have ever seen my kind, slightly dotty but always patient father, and I'm not sure I want to. 'He said he'd thought she needed to chat about her shorthand, but instead she'd grabbed hold of his hand and clamped it over her breast. Now I'm not saying he didn't enjoy it a little bit, we were younger than you are now, and he is a man, but I like to think he was more stupid than anything. I mean men can be quite naïve, you know, about the signals they're giving off. Some women who are desperate to get a man can do things that aren't really playing the game.' She fixes me with a look of determination I don't often see on her face; in fact, I think the last time I saw it was the day of my maths GSCE. 'But sometimes it's worth seeing past the silly stuff isn't it, looking at the man?'

I nod. What Stella did wasn't exactly playing the game, not the one of sisterhood and solidarity anyway. And Liam probably had been a bit stupid, and all the attention and neediness had fired something up in him he didn't know he had. His inner caveman. None of us knew he had that, and I think now he rather wished it had never escaped.

But Jake is different.

'Tomorrow, Mum. I don't want to spoil Jess's day.'

'That's a good girl.' She hugs me on impulse and nearly takes my eye out with something shiny that is sticking out of her hat. 'Now is my hat straight? Chop chop then, they're waiting.'

The helicopter is still sat on the grass, and there's no sign of Stella or Liam when the photographer announces he's satisfied, and we all head in for some more photographs in the grand entrance hall.

I now have two mantras in my head. *I can do it* and *don't fall for his charms*. The problem is, all this standing close business is playing havoc with my self-control. I'm not cut out for the acting lark. Every time he puts his arms round me, his fingers settle on my waist and I want to either lean in against him, or scream at him to stop it. And I can't do either.

But I can accidentally stand on his foot, and jiggle him with my elbows. It doesn't seem to be working though because he keeps getting closer, until I can feel his warmth on my ludicrously exposed shoulders and neck (whatever happened to bodices and being buttoned up to the chin?). My only other option is to take a 'to hell with it' view of this and throw myself at him. I am sure that if I was to use up some of my sexual frustration I'd feel much better.

Well, that's my theory.

Alternatively it could leave me feeling shit when he drives off tomorrow into the sunset, to go back to his relationship-free zone.

It would be weak to give in to his charms, but it would be strong to make the first move, wouldn't it? A strike for independent women everywhere. And who knows, maybe I could persuade him that he can learn to trust again.

I think I have realised that Liam was just a blip and that not all men are bastards. Jake has helped me do that. He has helped me realise I can wipe the slate clean and I am ready to move on. But something tells me that his hurt runs a bit deeper and is a bit more complicated.

All this thought about being a strong woman and taking control is making me feel rather randy though. I'm wishing I could just do it, and have one last fling for my own sexual satisfaction.

'Last one, all smile!'

There are smiles of relief all round, apart from mine. Jake has just squeezed my buttock and I rather think the expression on my face is not appropriate for a maid of honour.

Harry is guest of honour at the wedding breakfast. Personally, I wasn't convinced it was the best idea when Jess first mentioned it while we were posing for the photos, but I have changed my mind when we enter the reception hall for pre-dinner drinks.

Harry is looking very pleased with himself, and there are only a few traces of the sporran still stuck to his chin. He keeps smacking his lips together and rubbing his face along the floor – scooting along at high speed with his bum in the air – so I think there must be a bit stuck in his teeth, but he's very resourceful so I'm sure he will sort it out.

Jess managed to produce a little tartan bandana, which he's currently doing his best to pull over his head with his front paws, in between the attempts to get the fluff out of his molars. He's got his own bowl and food, and as luck would have it, Jess has given Harry Stella's seat and Jake has been given Liam's, so that the top table is still full.

Jess has even asked her mum to make sure his name is on the place setting.

We all heard the helicopter take off while we were posing for the final photograph, and there was a collective sigh of relief.

'You don't know where my sporran is, do you? It's rented and they'll charge me for it.' I really didn't expect to hear Liam's voice, surely he should be in the helicopter? But when I look up from my glass of bubbly it is definitely him. He sounds tetchy and he keeps glancing at Harry, and seems the tiniest bit nervous. His hands keep gravitating towards his groin, and he's got a nervous twitch, as though he's expecting an attack any moment.

Liam has never been keen on dogs, another of those pointers that I should have spotted earlier. A man who loves pets has to be far more trustworthy, if the pet loves him back of course.

'What the hell are you doing here?' I really cannot believe that Liam is so pathetic, and cruel that he's sent Stella off on her own. Though he is scared of flying. Milk Tray man, he is not. 'Shouldn't you be at the hospital?'

'Well...' He looks round and drops his voice so that I have to lean in a bit to hear. 'She's not actually gone.'

'She's not gone?' Unfortunately I forget to lower my own voice and I'm a bit shouty, so a few people look our way. But it was a shock. 'She's had the babies here?' I glance round, though to be honest I don't think Stella is going to come gliding down the fabulous staircase with a baby in each arm. She didn't seem that keen on joining in before she gave birth, and now she'll have stitches in unmentionable places and be leaking milk.

'No, not yet.' Liam's voice drags my mind away from my personal horror movie. He's looking a bit shifty. 'She's in our room. Resting.'

'But her waters broke.' I'm pretty sure that once that's happened there is no going back. You're on a countdown to the pain and pushing part.

'No. Her waters didn't break.'

'What?'

'Shh.' He does a frantic keep it down motion with his hand, but it's too late. Jake has heard.

'Everything okay, honey?' He nods at Liam. 'Surprised to see you here mate.'

'Fine.' I ignore the little shiver that brings goose bumps out on my arms as his warm fingertips land on my shoulder. 'Liam was just telling me that Stella's waters didn't break, and she's not had *their*—' it's a bit cruel, but I have to emphasise it '—babies, and she's not actually gone in the helicopter either.'

'With Prince Harry?' His eyes are twinkling.

'He was not Prince Harry.'

'How can you be sure?'

'Well, for one, Ruby would have got her mitts on him if it was, and two, Harry is far too busy these days.'

'You sound like you've got inside info?'

He's still looking amused. It's quite disconcerting, and makes it quite difficult to remember how much I hate him. Well, not hate him, but am trying not to like him.

I suddenly realise Liam is sidling off. 'But I saw her waters break!' Well, I saw a soggy mess, and heard her swearing about the state of her new frock. That stops him in his tracks. He sidles back so that he can talk in a whisper and still be heard. 'We all did.'

'Well, er, I'd given her a hot water bottle to help with her backache, and she brought it into church and she sat on it.' He looks genuinely embarrassed.

'Sat on it?'

'Hard.' He smacks his hands together, which makes me jump. 'Luckily it wasn't that hot, more kind of...'

'Body temperature?'

Liam nods. 'When we helped her move from the pew,

326

she owned up. She said, she was bored enough to fake her own fucking death if it would get her out of here.' He winces. 'And if she hears me say *Sam says* once more she won't be responsible for her actions. It was a bit late cos we'd already called the helicopter, and I think, well, don't tell Jess and Dan, but I think she thought even if her waters hadn't broken they'd still give her a lift out of here.'

'And?'

He shakes his head. 'They wouldn't. They said she's quite healthy, and the babies are fine, so she's in our room with a pile of magazines and afternoon tea.'

'Oh. Should I go and check she's okay?' I really don't want to.

'No!' Liam, who has been talking in hushed tones almost explodes. 'She might try and murder you or something. Oh God, why did I think bringing her here was a good idea?'

Why did he think shagging her was a good idea?

'She told me to piss off and enjoy myself with my stuck up friends.' He is very dejected. 'The sporran?'

I shake my head. 'Though to be fair, even if you do find it, the hire shop will probably still charge you. It's been through rather a harrowing experience I'd say.' I am trying to keep the smug smile out of my voice, but I think a little bit might be creeping through. 'I did see him dig a hole and bury it.' I'm digging my nails into my hand so I don't start to smirk, or worse, laugh. 'Then he pulled it out and shook it, er, clean, then he held it between his paws and started to try and shred it.' I suddenly realise I'm doing an impression and stop.

'Oh.'

'Ahh that's what you're after, is it? I might be able to help you there!' Jake smiles. He puts a hand into his pocket and starts to fish something out.

'Fabulo—' Liam brightens up, but then his voice tails off as with a dramatic flourish Jake holds the item in question up in the air at eye level. It dangles forlornly. What was once a proud manhood covering sporran, now looks more like a toupee.

'Fucking hell, is this a joke?'

'No joke.' How Jake keeps a straight face as he presses it into Liam's hand, I have no idea. He closes Liam's fingers over it. 'No need to thank me, catch you later mate.'

I make a dive for the ladies', fishtail swishing. If I turn back and see his poor little face it might create an emergency wetting-myself incident, and that would never do.

Chapter 24

There has been a disaster. Not on the working out how to go to the toilet in a very tight, fishtail dress. This is worse.

Ruby was in the washroom when I finally accomplished the task, and the smile she gave me wasn't exactly friendly.

'I can't wait to hear your speech. Going to tell us all about how you and lover boy met?'

Speech? Speech! Fuck. 'Oh no, no.' Where did that silly giggle come from? I feel sick. 'Just a few words about the bride and groom.' I've put the posh voice on that Mother uses, I find it works when I'm trying to avoid hysteria. 'You know.' I don't know if she does know, but I don't.

I hadn't forgotten. How could anybody forget something that important, something their best friend had asked them to do? How could anybody forget that they were going to deliver a speech to a large room full of family and friends?

Okay, I had forgotten. With the boyfriend thing, followed by the baby thing, I'd clean forgotten about writing my speech.

'Can't wait.'

Ruby's tone is dry. She knows.

'Haha, me neither.' Bugger. 'Must go!'

'I need a pen.'

'A pen?'

'And your brain.'

'Really?' Jake raises an eyebrow.

'I've got three minutes.' It might be more than three minutes, in fact I could spend all the meal writing it, but people will interrupt. I will be put under pressure when the dessert arrives and I know my time is imminent.

People will wonder why I've left it so late to write. People will think I don't care. Jess will think I don't care. I will leave a dark mark on an otherwise perfect day.

I have to write my speech before they all finish their bubbly and take their seats.

'A whole three minutes, hey? Maybe we should sit down.'

'Sit down. Yes.' Oh God, I can't even think straight, let alone write a speech. 'My hands are shaking, I won't be able to write.'

'I'll do the writing. Calm down.'

'I don't even know where we're sitting.'

'That bit is easy.' Jake slips his hand under my elbow. 'Trust me.'

I want to trust him, truly, but we're only halfway across the room and I know I can't do this. 'I can't do it, I just can't do it!' I can't breathe, my laces are too tight, I need smelling salts, and I'm having the type of hot flush you're not supposed to have until you're at least fifty. I need to get out of this dress, I need to lie down.

'Calm down.' Jake puts his hands on my shoulders to stop me dancing about. It kind of works, but not really. I'm still jittering. 'Can't do what?'

'The speech. Jess has asked me to do a speech after Liam does his, and I can't.'

'Why not?'

'It means standing up in front of everybody.' I've never been good at that type of thing.

'Stay in your seat then.'

'I haven't prepared, what am I going to say?'

'Why haven't you prepared? I could have helped you if you'd asked.'

'I forgot.' After I saw that picture of you and your offspring I clean forgot everything. But I can't say that, it would be mean.

'You forgot?'

'Well, er, at first I might not have been listening properly when Jess mentioned she wanted me to do one and I just said yes. Then when we got here she checked I would still do it.'

'And you said yes.'

'Definitely.' How could I say no? 'She wanted me to. She's my best friend.'

'Oh.'

'I can't, I really can't.' Why on earth did I say yes? Twice. 'I don't do public speaking.'

'Here.' He somehow magics up a paper bag and thrusts it towards me.

There is nothing in it, not even the smallest box of chocolates. He grins, and does that eyebrow lifting thing that I've got quite fond of.

'This really isn't the time to palm off your rubbish on me.'

'You got me.' He laughs, then goes serious. 'It's to help with breathing. Well-known technique to stop panic attacks.'

'And you've got it because?'

'Your dad said you'd panic.'

'He knew I had to do a speech?'

'No.' He grins. 'He just heard Ruby mention it a few minutes ago, before she headed off to ambush you, and he suggested you might need some moral support.'

'I can do this.' I close my eyes, wave my hands about, palms facing the floor like I've seen them do in the yoga class in the park near work, and wait for the zen calm that is supposed to descend. I am not bricking it, I am in control.

'You *can* do this.'

How can you feel empty and sick at the same time?

Jake drapes his arm over my shoulder and his fingertips hit my skin. Red Rum wouldn't have seen me for dust if I could make a run for it now.

'You'll be brilliant.' It isn't just that husky voice, it's his warm breath on my neck, the indecent tingle that follows the accidental boob brush of his arm. 'It isn't public speaking, it's just chatting to friends and family, people who love you.'

Liam had never made anything tingle, even after ten minutes of warming his hands up and preparing to attack. Though it was probably the time he spent preparing, that killed dead any chance. The closest he'd got to setting me on fire was when we were kids.

'What are you thinking about?'

'Liam giving me a Chinese burn.' Strange how your mind works when you are panicking, isn't it? I wonder if this is the type of thing I'd think about if I was faced with a man-eating tiger and certain death?

'Is that some kind of euphemism, or a strange pre-sex warm up routine?'

'It was the last time he made me tingly.'

'Oh.' He frowns and moves his arm. Okay, talking about tingles with your ex isn't normal behaviour, but as we've firmly established that Jake never was, and never will be, a proper boyfriend, it doesn't matter, does it?

'It hurt, so I stamped on his foot so hard his mum had to take him to A&E.'

'What kind of wuss goes to A&E?'

'We were only four at the time, so it was reasonable.'

He's lost his frown, and the hint of a twinkly is back in his eye, and I want to make it come back properly. I shouldn't. It's silly when all this is nearly over. But I like him.

'Sam, you make me all tingly.'

'Don't you dare! It's no wonder I'm confused, is it?'

'Sorry?'

Oh bugger, I said all that out loud. 'You have no right to say I make you tingle when you're about to leave me. Oh shit, they're all starting to come in. Give them more champagne or something! Help me!' I can sort out tingles later, right now it is the speech that matters. 'I'll tell her I can't do it. I have a sore throat.'

'You'll ace it.'

'I won't. I'm fat and ... and...'

'You're not fat Sam.'

'You have to say that, I'm paying you.'

'I don't *have* to say anything. I mean it, you're gorgeous.' He gives a frustrated sigh. 'Why do you think you're fat?'

'I'm being daft, aren't I?'

'Stage fright.' He smiles. 'We all get it at some time or other. Our whole life flashes before us.'

He's right. I've not even thought about being fat the last few days, whilst I've been with Jake. 'Even the podgy bits.'

'Especially the podgy bits.' He laughs. 'And the wetting yourself bits, and being chased out of the playground by all the girls. You're perfect now though. Do you think I'd have agreed to do this if you weren't?'

'You did it because I liked dogs. You said so.'

'No, I didn't. I said I wouldn't have done it if you hadn't.' He grabs me by the shoulders and propels me back into the washroom, which luckily Ruby has now left. 'Look!'

I look. He's standing behind me, staring into the mirror

with his gorgeous eyes. They're lovely, flecked with different colours. Mesmerising. He really does look good in a suit, not just a bit good, he looks movie star good. Which he is. I'm glad he ditched the kilt though, because even though he has got good legs, I prefer them in trousers.

'Did you really wet yourself?'

He mock-frowns at me. 'If you put that bit in your speech I will personally spank you.'

Which sounds quite tempting.

'Now, look at yourself woman, not me.' He gives me a little shake, still chuckling. Then he sobers, and his grip tightens slightly. His voice soft in my ear. 'You're sensational.'

I divert my gaze, so that I'm staring into my own eyes. They're very nicely made up, the make-up lady has done a perfect job, and the hairdresser has managed to banish every trace of frizz so that I look super sleek. Even after the dash around in the church, I still look fresh.

And to be honest, totally honest, I don't look wrong in this dress. It's pretty damned flattering – it's kind of holding in my stomach and propping up my boobs and telling me I've got a hint of a waist. I still look like I did at the start of the afternoon when I was with Beth and Sally.

'You're exactly the weight you are meant to be, and it suits you. It *is* you.'

'I can do this.'

'Totally. You don't even need to write anything down, do you? You can totally do it, Sam, all you have to do is talk a bit about what a wonderful friend she is, and that's easy.

Isn't it? You love her. You love her enough to go out and find a man to come with you, you love her enough to lie to her and your family.'

'Er, I might have told them a little bit.'

'Not them as well.' He shakes his head, but he's still smiling.

'I couldn't help it. It was your fault actually.'

'My fault?' The smile slips a bit.

'I'll tell you later.' I sigh and squeeze his hand. He's nice, I can't hate him. It's totally my fault that I misread the signs and thought that, because I'd fallen for him, the feeling was mutual. Why is life never straightforward, with fairy tale romantic endings? 'Come on. We need to find out where we're sitting.'

'Oh no. That's you, is it Samantha?' Jess's Aunt Annie points at my place name and looks very put out. 'What a disappointment.' And this is before I even start my speech. 'Why hasn't it got your full name on the card? It just says Sam.'

'Well, I don't know, I...'

'Hi, I'm Jake.'

Aunt Annie smiles and looks slightly appeased, but still not happy. 'How lovely.' She glares at me. I really don't know what I've done to upset her, I'm sure I've only met her a couple of times, and she hasn't been staying over at the castle so I couldn't have said anything untoward after several cocktails. 'I thought you were two gay men, Sam and Jake. What a let-down. Oh well, I suppose we'll just have to make the best of things. Gay couples tend to be so much more entertaining though. Sit down, sit down.'

'Oh, I'm so sorry.' Jake dazzles them with his best mega-watt smile, and treacle-smooth tones. 'But, we're on the top table now. Come on, Sam, Harry's waiting.'

Harry is. He's already sat in his seat, one napkin round his neck, the other in his mouth, and he's eyeing up the table decoration.

Jake smiles apologetically at Aunt Annie. 'Harry can always come and sit with you in the spare seat?'

'Oh yes, yes. He'll definitely be entertaining. Harry's a hoot!' I nod vigorously. This will get me in Annie's good books (I don't like being disliked) – I mean, shove a cute dog in any woman's face and she feels instantly better, doesn't she?

'Harry? Goodness me, I didn't realise he was still here. Now he *will* be entertaining.' She's gone bright pink and is fanning herself.

'Oh yes, he's still here.' I look at Jake, perplexed at quite how enthusiastic Annie is.

Before anybody can say another word, Jake whistles. With an excited bark, Harry leaps off the chair and bounces our way, dodging table legs as he goes. There's a piercing shriek, then Annie is off, heading in the opposite direction at a speed you just couldn't imagine her capable of, with the dog in hot pursuit.

Which wasn't what I expected at all.

Annie's husband, Albert, who has been watching the

proceedings silently, suddenly gives a broad, toothy grin and winks. 'I think she thought you meant Prince Harry, love, not Harry the dog!' He chuckles. 'Not seen her move that fast for years. Not for you to know she's allergic, is it?' He nods. 'I'll be off to get her back then. Shame you're not gay and there's no prince here though, would have given her something to tell the neighbours about when we get home.'

Chapter 25

'Dance with me.' Liam is drunk. Very drunk. He has to be, or else he wouldn't be barging in when I'm standing next to Jake, and he wouldn't be within a million miles of the dancefloor.

The wedding breakfast is over, and Jake was right – my impromptu speech went down incredibly well. Jess rushed over and kissed me when I finished, and John smothered me, and Mum shouted out 'that's my daughter' several times, and I got quite an ovation.

And now, after my exhilaration high, I'm feeling a little bit apart from all the laughter. I'm an observer, acutely aware that when the clock strikes midnight (well, maybe a bit later) the man standing behind me will disappear and all this will be over.

I don't need my very drunk ex interrupting the last few magical moments. I just want to stand here quietly, and think about what comes next.

'Oh come on, Samantha.'

'Shouldn't you be with Stella?'

He ignores me. 'Look, I know you don't love me anymore. But you can dance with me, can't you?' He sways closer, and I try and sway further away. Which is tricky when I'm slap bang up against Jake. 'For old times' sake.'

He's right. I don't love him, but it's more than that. I just don't like him at all. It's as though something inside me has flipped and he's a stranger. There's nothing left. I don't even want his hands touching me, it would feel, well, weird. He also has beer-breath. My best escape plan might be to duck down so that he's left face to face with Jake.

'Liam, we never danced, you never would.'

'Rubbish, I'm an ace dancer.'

'When you were eleven, at the school disco maybe.' He wasn't that good then either. He was one of those helicopter dancers that throw limbs out in all directions and sends people scurrying for cover.

'Sammy, I can't do this, you've got to help me.'

'Don't call me Sammy.' He must be even more drunk than I thought.

'I'm not ready to be a dad, Sammy.' He's said it again. 'I'm immature. You said so, Stella says so, everybody says so.'

'Well, everybody is bloody right, Liam.' The whole Sammy thing has wound me up, along with the fact that he keeps trying to dodge his responsibilities and isn't where he should be – with Stella. I am also cross that he's forced me up against Jake, who I have been desperately avoiding bodily contact with for self-preservation reasons, and who is also dodging the whole baby issue. It's been a long week and soon I will be free to go back to my normal life, but before I go I am determined to speak my mind. To both of them. 'You are an idiot, Liam, and it has absolutely nothing to do with me. I don't have to dance with you, and I don't have to help you. Those babies of yours are probably going to be born with more of a conscience and more grown-up than you are. They didn't ask to be born, did they? You had a choice but they haven't.' I realise I'm poking him in the chest. 'They're landed with you whether they want you or not. If you didn't want them you should have kept your twinky-winky in your trousers, shouldn't you?'

Liam lurches back a step, and Jake laughs.

'Twinky-winky? Who calls it that?'

'You don't like me, do you?' Liam has a glazed expression and looks like he might burst into tears any second.

'Not much Liam, not right now. You should be with Stella, helping her, not feeling sorry for yourself down here.'

'She doesn't want to dance with you, mate. Go upstairs and look after your wife.' Jake pauses, and puts a territorial arm round my waist.

'She's not his wife.' I hiss sideways, but he ignores me.

'Sammy is dancing with me, aren't you?' I am going to kill Jake, or change my name by deed poll to something you can't abbreviate.

'You know what? I don't want to dance with either of you.' I spin free, and am pleasantly surprised that I don't fall over, just wobble – it's a bit of a dodgy manoeuvre in these shoes after so much wine. 'I think it's time you both took a good long look at yourselves.' I fold my arms, lift my chin (because I really can do this), and give them both a stern look.

Liam staggers back, Jake gives me his puzzled spaniel look, and I glide off imperiously. I am in control. I have this. Well, I do for the first three steps, then I collide with Jess. Who wraps me in a drunken bear hug.

'You tell them, Sam. God, I am so proud of you, you are totes amazing, girl.'

I should like being amazing, but all I want to do is cry.

'Oh buggering hell, Jess, why I can't I just be normal?'

'You're far too special to be normal, Sam, that's why I love you so much.' She hugs me harder, and a couple of tears pop out of my eyes. 'What's the matter?'

She's dragged me to the side of the room where it's quiet, and I'm feeling all emotional, and this week has all been so good, and funny, and mixed up, and all of a sudden I have to let it out.

'It's nearly all over with Jake.' I want to cry, in fact I think I am. 'It'll end tomorrow.'

'Oh my God, you can't say that!' She puts her hand over her open mouth. 'He is mad about you. He loves you.'

'He doesn't love me. Oh Jess, I've been such an idiot, I've fallen for him and it's all a total sham, and I don't want to go home and it all to end.'

'It isn't a sham, Sam, don't say that.'

'He's not mad about me.' Though he might be mad at

me, after this. But it doesn't matter, we're going home tomorrow, so it doesn't matter if Jess knows.

'Is this about the baby?'

'No.' I blink away the wetness in my eyes, and a big fat blobby tear plops onto the front of my dress. 'It's not his baby.'

Jess frowns. 'So, he, you...'

'Jess.' Oh God, this is difficult. So I squeeze her tighter and close my eyes. 'I'm paying him.' There is silence. No shriek. I count to ten. Still no sound. I open one eye.

Jess is staring at me. I've never seen her speechless before. This is a first.

'You're paying him for what?'

'To be my boyfriend.'

'What?'

'Please don't tell anybody!' I don't need total humiliation. 'Not even Dan.' It's probably very un-best-friend-like demanding somebody lie to the man they've just married. But if she tells Dan, he might tell Liam, who'll tell Stella, who will tell everybody who fills their car with petrol when she gets home. Before you know it, Jeremy Kyle will be inviting us over. I gulp down the lump in my throat. 'I couldn't find a real boyfriend in time, and so I found Jake. Please don't tell anybody, not until we've gone in the morning. Please? Cross your heart...'

'And hope to die. I promise. But...' She lets go of me. 'Oh Sam, you don't have to end it now, that's not all an act. I know it isn't. Just look at him.'

I look. He's watching us from the other side of the room, and for once I haven't got a clue what he's thinking. I can't read the expression on his face at all.

'I think I need some fresh air.' I pull away from my best friend.

'Sam?'

'I'm fine, go and dance with Dan, he's waiting for you.'

'But...'

'Go.' I hug her back properly. 'This has been the best wedding ever, Jess.'

'It has, hasn't it?' She's grinning, flashing glances at her gorgeous husband. 'You will talk to Jake though, won't you Sam? I'm sure he...'

'I...'

'You need to. For me?'

'I know I need to. For me, actually. This isn't all about you, you know!' We laugh together, then she leans in close and whispers in my ear. 'He likes you.'

'I liked him.'

Harry thinks I am amazing too. His tail is wagging so hard when we get outside, I'm a bit worried he might fall over.

He stops wagging and is sick.

'That's what comes from eating too much food!'

He bounces off, obviously feeling much better. It's a shame I can't solve my own problems that easily.

It's a beautiful evening, a massive sky that stretches on forever, and the air has that slight crisp edge that comes in with the dusk. I've always liked that cusp between night and day, that sense that everything is suspended for just a moment. That magical time when it's all about promises and what could be, rather than what has been and what went wrong. Even the air is expectant, and the sky shimmers with the colours of change and new beginnings.

There's a coolness to the air that's refreshing, and it stamps on the claustrophobic feeling that's been building inside me. Out here I'm free. I can do anything, be anybody. Drop the act.

There's a splash and I'm a bit surprised to realise that I've wandered down to the loch, and Harry is jumping about in the shallows, pouncing on imaginary prey.

I kick off my heels, and let my toes curl into the soft damp earth at the edge of the loch. I could walk in now, into this cold water. I hate water, hate swimming, but maybe right now that is what I should do. Prove to myself that I really can do anything.

Anything. Be on my own. Wait until *the one* appears if he ever does. One that can make me tingle inappropriately, make me laugh, and hasn't got a brood of children hidden away somewhere.

Harry barks with excitement, then splashes in the shallow water at the edge.

Harry can do it, I can do it. Here, at this part, it shelves quite steeply. A few steps and I will be in up to my thighs. I can swim, Dad made sure of that. I've just chosen not to. Until now.

I take a step. Good God, it's fugging (as Sarah says when we're in work) freezing and I'm only in up to my ankle bones. Maybe the whole water and swimming thing should be put off until I'm somewhere hot and sunny, maybe Scotland demands a different kind of challenge. I need to face a different fear. Like drinking too much whisky.

'Stop! What the hell...'

I'm grabbed from behind, Harry starts to bark, I lash out (like you do) and twist round. It's Jake, and I might possibly have kneed him in the groin which could account for him stopping mid-sentence. And we're staggering backwards off balance.

Doesn't he know I've changed my mind? I don't want to go in the water, and I'll ruin this dress, and...

He's got a proper grip on me now, and we seem to have stabilised.

And before I can object he's kissing me. Gently.

'Stop.' It's bloody hard, but I can't let him do this. I just can't, it's taking the whole pretence too far and I can't let myself be used or lied to. I push as hard as I can against his chest and he stops. And we wobble. Mainly, I think, because I have lost all feeling in my feet, I no longer feel like I have feet. They are blocks of ice. 'Move, quick.' This time I pound on his chest, and he does move, so that we're back standing safely on the edge of the water rather than in it. I lift up a foot, prod it with my finger. It is definitely still there, just numb.

'Sam, what's up?'

'Cold feet!'

'I don't mean that, you know I don't. Sam, look at me.' He puts a finger under my chin so that I don't have much choice. 'I don't understand what's gone wrong, I thought...'

He doesn't say what he thought. But I don't want him to. I don't want to hear. I forget about my feet, it's hard to think of anything but him when he's staring into my eyes like that.

'You've been avoiding me.'

Full marks. But if I didn't I might cry.

'Did I cock up in some way?'

Only in a minor *you snogged me and now it's all over* kind of way. 'It's not you, it's me.' Gawd, can't I come up with something more original than that? But it's true.

'Sam, for God's sake, talk to me. Please.'

I've never been good when people say please. But maybe now is the right time. I can't spoil anything now, why wait until tomorrow? Deep breath time.

Before we say goodbye forever, I'd like to know why this would never work, why he'll not even give it a chance, but I don't really know where to start. 'You don't have to act anymore, Jake. It's nearly over.' I shrug. 'You can just go back to normal life tomorrow and forget all this.'

'I'm not acting, Sam. This is me being me. And I'll never forget all this, it's been amazing. And so have you.'

'You've been brilliant, I must say.' I put my posh voice on, and sound like Mum, because otherwise I might cry.

'Totally convinced even me.' I blink to keep the dratted tears away.

'Sam...' He looks uncomfortable, and is messing his hair up. 'We agreed what we were doing at the start. I thought we understood, that you were happy...'

'I was happy, but I'm not now, and I don't know if you've lied to me, or—'

'I have never lied to you!'

I know the baby isn't what I really want to talk about, but it strikes me that it's the thing that has hurt Jake most. This is why he needed a distraction. If I find out why, then maybe I find out if there will ever be the smallest inkling of hope that we could see each other again. 'Well...' I fumble about trying to unlock my phone. 'What's this then?' I'm still fumbling, trying to find the message from Sarah. As confrontations go it's losing impact a bit. 'This!'

I thrust the phone forward so forcibly he has to lean back so that his nose doesn't get squashed.

'Oh.' He takes the phone out of my hand and even though I'm cross I can see that his fingers are trembling, and his voice has an unfamiliar edge to it. He's trembling nearly as much as I am.

He touches the picture with the tip of his finger as though he can't help himself, and the tears well up in my eyes but I don't know why. 'Yes, that's Laura's baby. This is the first time I've seen this picture though.' There's a crack in his voice which brings a lump to my throat and I almost wish I hadn't said anything. Almost.

He thrusts the phone back in my direction, face down, closes his eyes briefly, then runs his fingers through his hair again and looks up, over the top of my head. Not meeting my eye. He's gone pale.

'What do you mean the first time? It's you! It's your...'

'It is me.' He's ignoring the 'your' bit. 'But I didn't realise anybody had taken a photo, let alone passed it round. Where did you get this?'

'Facebook.' I feel a bit guilty saying it, like I've been snooping.

'Oh God, I am such an idiot, I should have known she was up to something. Sorry, it was just a shock, seeing...' He takes a deep breath then seems to refocus. On me. 'Hang on, you still think this is *my* baby, don't you?' He's staring at me, and it isn't in a nice way. The short laugh isn't particularly jolly either. 'I thought I explained...'

'No, not really.' I do believe him, deep down. He's never given me a reason to doubt him. 'But it says Proud Daddy moment.' With exclamation marks. I point out the obvious. 'You said she was your ex and that you just shared a dog, and it wasn't your baby.' I've lost my posh voice.

'She is my ex, and it's not my baby.' His own voice is soft. Hurt.

'But you're not over her, are you, there are pictures of you together, and even if you're not the biological...' I need to know, even if it kills me inside.

'Sam.' He doesn't seem upset now, more like frustrated. In fact he sounds a bit like my maths teacher did when he said that of course I could solve simultaneous equations (I couldn't). It makes me even angrier.

I wave the phone about speechlessly, and tap the display even though it's black now and there's nothing to see. 'You said it still twinges, but it's more than a twinge, isn't it? It's full blown toothache.'

'It's not more than a twinge, Sam.' He pauses. 'More like an aching loss, after the extraction.' His voice sounds hollow, empty. Defeated, which makes me feel horrible and empty inside.

Oh God, an aching loss, that is worse.

'But it's not what you think.' His tone is gentle now. 'This is not because of Laura.' He raises an eyebrow, but there's the hint of a smile on his face. 'I miss the baby, Bella. Annabelle. Not Laura.'

'But she isn't...'

'Bella isn't mine, no. She's Mark's.'

'Mark's?' Who the hell is Mark?

'Mark is Laura's fiancé, they had a big party to celebrate their engagement on Friday, they're getting married in September.'

'Married? But you, she, the photo ... it says...'

'That photo is more than a year old, I don't know why it was on Facebook.'

'Sarah spotted it.'

'I won't ask why.' I haven't asked her either, that bit kind of escaped me. But I make a mental note to. It could be quite innocent, she could have just been looking at Amy's profile. Or she could have been in full-on investigative mode. She gets bored at work, especially if I'm not there. 'I honestly didn't know Laura had taken it, let alone posted it. She knew I'd say no if she asked.'

'But it says...'

'I know what it says, Sam! I could strangle her. I reckon she did that to make Mark jealous. Okay.' There's a long pause as though he's planning his speech. 'We split up a couple of years ago because she had a fling.'

'A couple of years ago?' This sounds more positive.

'A couple of years ago.' He nods. 'She'd got pregnant.' He stares at me and waits for it to sink in. 'I know how it feels Sam, I knew how you felt which was partly why I wanted to help you.'

'Oh.'

'Mark was engaged to somebody else at the time, and refused to end it. Then just before she had the baby, me and Laura bumped into each other. To be honest I thought it was pure coincidence but I reckon she had it all planned out. She said she'd made a massive mistake, she still loved me, she wanted to try again.'

'Try again?' This is sounding bad.

'Try again.' Another nod. 'So we did.'

'You did?' Oh shit, this is very bad.

'We had a brief reconciliation and I was around when Bella was born. But...'

'But?' Please make this the bad for them, but good for me bit.

'But I realised it was hopeless. We didn't love each other, she was just desperate. I won't say she was using me—' I might, but that would be uncharitable and nasty '—but I think she panicked over the whole single mother bit, she wanted the perfect family and she'd blown it.' He shrugs. 'So we split. The final split, over, completely.' He waits again until I nod, and show I understand. 'But Bella is lovely, I used to see her when I went to pick Harry up.'

'You did?'

'She's cute, Sam.' He grins. 'Like you.' The grin drops. 'We've kept it pretty amicable, then about six months ago, Mark got in touch with Laura. He'd split up with his fiancée, said he'd made a massive mistake. I reckon she'd been dropping hints all over the place that I was bringing Bella up, and it hit a nerve.' He grimaces. 'She'd just been using me, and that photo is probably part of it. Anyhow, he proposed, so everything in the garden is rosy.'

'Except you're not.'

'I'm feeling a bit … I don't really know what the right word is.' He frowns.

'Bereft?'

'Maybe. I don't miss Laura, Sam, and I haven't loved her for a long time, but this is like the final cut. Her getting married means I've lost Bella.'

'But surely you can see her? I mean, Laura can't be that mean, she lets you see Harry.'

'It's not Laura that's made the decision, it's me. It wouldn't be fair on any of us, it would be a bit weird and confusing for Bella. It's time to move on, Sam.'

'Which is why you came here. You needed a distraction.'

He gives a wry smile. 'So Amy says. But that wasn't really why I said yes, it was you.'

'Me?'

'You. Haven't I told you I fancied you the moment I saw Tank dragging you through the mud towards me? You were so gutsy, and so funny, and so generous doing all this so you wouldn't let Jess down.'

As moments go to tell the grandkids about, if we ever have them (I'm jumping ahead a bit here), and if they ever ask how we met, it's unusual – I'll give it that.

'I have to admit you were a bit prickly at first—'

'I was not!'

'Like a porcupine, and so bossy.'

'I am not.'

'All those rules.'

'There was only really one, the no sex one.'

'True, and that's a bloody frustrating one, I'll have you know.' He turns serious again. 'The more I got to know you the more I realised that there was a pre-Liam version, the real, funny Sam, waiting to explode into the world. The one with dreams, and funny dances. And when I found out about what he'd done to you, it gave me a reason to say yes.' He pauses. 'Because I couldn't admit to myself that I just wanted to get to know you better, not at the start, not when I'd told myself I didn't do relationships anymore.'

'Why didn't you tell me about the baby?' This is important. There have been too many secrets, from Liam, from Laura, from me.

'It didn't seem important. Well, it's not important. Laura is just an ex.' *Just* an ex, I like the sound of that.

'You weren't married?'

'Nope, we weren't married. What about Liam, is there anything you've not said?'

'Liam is just an ex.'

'Just? You seemed pretty wound up back there.'

'Because he's a jerk, a selfish jerk. Not because I still like him.'

'Ah.'

'It took me a while to realise, because I've not had that many proper, serious boyfriends. Liam was my first proper boyfriend.' And so I believed him, believed in him. You do, don't you?

'Maybe I can be your last.' He seems to have somehow snuck even closer so that I can literally feel his body heat, and the warmth of his breath against my neck.

'Nobody can hear, you don't have to say that.' My voice seems to have developed a wobble.

'But I want to say it.'

It has to be nerves that are making my legs shake, not the fact that he's just rested his warm hand in the small of my back.

'Cold?'

'I'm fine.' It comes out as a squeak. I'm indecently red

hot if he must know. His hand brushes my cheek, then he tucks my hair back behind my ear and I've got a new set of goose bumps. God, he is good at this. I'd give him an Oscar any day.

'I mean it Sam. I could be your last. If you wanted me to be?'

'We hardly know each other.' I mean we've spent nearly a week in bed together, and acted like we know each other. But that doesn't count.

'Well, maybe it's time to remedy that.'

He's hard and firm, and that's just his lips, not to mention all his other bodily parts that are pressed against me. And it is bloody amazing. Jake Porter is kissing me in a teasing, gentle way, and he doesn't have a baby, or a wife. Just half a dog.

In fact, it's so amazing we seem to be staggering back towards the water.

'Oh my goodness!' The loud shriek startles both of us, and Harry. He leaps at us, barking like a mad dog. We lose our footing, stagger back and end up both sat in the shallow water. 'Another Mr Darcy moment! He's rescued you again, how wonderful!' Mother is leaping about and clutching her hands together as though she's won the lottery. Her enormous hat is bobbling about on her head, but she's oblivious.

'Go away!' We shout it more or less in unison, and miraculously she does, which is a total first.

Chapter 26

There is a heavy weight across my legs. A slightly furry heavy weight. And it is not Harry, because he is licking my nose.

Which means ... I dare to open one eye and glance to my right. Jake has one eye open too, and he's looking straight at me.

I close the eye and re-open it. He's still there. There are no cushions down the middle of the bed. Which means it wasn't a dream. It happened. I have had wild sex with Jake Porter in a four poster bed!

'Breakfast in bed?'

'Sure.' The sheet is pulled up to my chin on my side, so that saves the embarrassment of floppy boobs. Mine always look much better in a bra, and when I am stood up. Once I lie down they migrate to opposite sides of my body as though they want to hide under my armpits.

'I'll go and get it.' He flings the sheet back on his side and I know I should close my eyes with girly embarrassment, but I can't. Well, I pretend to, then peek. I need to remember this, it will be part of my 'I can do it' mantra when I get home. I should probably capture the moment on my mobile, because my memory isn't that good, but that might seem a bit forward. And Jake might not understand, he might think that I am like Laura and will be posting the picture on Facebook with 'Proud shag moment!!' as a caption.

'The full works?'

'Yes please!' I might have said that a bit eagerly, and feel myself go red, but he just laughs. Then winks. Which makes me blush even more.

'We can do that after breakfast.'

I didn't know your toes could actually curl during sex. I also didn't know tongues were that long, or strong. I didn't know that giggling just before an orgasm made it better. And I didn't know that falling asleep in a man's arms could make you feel the safest you'd ever felt.

I also didn't know that toast crumbs in bed and drippy butter on boobs are a good thing. Which I discover when he comes back with a tray of toast and coffee. He's actually licking said butter up when he drops the bombshell. Between slurps.

'I got a text from my agent when I was collecting breakfast.'

'Mmm, that's nice.' I'm actually talking about what he's doing – it's very nice, so nice that I'm not really capable of registering what he's saying. This bed really is the biggest, softest bed I have ever been in. And it smells nice.

'I've got to go to Greece tomorrow morning for two months' filming.'

He says it like I'd say, *hang on: I need to get that pizza out of the oven*.

My dreamy, sexy state has a bucket of cold water thrown over it. 'Oh, that's nice.' Nice is sometimes the only word. When what you really mean is horrible. Cruel. Totally unexpected. Not nice at all. Not remotely. My after-sex glow fizzles out like a cheap sparkler. 'Tomorrow morning? But we're in Scotland!' I sit up abruptly, and might well have given him a black eye. And just like that I know this is over. We're heading back to reality. Normal life.

Jake is off to do his jet-setting, glamorous acting thing, I am going to the travel agency on the high street.

My dreams of romantic dinners, lazy Sunday mornings and walks along the river pop, like giant bubbles, splattering the world with damp unpleasantness.

'He sent it the other day, but I've not been checking my phone. I switched it off. I kind of cut myself off from the real world.' He shrugs.

That's what I had done as well, and it had been lovely. Apart from the Liam and Stella bit. And the shock of his baby-that-wasn't bit.

'Two months?'

He nods. 'At least.'

'There's something else, isn't there?' He's cuddling Harry now, glancing out of the window, not really giving me the full-on attention that I've become used to. I've got an empty feeling of dread that has nothing to do with going home.

'Laura.'

'Laura?' This is not sounding like the happy-ever-after that I'd thought might go with waking up in a four-poster bed in his arms.

'She's co-starring. We've only ever been in two films together but apparently the director liked what he saw.' By 'what he saw' I presume he means chemistry, but I'm not going to say it.

The bed seems a bit lumpy. I don't want to stay in it a second longer. I brush him and the crumbs aside and am pulling my knickers on as fast as I can.

'You could come out for a few days, get a cheap flight?' He's still lounging on the bed, looking all film star-ish.

'I've used up all my holiday quota coming here.'

'Don't be sad, we can stay in touch.'

Staying in touch works when you're already in a relation-ship, not when you've had six days, three snogs, and one shag. The first two meetings don't count. They were job interviews. We've not even had a proper date.

He's excited though, I can tell, and it just isn't fair for me to act like a spoilt child. But I'd just thought, hoped, that when we got home we could meet up. See if this was as good as it seemed.

Apparently it is not. It has already passed its sell by date. He is heading off to Greece with his ex.

And there was I, thinking that shared crumbs in bed

and a late night ducking in a loch counted as something more meaningful than foreplay.

I do know he fancies me, and I fancy him rotten. But last night must have been about mutual lust, and pent up emotions after being flung into close proximity for a week. It has nothing to do with a proper relationship.

Or maybe the fact he's so pleased to escape me is all my fault. I did do my best to cock things up, I accused him of lying (which he didn't), of having a baby (which he hasn't) and of being married (which he isn't). I've screwed everything up. Relationships are about trust, and I haven't trusted him at all.

So he's going to Greece for a cooling-off period, otherwise known as escaping. For on-screen snogs with the glamorous Laura. I presume there will be on-screen snogs, and that it's not a Greek tragedy where he runs her over with his chariot.

I don't want it to be a modern day romance. I want there to be tragedy involved.

'We can go out when I get back home?'

'We could.' But inside I know we probably won't. 'Sometimes the timing isn't right, is it Jake?'

'Sometimes you have to make it right, Sam.' He says it seriously, but without pressure.

'I'm sure it will be very exciting in Greece.'

'I'm sure it will.' He's studying me as I hop round the room pulling on my clothes. 'It's a good part. Filming wasn't supposed to start for weeks though, they've pulled it forward.' He waves his phone. 'Missed a lot of texts apparently.'

'Fab.' I start throwing everything else into my suitcase. 'Better get a move on, I'm sure you need to rush home and learn lines or something. You can tell me all about it in the car.'

'I will. Shall I get that? Probably your mum.' I've been trying to ignore the knocking on the door because I need to get my head round this and work out how not to cry the moment anybody talks to me. But it's too late, he's opening the door. If anybody comes in now and cheerily says 'how are you?' I'm done for.

'Where the fuck have you been?'

Okay, not quite what I expected. And the stranger at the door is not directing the comment at me, but at Jake. I stop throwing stuff into my case.

'I've been trying to get hold of you for days.' He's tall, slim, blond and fidgety. He looks stressed. And angry.

'I told you I was taking a few days off.' Jake's voice is smooth, but I can see the twitch at his temple. He's not happy. 'I presume Amy told you where I was?'

'She was a bit awkward actually, until I explained that if I didn't get hold of you today the whole thing would be off. It's been brought forward.'

'Honestly Jake, what on earth are you playing at?' Harry gives a yelp of recognition and hurls himself towards the door as a woman steps in. A woman I recognise. She doesn't look as glamorous as she did in the photo that Sarah sent me. But it's her.

'Laura, what the hell are you doing here?'

'Keeping my husband-to-be company of course.' She smiles, and slips her hand through the crook of the man's arm, and he smiles back.

'Hi there!' I wave. He's still my date, I've paid up until the end of today, so they are not going to ignore me. 'I'm Samantha. Pleased to meet you, and you are?' I shove a hand in his direction. He looks slightly baffled, but automatically takes it.

'Sorry, darling.' Jake puts a possessive arm round my shoulder, and even though I know he's acting again, it's worth it – just to see their raised eyebrows. 'This is my agent, Mark, and...' He pauses. 'His fiancée, Laura.' Which is tons better than him saying 'my ex'.

I blink as it sinks in. He'd not told me that bit. He'd omitted to mention that 'a text from my agent' equated to 'a text from Mark'. Father of the baby. No wonder he felt bloody betrayed!

'I've just discovered that even more congratulations are in order, he's also her agent now as well as mine. Though he wasn't when she got cast as my leading lady, were you Mark?' His tone has that dry edge and Mark flinches, but doesn't respond.

This is all starting to feel very awkward, and weird, and horrible,

'Hurry up and pack, it's taken us hours to get here.' Laura has patted Harry and now shoos him away. I haven't offered to shake her hand, I'm not sure I want to.

'Well, you'd better both set off back then, you don't want to miss the plane, do you?'

'The three of us are all on the same flight.' Mark dips into his pocket and pulls out tickets with a flourish. I rather suspect he had aspirations of acting, but ended up managing instead.

'Leave my ticket, I'll see you at the airport tomorrow. I'm going home with Sam, aren't I?'

I nod, but my face feels all achy and wrong when I smile. I can't say no, can I?

By the time we cross the border back into England I know that it is not a Greek tragedy. Or an island murder. It is a romcom, which is the most depressing thing I can think of right now. Romcom means flirting and fun.

Apart from polite discussion about the film, we don't talk much other than when he tells me I've taken a wrong turning or offers to drive. He puts his hand on my knee at one point, but when I jump and nearly steer the car into a ditch he thinks better of it. We both remember the Landrover experience day.

It seems like the longest drive I have ever been on, and nowhere near as much fun as when we were heading up to Scotland a few days ago. But that was when he made me laugh with silly jokes, and Harry kept licking my ears. Even the dog senses the strained atmosphere, and spends most of the journey asleep in the footwell, occasionally waking up and scrambling onto the parcel shelf so that he can check out the scenery.

I've been driving slower and slower as we get nearer to home, and practically crawl into the station car park in first gear.

'So, here we are. Safely home!' I really am turning into my mother.

'Here we are.' Jake looks at me, and Harry sticks his head through the gap between the seats and rests his head on my shoulder.

'I could drop you off at your place.'

'Here's fine. It's been a long drive, and the train's quick.'

'Jake, I—'

'Sam, we—'

We speak at the same time. Then both stop abruptly. It's awkward. Like a first date, except it could be the last.

'Ladies first.'

'Thanks for this week.' I swallow hard, determined to be sensible. Strong.

'You're welcome.'

'It's more than just the boyfriend bit.' I stare into those lovely eyes of his and wonder if I'll ever see them again, apart from at the cinema when he's famous. 'You made me feel good. You gave me back "me" if that makes sense. Thank you.' I'm blabbing on to stop myself saying that I want him, but I still mean what I say. There had been too much compromise while I'd been with Liam, and I'd not even noticed the real me drifting away until suddenly our relationship was over, and I felt like nothing was left. I feel like crying, but I can't help but smile at him.

'I didn't do a thing, darling. You did it all yourself. You keep working on it, and you'll get everything you want, Sam.' He cups my chin in his hand. 'You can do anything.'

'Good luck with the filming, this is your big break!' His big break, our big break.

'Could be. I can't not take it, Sam.'

'I know, I never said you shouldn't!' There's a hollow in my stomach, and my throat is all blocked up. Our lives are totally different. He rushes off to exotic locations, spends time with his glamorous ex, and glowers at his agent. He is complicated and confident. I have Sarah, cocktails and takeaways.

'But you don't seem happy.'

'I'm happy, over the moon.' I smile my happiest possible smile. 'Back to work tomorrow!'

'You should come out, just for a few days. I can book the ticket.'

'I can't, I told you. I've got a job, stuff to sort out.' And I don't want to see him in a clinch with Laura, just thinking about it makes me shudder. If I knew him better I might be rash, just ditch everything. But I don't know him better.

'I'll skype you, and maybe a date when I finish filming?'

'That would be nice.' This time I say maybe, not no. Because my heart doesn't want to be sensible. And it will be months. By the time he comes home, our time together will be a distant memory.

Jake has been worth every penny. But this is the saddest goodbye ever. I kiss Harry and bury my face in his fur.

'You'll be okay?'

I nod. 'I wish you'd stop asking. I'm a big girl now, I'll be fine.' And I will be. Harry licks my hand, my salty face. Tidying up the tears I hadn't cried – except it appears I have been a bit leaky. I thought I'd got away with it. 'Dust in my eyes, from having the roof down.'

The corner of Jake's mouth lifts, but he looks sad, not smiley. He dips his head closer to mine and those dry firm lips of his brush against my own, and when Harry snuffles and pushes his nose between us it's almost a relief. I can't do a big passionate snog outside the station, then watch him disappear. 'Sure.' His thumb rubs lightly over my cheek and I really, really want to lean into his hand. But I don't. I pat the dog.

'Come on, Harry.' Jake ruffles his hair, and then mine. 'Looks like it might be me and H against the world together now. Laura texted me earlier, she's finding the baby a bit demanding, asked if he could stay at mine for a while when we get back from location. I don't think Mark is keen on him.'

He hands me an envelope as he gets out of the car. The same envelope I'd stuffed in his bag this morning. With the money in.

I push it back. 'You've got to take it. It's yours, we had a deal. You have no idea what I had to go through to get it.'

He smiles, but it's a sad smile. 'I daren't ask.' Then even

the sad smile falters and he's just looking at me. 'I don't want your money, Sam. I just wanted to be the man who makes you smile.' He taps me on the tip of my nose, and then they both go. Walk out of my life. Man and dog.

Maybe I need a puppy in my life, not a man. Maybe visiting that dog's home wasn't fate's way of introducing me to Jake, but of telling me I need a dog. Just not Tank.

Chapter 27

I will be 30 when I wake up in the morning and:

1. I don't have a boyfriend or husband, and the closest I've got to a maybe has left the country
2. I'm not rich and about to be whizzed off to Monte Carlo
3. I don't have a Ferrari
4. The only thing I love about my job, if I'm honest, is Sarah
5. I'm still not thin (but am happy as I am, so should probably delete this one).

There are many good bits –

1. My family are deluded about points 1, 2 and 3
2. Jake said I am the size I'm supposed to be. I have now realised that 'thin' is not me. This is me, and I am sensational (according to him). I have written this on the envelope he gave me, next to the 'I CAN DO IT', but in smaller letters as there wasn't that much room left.

When I say many good bits, *many* might not be an appropriate word, but I might think of more positives to add later.

I have realised though, that I am still living a lie. Despite nearly telling my parents that Jake was not a real boyfriend, I still haven't done it. I also kissed him in the loch. They saw us whizz off together the next morning looking like we'd barely slept (we hadn't). I never told them that we were in a hurry because Jake was fleeing the country with his ex and her lover, and it was over before it had barely begun.

I will write a round-robin text tomorrow, like people do at Christmas and New Year, and I will explain.

Hi all, well what a busy decade I've had and what a relief that I am now in my thirties and mature. Sorry about the little white lie that Jake was my boyfriend when he wasn't, but he actually was briefly, but now he isn't again as he has a starring role to play in Greece (Mother will probably think it's a re-make of Grease and he is the new John Travolta, but you can't spell everything out in a text). *But I have good news! Jake was excellent in bed, and is the master of toast buttering. See you in my thirties! Sam x*

Something like that will do, but I will re-read it before sending. But now I am going to have an early night and prepare myself for departing my twenties. Tomorrow I have work, and then a surprise celebration with Sarah.

I'm not sure I should have agreed to the surprise bit. I am officially too old for surprises – especially the Sarah type. Appletini guy still hasn't recovered from the marshmallow surprise which he thought was something to do with hot chocolate. He will never look at a marshmallow in the same way again. I will say no more, other than they go very soft and sticky if put in warm places and can take a lot of dislodging. Which Sarah says is the whole point. She says it was a stamina test and he passed with flying colours.

***

Thirty does not start off with a bang. It is very sedate, which I hope is not a sign that this is how the rest of my life is going to be.

Work has been quiet. We've hit the lull. Most people have already booked their summer holidays, and some organised people have booked their winter ones too. The less organised people are actually on holiday, packing, unpacking, or thinking about how they're going to pay the balance. Which gives me time to mentally prepare for the next decade of my life, and for this evening.

Things I must do now I'm thirty:

1. Buy anti-wrinkle cream (I have never looked after my skin properly, but as thirty is the new forty I think I should).
2. Write a five-year plan.

3. Decide what I really want to do (see point 2 – I am no longer sure that travel agency work is my true vocation or fulfilling in any way other than the holiday discounts).
4. Oops, scratch the cream – Sarah has just told me I've got it the wrong way round. Forty is the new thirty, thirty must therefore be the new twenty and so I need not worry, yet.
5. Get a dog.

By the time I've written the list, and tried to come up with some alternative careers for which I'm qualified (I'm not entirely convinced that the dog-walking scenario will work for me – I don't like early morning walks for a start, so am back to concentrating on travel), it is 5.30 p.m. and time to head home. Sarah gives me a hug and tells me she will be at my house for 7 p.m. so that she can check I am dressed appropriately before we hit the town, or wherever it is she's planning to hit.

I am trying on the third dress, and thinking about point five on my list, when the doorbell rings. I'm not sure I want a teeny-tiny handbag dog because I'd probably forget it when I'm rushing round in the morning, and might sit on it. This would be disastrous on many fronts. I would be distraught about hurting it, and my bank manager would no doubt be disappointed at the vet's bill. I also don't want a big strong dog like Tank, I'd end up looking like a body-builder if I had to hang on to his lead. I really just want a medium-sized dog. A dog like Harry. With an owner like Jake.

I can't believe my stupid head has taken me down this cul-de-sac. One minute I'm thinking about cute canine companions, the next *he* is on the scene again.

But I do miss Harry. And Jake.

I might agree to see him if he ever comes back from Greece, and he wants to see me, and he calls. But so far, things have panned out exactly like I thought they would.

He did ring from the airport after he'd landed, but it was awkward. And he has sent the odd text, but texts just aren't enough are they? I mean you can totally misunderstand what somebody means. And it has been a whole five days since I dropped him off at the station. He did ring when he arrived on location as well, but the line crackled and then we got cut off. I don't think it's very good for communication on remote Greek islands. Then there was a text saying that maybe we should cool it until he came home.

Cool it? It is so tepid warm that we will soon be entering chilled territory.

See? This is what happens when somebody throws in a few extras for free and you think they actually mean something.

I had spent quite a bit of time since I came home looking online at flights to Greece. Maybe as a go-getting thirty-year-old, I should grab my chances while I've got them, pull a sickie and go and see him. But the fact that we haven't had a meaningful conversation since he went, and then I got *that* text, has stopped me pressing the 'book now' button.

I did also have 'avoid men like the plague' on the list I wrote when I was in Scotland, and I am beginning to realise that my sub-conscious did actually have a valid point, before Jake led me astray in the loch.

Dress number three looks dowdy. It belongs to the type of girl who has been cheated on. Not the type of thirty-year-old who is determined to be the best she can for her own sake. I pick up dress number four.

Sarah has insisted on taking me out for my birthday, but has refused to say exactly where we are going. Which leaves me slightly afraid. I hope it's not some kind of club where you're expected to stick pound coins between a man's naked buttocks, or the local pizza parlour. I've not got anything against men's buttocks, or pizza, but after rather a depressing day at work I have decided it would be quite nice to see in my thirtieth year in a slightly more sophisticated way than I greeted twenty.

'Are you nearly ready?' Sarah is in the bedroom doorway, studying her long black fingernails which I'd say are danger-ously long if we're talking about sticking pound coins anywhere. So I think I'm safe there.

The doorbell goes again. 'Is this suitable?' Dress number four is definitely sexier than number three. It definitely doesn't say invisible woman who doesn't mind being two-timed. Maybe it is a bit too bright and stand-out-ish though?

Sarah nods. 'Yeah, you'll do.' She doesn't sound too sure, seeing as she picked the place. She also seems uncharacteristically twitchy. 'Ready?'

'Do?' I look at her more closely. 'Do' is not good. It is the type of thing people say when they haven't even looked at you. It is the type of thing elderly aunts say before they wipe an imaginary smudge off your cheek with their spat-on hanky. It is not the type of the thing you say about a woman wearing a dress like this. Well, at least I hope not. Sarah has got very high heels, leggings and a sleeveless top on. 'I'm not over-dressed?' Our taste in clothes is very different, and she moves from goth to ditsy to vintage effortlessly. If she was taller she'd probably make the perfect model. A constantly changing canvas. I won't say 'blank canvas' as Sarah is anything but blank.

'Oh no, no.'

'Too tarty?' I've got a bit of a cleavage thing going on, and this dress is quite short, and my mum always said you do legs or boobs, not both. But times have changed.

'You can always wear a jacket.' She's not even looking at me, she's looking at her watch.

'Sarah!' They're not exactly falling out, just a little bit uncovered. Shit. 'I need to get changed, I haven't got a jacket this colour.'

'Cardi?'

This is very un-Sarah like. Sarah is not a cardigan type

of person. Sarah isn't the type of person who ever considers that there can be too much cleavage. Maybe she thinks mine have gone droopy now I'm thirty, and shouldn't be on show? Or maybe she's arranged something very special for my birthday, looking at the time is also very un-Sarah like.

Oh no, I feel sick. 'You've not arranged a surprise party?' She knows I don't like being the centre of attention, and I particularly do not want to draw attention to myself on my big birthday.

'What?' She looks blank. 'Oh, no, no, don't be daft. Are you ready then?'

The doorbell goes again, which is a bit annoying, I could do without the pressure. 'Who the hell is that? Shall I ignore it?'

'Answer it, it's your birthday, it might be flowers.'

'At this time in the evening? Oh yeah, sure.' At any time was what I mean, but it sounds a bit defeatist on my birthday. 'My mum, more likely.'

'Didn't you tell her we were going out?'

'I did. She thinks you lead me astray, she's probably brought condoms round.'

'Condoms?'

'She still treats me like I'm seventeen sometimes. I think that's down to her spell working for the family planning clinic, she used to throw condoms at all the kids like they were sweeties, big bags of them.' I hold my hands out to demonstrate. 'Massive bags.' She probably took a stash when she left, just in case. 'If you ever need some, just let me know. I have to hide them, God knows how many times a week she thinks I have sex.'

'My aunt doesn't think I ever have sex.' Sarah grins, but seems back to her old self, so I can relax. 'I'll always be her sweet, innocent little darling.'

'I can't imagine you ever being sweet and innocent. Oh shit, whoever is at the door is persistent. Are you sure this dress works?'

'Positive. Now answer the bloody door and then we can start celebrating.'

It is not my mother at the door. It is a walking bunch of flowers. But there is no florists van, and the man holding the bouquet over his face doesn't look much like a delivery man. His clothes are all wrong.

He moves the flowers.

'You're in Greece.' Since I got back from Scotland I have spent most of my time looking at Greek holiday catalogues and wondering if it is me that's got this wrong. The new improved, go-getting me should surely have grabbed her chance and jetted off for a bit of on-location fan-girling – not gone to work and written out a list of what she was going to do in the next five years. Go-getters don't plan, they do.

They make the most of it when a man says he wants to be the one who makes them smile.

I smile.

'No, I'm not.' He grins back. 'I was in Greece, then I came back.'

'You came back for my birthday?'

'I came back for good. I realised I was making the biggest mistake of my life. I couldn't miss your birthday, so I told Mark to stick his contract.'

'You did?'

'It was never going to work, I've hated his guts ever since I found out about him and Laura. I don't know why I didn't sack him straightaway. I guess the final straw was finding out that he's now representing her as well.'

'Don't you need an agent though?'

'I've found a new one, and I've got a screen test for a new job in Cornwall in three weeks which my agent is really positive about. He says they're keen, they asked for me. I thought that gave me enough time to persuade you to come. And to wish you happy birthday.' He's so close I can smell him, and the flowers. If he kisses me now we will have crushed roses, but I don't care.

'You didn't call.'

'Reception was crap on the island, and I didn't want to talk to you on the phone. I thought you'd understand me being quiet for a couple of days, I literally booked a flight back the day after we arrived. I told myself that the next time I spoke to you I wanted to be able to see you. I needed to look you in the eye and be able to say sorry.'

'For what?'

'For not telling you about Annabelle, for just waltzing off to Greece with my ex and her fiancé.'

'It was work, you had to, I get that.'

'I was walking on to that plane and asking myself how I'd have felt if you'd walked away from me with Liam.'

'I wouldn't have gone...' I'm trying to keep a straight face, but it's tricky. '...if Stella had been there.'

'Holy crap, *that* is the dog's bollocks.' Which is a bit OTT even for Sarah, who interrupts what was building up to a proper romantic moment. 'Coo-ool.' She gives me a none-too-subtle nudge, and when I look she is goggle-eyed not at Jake, but at the car which I have failed to notice. Despite it being parked at the bottom of my drive. Being shiny red. Being a Ferrari.

I was busy thinking about Cornwall, and kisses.

'Can I come in?'

'Well yes, but we're off out.' I don't want to be rude, but Sarah has arranged this and I'm not about to dump her just because a man turns up with flowers. Not even a man with a Ferrari.

Sarah giggles. 'We're not off out, you are. This is the surprise.' She does a ta-dah and flings her hands open in Jake's directions.

'Jake's the surprise? You knew he was coming?'

'Yep. Jake told Amy, who told Tim, who rang your mum, who came to see me. And...' She dashes down the hall and wrenches open the door to the under-stairs cupboard. 'I packed this.'

It's my case.

'Why do I need that?'

'Because I'm taking you away.' Jake grins, and looks uncharacteristically awkward. 'If you'll come?'

'Of course she will, of course she will.' Sarah grabs the flowers off him. 'Does she look okay? She can change.' She's like a ping-pong ball rocketing between Jake and me. 'I wasn't sure what was suitable!'

'She looks fantastic.' He's not taken his eyes off me, which is making me all squishy inside. And he's not even looking at my cleavage. I think about pointing it out.

'You don't think the dress is too booby?' Sarah solves the issue. 'Too much? Not enough? We did wonder. And I wasn't sure exactly what you had in mind.'

'Not at all. Perfect for what I've got in mind.'

I'm not sure I like being talked about when I'm present. 'But I've got work tomorrow.' Which is a shame, if he's got something really dirty in mind, and after all it is my birthday, I should be able to enjoy myself before I have to seriously consider full-blown adulting.

'I fixed that, you've got a day off.' Sarah is bouncing about like Tigger. 'Isn't it brill?' She grabs me so that we can jog about together, and a few flowers come to grief. 'I'll put these in a vase, shall I?'

She's right though. It is brill. Totally brill.

But then I remember. 'You sent me a text saying that we should cool it.'

His smile falters, then he frowns. 'No, I didn't.'

'Yes, you did.'

'Look, I promise you I didn't.' We compare phones, this

is important. Important enough to halt massive birthday surprises for. I can't go away with Jake and my suitcase if he is the type of man who wants to cool things when we've been apart for a few days.

I have received the text, but according to Jake's phone, he has not sent it.

'You deleted it!'

'Or somebody sent it, then deleted it.' He pauses, then frowns. 'I bet this was Mark and Laura, they were fuming when I said I was coming home and messing up the film schedule. And Laura knew how I felt, she knew I was coming back for you. I reckon this was her way of trying to give them time to change my mind.'

I must admit, this all sounds a bit dubious, but Jake is tapping away at his phone angrily and we are all hovering in the hallway instead of having a wonderful birthday celebration.

His phone pings. Several times. There are several messages. 'Here, look.' I look. 'It was Mark, I should have guessed. Laura doesn't say cool, but Mark does. He's all about cooling off periods.'

'Oh, heavens above, look at that car, isn't it a lovely shade of red?' Mother has arrived, barged in the front door, kissed my cheek and thrust a present at me, all the while never taking her eyes off the car. 'You always wanted a red car, didn't you, dear?'

'I always wanted a Ferrari, Mum. Not just a red car.' I look at Jake, he is looking back, his phone still in his hand.

'I'm telling you the truth, Sam. Honest. Can you trust me on this one?'

'Oh dear, oh what a shame.' Mum is totally unaware of the dramatic situation she is slap bang in the middle of. 'Never mind dear, at least it's a nice shade of red.' She pats Jake's hand. 'At least you tried your best.' He isn't really listening. He's waiting to hear my answer.

I take a deep breath. 'I can trust you.' I don't mean it to come out as a little conspiratorial whisper, but that is how it sounds.

It is so small and conspiratorial though that it has bypassed both my parents.

'It is a Ferrari, Ruth.' Dad kisses me on the cheek. 'Happy birthday, love.' He too, is staring at the car. 'Mind if I...?'

'Be my guest,' Jake says and Dad wanders back outside to study the car more carefully. I do hope he doesn't get in, I don't want a stowaway. Not even Dad, who I truly love and isn't any trouble at all, but today is about me, and Jake, and my Ferrari.

'Oh well, if it is a Ferrari what are you complaining about Samantha?'

'I wasn't complaining, Mum.'

'I do hope you're not going to turn into a misery guts as you get older. I'm sure you won't let her, will you?' She grabs Jake's arm and practically simpers, it's obscene.

'Sam isn't the miserable type.' He doesn't object to all this manhandling by my parents, he just nods and smiles like a well-behaved boyfriend. Which he isn't. I don't think.

'True, true, she has always been so fun-loving until she moved in with that Liam. Did you know he's got two baby girls? Juliet said he's applied for extra hours at the bank, not that I blame him with that woman. We're not keeping you, are we?' She pauses for breath.

'Yes, Mum, you are.'

'I'll tell Juliet the September wedding is still on, shall I? Come along David, come away from that car, you're holding them up. We don't want them missing their—' She puts her hand over her mouth and shrieks. 'Goodness me, I nearly gave the game away. Well, happy birthday darling, we can all go out when you get back, can't we? Supper?'

I want to say no, but Jake speaks up before I get a chance. 'Hopefully Mrs Jenkins, though it's fingers crossed for the starring role, so it really does depend on the filming schedule. I'll get you tickets to the premiere, shall I?'

'Oh my goodness yes, wouldn't that be lovely? Is there a red carpet, will I need a new frock. David, David, did you hear? We're going to be mixing with royalty.'

I raise an eyebrow in Jake's direction and he just grins. 'Shall we go?'

I look at Jake, I look at Sarah and I realise that he really has been the man to make me smile. I can't stop. 'Sure.' It was supposed to be casual, but comes out all croaky. When he opens the car door I positively swoon into it. It's all sleek and shiny, and smells nice.

'Wait a moment, Samantha, Samantha!' My mother is

delving in her handbag as Jake closes the door. Oh my God, she's going for condoms, I just know she is.

'Move, quick!' Jake puts his seatbelt on far too slowly. 'Quick!'

He finally starts the engine, just as she yells triumphantly and holds a bag in the air. 'Here they are! Wait, Samantha, I've got...'

We never hear what she's got because we roar away from the kerb in a very satisfying way. Honestly, do mothers embarrass you for the whole of your life?

Looking back in the wing mirror, the bag does look a little on the small side, it could have just been sweets for the journey.

I don't care though. It's always safest to move first and ask questions later.

'What the hell are you doing?' Jake is laughing as he turns out of the end of the road. 'You look like Harry when he's spotted a squirrel.'

'Smelling the car.' It is gorgeous. Opulent is the word. It's also a way of hiding the fact that this feels a bit awkward, a bit first date-ish and I'm not quite sure if we're carrying on where we left off (bed head hair and obscene lust) or he's just giving me a non-carnal birthday treat.

'Have you never smelled leather before?' He is amused, but slightly awkward too. A bit Mr Bean-ish if I'm honest. Though of course he doesn't look like Mr Bean.

'Not like this. It smells of posh, of rich.' It's nice, and so is the hand resting inches from my knee. He moves one finger, just far enough so it catches my leg. That is so not first date-ish. I gulp and start counting trees. Which makes me a bit dizzy, the speed we're going.

'Equity rates have gone up then?' That comes spurting out to distract me from the warm feeling that seems to be creeping into places it shouldn't, and the fact that the tree counting is making me feel a bit nauseous.

'Sorry.' He gives a deep rumbling laugh that fills the car and warms me up even more. 'It isn't mine. Spielberg hasn't rung yet.'

'How disappointing, I'm surprised after your sterling performance in Scotland.' I fiddle with opening the window and closing it so that I don't have to look at him. I'd like to just sit and stare at him, and stare some more. But is it really a good idea to let him know how desperate I am to have his hands on me again? How totally sexy I find him? 'I'd have thought Richard Curtis would have been onto you like a shot.'

'News obviously hasn't crossed the border, once it does we'll be buying his and hers models.'

I quite like the 'we' bit. Maybe it is safe to unclamp my knees, which I've been squeezing together. 'I bet Harry's glad you're back from Greece. I bet he's missed you.' Dogs are safe ground. You can discuss dogs with anybody, total strangers in fact, and not be considered abnormal or forward.

'I missed him, but I can take him to Cornwall with me.' He puts his hand back on the steering wheel, ignoring the fact that I've now relaxed my legs, and stares ahead. 'I've missed you too, Sam.'

'Really?' I quite like the fact I've been missed.

'Really. A lot. You're a pain in the neck if you must know.'

'That's one of the nicest things you've ever said.' Though the wanting to make me smile thing was even nicer. I'm beginning to think thirty might be getting off to a good start. 'I've got a bit of a confession actually.'

'Oh?' His foot dithers on the accelerator and we do a mini bunny hop, then normal service resumes.

'I looked at flights to Greece.' It sounds like it was a good job I didn't act impetuously and rush out there, we might have been on passing planes in the sky.

'So you missed me too?'

'Just a little bit.'

He's grinning, even though he's still looking ahead. Then he turns and glances my way, his lovely eyes all wrinkly at the corners.

'Maybe a medium-sized bit.' Or even a whopping big bit, but I'll save that for later. 'I thought I'd frightened you off, that you'd run away.'

'Honey.' He's doing that honey thing again, complete with sexy drawl, I've rather missed it. 'I don't run away from girls, especially ones I fancy the pants off.'

'You fancy the pants off me? Really?'

'Totally! I'll demonstrate later, I'm good at getting pants off.' And he does that cheeky wink and dirty grin, which makes me feel a bit hot and bothered so I go back to stroking the car upholstery.

'Where are we going?' I've realised that we have crossed the sign that thanks us for visiting my town and seem to be heading for the motorway.

'Surprise. It's not far, sit back and enjoy the trip.'

'So if this isn't your car, whose is it?'

'Let's just say one or two people owe me favours.' He trails his forefinger down my arm slowly and I gulp. Oh my God, what have I let myself in for? Is he part of some kind of mafia gang? Do you still call it abduction if you go willingly?

We zoom past a Mercedes in a very satisfying way. I really should stop worrying about things and live in the moment. That's what calm, happy people say isn't it? That is how I will live my life. For now.

Chapter 28

'**B**loody hell.' I am so busy deciding I will live in the moment that I missed the fact we've pulled off the main road and are speeding across shiny, black tarmac, and now we are spinning. Fast. 'Shit.' We're going to die. But at least I'm dying with a man at my side, in a red Ferrari.

Hell, we are doing a Jeremy Clarkson, or rather the car is, spinning round and making screechy tyre noises that are even louder than my screams.

We stop. I breathe. And blink. 'Where the hell are we?'

'Sorry, I've always wanted to do that.' Jake grins. 'It's a private airstrip. Your chariot awaits.' He indicates out of the window and I look. It is a plane. A tiny plane. Like a toy one. He drives closer, more slowly with no spinning. It is bigger than a toy plane. Slightly. He turns off the car engine. 'Ready?'

'Can we do the spinny car bit again, now I know what to expect?'

I don't have to ask twice. Jake is well up for it. It is quite like you imagine Top Gear to be, when you've got an almost deserted airstrip and a car that will go really fast. I have never ever done a handbrake turn. By the time I was old enough to have boyfriends who could afford proper cars, I was going out with Liam. Enough said.

We're both laughing hysterically by the time Jake stops the car. I feel more alive than I ever thought possible, every bit of me – apart from my toes because I jammed them down on the floor to brace myself as we hit the corners.

'We're honestly going in that?'

'Honestly. Come on, I'll get your case.'

'Shit.'

'I didn't think ladies swore.'

'They don't, and they don't do this either.' And I grab him before he has chance to get out of the car, and kiss him. He actually looks rather chuffed with himself. He has the same look that Harry had when he managed to get a grip on Liam's sporran.

'Come and meet my mate Andy. It's his plane, he's taking us to Paris.'

He takes my hand in his and helps heave me out of the car. I really am going to have to read up on how to get out of car like this, just in case it happens again. 'Paris?'

'Paris.'

I'm still saying it over and over again as we walk up the steps. 'Paris!' I can't stop saying it.

I'm ashamed to say I have an overwhelming desire to kiss him again, at the top of the steps before he's even in the plane.

'Sam.' He leans across to check my seatbelt is done up, and his lovely lips are so close to mine I'm tempted to steal a kiss again. 'Do you want to know what really made me dump Mark and come back for you?'

I wait.

'You taught me to trust again. You taught me to trust my heart, my instincts and who I want to be. I wanted to, but I was scared before.'

'Oh. And who do you want to be?'

'I want to be as brave and determined as the gorgeous and funny girl I'm looking at right now. I want to be the man who whisks his girl off to Paris for her birthday, and I want to be the man who makes her smile, if she'll let me?'

I grin inanely.

'And I want to have a close look at that bluebird.'

And that, dear reader, is how I ended up drinking champagne and contemplating the benefits of being a member of the mile high club on the evening of my 30th birthday. I didn't get full membership – there wasn't quite enough time. This was Paris, not some far flung destination, and he is a man who likes to prepare properly, thoroughly, for each role. But I think my dress was quite a suitable choice.

I will leave it to your imagination to work out what actually happened during the flight, but let's just say I didn't know method acting involved THAT.

Acknowledgements

My thanks as always to my amazing, kind, and talented editors Charlotte Ledger and Emily Ruston. Thank you for all the words of encouragement, and your support, hard work and advice, I feel incredibly lucky to be able to work with such talented people.

Thanks also to my fabulous, and funny, agent Amanda Preston, your enthusiasm is infectious and your advice invaluable.

And a big thank you to you, for reading this story, and being so supportive.